THIS LOVE FORBIDDEN

His hand shook. He inhaled the essence of jasmine she always wore. "I would claim you for my own if I could," he murmured.

"Speak not so," she cried, "for you cannot. Yet my heart has always been yours."

He placed his mouth over hers and gently parted her lips to sample the sweetness within. At first she stiffened in surprise, and then her arms came up around his neck. Her body was on fire with sensations far beyond anything she had ever dreamed existed. With a groan he pulled her to him and began to claim all of her at last . . .

D0976432

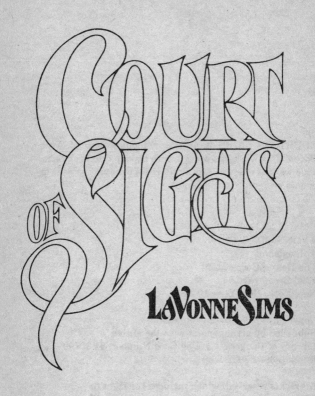

Court of Sighs

LaVonne Sims

AVON
PUBLISHERS OF BARD, CAMELOT, DISCUS AND FLARE BOOKS

COURT OF SIGHS is an original publication of Avon Books. This work has never before appeared in book form. This work is a novel. Any similarities to actual persons or events are purely coincidental.

AVON BOOKS
A division of
The Hearst Corporation
1790 Broadway
New York, New York 10019

Copyright © 1984 by LaVonne Sims
Published by arrangement with the author
Library of Congress Catalog Card Number: 84-90799
ISBN: 0-380-86082-1

First Avon Printing, May, 1984

Acknowledgments

No book finds its way to the marketplace through the efforts of an author alone. In my case, that is particularly true. There is my mother, who loved, nurtured, and encouraged dreams, and my father, who provided constant mental stimuli while broadening my view of the world. From them both I inherited a reverence for learning and books.

I could not have completed a sentence without the research and literary work of others, many more gifted and knowledgeable than I will ever be. The combined works of Edgar Snow, Hayman Kublin, and Rene Grousset, to name only a few, gave me an insight into a time before my birth. Through the writing of Ida Pruitt and the eyes of Ning Lao t'ai-t'ai, I was given a unique glimpse of everyday life in pre–World War II China. But it was Pearl S. Buck, more than any other, who fired my youthful imagination and inspired admiration for a great and ancient culture. Her love for the Chinese people, which shimmered from every sentence of so many of her books, provided my first beacon. It shines brightly still.

To enumerate all who have given support and encouragement on a personal level would fill tomes. Still, I cannot forgo a very special thanks to "The Group": Vince Andrew, Denise Herberger, Sid Knoch, Ron Montana, Richard Russo, and Bonnie Young. Without their criticism, I would have slept better—and failed.

I owe a debt of gratitude to Peggy Crites, my secretary, who looked up the words, typed her fingers to the bone, and waited with me; to my agent, Charles Stern, and his wife, Mildred, who never stopped believing; to Judith Riven, my editor, who allowed me the dignity of compromise; and to Susan Coon, who taught me the true meaning of "professionalism."

I also wish to thank Doug Lee, Susan Ma, and Brian

Tam for their help, patience, and tolerance; Elva, Laura, Marsha, and Tony for their love and encouragement.

As for my family—my husband, Bill, and children Debbie, Lori, Jay, and Michelle—there are no words eloquent enough to convey my love and gratitude. They see my worst side and give back only their best. Every writer should be so blessed.

L.S.

This book is dedicated to Bill,
who held my hand through it all,
and to the memory of Pearl S. Buck. . . .
I hope she would approve.

THE WEDDING

Chapter One

Sweeping off the Gobi, the northwestern wind howled. No vehicles traversed the narrow streets of Tanpo. Warehouses and granaries were locked tight. The sand-laden night sky flashed copper in the wake of a lightning bolt as peals of thunder rolled over the highland valley. Rain began to fall in huge drops, first one and then another. Within moments they joined to form a solid curtain, drenching the houses of rich and poor alike.

In all this small city, few houses boasted more opulence than the House of Tse, whose inhabitants slept snugly surrounded by walls four feet thick and twelve feet in height. But stout walls and abundant wealth do not stay the wrath of heaven, and in the courtyards willows bent low. Fishponds churned. Once more lightning cracked overhead.

Illuminated by the storm's fury, a small feminine figure moved hurriedly along the labyrinth of pathways which led to the family temple. The girl was shivering as she reached her destination and grasped the slippery brass ring of the temple door. Only after a third mighty heave did the door swing outward, creaking on ancient hinges.

With one swift, furtive glance behind her, she stepped into the dim candle-lit interior, where for generations her ancestors had worshiped and been worshiped in turn. White silken sleeping garments showed from beneath her rain-soaked robe. A cascade of raven hair fell dripping to her waist. Red dye pooled around her feet, running from the tiger-faced slippers she wore. Her chest rose and fell in ragged breaths. Her beautiful elongated eyes were wide, almost frightened, as she moved quickly around the spirit wall and into the main room of the temple.

Before her stood a scarlet-covered altar table, and

slightly beyond, the family shrine. Wisps of smoke spiraled upward from a row of joss sticks. In the left corner of the shrine, taking a subservient position to her male counterparts, sat the likeness of Kuan Yin, Goddess of Mercy. This small statue wore a robe of red silk and a headdress of finest gold.

The girl looked at the goddess for long moments, her lower lip trembling slightly. "Merciful Mother," she finally whispered, "it is I, Golden Willow. I come . . . I come to beseech you, Most Blessed One . . ."

She stopped suddenly and groaned. Falling face down, she began to beat her forehead against the cold gray floor tiles. Sobs shook her body from head to toe.

Looking down upon the supplicating form of Golden Willow, the eyes of Kuan Yin remained chill and quiescent, while, outside, an early winter gripped the mountain city of Tanpo.

"Eat, My Lady." The little bond servant, Crystal, nudged a bowl of steaming pork dumplings toward her young mistress. "If you do not take nourishment, you will be pale and weak on your wedding day."

Golden Willow looked at the food and her stomach churned. The skin around the edges of her face and along the line of her high forehead tingled painfully where it had been plucked of any rebellious fringe in preparation for her coming nuptuals. Likewise had all feminine growth been removed from her lower body. Her flesh glowed beneath the loose wrapper she wore, for she had just finished being bathed, oiled, and perfumed for hours on end. Her insides were icy with fear.

"I will take only a little tea, Crystal, thank you."

The servant opened her mouth to protest, but closed it without speaking as the heavy curtain covering the doorway was pulled to one side.

Golden Willow's mother entered the small sitting room, her vast bulk supported by her own aged serving woman, Chu Ma, and a dragonhead walking stick.

This imposing woman clicked her tongue upon seeing the small feast which had been spread upon the table. "Do not stuff yourself, Daughter," she said, "or you will look like me before you can conceive your first son. Somehow I

do not think your groom would approve such alteration."
She did not notice the color leaving Golden Willow's face
at this mention of the first Chang son.

Always a staunch defender of her young mistress, Crystal spoke up, albeit with respect. "My lady has a very delicate appetite, Madame. Indeed, just this moment I was
encouraging her to partake of at least a few morsels." The
worried look she then turned on Golden Willow caused Madame Tse to scrutinize her daughter more closely.

As for the latter, she kept her lashes lowered to hide the
tears that threatened to spill down her cheeks at any moment. The emotions she was experiencing were made more
intense by her knowledge that they could not be shared,
not even with her mother or Crystal, who was more friend
than servant. The guilty secret she harbored seemed about
to tear her apart, and only with tremendous effort was she
able to prevent screaming out her anguish. Picking up a
teacup, she brought it to her lips and pretended to drink.
The fingers twined around that cup pressed the porcelain
so firmly that they were white and bloodless.

Without taking her eyes from the face of her daughter,
Madame Tse spoke to Chu Ma. "Help me sit, Old Bone,
and then you and Crystal are to leave. I would spend a few
final moments with my daughter alone."

The task she assigned the serving woman was not easily
accomplished, for in addition to her abundant size, Madame Tse was truly crippled. Her bound feet were no more
than stumps and would have served even a slim woman
poorly. Chu Ma grimaced both from exertion and sympathy as she guided her mistress to a large ebony chair and
helped lower her onto its cushioned seat.

After the servants had slipped quietly out, Madame Tse
pulled a fan from the sleeve of her green satin robe and
cooled herself despite the harsh weather that prevailed
outside.

Golden Willow stood, but still did not look up. "Let me
pour tea, Mother. It is Cloud Mist, your favorite."

Madame Tse closed her fan with a decisive snap. "I do
not care for tea. Sit now." Rapping her long nails on the
carved arm of the chair, she looked intently at her only
child, at a loss as to just how best to approach the conversation she wished to pursue.

Golden Willow took her seat again and folded her hands tightly in her lap so they would not shake. The room was silent save for her mother's rhythmic tapping. Outside, snow drifted to earth, wrapping the myriad courtyards about the House of Tse in pristine splendor. Fishponds were frozen over, their brightly colored occupants trapped deep in winter's sleep.

At last Madame Tse cleared her throat, but instead of broaching her subject with the finesse she had intended, she blurted out her concern in a single blunt statement. "You fear the marriage bed."

Startled by such plain words, Golden Willow stared at her mother. Her cheeks flushed scarlet.

"Well," said Madame Tse in an exasperated tone, "it is not an unusual thing for a maiden to fear, after all. And a curse on me for not speaking sooner! It is plain to me that you are greatly disturbed."

"I . . ." Golden Willow began, but instantly changed her mind. Better for her mother to believe that maidenly reserve was at the root of her unhappiness than to suspect the truth. She looked down at her hands without really seeing them.

Madame Tse forced a cheerful laugh. "It is not as terrible as you might imagine, child. Oh, I know what you are feeling, but you need not worry."

And so in a half-joking, tender sort of way, she began explaining the simple, carnal mysteries of marriage.

In the chilly corridor, Crystal stood with Chu Ma. It was impossible not to eavesdrop through the door hanging. She was wide-eyed as she listened to the intimate details being expounded upon by Madame Tse.

Chu Ma cackled softly behind her hand, only to be given an indignant glare. "I see no reason for amusement," the girl whispered. "These things Madame tells my mistress, why, they are . . . are . . ."

"Yes?" Chu Ma grinned like a wise old monkey.

"This business with men," Crystal sputtered. "It seems . . . well . . . little better than *dog* business!"

At this Chu Ma had to draw an arm across her face to muffle her laughter. When she finally managed to contain her mirth, she said, "I can just see telling my man such a thing. Aie-e-e, how he would beat me! 'Old Bone,' I would say. 'You were just like a rutting cur when you made sons upon me!" Again she laughed, and went on doing so until she began to choke and wheeze.

Crystal grew alarmed at the old woman's color and drew her away from the door. "Hush, Ancient Mother, lest you kill yourself with glee."

While Chu Ma wiped tears from her eyes, Crystal grew increasingly pensive. "My poor, poor mistress," she murmured.

Chu Ma heard this and gawked at her in genuine surprise. "I do not believe my ears. *Poor mistress* indeed! What woman does not want sons? Is it not our duty to bring them forth?" Once more she donned that disconcertingly wise expression. "The duty is not entirely unpleasant either, girl, as you will no doubt soon learn."

The color washed from Crystal's face. "I shall not! I shall do without sons if I must become a beast to have them!"

Madame Tse's voice called out to them. "Chu Ma! Chu Ma! Where are you, woman? It is past time for me to retire."

Both servants went in, immediately sober, their faces passive, as if they knew nothing of what had transpired between mother and daughter.

After the two elder women left, Crystal followed Golden Willow into the bedchamber. Large stones sat heating on the brazier and she took them up with tongs, transferring them quickly onto a heavy quilt. This done, she wrapped them tightly and carried them to the bed, where she tucked them beneath the coverlet. Golden Willow stood silently by, her eyes strangely glazed.

"Come, Mistress." Crystal took her by the hand. "Will you not have at least a bowl of soup before you sleep?"

These two girls, of an age and nearly equal in size, stood looking at one another. Crystal swallowed hard. "It will not be so bad, Mistress. Really, it will not. Chu Ma told me—"

Golden Willow buried her face in her hands. "Do not speak to me of marriage or beds or husbands." Her voice was muffled and trembling. "Speak not, Crystal, for to hear more is to die!"

Chapter Two

*I*t was not yet dawn. Behind the heavy velvet canopy of her bed, Golden Willow stirred but made no attempt to rise. She kept her tear-swollen eyes tightly closed. She had slept for only a short while, and then fitfully, beset by dreams she now refused to recall. She knew Crystal lay on a pallet nearby and that it would take only a soft whisper to summon her. Golden Willow did not make a sound.

The day is here, she thought. It is here and there is no escape. All my life I have known that it would come, that the eldest Chang son would become my husband. So why is my stubborn heart so wayward? Why do I insist on clinging to childhood's foolishness?

Not for the first time, she cursed the gods for allowing her to glimpse that *other* face, the one that had been so familiar to her years ago, the one she had constantly longed to see ever since. How much easier this day would be if that secret wish had never been granted!

Almost against her will, she let her mind drift back in time to a bright spring day in a huge garden courtyard. She had been only a child of six then . . .

"Golden Willow! Look at me, look at me! I am a bird!"

Perched atop a boulder, a little boy held out his arms and waved them like the wings of a young falcon, his left leg suspended behind him. Golden Willow gasped and put her hands to her cheeks. "Please come down, Fengmo! You will fall and be killed!"

But the boy paid her no heed. He only laughed boldly and increased the tempo of his arms.

Suddenly, another boy leapt from a nearby shrub, screaming loudly. Startled by this outburst, Fengmo flapped wildly, clawed the air in an attempt to regain his

9

footing, and finally toppled to the ground with a thud. His tormentor gave a cry of victory and took his place.

"Oh, Kao, you brute! See what you have done!" Golden Willow ran to the limp form at the bottom of the boulder.

Fengmo was very still.

"Come back. Come back, little soul," she crooned, sure that life had fled the body of her friend and could be coaxed back only with the utmost tenderness.

"Look at the great eagle now," Kao snorted. "Why, he is no more than a fuzzy chick."

Tears sprang to Golden Willow's dark eyes as she continued to exhort the soul of Fengmo. A moment later his eyelids fluttered and he leapt up. Gasping for breath, he shook a fist at Kao.

"I will punch your nose," he wheezed. "Come down from there and I will beat you!"

Kao sat down on his haunches and indolently picked at his newly grown incisors with a thin sliver of a chicken bone. "I would come, but I fear I would have to knock out yet more of your poor teeth. You have so few to spare, Little Brother."

Instantly Fengmo pursed his lips in an attempt to hide the offending gap, a ploy which made speech difficult. "You have never done such a thing, Kao. My teeth came out of their own accord, and Mother said that is as it should be. Soon I will have new ones just as you do."

The other boy laughed contemptuously. "You only deny the truth in order to impress this silly female. But I care not a bit what *she* thinks"—he snapped his fingers to emphasize this point—"though it is *I* who must wed her someday. In fact, I think when I am grown and big I might refuse to do so. She is an ugly thing, and unless she changes greatly I will not have her."

Golden Willow and Fengmo gasped in unison. Even at their tender ages they knew such talk was not proper between boy and girl.

"Be quiet, Kao!" Fengmo was now more incensed for his friend's sake than his own. Seeing her mortification, he began to climb the boulder again. His little mouth was set in a grim line.

Kao was a full two years older than Fengmo and at least a half-head taller. Nonetheless, he came to his feet quickly when he saw his younger brother ascending with such determination. With a premature cry of alarm, he scurried down the opposite side and ran into the cover of a nearby bamboo grove.

"Come down, Fengmo," Golden Willow pleaded. "He is gone now."

Almost overcome with frustration, he did as she asked. "That Kao," he grumbled. "He never did knock out a single one of my teeth!"

She put her hand on his arm. "I know how good and brave you are, Fengmo. I know too that Kao has a heart like a snow pea."

Just then a woman's clear voice called from the forecourt. "Chang One! Chang Two! Come now. Your father wishes to see you."

Kao streaked from his hiding place. Fengmo and Golden Willow exchanged a look of disgust when they heard him crying. "Mother, Mother," he wailed. "Fengmo threatened to beat me and break my new teeth. He hates me and I do not know why!"

"There, there, little dumpling," soothed Madame Chang. "Fengmo! Come here at once!"

Stiff legged, hands clenched at his sides, Fengmo turned from Golden Willow and began to march away. He took only a few steps, however, and then stopped. He looked at the ground rather than at her. "I hope he *does* refuse to have you, for perhaps then my parents will insist you wed the Second Son."

Golden Willow's voice quivered with emotion. "I hope so too," she whispered.

She watched him run away, and her heart felt as though it was growing bigger and bigger. The sensation was sweet and yet somehow strangely painful.

Golden Willow never forgot her love for the stalwart boy. Yet, as custom dictated, they were separated when they reached the age of eight and were no longer allowed to romp and play in the same courts while their parents visited. Discipline became very strict.

In one way, she had been very lucky in the years that followed. Her father was a kind and enlightened man. Against all her mother's wishes he had left her feet un-

bound and allowed her an education, not only in needle-
craft and music, but in literature and art as well. She was
tutored in mathmatics and could soon do sums better than
most males.

"Who will want such a wife?" Madame Tse had ranted.
"Her feet will look like those of a peasant, and she will be
too smart by far! I tell you Madame Chang will never have
a daughter-in-law like that!" On and on she went, and had
Master Tse seen any evidence that his daughter had no desire for learning, he would have stopped her education immediately, just for the sake of domestic harmony. This was
not the case, however. Golden Willow was diligent. Sometimes he would pass her private courtyard and peek in to
see her lying upon a quilt beneath the plum tree with a
book in her hands. Her face was always intent and her
eyes glowing at these times, and he knew that he had done
well by her.

There was, however, one drawback to all this learning
that Master Tse had not considered. Interspersed among
the classics Golden Willow read were other stories, tales of
romance between the heroic men and women of old. These
accounts fired her already fertile imagination. When she
was not actually reading, she fantasized. In her dreams,
Fengmo became the brave warrior and she the empress
who bestowed honors upon him. At other times, it was he
who ruled and she became his adoring consort. And all the
while she was dreaming, she longed to see his face, to
know what sort of person he had become.

Thoughts of Chang Kao she put far from her—always.

Then, three months before Golden Willow was to be married, Heaven chose to intervene in a most cruel manner.

She had been rushing through a courtyard on some errand she no longer remembered. It was autumn. The skies
were overcast, though the weather was still clement
enough. That day her hair had been plaited into coils and
wrapped close to her ears. Gold and jade filigreed pins,
wrought in the shape of butterflies, were stuck in each of
these coils, and their ingenious wings fluttered in the
breeze as she ran along. Instead of a robe, she wore wide-
legged trousers and a matching jacket of apple green silk.
Her feet were tiny, for all their being unbound, and the
shoes she wore made them seen even smaller. Intent upon

her own thoughts, she did not look up as she entered the main courtyard. A puppy trotted at her heels. When the shaggy little creature began barking in a high-pitched voice, she scolded him and at the same moment collided against the back of a young man.

Stepping quickly back, she said nothing, thinking at first that it was one of her male cousins, or a servant.

This was proper, for in the city of Tanpo customs were closely observed, especially among wealthy families. The separation of the sexes was so complete that even blood relatives did not speak if they were young, unmarried, and of opposite gender. Contact was kept to a minimum and conversation all but forbidden.

Sidestepping, she kept her glance on the ground just in front of her.

"Golden Willow. Is it truly you?" What came to her ears was little more than an awed whisper.

Surprised, she completely forgot propriety and whirled around to look straight into the eyes of Chang Fengmo. In that brief instant, time itself seemed to halt. She felt suddenly light-headed. Her heart tripped like a temple gong, beating so loudly she feared the entire household would hear.

"Golden Willow, do you not recognize me? It is I, Fengmo." She put a silencing finger to her lips, but he paid no heed. "Am I so different then?" he asked.

She looked to the right and left. No one seemed to be near. The puppy was still yipping excitedly. She scooped the dog up.

"Why are you here?" she whispered, not realizing how lilting her voice was. "You should not be within these courts!"

"My father had a message for yours, one that he did not wish to entrust to a servant. I have just delivered it and am leaving."

"Then go . . . please!"

"Not until you have answered. Am I so different that you no longer know me?"

Again she gave a frantic look around her, and said in a shaking voice, "You are the same and yet not the same. So tall . . ." The words trailed away, but she could not force herself to show modesty. She looked into those dark, almost black eyes. She memorized the firm jaw and well-defined mouth. He smiled and she saw how straight and startlingly white his teeth were.

"*You* have changed greatly. You are even more beautiful than I had imagined." He was whispering again.

A new and unexpected sensation seeped through Golden Willow as she watched his lips move and listened to these words. The emotion both dismayed and frightened her. "Speak no more," she implored. And without another word she turned and ran from the courtyard.

That night and every night thereafter, her dreams were filled with him. Over and over again she saw his face, heard his voice, and imagined that she felt his touch. By contrast, her days were a misery. Preparations for her wedding monopolized the entire household. After all, a union between the mighty houses of Chang and Tse was a momentous event. There were robes to be sewn, gifts to exchange, and a myriad of other details to attend to. Try though she might, she could not ignore this commotion.

Finally, in sheer desperation, she had gone to the family temple and prayed to the Kuan Yin, but to no avail. Her dreams still came and time rushed madly on.

"Mistress, it is time for you to rise."

She felt the gentle shake of Crystal's hand and opened her eyes. Moving like an old woman, she sat up and pushed back the coverlet. The tea given her was tasteless. Female servants began to enter the bedchamber.

She said nothing as she was bathed yet again, dressed and groomed. While the other women chattered and giggled with excitement, the mind of Golden Willow grew numb. Her last clear thought before the wedding headdress was set in place was, *At least I will see him sometimes. May Heaven help me, I shall live for that.*

Chapter Three

"Long life and many sons to the House of Chang!"

Firecrackers popped and peasant children gawked as the bride's swaying litter was carried through the massive gates of the Chang compound. It was borne on the shoulders of four porters, all dressed in red. The main courtyard was filled to capacity. Friends and lesser family members smiled and nudged one another as the litter was set gently down.

Master Chang watched his wife separate herself from a large group of women and gracefully approach the curtained vehicle. A hush fell over the gathering. The family priest began chanting the ritual litany. A cymbal rang softly. Madame Chang lifted the tassled drape and everyone expelled a sigh upon seeing the veiled figure of the bride.

"How straight and proud she sits," murmured one woman.

"She is slim as a bamboo," said another.

Madame Chang extended her hand, and after the briefest pause the bride took it. Together they made their way to the family temple where the groom waited. Master Chang followed. After him came Master Tse and his three young sons, then the first and second Tse wives together, and finally a myriad of uncles, aunts, and cousins.

The first and only daughter of the House of Tse, the bride, was dressed in a bright red robe. A sash of cream-colored silk shot with gold thread circled her waist. The traditional jeweled headdress covered her head, and her face was hidden behind a veil of minute beads.

The actual marriage ceremony was brief and simple. Through the residing priest, the bride was presented to the ancestral tablets. Then, as all brides are, she was exhorted to be a proper wife, a cheerful provider of fine Chang males. Her surname would not officially become Chang until the following morning when she presented the blood-stained sheet of her marriage bed to her new mother-in-law.

The bride took her place beside Chang Kao and the entire procession retired to the dining hall where the families would feast and be entertained by jugglers, acrobats, and magicians. This revelry would continue long after the newlyweds retired to their own court. The next morning the main gates would be opened, and for three days the less fortunate of Tanpo and the surrounding countryside would be invited to feast also.

Master Chang was a generous man, but even he winced a little at the cost of such an affair. He tried not to notice the heaping platters of rich foods being served. The dowry had been considerable, after all: one silk shop, a granary, and five acres of farmland. Moreover, he would not have his eldest son wed in less than the best style. To do so would have caused a loss of face before friends and business associates.

He looked down the main table to where Kao sat with Golden Willow, the daughter of his closet friend, Liangmo.

May they be truly happy, he thought. Perhaps marriage will help settle that wayward son of mine.

Surveying the rest of the cavernous room, his heart swelled with pride. Down to the most distant cousin, this family of his was a fine lot. Faces gleamed with good health. All were garbed in satin or silk. No one could say that a single member of the Chang family was not well fed and at least minimally prosperous. If they did not own land or shops of their own, they were employed in one of his private enterprises. Many of these folk lived beneath his roof.

At the table just below him there was a group of young men, six in all. Three were the sons of Tse Liangmo, offspring of a second marriage. But the other boys belonged to Master Chang, and he was extremely fond of them.

Chang Hsu was only seven, still chubby and the possessor of an angelic face. A deceiving fact if one did not know him, for he was bold and full of mischief. His present goal in life seemed to be to outdo his elder brother, Tan, whenever possible.

Chang Tan was eleven, and bent on becoming a soldier, even though his entire family might disapprove—which he knew they did.

Last, Master Chang let his gaze rest and linger on his second son, Fengmo. He would not admit, even to himself, that of all his seven children he loved this one best. The boy was tall and slim, with broad shoulders. When he moved, his carriage displayed the subtle grace and strength of a leopard. More important, however, was his spirit. Fengmo was honest and straightforward in his personal dealings. He did not use subterfuge or petty intrigue to get his own way as Kao so often attempted to do.

Today Master Chang was well pleased with everyone. His family surrounded him. Chang Kao was well married, thus assuring the beginning of a long line of heirs. There was nothing he could think to wish for that he did not already have.

Tse Liangmo sat next to him, and Master Chang gave him a hearty slap on the back. "You and I are more than just friends now, Liangmo. We are almost relatives!"

Both men laughed. They had been friends since childhood, and today they were realizing the beginning of a plan. There were to be more joint weddings in the future of these mighty clans.

Perhaps soon, they dreamed, two great houses would become one.

The dining hall rang with laughter and applause. A small stage had been erected at one end of the room, and acrobats tumbled, twisted, and jumped about upon it. At the moment, attention was centered on a female contortionist. Golden Willow found it hard to believe a body could be forced into such unnatural positions. She started involuntarily when the hot breath of Kao whispered into her ear. "I hope you will prove to be so agile, Wife."

She was not certain exactly what he meant by this remark, but she colored deeply. For the first time she was grateful for the heavy headdress she wore. It was not yet proper for him to address her in public, and she looked between the beads of her veil to see if anyone had taken notice.

All seemed intent upon the stage—except one. Fengmo looked directly at her. His brows were drawn down in a scowl and his face seemed pale. She closed her eyes so she could not see.

The act on stage finished, and after the excitement died away, the hall became quiet. It was dusk, and servants went about lighting more lanterns. When they had finished, all heads turned toward the main table. Men smiled outright, and women behind their fans. The younger children looked questions at one another.

It was time.

Golden Willow feared she would faint before she was finally able to stand. Her head throbbed painfully beneath the weight of her headdress, and tiny beads of perspiration formed on her forehead. It was she who must leave the hall first, accompanied only by Crystal. Toasts would then be said. Afterward, the men would regale Kao to the moon gate of his new court. Jests and good wishes would be called out to him as he entered to formally claim his bride.

There was an old servant waiting, torch in hand to light the way, when Golden Willow and Crystal came out of the dining hall. It was snowing lightly and the pathways were slippery, forcing them to walk with care. Even so it seemed only seconds before they reached their destination.

In the dark it was impossible to clearly see the courtyard they entered. Golden Willow would not have taken notice in any case, for she was nearly wild with fear. At that moment, her terror was enough to overshadow even her personal unhappiness. But she intuitively knew that had she been going to await Fengmo, her emotions would have been very different. No doubt she would still have been apprehensive, but her uneasiness would have been mingled with a sweet sort of anticipation too. She would not be frightened witless. Nothing she knew of Kao, not a single memory, helped alleviate her terrible tension.

The old servant left them in the court. Golden Willow began to shake as Crystal led her inside and through the sitting room to the bedchamber.

"Sit, My Lady," Crystal said. "Before all else I would remove your headdress. It is so heavy I wonder that you can hold your head up."

Golden Willow did feel dizzy when the thing was lifted away. Her teeth started chattering when her robe and undergarments were removed, though the room was heated by braziers in every corner. Silently, she submitted to being freshened. Tradition dictated that a bride be perfumed just before the entrance of her husband. Each of the seven orifices must be anointed with fragrant oils. This too was done, and finally she was robed in her sleeping garments, which felt as though they were made of ice rather than white silk.

Her anxiety increased as she turned toward the bed. It looked huge, and indeed it was very high. She had to use a small stool to get up and sit upon its edge.

Crystal hesitated. It was all she could do to smile and say the expected words. "May you conceive this night, My Lady, and present your husband a son." With this she bowed deeply and left the room.

Never in her life had Golden Willow felt so utterly alone. She could feel her heart pulsing at the cleft of her throat. Slowly, she took several deep breaths in an attempt to calm herself.

I will not be shamed by my own fear, she resolved. Chang Kao is to be my lord and I must accept him. He is a man now, and no doubt much changed. Since I cannot love him, I will at least be diligent in my duty.

Opening the door, Kao looked upon his new bride. She sat demurely on the edge of the bed, her feet resting on the step stool. Her hands were folded in her lap, her head slightly lowered to show proper modesty. Her hair, so dark that in the lamplight it gleamed blue-black, formed a cape around her back and shoulders.

He stood there for a moment, face flushed from the huge quantities of wine he had imbibed. His eyes raked her from toe to crown. A smile spread over his face.

Closing the door, he quickly walked to the bed and began immediately to undress. In his haste he ripped the sash which held his robe together, and cursed aloud.

Golden Willow did not move. Only the tempo of her breathing increased.

"Look at me," Kao commanded

He stood before her completely naked, feet planted wide apart, arms akimbo. His body was thick and smooth, almost hairless.

When she did not respond, his smile disappeared. "I say look at me, woman!"

His voice lashed out and she started. Slowly her head came up. She gasped slightly when she saw the jutting appendage he displayed. Her eyes widened and the color drained from her face. She appeared frozen.

Kao laughed and began rocking his lower body from side to side. His manhood hit the skin of his upper thighs, first left then right, making soft slapping sounds. "Will I not make many fine sons?"

He laughed again, but it was far from a mirthful sound. When he smiled, his lips drooped at the corners. His narrow eyes glittered.

He stopped moving. "Touch me."

"Please, My Lord . . ." Her voice was little more than a whisper. She swallowed convulsively.

"You will do what pleases me, Wife." So saying, he reached out as if to take her hand and force it.

Suddenly, Golden Willow came to life. With a wild cry she jerked away and scurried back onto the center of the bed. Gathering the quilt around her, she attempted to cover herself. "I am your wife, My Lord, and I will do my duty since I must. But I am no slave!" Her breath came in small pants.

In a single swift motion, Kao pulled the quilt from beneath her, causing her to sprawl sideways. The light shift she wore rode up around the tops of her thighs. There was the sound of cloth tearing and one white shoulder was exposed. The soft skin of her upper breasts was clearly visible.

"So, you will resist me," he chuckled. "It is what I might have expected. But do not think I care, for I do not. I like to have a woman fight sometimes."

Golden Willow tried to sit and right herself, but became tangled in her own hair. With an almost animal-like snarl, Kao leapt upon her. The scream that rose to her lips was smothered by the crush of his body.

Chapter Four

The first day of feasting was over. The dining hall was quiet and dim. Many of the brightly colored lanterns had been doused and servants moved sluggishly about, clearing tables and smothering yawns. In a few hours it would be dawn.

Fengmo sat alone at one table. For all the wine he had consumed, he was still sober and wide awake. His jaw hurt from clenching his teeth together, but his face remained passive, almost expressionless. He had learned long ago to don this mask and hide behind it. When, in the past, his mother had chastised him and blamed him for the wrongs of his elder brother, Fengmo had refused to let her see how her rejection affected him. Pretended indifference became his shield against pain.

Yet, he had never known the raw hurt he experienced now. He could not keep his mind from tripping over the many courtyard walls and into the apartment where at this very moment a marriage was being consummated.

Heaven take these visions from me! he screamed inwardly. For a moment he let his guard down and covered his face with his hands.

Master Chang entered the dining hall. He stood watching the servants clear away platters of leftover food and other debris, and once again he tried not to mentally tabulate the money that was being spent, telling himself that he would be richly repaid in grandsons. Expelling a deep sigh, he turned and was about to leave when his eyes fell on the lone figure of his second son.

Ah, he thought, the boy has had too much to drink. I will help him, for he is almost asleep there.

Lost in his sorrow, Fengmo did not hear his father approach. When he felt a hand rest on his shoulder he was taken by surprise.

Master Chang almost exclaimed aloud when his son looked up. This was not the face of a drunkard. No, the expression stamped on Fengmo's features seemed vulnerable and somehow completely helpless.

"Oh, Father. I did not see you come in." Instantly, the mask was back in place. "I thought you had retired long ago."

Master Chang was confused. Had his eyes played him false in the dim light? It was very late and his old bones cried out for rest. Still, for a moment he hesitated, and then, with a flash of insight, he put all thought of his warm bed away. He motioned to a nearby servant. "Go fetch my fur robe," he said. "And bring one for my second son here also."

"What is it, Father?" Fengmo asked. "Is there something wrong?"

Master Chang shrugged. "Nothing really. It is just that I cannot sleep after all this feasting. The tea house on the Street of the Golden Bridge seems to be calling me. If you are not too tired, I thought you would like to accompany me."

Fengmo stood. "I will be happy to go, for I too am restless." He knew that anything was preferable to being trapped with his thoughts in the quiet of his own room.

So the two went on foot, without even a servant to light their way. Neither spoke. The silence between them was comfortable, however, and made more so by the snow drifting down all around them. It was almost as if they were the only souls on earth.

The tea house, known for its delectable foods and exquisite flower girls, was warm and surprisingly busy. From dusk to dawn a man could come here and relax or gamble, eat or cavort, as the mood moved him. Many of the men who had been wedding guests were sitting in the large main room. Several called greetings and congratulations when they saw Master Chang and Fengmo enter the foyer.

A plump woman of middle age approached them immediately. Her face was thick with rice powder and she wore an elaborate wig.

"Ah, Master Chang," she gushed. "What a surprise to see you. A great honor. I hear your eldest son was wed today. Congratulations!" She smiled coyly at Fengmo. "Surely *this* is not the bridegroom."

"This is my second son, Madame Ying," he answered. "My fine second son." The pride in his voice was obvious.

"He is fine indeed!" Madame Ying raised a thin eyebrow at Fengmo. "And so big!"

This was true enough, for Fengmo's mother came from northern China, where people grow larger, and he had inherited his height from those hearty ancestors.

Madame Ying was prepared to lead them into the main room when Master Chang decided otherwise. It was noisy there and always filled with smoke, loud music, and the rattle of dice cups.

"Give us a private room, if you please," he said. "We seek only a little peace and quiet conversation."

Nothing could have pleased Madame Ying more, for such a request meant a much larger profit. She quickly suggested they order green winter melon and offered to make two singing girls available for their pleasure.

Master Chang looked to see if this idea appealed to Fengmo, but the latter stood back a little and seemed not to have heard.

"We will take the melon," he decided. "Make sure our tea is the kind called Eyebrow of Longevity. As for the girls, send only one songstress and make sure that she is small and pretty. See also that her voice is soothing and her ways quiet."

"I have only one such songbird," said Madame Ying, rubbing her fat hands together. "She is very serene and dignified. Unfortunately she is sleeping, and so . . ."

Master Chang knew these subtleties by heart. "Well," he responded, "perhaps she would be willing to leave her bed for a little extra silver."

"No doubt, no doubt," the woman laughed. "I will fetch her now, and if she is lazy, I will give her a good pinch." She clapped her hands sharply and a male servant appeared as if from nowhere. "Take Master Chang and his second son to the Room of Three Cranes and see to their needs at once." She then instructed him carefully in what to serve and went herself to get the girl.

Fengmo had been to small tea houses before—modest places that boasted only one or two flower girls, usually older ladies who were too worn or homely to serve in a better house. He had visited these low-class establishments with his friends, but only a few times, for he always felt guilty when he did so. Above all he could not understand it when one of the other young men went into a back room with those slatternly women. He connected his own sensual longings with beauty and would not have it otherwise. After a while he was so sickened by the crude jesting and actions of his friends that he began to make excuses and soon quit going with them altogether.

This tea house was very different, but in his present mood Fengmo was oblivious. The insinuating looks of Madame Ying and the opulent surroundings were lost on him. He followed the servant and his father down a narrow corridor and into a small room with a window that overlooked a lake. It was frozen over, but visible nonetheless because bright lanterns had been strung around it. The room itself was decorated in black, red, and gold. In place of regular furniture there was a low table with cushions to serve as seats. Likewise a low couch, narrow and long, occupied one corner. The air was fragrant with essence of sandalwood.

Most unusual were the paintings which monopolized every wall. They were of girls dressed in loose colorful robes, who at first glance appeared to be only relaxing and smiling prettily. But upon closer inspection it could be seen that their repose was far from natural. In each case they were partially exposed. Many were touching themselves in a suggestive manner, and a few were actually using devices of self-gratification.

Fengmo sat down on a cushion, a polite half-smile upon his face, without really seeing any of this. As for Master Chang, the decor was so well known to him after his many years of patronage that he was immune to it. He wished only to share a few quiet moments with his favorite son.

The servant left them and returned a short time later with tea and a large plate of crisp melon slices. Of her own accord, Madame Ying had instructed him to bring a bowl of spiced pork and vegetables as well.

After the man served them and left again, Master Chang looked at Fengmo closely. It suddenly occurred to him just how little he knew his son. Oh, he knew the general characteristics and personalities of all his offspring, even the girls. But like so many parents, he thought of them in broad terms. His children, especially his sons, he considered simply extensions of himself. Tonight, for some reason he could not clearly discern, he wanted to learn the real timber of Chang Fengmo.

Though this should have been easy, it was not, for Fengmo sat there drinking his tea and saying nothing. The boy hardly touched his food.

To begin with, Master Chang spoke of general things, casting about the entire time for a subject that might spark his son's interest. Fengmo only nodded and answered in courteous monosyllables.

Finally, Master Chang thought of a topic that seemed in keeping with the day's events. "Soon it will be your turn to wed, my son." He smiled in a conspiratorial way. "I should not tell you this, but your mother has been speaking to the go-between about you. We think that perhaps the first daughter of my friend Quan Tou would . . ."

Fengmo's head snapped up, and to his father's astonishment, his eyes were ablaze. "I will not wed, Father. Do not speak of it!"

Master Chang was speechless. What sort of foolishness is this? he wondered. He is not overly religious by nature, nor given to priestly study. So why? Then he almost laughed aloud, thinking he had overlooked the most obvious explanation. This is not Kao after all. I would wager this second son of mine has never been with a woman! Why, no wonder he is moody! All this talk today of marriage, and him still untried!

Madame Ying chose just that moment to enter with a girl who was clad in a beautiful long robe that flowed out behind her. All at once Master Chang was very glad he had been willing to pay extra in order to secure the services of this particular female. She was lovely, with modest eyes and tiny feet. Her skin was a pure ivory white. He was even more gratified when he saw Fengmo gaze at the girl with what appeared to be longing.

"This is Sweet Harmony," said Madame Ying, "and the name suits her well." She cast a long sideways glance at

Fengmo. "Indeed, this one pleases with more than her voice. A talented flower she is."

Immediately, the girl knelt on a cushion and began to sing without benefit of accompaniment. Her voice rose and fell in perfect pitch, making even Master Chang tingle with its sweetness.

Fengmo watched her with fascination. Her oval face was very like the one dearest to him, though not so beautiful. For a moment he was mesmerized. Then he began to notice all the small differences.

No, this girl's features were not so finely shaped. The bridge of her nose was just a bit too flat. Her body was shorter and rounder than the one he had once seen dressed in green silk. He turned away and gazed out the window at the frozen lake.

Madame Ying frowned.

Master Chang saw all this, and was also perplexed. He had seen Fengmo show open interest and then, for some unfathomable reason, lose it just as quickly. He motioned Madame Ying to leave the room and turned back to his son. The girl continued to sing softly.

"She is pretty, is she not?" Master Chang prompted.

Fengmo looked back at the girl. "Yes, Father. Very pretty."

"If this one does not suit you, I will have another brought at once."

Seeing the pains his father was taking, Fengmo hastened to reassure him. "Oh no, Father, this one is very good. I enjoy her voice. It is soothing."

"I only wondered," Master Chang ventured, "because you seem so distant. But come to think, you have not been quite yourself all day. If you are troubled about something, perhaps I can be of help."

No one can help me now, Fengmo thought. He could not say this, however, and he knew he must say something. "It is nothing, Father, except that my life is passing and I accomplish nothing with it." He sighed deeply. "I am a man now, after all, and I should be busy. The days hold no pleasure for me."

These words seemed grave for one so young, and yet Master Chang was pleased. It was a good sign for a young man to be serious and concerned about his future.

The next thing Fengmo said surprised even him, for the idea came to him unexpectedly. "Perhaps I should leave home, Father. I can go across the sea. Many young men are doing this nowadays. It is said there is much to be learned from the foreign devils. I could even learn to read their letters and speak in their tongue."

Master Chang's heart plummeted. Of all his children, he knew he would miss this one the most. He did not want Fengmo to be so far away, but he knew he must proceed with care. "What would such a learning benefit you, my son?"

"Why, I could take care of all the business we do in foreign goods, Father."

The more he talked, the more this new idea appealed to Fengmo. Suddenly, he felt he must get away at all cost. He could not stay in the same house with Golden Willow and know that she could never be his.

"Let me go, Father," he pleaded. "We have been stocking our shops with many foreign goods of late, and my knowledge could save you much."

Master Chang was a very astute man in most ways. He heard the desperation in his son's voice and again began to feel there was something afoot of which he remained unaware. Still, he could not quite give his consent to this plan. He decided the best course would be to delay his decision. He was too tired to think things out so quickly.

He smiled and scratched his head. "Let me consider what you have said, my son. You may be right. We will talk more in a few days' time."

Both men leaned back now and pretended great interest in the girl. When she finished her song and inquired if they would like another, Master Chang smothered a yawn.

"My son would like one I am sure," he said. "But I am an old man and must get myself home."

Fengmo made as if to rise, but his father motioned him to remain seated. "Please stay. I will pay before I leave and you may take all the pleasure you want." He looked meaningfully at the girl. "Come home only when you are ready."

On his way out he stopped to speak to the servant who waited in the corridor. "Take wine to my son. I will pay you to see that he gets safely home."

* * *

Now that Fengmo was alone with the girl, he could not help but look at her, for to do otherwise would have been extremely rude. The wine arrived and he sipped it slowly. At the same time he began to notice the pictures hanging on the walls. Unconsciously, he blushed.

Sweet Harmony watched from beneath lowered lids and guessed the truth. This good-looking young man had never been with a woman.

For her next song she chose a tale of love and sadness, allowing one silver tear to run down her cheek. Finally, her melody and the wine did their work. Fengmo's mind grew hazy. His eyes lingered on her throat.

When her song ended, she stood. With a rustle of silk she moved to kneel behind him. Placing a cool finger on each of his temples, she began to massage. Her hands worked down his neck and under the collar of his robe to his shoulders. "You look weary, Young Lord," she murmured. "Come, lay yourself on the couch yonder and I will soothe you."

He did not resist as she helped him rise and led him to the couch. She left him for only a moment to go out into the corridor and tell the manservant they were not to be disturbed.

Fengmo looked up at her when she returned. His eyes were slightly glazed. He could not remember her name. When he spoke, his words were slurred. "How are you called, little flower?"

She smiled. "They call me Sweet Harmony. I bring peace to men's souls."

So saying, she stretched out beside him. Her small hands began to move over the length of his body, stopping to stroke here, press there. She used all the knowledge of her profession to give him pleasure. Soon she could feel the heat coming from him and he began responding in kind.

Fengmo was caught up in another world. Her body was round and soft, her flesh smooth as silk. He gave himself over to the fire coursing through his veins. At his moment of completion another form appeared on the black velvet of his mind, however, a figure dressed in a robe of red with a cream-colored sash. He could not see the face hidden beneath a beaded veil.

"Golden Willow!" he cried out her name.

Now, flower girls are many things. Those who are wise keep the secrets they learn to themselves, for they often see the souls of men exposed in a way they would be at no other time. Sweet Harmony knew of the wedding that had taken place that day, as everyone in Tanpo did. She knew too of Golden Willow, and found herself moved beyond belief at the tragedy she had become privy to.

Chang Fengmo seemed to know what he had disclosed, for his muscles went unnaturally tense and rigid. He quivered.

"Let it go," Sweet Harmony whispered in his ear. "Let your sorrow break, Young Lord, or it will poison you."

For a very long time she lay beneath him, and she held him close against her while he wept.

Chapter Five

Crystal moved quietly about the sitting room, trying not to think of the sounds that had kept her awake throughout most of the night. It was no use. She could think of little else.

How she loathed Chang Kao already! He was a monster! *I will never allow a man to touch me,* she told herself vehemently. *Chu Ma lied. No woman could take pleasure in such things!*

Over and over again she had heard feral grunts and cruel laughter coming from behind the bedchamber door. Only once, early in the evening, had she heard her mistress. The words Golden Willow had spoken were not clear, but Crystal could tell they were exclamations of anger. After that there had been only the animal moanings of the eldest Chang son.

The sitting room was spacious, and in other circumstances she might have taken pleasure in it. There was a fine teakwood cabinet. The small table and two chairs were intricately carved in a lotus pattern, with rose-colored cushions on the seats. A thick blue Peking carpet covered the tile floor. There were two decorative screens, and lovely scrolls depicting the four seasons hung on one wall. Everything was scrupulously clean and fragrant. The furniture shone from a thorough waxing.

After the braziers were lit and glowing, Crystal found a ceramic jar and went outside. She pulled her jacket tightly together in front. The pathway was covered ankle deep in snow, and by the time she reached the moon gate, her cloth slippers were soaked through.

"Good morning!"

31

Stepping out onto the main path, she turned toward the voice. A toothless old man stood there smiling, a large shovel in his hand.

"Hello, Old Father," she smiled back. "Can you direct me to the water shed? I would prepare tea for my mistress."

The old man laughed. "Ahhh, are those lovebirds up so early then?"

The smile immediately left Crystal's pretty face. "They are not, though it is no concern of yours."

"Forgive me," he said. "In my old age, I rattle on without thinking."

This gardener was no fool. He might be a man and older by far than this snip of a girl, but it would be she who ruled the servants one day, for she was personal maid to the future mistress. With all courtesy, he gave her directions and resumed his work clearing the paths.

There were already servants at the shed when Crystal arrived. She patiently waited, conversing as little as possible because she wanted neither to listen to the ribald jokes nor to answer questions. When her turn came and her jar was filled, she thanked the waterkeeper and asked, "Might I return after a time and receive hot water aplenty?"

The man nodded. "To be sure," he said. "I have two grown sons who will haul it for you as well. The lazy fellows are abed now, but I will bid them rise at once."

Satisfied, she bowed and left. Upon reentering the apartment, she almost cried aloud to see her mistress already up.

Golden Willow was standing in the middle of the sitting room. When she saw Crystal, she put a finger to her lips. "Speak but softly," she said. "He . . . the master still sleeps."

The fact that she did not refer to Chang Kao as "my husband" or "my lord" was not lost on Crystal, who set about making tea at once. From the corner of her eye she watched her mistress walk slowly to the table and sit down, wincing slightly.

Why, she is in pain! Crystal realized. I must make all haste!

* * *

The water was hot and soothing. Golden Willow sat shoulder deep in the Soochow tub, which in reality was more a human-sized jar than anything. It was equipped with a small smooth seat, which enabled her to submerge almost completely. In addition to the scent of jasmine, Crystal had added healing salts to the water, and these helped relax her aching muscles. She tried to ignore the fact that they also made her torn flesh burn. She bit her lips to keep from crying out, for above all she wished to cleanse the filth from her body.

Soap and perfume may purify my flesh, she thought, but a part of my soul will be forever black!

Unfortunately, her time of ablution could not be prolonged. She feared Kao would rise, and more, she feared he would summon her again. Knowing in advance that it was futile, she prayed his drunken slumber would last for all time. She fought the waves of helplessness that threatened to engulf her.

As Crystal patted her gently dry, Golden Willow tried not to see the tears that glistened in her servant's eyes. Together they went to an ebony chest, which had come with her from her parents' home, and selected a robe for her to wear to the courts of her new mother-in-law. Neither of them spoke of the need to choose a style that would cover her throat, which was mottled with dark bruises. Just above her collarbone there were also angry red indentations where Kao had bitten her.

"This blue one, Mistress," Crystal suggested. "The color suits you very well." And indeed it was exquisite, a heavy brocade with wide, flowing sleeves. The stiff collar would reach almost to Golden Willow's chin.

Soon she was dressed. Crystal groomed her hair with a large sandalwood comb, all the while speaking in a low, gentle tone.

"There are so many servants here, Mistress. Even the House of Tse cannot boast so many. And you should see the water shed. There are *three* caldrons there. I met one gardener, a dear old man. I am sure he has already cleared the pathway in your courtyard."

Golden Willow knew her loyal maid was trying desperately to distract her, and she was grateful. But she kept thinking of the task that lay ahead. In order to present evidence of her virginity to Madame Chang, she would have to wait for Kao to wake. The idea appalled her.

Coiffure finished, she stood. "Go to the cabinet, Crystal," she said, "and bring me a bed covering."

The bond servant looked perplexed as she obeyed. Her confusion increased when Golden Willow bid her spread the giant cloth upon the floor.

"Rumple it," Golden Willow commanded. "Here, let me help you."

Crystal's eyes widened at the sight of her mistress down on hands and knees wadding the cloth into a heap. For a moment she feared Golden Willow might be losing her mind. Then, suddenly, she understood and rushed to help.

"Bring me a small knife, or a pair of scissors," came the next command. Golden Willow began pushing up the sleeve of her robe. There could be no evidence of a wound on her hands or fingers.

"No!" Crystal gave a soft cry of alarm. Putting her hand out, she pulled the sleeve down again. "I will do it. Who will know your blood from mine?"

She did not wait for a response. With quick steps she went back to the cabinet and returned with a pair of sewing shears and a small scrap of cloth.

"You must not, Crystal. It is my responsibility. If your wound should become infected . . ."

But it was too late. Even as she spoke Crystal drove the points of the scissors into the flesh of her own forearm. She then moved to the center of the bed covering and let fall drops of bright red blood.

Golden Willow stood. "It is enough. Come here and let me help you."

Her hands shook as she tightly wound the scrap around Crystal's arm and, when it had stopped bleeding, tied it in place. She looked at the maid squarely. "Please believe that my deception is not complete, Crystal. I was truly pure. There *are* stains upon that other . . ." She swallowed hard and tried to continue. "It is just that I do not want to see . . . am afraid . . . do not want to disturb . . ."

"Hush, My Lady. Who could know your innocence better than I?"

A moment later they were in each other's arms. Crystal held Golden Willow close. "Do not fret, Dear Mistress. Somehow all will be well. Her words carried a conviction she did not feel.

Madame Chang had been up since first light. This had been a habit of hers since childhood, one she could not break even when she was exhausted, as she was on this morning. She stood looking out a window that opened onto her front courtyard. Tiny icicles sparkled from the tree branches, and blue shadows fell onto the snow that covered everything but the stone path. Her heart felt as chilled as the surroundings. Guilt weighed heavily on her mind.

"Madame."

She turned to see that her serving woman, Li Ma, had entered the room. "Does my daughter-in-law come so soon?"

"Yes, Madame. The gardener just sent word that she has left her court. She will be here any moment. Come now, all is ready."

Madame Chang moved to the table and sat down. Her chair was high, with a tall, imposing back, almost a throne in appearance. On the table before her was a pot of tea and a bowl of small winter oranges. Cups and plates were also set neatly in place.

There was a light tap on the door. She nodded and Li Ma went to admit Golden Willow.

She is beautiful, Madame Chang thought, but too proud, I fear. Life will be difficult for her if she cannot be humbled.

Golden Willow stepped forward, keeping her head slightly inclined. The bed covering was draped over her arm and covered with a piece of pure white silk. Li Ma took it from her and brought it to her own mistress. The silk was lifted. Madame Chang looked at it and then at Golden Willow.

"Welcome, Daughter," she said. "Please join me." She signified the chair to her right.

Golden Willow approached the table and took an orange

from the bowl. With deft fingers she peeled it, leaving the skin in one piece. She then separated each section only at the top, forming a perfect flower. This fruit she put on a plate and offered to Madame Chang, who accepted it with a gracious bow.

This ceremony concluded, Golden Willow took her place at the right side of Madame Chang and allowed Li Ma to pour tea for them both.

The air was crisp and the sky an almost blinding blue as Golden Willow left her mother-in-law's courts. She had not gone far when a long shadow fell across the path in front of her. Shivering, she pulled her cape close about her. Somehow she knew before she raised her head who would be standing there.

Fengmo drank in the sight of her. There was a spot of color on each of her cheekbones, and the cold had turned the tip of her nose slightly pink. Even so, her face seemed perfect, surrounded as it was by a hood of silver fox fur. He opened his mouth to speak but could not.

They stood like that, gazing at one another for what seemed an eternity.

"Golden Willow," he finally managed.

"Shh." Her hand reached out and she placed a single finger on his lips. It was the first time she had touched him in over nine years. She spoke, and her voice was surprisingly controlled and calm. "You will always be my heart and soul. But we must not speak again, or even look at each other, until after you are wed."

"I cannot."

She drew her hand back and it disappeared within the folds of her cape. "You must."

They could not remain there, and it was she who forced herself to walk away. He watched her until she was out of sight, and then ran inside a nearby compound and slammed the gate behind him.

What neither Fengmo nor Golden Willow realized was that they had been observed. On his way to see his wife, Master Chang had come upon them and stepped quickly behind an ice-covered shrub. He had not been able to hear their brief conversation, but his eyes had shown him the truth.

"By the gods!" he cursed under his breath, and suddenly he knew what he must do.

Chapter Six

Married life began to take up a certain pattern. The long nights Golden Willow spent with her husband were still an unending horror, with Kao lustful and ever ready to debase her. Things might have been easier had she been willing to submit to his constant demands for the perverse, but this she would not do; and since he could not force her in the ways he desired, he often grew violent, even striking her on occasion. The blows he dealt were carefully premeditated, however. He never struck her in the face. Such mistreatment would have given evidence, and he feared his parents, especially his father, would take a dim view of his brutality.

One night became much like another. Kao unceremoniously disrobed and in the foulest possible terms made his coarse demands. Without words, Golden Willow defied him. She would lay on the bed rigid as stone, neatly dressed in her night garments. Gnashing his teeth in frustration because she refused to speak or look at him, Kao called her vile and filthy names. When this failed, he would clutch her chin and force her to face him, an action he soon gave up. He was by nature a base coward, and the hatred and contempt he saw snapping from her eyes at those times had a strange way of unnerving him. On the nights he was able to resist hitting her, he still ground into her with a bestiality that left her torn and battered. There was never a morning when she rose without marks on the tenderest parts of her pale flesh.

As for her days, they were a pleasure by comparison. Kao was not the sort to bestir himself early, thus allowing her time to bathe and be groomed in peace. Once he did get up and appear in the doorway, yawning and scratching,

Crystal made it a point to stay close by. It would have mattered little in any case, because no sooner did he finish his morning meal than he hurried to slick his hair, dress, and rush off to meet his friends for a day of gambling.

Golden Willow was overwhelmingly grateful for this second vice, for it meant she need not see him again until the family gathered for the evening meal.

Except for the quiet company of Crystal, she had been most often alone while still living with her parents. This had not been disturbing at the time because she had found such contentment in her studies and beloved books. Now, however, she did not desire long hours in which to dwell upon her circumstance. Thankfully, she was not allowed much solitude, for Master and Madame Chang had two daughters. The eldest, New Moon, was not quite two years younger than Golden Willow. Following close behind her in age was Moon Shadow, a pert fourteen-year-old who kept her older companions in constant but delightful turmoil. Had it not been for these two, the new bride would have found life a great deal more difficult to bear.

After Kao left one morning, the three girls were gathered, as had become their habit, in the warm apartment of Golden Willow. Outside, the snow had given way to a chill drizzle. A tray of sweets and a pot of steaming tea had been prepared for them by Crystal, who then occupied herself with a bit of sewing in one corner of the sitting room. A slight smile tugged at the lips of the serving girl as she listened to the idle talk going on at the table. Her mistress was understandably more subdued than her guests, but from time to time Golden Willow would laugh in her silvery voice. For this Crystal thanked all the gods. In the beginning, she had feared misery alone would kill the one she served, and whom she loved above all people on earth.

"Sister!" New Moon scolded. "Put that terrible book away at once! Better yet, feed it to a fire. You know how our mother disapproves of such reading!"

"I am *not* reading," Moon Shadow retorted. "Who could read such a book, I ask you? Only a foreign devil could make sense of such silly characters. Why, just look for yourself. They are all written in squares or circles or straight lines." Obligingly, she held up a publication, an American movie magazine. New Moon and Golden Willow could not contain their curiosity at a large picture showing on the proffered page.

"Oh!" gasped New Moon, forgetting her own reprimand. "How bold those women from across the sea are!" She reached out a hand to take the magazine but Moon Shadow snatched it neatly away.

"It is as you say, Elder Sister. We should not read such books. I'd best toss this into a brazier."

Watching these two, Golden Willow was forced to hide a smile. New Moon scowled and struggled briefly with her earlier convictions. Moon Shadow rose as if to make good her threat, but the glint of satisfaction in her eyes could not be missed.

"Wait!" New Moon protested, and then quickly lowered her voice in an effort to restore her dignity. "Perhaps you were correct after all, Little Sister. As you say, we are not reading vile foreign words. What can it hurt if we inspect a picture or two?" She looked wistfully at the magazine. "Quick now, turn it back to that picture, the one that showed a white-haired female."

Both she and Golden Willow moved to stand behind Moon Shadow and look down over her shoulder while she smugly turned the pages with deliberate slowness. At last the picture they sought reappeared. The face and upper torso of an American film star gazed up at them.

"Ahhhh!" The three murmured in unison. Golden Willow looked up and beckoned to Crystal. "Come," she said. "You too must see this."

After joining the others, Crystal also uttered an exclamation of shock. "Why, Mistress, her bosom is all but bare! And so large!"

"Perhaps she is nursing a child," New Moon suggested, but Moon Shadow gave a snort of derision. "Of course she is not. All those women from across the sea are built so. It is a wonder they can stand erect."

"How terrible," breathed Crystal. "Her face is young and yet her hair is already white as the winter snow."

Again Moon Shadow spoke with an expert's voice. "It is not age, Crystal, nor even worry that makes her hair white. I once saw a foreigner, a man who came to Tanpo for a short while to practice his medicine. His hair was like flames shooting up out of his scalp. I tell you these foreigners are born with all different sorts of hair and eyes."

The others fixed her with a doubtful stare, shuddered, and then resumed their study of the picture.

"This one has eyes like glass," said New Moon, transfixed. "I fancy I can see her soul right through them. For all her bright smile, I think she is very sad."

Golden Willow and Moon Shadow nodded their agreement while Crystal continued her close examination, turning her head this way and that. "Perhaps she is sad because she knows she is so ugly," the serving girl suggested.

Golden Willow and New Moon agreed most positively, but Moon Shadow remained silent for once. She did not find the foreigners at all ugly. Rather, she thought them most fascinating, especially when they had a lighted cigarette dangling from between their lips, with wisps of smoke spiraling upward. The other girls did not notice her lack of comment, however, and she turned to another page, which prompted new discussion. A few moments later they were interrupted by someone scratching upon the door leading in from the courtyard. Crystal rose to answer the summons. When she returned, she spoke to Golden Willow. "That was the gateman, Mistress. He informs me that the Madame, your mother, arrived a short while ago. She is with your husband's mother now, but will call upon you shortly."

Pleasure flickered across Golden Willow's countenance, only to be extinguished in the next instant. This would be the first time she had seen her mother since the wedding three weeks before. She knew the effort it must have cost Madame Tse to adhere to courteous standards. Had she come a moment sooner, she would have appeared rude and overinquisitive about her daughter's welfare—an insult to the House of Chang.

Golden Willow gathered her courage tightly about her, knowing it would not do for her to fall weeping into the arms of her beloved parent. To do this would prove disastrous, for Madame Tse, were she to learn of Kao's cruelty, would undoubtedly whisk her daughter away at once, thus bringing shame to both families. The great houses of Chang and Tse had been united in friendship for at least five generations, and Golden Willow refused to allow that bond to be destroyed on her account. Nor was she willing, even under the circumstances, to be taken home where she would be trapped forever, branded a used woman and unable to wed again. If this were to happen, she knew she would never more glimpse the face of her heart's delight. Still, she wondered at her own ability to play the happy, blushing bride before her mother. It would not be easy.

New Moon and Moon Shadow made an exit, still engrossed in their magazine, while Crystal set about replenishing the sweetmeats and tea.

Less than an hour passed before the bulk of Madame Tse filled the small, tiled foyer. Chu Ma stood there too, shaking the rain from an oiled umbrella, while mother and daughter embraced. The two looked long at each other before Golden Willow took her mother's hand and helped her into the sitting room where she knew the playacting must begin.

That night the last of the storm subsided. Thin fingers of fog trailed through the streets of Tanpo, intertwining, until the city was literally shrouded in a thick, silent blanket. The hour was growing late as Madame Tse squinted over her embroidery. For all her weight, her fingers were still slim and nimble as any girl's, and they deftly plied the needle and fine strands of silken thread. While she appeared completely engrossed in her work, she was not. Her mind raced over the topic she wished to discuss with her husband.

Master Tse sat across from her in a matching chair, his feet resting on a low stool next to a glowing brazier. Those feet were clad only in white cotton stockings, and he wiggled his toes toward the warmth. Spectacles rested on the end of his nose to assist in reading the clothbound volume he held open before him. Though he acted to the contrary, he was not unaware of the many deep sighs his wife had expelled over the past hour.

The sound of voices came from the corridor just beyond the curtained doorway, and a second later Chu Ma and her husband, Old Chu, entered. On a brass tray Chu Ma carried a covered pot filled with delicious beef broth such as the mistress and master liked to sup in the evenings,

and also two lacquered drinking bowls. Likewise, Old Chu
held a long-stemmed silver pipe for Master Tse to enjoy afterward. Both servants quit speaking once they crossed
the threshold of the cozy room, but the scowls upon their
faces left no doubt that they had been quarreling as usual.
Their long and varied arguments had become a joke
among the entire staff.

Madame Tse looked up. "Please set the tray down for
now, Chu Ma," she instructed. "We will not partake just
yet."

Master Tse knew this was an indication that she wished
to speak with him, but he did not raise his glance from the
book. His curiosity was aroused more than ever when she
excused the servants and laid her sewing aside. Still, he
pretended to go on with his reading until she coughed behind her hand. Only then did he allow himself to look up,
questioningly.

Showing the proper respect by never quite meeting his
eyes, Madame Tse began. "I went to see our daughter today, Husband."

"Oh?" He kept his voice purposefully innocuous since it
was considered unseemly for a father to show too much interest in a mere female offspring. "I trust she is well."

Madame Tse's brows furrowed. "This is why I wish to
speak to you. I am not at all certain our daughter *is* well,
though she spoke no word of complaint."

Master Tse struggled for continued neutrality. "Was she
melancholy, then?"

"No, not even that. She said much to me of her new life.
In fact, I think she spoke much more than is common for
her. I hardly had time to slip in a question or two. Moreover, it is not what she said that leaves me disturbed, My
Lord, but what I feel she did *not* say."

"I am not sure I follow your meaning." Now Master Tse
dropped all pretense. His voice was warm with interest
and he allowed his thumb to slip from the place it had been
marking in his book. He knew his First Wife to be a very
intuitive woman, and concern for his favorite child welled
up in him whether he wished it to or not.

Slowly, choosing each word with care, she went on.
"Well, she spoke much of the two Chang daughters. It
seems that in spite of their age differences they have be-

come fast friends. This pleases me, for there was no real companion here for our girl. She was too often alone.

"But while she and I talked, she said nothing of her new husband. When I finally inquired, she simply told me that he was well and then went on to speak of something else. No matter how I circled the subject of Chang Kao, she seemed to avoid it."

Suddenly, Master Tse wished for his pipe. He always felt more able to think clearly when he had it to puff upon. He put the longing aside, however, for he did not wish to call in Old Chu just yet, though he was convinced both servants were at that very moment hearing every word spoken. Instead, Master Tse scratched his head with the long nail of his right little finger. "Perhaps she thought it would be immodest to discuss her husband," he suggested.

"Pffft!" His wife waved the idea aside. "I have yet to meet the bride who is not brimful of talking about her lord—what robes he prefers, what tea he likes, which newly discovered bad habits he may possess, or his good qualities. Besides, why should she feel a need for modesty before me, her own mother, now that we are both married women?" At these last words she flushed ever so slightly, and the guilt that had been troubling Master Tse so much of late began to prick him yet again.

"What do I know of such female matters?" he retorted, almost irritably. "If there was no reason for reticence, why did you not just come out and ask our daughter the things you wished to know?"

She hesitated. "I was going to do exactly that, My Lord, but . . ."

He looked at her closely and saw that she was even more upset than he had imagined. "What is it, Little Flower?" His voice was gentle. It was the first time he had used her given name in a very long time, and he saw her lips tremble. Tears glistened in her eyes.

Madame Tse tried to still the inward quivering his tenderness evoked. The sound of her name spoken so softly brought back memories of better and happier days. She forced herself to continue with the matter at hand. "I *am* troubled, My Lord. When our daughter bent to pour my tea today, her robe fell open just slightly. I would swear I saw a

dark bruise at the bottom of her throat, just along the bone
to her left shoulder."

Master Tse, who had been leaning forward, now sat back
abruptly. The expression that came over his face was one
she had never seen before, one that was almost frightening. The muscles in his jaw twitched and he narrowed
his eyes. "Do you imply what I suspect, Madame?" he
rasped.

Madame Tse began to wring her hands. "Oh, I do not
know what to think! It is barely possible I saw a shadow
and no more. Or perhaps there was a bruise and it came
from some natural source, though it seemed in a very unlikely place." Tears began to spill down her cheeks. "I only
know that I am mightily worried about my Golden Willow!"

The angry red which now suffused her husband's face
told her that she must calm both herself and him. "Let us
not leap to conclusions yet, My Lord. Indeed, for the sake of
friendship and honor, we *must* not. Forgive me for being
such a burden, but the need to speak and share my fears
was very grave."

Master Tse took several deep breaths to clear his mind
and bring his emotions under control. "You were correct in
doing so, Little Flower." Again he spoke her name. "Put
your worries to rest for now, however, and leave it to me. I
will seek the truth in my own way. Can you do this and
find peace?"

Her answer came in a whisper, and without intending
to, she let her eyes meet his in a long gaze. "Yes, My
Lord."

Master Tse was the first to look away. I have been most
unfair to this good wife of mine, he thought, and his nag-
ging conscience finally struck him to the marrow of his
bones. To cover his feelings and a sudden new resolve, he
cleared his throat and called out gruffly for the servants to
enter. The pair came at once, wearing their passive masks.

The broth was served in silence. From time to time master and mistress peered at one another over the rims of
their bowls, but when their eyes chanced to meet they both
looked quickly away. The servants too looked at each
other, and for once they shared a smile. After the bowls
and pot had been cleared away, Old Chu fetched the pipe.

Standing dutifully beside his master's chair, he lifted a brown paper spill from a nearby urn and lit the fragrant tobacco. Master Tse puffed deeply three times, rested, and then Old Chu lit the pipe again. So it went: light, three puffs; light, three puffs.

Almost afraid to hope, Madame Tse smothered a yawn that was not quite genuine. "I grow sleepy, My Lord. You must excuse me." She spoke to her serving woman. "Come, Chu Ma. Help me to retire."

While the aged servant assisted her, the mistress dared not look at her husband. Her heart plummeted when he made no reply, not even to wish her a pleasant sleep. She was nearly to the door before he spoke over his shoulder.

"I also will retire soon." His voice was more abrupt than usual. "See that there are heated stones aplenty to warm my old bones. I will have Chu here fetch my slippers from the Second Court."

With one hand on her dragonhead walking stick and the other on Chu Ma's shoulder, Madame Tse hobbled down the last chilly corridor to her apartment. She was out of breath, and the gasps she emitted clouded the air. Her girth and the tiny stumps which served as her feet made each step a trial, but now she hardly noticed the agony shooting up her legs. She pulled aside the silk hanging that covered the door to her apartment and went in. Chu Ma helped her sit down in the nearest chair to rest for a moment.

"You heard the master," Madame Tse said. "Hurry and do as you were bid."

"I heard, Mistress." Chu Ma's old face creased in a grin. "As for the stones, they are already warm and resting on the brazier in your bedchamber, though I do not think the master will have need of them to keep warm tonight." The old woman cackled.

Madame Tse shot her a threatening look. *"Pei!* You need your ears boxed for such boldness. What a disrespectful servant you are!" But she too smiled—the secret smile of a bride. After Chu Ma left, she struggled up and made her way to the dressing table. Lifting the lid of her toilet case, she stared at her reflection.

How she had changed since coming to this house! Her

face was no longer the perfect oval it had been, and her
eyes were not shining with health. Her cheeks, indeed her
entire body, were bloated from the eating of fatty foods and
sweets. There were wings of white hair on each side of her
head. "I should not look so at the age of only thirty-three,"
she said aloud. "It is no wonder my husband does not leave
his slippers beside my bed."

No! Her mind rebelled. It was not because of her looks
that Liangmo no longer favored her. She had not always
been fat and gray. Her body had changed only after That
One had come into the house. It was not until then that she
began to seek solace in rich foods and care less for how she
looked.

When not involved in the running of her home, she sat
and played mah-jongg with her lady friends, eating and
gossiping. Sometimes the gambling was done in her own
rooms, or sometimes at the house of Madame Chang or Madame Ling, each taking turns. But even when not so involved, she ate from sunup to sundown. It seemed the only
pleasure left her, except for her daughter.

Madame Tse sat back in her chair and shook her head. A
slow, wistful smile curved her lips as she remembered how
shy she had been when she first entered this house, the
great and renowned House of Tse. Her greatest fear had
been that the man she was to marry sight unseen would
despise her. And what if he were to be the foul-tempered
type? Or ugly?

During the wedding feast, she had stolen a glance at her
bridegroom and her young heart had tripped with happiness, for Tse Liangmo was *not* ugly. He was lean, but not
too lean, and he had fine cheekbones and wide-set eyes.

Madame Tse was one of those lucky women who, by accident and good fortune, had been allowed to marry a man
she might love. Liangmo was more than comely. He possessed a kind and mild disposition as well. He was an ar-
dent lover, and this was also lucky, for the fires in his
young bride were well kindled.

On their wedding night she had been as slim and lithe as
winter bamboo. The couple was spellbound and their affection soon grew so that it was agony for them to be apart at
all. It became a great source of laughter throughout the
household, and as might be expected, a child was very soon

conceived. In those days Madame Tse had been simply Little Flower, while the titles of Madame and Master were given to Liangmo's parents.

What a time of joy that had been! But joy cannot last in this life, and soon the coming birth was overshadowed by a bad omen. It happened at an evening meal while Little Flower was in her sixth month of happiness. Liangmo's father, the Old Master Tse, filled his mouth with hot pork dumplings. Indeed, they were so hot his tongue was scalded and he quickly sucked in air to cool the morsels. This action drew the dumplings down into his windpipe. He made no sound, and the other family members did not realize there was a problem until he fell from his seat, face engorged and purple. All the alarm and the backslapping done by his three sons, his cousins, and nephews did not save the old sir's life.

When, three months later, Little Flower began labor, the house was still deep in mourning. It was a hard birth and the midwife was in the birthing chamber for more than three days. Little Flower did not scream out. She only moaned and tossed from side to side, sure that in the end her agony could not but produce a son for her beloved. After the child was finally born, the young mother began to bleed profusely. The midwife worked frantically to staunch the flow, packing Little Flower's body with strips of cloth. At last the flow was stopped and she was given herbs to thicken her blood, cows'-flesh broth, and fish broth with red sugar. But alas, for all her pain she did not have the son she so desired. There was only a tiny female.

While all this drama took place, Liangmo waited outside the door of the birthing chamber. The air was heavy and rancid with the smell of hot blood. His eyes were shot with red and smudged black beneath. When the midwife emerged, he looked at her and the small bundle she carried. A lusty wail sounded and for the first time Liangmo looked down into the face of his daughter.

As if she could see and knew who he was, the baby girl quieted instantly. Her eyes, unlike most infants', were wide open. The young father put forth a finger and she clutched it. His heart stirred and he decided this was a beautiful child, girl or not. Smiling, he looked at the midwife and saw tears coursing down her cheeks.

"What is it?" he demanded. "The child's mother . . . she is not . . ."

"No, My Lord. The young madame lives, but I fear she will bring forth no more children. She is narrow hipped, and her womb is badly torn. She will conceive no more."

Liangmo took the baby in his arms and sat upon a chair. Without regard for the presence of the midwife, he bent his head down and wept.

It was a long time before Little Flower knew the extent of her misfortune. A nurse was brought for the child and, a little at a time, the mother recovered. Even when the first birth feast of her daughter arrived, she was not overly concerned that she was not yet with child again.

Old Lady, as Liangmo's mother came to be called after her husband's death, knew the truth, but her son begged her to be silent. "The midwife could be wrong," he reasoned. "Perhaps Little Flower *will* conceive. If that is possible, would it not be a bad thing to destroy her harmony with needless worry?"

In his heart of hearts Liangmo did not believe his own words, but he loved his wife and wanted to protect her from pain at any cost. He watched her sitting in their courtyard with Golden Willow, smelling the sweet flesh of the babe's neck and hands. It was a beautiful picture, and he decided that if there were never another child born, he would still be a happy man.

Eventually, however, Old Lady began to grow impatient. A year passed and almost another. Though she did not admit it even to herself, she possessed that brand of jealousy which is common to some mothers. The love Liangmo had for Little Flower somehow irritated her. "You are the eldest son," she would grumble, and her old mouth puckered with disapproval. "Your younger brother is already wed and he has a son. It is not fitting that you care for that wife of yours more than you do for the welfare of the family and the honor of your ancestors. It is *your* son who should be leader of our next generation. It is tradition." Nodding her grayed head, she ranted on. "It is time for you to look about for a Second Wife, my son. Do you think your own father would not have done so if my womb had been dried up before I gave him sons aplenty?" Old

Lady shook her finger in his face. "I tell you he most certainly would have!"

But Tse Liangmo could not bring himself to take a Second Wife. When the demands of his mother grew harsher and more to the point, he made excuses and half promises.

This state of affairs could not go on forever, of course. One day Little Flower was sitting in her courtyard sewing a red silk jacket for Golden Willow when Old Lady came and joined her. The older woman watched her granddaughter run about on sturdy legs, enjoying the spring afternoon.

"The child is fair," she commented.

"Thank you, Mother," Little Flower said proudly, and then immediately remembered her manners. "Of course, she is of small worth, being only a female."

Old Lady nodded. "That is true enough. What does it matter if a girl be fair or not? She need only be strong and able to be a good wife and mother."

Little Flower bent her head over her sewing lest the pain on her face show. She had criticized her daughter for the sake of courtesy only and did not much like her mother-in-law's agreement. Moreover, the fact that she had not yet given Liangmo a son was beginning to chafe sorely. The attitude of Bright Star, the wife of the Second Son, did not help either, for the woman was forever bragging about her newborn son, showing him to everyone. In secret Little Flower had begun drinking drafts that were rumored to help induce fertility. Yet there was still no sign of happiness within her womb.

Old Lady continued to watch Golden Willow, her face bland. She extracted a handful of melon seeds from her pocket and began to eat them. "Yes," she sighed. "Without sons, our family would become no more than a memory, no more than dust."

Little Flower pulled a fine gold thread through the cloth she worked, but said nothing.

"I have asked my First Son to take a Second Wife," Old Lady blurted out, but her wrinkled face still did not change.

The wooden sewing hoop Little Flower held dropped from her hands and clattered on the tiles of the court. There was a nursemaid attending Golden Willow and the little bondsmaid, Crystal, also a toddler, who had been purchased as a playmate and who would later become a servant. This nursemaid stood very still, a look of horror stamped on her face.

Old Lady cracked a melon seed between her teeth and spit out the husk. Nothing about her indicated that this was more than an ordinary, everyday conversation. Little Flower did not know whether to weep aloud or show her anger. Her body suddenly felt numb. She gave a weak little laugh. "Surely, Mother, you make a jest. My Golden Willow is less than three years old. I may be slow due to her hard birth, but there is not a doubt I will have happiness in me any day now. In fact, the seed may be already planted. I will bring forth a son yet, and then another and another!"

Old Lady turned her face up to the warmth of the sun and closed her eyes. She sighed deeply again. "I would not make such a suggestion if I thought there was a chance for you to prove yourself, Daughter. But there is no chance. You are barren."

"I am not!" Little Flower cried, forgetting all respect. She pointed a shaking finger at Golden Willow. "There is the very proof!"

"I say you are barren," Old Lady retorted in a voice cold and hard as iron. "So the midwife said, and so your own husband knows."

At first Little Flower only stared at the set features of her mother-in-law, but then her shoulders drooped. Her whole body seemed to shrink into itself like a wilting flower, for she knew the old woman spoke the truth.

"Did your eldest son say he wanted to take a Second Wife?" Her voice was dull, expressionless.

Old Lady waved her hand impatiently. "He *must* do his duty. It is not a matter of wanting or not wanting. He makes stupid excuses, but in the end he will do what he knows must be done." She looked closely at Little Flower. "You also have a duty," she added. "If my son thinks you are willing, he will do his duty more quickly. His love for you makes him weak. You must encourage him and let him know that you understand the necessity."

Little Flower did not answer. She could not meet the questioning glare of her husband's mother.

I cannot do this thing! her brain screamed silently. *He is my man! I will not share him with another, even if it means I am an undutiful wife!*

Old Lady shrugged elaborately and rose to leave, pausing only long enough to give Golden Willow a pat on the head. She decided to let her daughter-in-law think about the situation, and in the end, perhaps, see her duty clearly. She would not wait forever though. One way or another Liangmo would give her a grandson as he should.

After this terrible day in the courtyard, things might still have remained harmonious between Little Flower and Liangmo had the former managed to stay the creature she had always been. If she had stayed sweet of temper, loving and passionate, neither Old Lady nor anyone could have persuaded Liangmo to seek out a new wife. But ashamed and frightened, Little Flower began to let her grief and worry take hold of her. She could not speak her heart to Liangmo, nor he to her. A wall grew between them that neither seemed able to breach. Often she was swollen-eyed with secret weeping and she did not sleep well. She grew listless. Her only smiles were for Golden Willow, and her life began to revolve around that little girl, who went about completely unaware of the misery of her parents.

In frustration, Liangmo finally began to frequent the local tea houses to escape both the long face of his wife and the constant badgering of his mother. He still slept every night in the high bed he shared with Little Flower, but too often she would turn her back as though she hated him, and he could hear her muffled sobs in the wee hours of the morning.

The inevitable happened all too soon. At one tea house there was a small, birdlike creature named Peach Blossom. She played a stringed instrument with her long lacquered nails, and when she sang in a warbling, high-pitched voice, it was enough to melt the heart of any man. Liangmo was not only a handsome man, he was rich as well. He was, in fact, from one of the wealthiest families in Tanpo. With the weight he carried on his heart he was an easy target for the wiles of a clever flower girl.

Peach Blossom sang and lured. Her eyes alone promised unending pleasure of the flesh. She put forth all her con-

siderable efforts to tantalize. In the end she was successful,
for Liangmo was a proud and passionate man. His wife
turned him away, while this lovely creature let him know
there was no one on earth quite as wonderful as he.

A few weeks after he began bedding Peach Blossom, she
came to him and told him she was with child.

On the day he announced that he would bring Peach
Blossom into the House of Tse as his Second Wife, all turmoil broke loose. Old Lady had wanted him to take another, but not this! She had already been putting her head
together with the matchmaker. The fourth daughter of the
Sung house had seemed a perfect choice.

"Oh, what have you done?" she lamented. "You will
bring wild blood into our family with one such as she! And
how shall I hold up my head before my friends when they
learn I have a daughter-in-law of such origins?"

But Liangmo would hear neither the complaints of his
mother, nor those of his younger brother, nor his brother's
wife, no matter how much they screamed. They had demanded a male child of him at any expense. *Well, good,* he
thought. *Now perhaps they will have one!*

Only before Little Flower did he feel ashamed and contrite, and for this reason more than any other he avoided
her. He moved out of the apartment they shared and into
what came to be known as the Second Court, where Peach
Blossom was installed. When this Second Wife gave birth,
all rejoiced. It was a son—a fine, lusty, bawling son.

Being First Wife, Little Flower was considered First
Mother as well, regardless of the fact that she had not
given birth to the child; and on the day that son was born,
Liangmo had the midwife wrap the child, and went immediately with them both to his former abode as tradition dictated. The midwife knelt on the floor and laid the babe on
top of a rug which was spread before the ebony chair where
Little Flower sat. Once the infant was unwrapped, he
thrashed his arms and legs, letting out an enraged squall
at such indignity.

Little Flower looked down at the tiny scrap of flesh and
felt her heart would break with pain and longing, but she
held her thin body ramrod straight, her face showing only
an aloof, cool pride. She did not look at Liangmo when he
spoke.

"You are my First Wife," he said. "Likewise you are mother of my son and to any number of sons I might have."

He waited to see if she would pick the babe up, but she did not. She only inclined her head slightly. "Congratulations, My Husband," she said in a faraway voice. "He is indeed a fine son, but I fear he is cold. Take him back now to That One who is your Second Wife. Be sure that I will have eggs dyed red and a feast prepared that you might invite your friends for a celebration."

Liangmo felt like a man beaten instead of a proud new father that day, and for a very long time he felt like a dog every time he looked at his First Wife.

The years passed. Old Lady died, attended by none other than Little Flower, for Peach Blossom could not abide age or death, and Liangmo felt an unspoken bitterness toward the old woman who had given him life.

As for Little Flower, she never referred to Peach Blossom by name, calling her only "That One" whenever she was forced to speak of her at all. That One who had stolen her husband's love. That One who had given him sons when she could not.

And sons there were, for two more followed the first without a girl among them.

Now the eldest boy was nearly twelve years old. Madame Tse could not stand him. He had grown to have a thin, narrow face, and to her he always seemed somehow sneaky. The Second Son was solemn, if not discourteous, and Madame Tse neither liked nor disliked him. But the Third Son was different. He was four now, with a round cheerful little face. He looked much like his father and she loved this child very much.

On the little fellow's first birthday, the family had gathered for a feast, as was the custom. It was a special occasion, a naming day. The baby sat on the lap of the wet nurse, struggling to be put down. Finally, the nurse stood him on his fat legs, and he chose that moment to take his first steps, looking from one face to another for approval. When his eyes rested on the face of Madame Tse, he smiled from ear to ear and gurgled. Holding out his arms, he laughed and took six steps toward her.

"Oh, look, Lady," the wet nurse cried. "You and this

third little son must surely be soul mates, for he seeks you above all others."

Madame Tse's heart opened to the child that day. She scooped him up into her arms and nuzzled his neck while the family laughed and clapped, Master Tse loudest and longest of all.

Peach Blossom did not join in the merriment, however. She sat rigid with anger, but she dared not chastise the wet nurse openly as she would have liked to do. Madame Tse and her daughter, Golden Willow, were dearly loved by one and all. It was a terrible frustration for the former flower girl. She had been sure when she first entered the House of Tse that she would be able to dethrone the mistress in no time at all. But this had not happened. Even after that querulous Old Lady had joined her ancestors, Peach Blossom was barely tolerated by the rest of the family, and even that would not have been the case had she not given birth to three sons.

On various occasions, she had attempted to criticize Madame Tse to her husband. This tactic had also failed, for he would hear no evil against his first love.

"If you are so fond of that shriveled old womb, why do you not take yourself to *her* at night?" she had taunted him once as they were arguing and preparing for bed.

For a moment he had looked as if he was about to strike her. He flushed and his lips thinned. But then, all at once, the anger drained out of him. "I am not worthy," was all he would say. He turned his back on Peach Blossom that night, and for days afterward he neither spoke to her nor touched her in any way.

So more years passed. While Peach Blossom grew thinner, Madame Tse grew more rotund. The Second Wife hated the First, and the First the Second. And amidst all this, Golden Willow had grown into a beautiful young woman, the center of Madame Tse's life. It was the greatest pleasure of the older woman to embroider, and she had done so constantly for her daughter. Every robe and slipper Golden Willow wore had been hand decorated. The hems at the bottoms and sleeves of her robes were a montage of flowers and birds. Even the tables in her rooms had been topped with coverings rich in design. Madame Tse had never let a seamstress or anyone else do this labor of love.

Now that Golden Willow was gone, Madame Tse often did the same for the Third Son while Peach Blossom, who could not sew a stitch to save her life, steamed.

It had been after the birth of this last son that a kind of companionship began to develop again between mistress and master. Each evening, for an hour or two, they sat quietly together in one of the central rooms. Most often Master Tse read a book or examined some ancient scroll while Madame Tse worked on her sewing. Sometimes they talked of household matters, a disturbance between relatives or servants, or even shared a tidbit of gossip, something Master Tse had heard while gambling. Golden Willow they discussed as often as propriety would allow.

It was a truce of sorts for them, almost a show of affection, and until tonight Madame Tse had contented herself with these sessions, for she truly believed That One had forever won the heart of her Liangmo.

Now, Chu Ma coughed discreetly to bring her mistress out of her reverie. In her hand the serving woman held a pair of worn velvet slippers with frayed bottoms.

"Ahh," said Madame Tse, "and how is That One tonight?"

Her voice was honey sweet, but Chu Ma knew her mistress far too well to be taken in. She threw back her head and laughed.

"I would not dare repeat the foul words my husband said erupted from the mouth of the Second Lady, Mistress." She laughed harder and wiped tears from her eyes. "How he wished he could paint a picture for you, for he swore the face of That One was something to behold!"

"Hush, Chu Ma, you mean-minded thing," Madame Tse scolded, smiling. "Now go and fetch the stones for the bed and help me prepare for sleep." Madame Tse's eyes twinkled like those of a girl. "Then, get yourself out of here!" Chu Ma did as she was told and then removed the gold and pearl pins from Madame Tse's hair, which she combed and oiled with the fragrance of honeysuckle. She helped her disrobe and attire herself in pale green night garments.

"For once I wish I was less blessed with flesh," Madame

Tse grumbled. "Now that I carry all this fat, how shall I ever rid myself of it?"

Chu Ma smiled. "I think it will be no problem now, Madame. No problem at all."

Within minutes after Chu Ma left, Madame Tse heard the familiar tread of her husband's steps approaching. Even after all the years she still recognized that quick, slightly impatient sound.

The woman servant, Chu Ma, had closed the canopy around the bed before leaving, and now it was pulled open a crack. The face of Master Tse peeked in. He smiled a little shyly and the drape closed again. Madame Tse could hear him moving about, taking off his robe and putting it over the back of a chair as he always had. The oil lamps were doused, and when he crawled in beside her she could not see his face clearly. He stayed on his own side of the bed for a bit, lying face up.

Master Tse could feel the heat of his wife next to him. It radiated from her full breasts and rounded thighs with more intensity than the stones at his feet.

"I am glad to be back, Little Flower," he said softly into the dark. "Three sons are enough for any man." There was just a slight hesitation. "I have missed you."

"And I you, Husband." Little Flower held out her ample arms and welcomed Liangmo home.

Chapter Seven

The sun shone brightly for a change. The day was unseasonably pleasant and Master Tse decided to walk to his rendezvous with Master Chang. Due to his reconciliation with his First Wife he was more at peace with himself than he had been in years. There was a bounce in his step, and had he not been so abundantly happy, he would have groaned aloud at the stupidity he had displayed over the past dozen years.

What good is life, he asked himself, without the comfort of a good, wholesome woman? A man cannot even enjoy his sons if he is forever hounded by their mother.

When he thought of sons he could not help but think first of his eldest. Doing so now he cringed slightly, for never could he look at the boy without self-disgust. He, Tse Liangmo, had been made a fool in the oldest way possible. He was still grateful that his deceased parents and his younger brothers had not known how long he had lain with Peach Blossom before bringing her to the House of Tse. It was bad enough for a man to view a clown in his own looking glass without the rest of the world joining in the laughter.

Heaving a deep sigh, he dwelt but momentarily on his second boy. A quiet lad, Po, but there was something a bit disconcerting about him too. Even as a babe he had seemed to possess an unusually undemonstrative personality. One could never be sure if Po was happy or sad, angry or amused. The boy was a puzzle.

Master Tse let his vision range upward to the snow-crested mountains and on to the cloud-dappled sky. As he walked along, the townspeople called out to him and he waved back. The door of a small silk shop opened and the merchant came out. "Good morning, Honorable Master Tse," he bellowed. "Wonderful weather that Old Man in the Sky has sent, is it not?"

"Indeed," agreed Master Tse. "A day blessed by all the gods!"

The merchant smiled after him as he continued on. The exclamation seemed no exaggeration to Master Tse today. All things considered, the gods seemed kind. He did have one son, at least, in whom he completely delighted. That rosy-faced Lo'ting was enough to win any but the coldest heart. Yes, he decided, he had Lo'ting, and above all he had regained the love of Little Flower. He hummed a tune to himself as he turned onto the main street.

The Tea House of Quan Sung sat snugly between a bakery and an herb shop. It was certainly not the largest or most luxurious establishment of its kind to be found in Tanpo, but it was always comfortable and full of good cheer. There were no flower girls to entice or distract. Only the bluff fellow who ran it with his wife and eldest son. That proprietor looked up and a broad smile lit his face when he saw Master Tse, a frequent and highly valued customer. Not more than a moment later Master Chang also entered, and the man considered himself doubly blessed to receive two such wealthy men in his establishment at the same time.

After amenities had been exchanged, the two friends were led to a quiet corner table and served immediately. In a leisurely fashion they discussed several joint business interests and the favored topic of the day, the weather. Finally, however, the conversation began to lag a bit and Master Tse knew his companion must be patiently waiting to learn the exact reason this meeting had been requested. So, taking a deep breath, he began working toward his intended goal, at the same time praying the words he was about to speak and had practiced for the past two days would not injure his best friend.

"No doubt you are wondering why I asked you here today, Hai-teh," he began.

As courtesy dictated, Master Chang shook his head in protest. "Indeed not. There need be no excuse for us to meet and share a little conversation. However, if there is a matter you wish to discuss, I am more than eager to hear it."

"I hesitate because you will undoubtedly think me a fool for being so fond of that worthless female I sired."

Master Chang was taken somewhat aback by this confession, not because he felt there was anything amiss in his friend's statement, but because the worry of Fengmo and Golden Willow had been so much on his own mind. In fact, that very morning he had received a letter which he hoped would soon resolve the situation. Carefully, he prompted the other man to continue.

Master Tse put on a jovial front. "Oh, you know how women are, Hai-teh. They will find the littlest thing to worry over. Take my First Wife now. She is forever mistaking a hummingbird for an eagle. Two days ago she went to visit our daughter, the first time she has done so since our houses have been joined. And she fears . . . at least she seems to think it possible . . ." All the words he had planned were suddenly almost unspeakable. How was one to tell his best friend, the companion of his youth, that his son was a possible beater of females?

Master Chang saw his discomfort. "Come, Liangmo. How long have we known one another? We have been friends from our mothers' wombs. Speak if you have a question."

Master Tse looked at him miserably. "I would like to say my wife is being foolish and concerned for naught, Hai-teh. Perhaps that is indeed the case. I know her to be a very perceptive woman, however, not given to fantasy, and so when she is concerned I am also. Forgive me for saying so, but she fears Golden Willow is less than happy in your home."

The words seemed so unpardonably rude that he prepared himself for an angry explosion. When his friend appeared completely unperturbed it came as a surprise.

"You need not ask my forgiveness, Liangmo." Master Chang smiled. "We are both fathers, after all. I too am inordinately attached to my little girls. It would distress me greatly if I felt they did not lead happy lives." He became very serious. "We cannot always control these things, however. Let me ask you, did my daughter-in-law say she was unhappy for some particular reason?"

Master Tse hastened to correct this misconception. "Please, I would not have you believe Golden Willow is one of those overemotional girls who run weeping to their mothers at the least provocation. She made no complaint whatsoever."

"Then I fail to understand your concern." Master Chang put down his unexpected irritation as best he could, but his finger began tapping the edge of the wooden table impatiently.

Master Tse began to feel like a dog trapped in an alleyway. He would have liked nothing better than to be able to make some lame excuse and change the subject altogether, but his love for Golden Willow would not allow this. "It is all on account of a bruise," he blurted out. "My First Wife believes she saw an unusual bruise on our daughter, one difficult to receive by simply bumping herself in some mishap."

There, it was finally spoken!

As suddenly as it had started, the finger of Master Chang stopped beating its tattoo. His eyes narrowed as the implication of what had been said became clear. Color flooded his cheeks. It was all he could do to stay seated, and when he finally spoke his voice came out in an angry hiss. "I will pardon a foolish parent for the sake of our friendship, Liangmo. But this . . . this comes close to slander! I can well believe a young woman might be a bit melancholy until she adjusts to married life. A bride is often homesick. I will also admit that my son is not without reputation in Tanpo. He is perhaps a bit too spirited. But what you accuse him of . . . why, I tell you it is not in his nature!"

Now that the damage was done Master Tse refused to be so easily dissuaded. "Oh? And how can you know for certain? Tell me, Hai-teh, is he given to a bad temper? When he was child did he bully those younger than himself? You speak of friendship to me. Does not that same friendship prompt you to at least examine the situation with an objective eye?"

A cold dread crept into Master Chang's soul for he remembered only too well the times Kao had abused his siblings. Moreover, he knew full well the other man was equally aware of this fact. Years ago the two of them had talked of one such incident, and at the time Liangmo had been quick to give an understanding ear and reassurance.

It was not difficult for Master Tse to see the struggle taking place within his friend's mind. "Listen to me," he gently said. "I am not accusing your eldest son. I ask only that you be observant and watchful for the safety of one I hold dear. Is it too much I request?"

Master Chang was a bigger man than many. He slowly shook his head. "It is not too much, dear friend, not too much at all. I say again, I think you are wrong and mistaken in your concern. I believe this to be true. But I will not be willfully blind in the matter. I intend to watch and even discreetly question those who might know for certain."

They both knew he meant the servants, for those humble folk were always an amazing font of information. Master Tse was satisfied. His eyes rested kindly on the face of Hai-teh. "I most humbly thank you," he said, "and ask you to forgive me for having damaged our relationship. It is the last thing I wanted."

Waving a dismissing hand, Master Chang forced himself to smile. "Think not that, Liangmo." He signaled the proprietor for more tea. "You and I will be friends—no, more than friends, almost brothers—until we grow old and gray."

For all these confident words, the remainder of their time together was subdued and strained. Very soon they made an excuse to bid farewell and went to their separate homes, each wrapped in his own thoughts.

A child was ill in the Chang household. It was only the third son of a second cousin, but Madame Chang always waited upon the ill in her domain, even the servants. Now she laid a cool poultice upon the little boy's flushed brow while both his father and mother stood nervously above her.

"What do you suppose it is, First Mother?" The wife of the cousin twisted her hands in despair. "He has always been bright and healthy, with hardly a cough in all his four years."

Madame Chang rose and addressed the pair. When she spoke it was in her most reassuring tone. "I fear he has that fevered rash brought to us so long ago from across the sea. Within a few hours I believe you will see his body covered with tiny red spots."

The child's mother began to weep and Madame Chang put a slim hand on her shoulder. "Try not to worry. The disease is serious enough for concern, but not often deadly. Keep him well covered and have him drink broth and as much water as he will. More than this you cannot do." She looked at the other children standing wide-eyed and frightened in the doorway, two boys and a tiny girl, and then back at the distraught parents.

"This will present a problem," she warned. "We do not wish the illness to spread throughout the house. Who has your Little Three been with these past two days or so?"

The mother stopped weeping for a moment and thought. "Let me see," she said. "Two days ago my mother came, but she suffered the rash as a child and I am told it visits a body only once."

Madame Chang nodded. "Have there been others, children perhaps?"

"No," the woman answered positively. "You will remember how cold it has been until today, First Mother. I kept all my little ones indoors, not like some I know, and I have had no visitors except my own mother."

The two rooms in this small apartment were very neat. The children were all clean and clear eyed. Madame Chang hoped all would be well with the inhabitants there. She hated to disturb the mother further, though she knew she must. "There is a chance that the other children will become ill also," she said. "Unless you and your husband have been sickened this way before, neither are you immune."

"I have," the boy's father offered. "I was sick just like my Little Three here when I was about the same age."

"Good," said Madame Chang. "I also am protected. But you must hang a white cloth on your gate to warn others away, and above all keep your family within your own court until the danger is passed."

Since there was nothing more she could do, she took her leave. The cousin escorted her to the gate. It was obvious the fellow was worried. "My wife is a tender mother," he said, not without pride. "She will not rest until this business is finished. Perhaps I will not go to the warehouse for a while."

Had it been another speaking, Madame Chang might have suspected the man of finding an excuse for laziness, but not in this case. She nodded. "I am sure my husband, your cousin, would approve. It has come to my ears that your good wife is with child again, and being so, she will be more than ever easily upset. She will need your help." Giving the man her warmest smile, she said, "I will pray the gods send you another son."

"Thank you, Madame Chang. In all humility might I ask that you also light a joss stick for out Little Three? All in the House of Chang know that heaven pays you special heed."

Accepting this compliment with magnanimity, she nodded again. Her special ability with the gods *was* in fact a rumor, but one which privately pleased her very well.

The man opened the gate for her. "Do you remember the foreign doctor who used to live on the Street of Two Geese, Madame? He was a frightening one, he was, with his head all aflame." The cousin did not notice the suddenly stiffened spine of his listener, nor the fact that she did not answer. He went on. "I am not above wishing he were here in Tanpo still. Perhaps a foreigner could cure a—"

"Do not speak so!" Her voice lashed out, cutting him off in midsentence.

The cousin was amazed to find a look of pure rage stamped on her features. Knowing that somehow he had angered her, he hastened to apologize. "Forgive me, Madame Chang. I did not mean to imply your expert care was lacking in any way. Indeed, I am sure—"

"Fool! I know my own worth! My pride is not so easily wounded." Her next words were ground out from between clenched teeth. "Those foreign medicine men are dangerous! They are foul, every one of them!" With that she turned and stalked through the open gate, showing none of her usual grace and aplomb.

Flabbergasted, the second cousin watched her go. His mouth was agape with shock, for never had he seen her act anything but completely controlled. Her reaction was all the more inexplicable because the cousin was *sure* the doc-

tor he mentioned had been called to this very house some
years back.

Shaking his head, the man pulled the gate closed and
then turned his mind back to the problem at hand. With
hurried steps he went inside to fetch a white cloth of warning.

That night, during the evening meal, Master Chang
looked across to the lower table where all the female members of his immediate family were seated. He observed
them in a way that would not draw attention, but observed
closely nonetheless. His gaze tripped quickly enough over
his two daughters, who were smiling and talking in high
animated voices. His wife appeared unusually restive, but
this he did not dwell on either. For the most part his attention fastened itself on his new daughter-in-law.

The girl is beautiful, he thought, and as graceful as her
name. If that First Son of mine has a grain of sense, he will
count himself fortunate.

Of all those at the table, only Golden Willow was aware
of his scrutiny. Consequently, she kept her eyelids modestly lowered and her face even more composed than usual,
presenting a picture of perfect calm. Only a person very
near her could have seen the rapid pulse at the cleft of her
throat, or the slight trembling of her hands as she moved
the food about on her plate with a set of delicate ivory chopsticks. Though she knew it was impossible, she had the un-
reasonable fear that somehow her father-in-law knew her
deepest secret. When he finally turned his attention elsewhere she breathed an inaudible sigh of relief.

Master Chang saw nothing in the girl's appearance to
give him pause, and had he not known otherwise, he would
never have guessed she was anything but happy and sublimely content.

Sitting on his right were Kao and Fengmo. He looked at
them now and wished with all his heart that one day they
would both be contented husbands and fathers. They were
such good-looking young men, each in his own way. Their
black hair was cut in the modern short style and their skin
gleamed with good health.

Having finished his meal, Kao lit a cigarette, enjoy-

ing a habit his father thought somewhat less than manly.
Fengmo was silent, as he seemed always to be these days.

It was difficult for Master Chang to enjoy his food that
evening. Later, when he tried to sit in his library and read,
he could not concentrate at all. His mind kept returning
either to Kao and his marriage or Fengmo and his frustration. Finally, he slammed the book down and massaged his
temples in an attempt to relieve a throbbing headache. His
eyes fell on a letter which rested on the table at his elbow.
Picking the missive up, he scanned its pages for the tenth
time.

I will speak to my Second Son tomorrow, he decided.
That, at least, is a problem I can solve.

Fengmo stood in one of the many Chang storerooms. All
around him were shelves filled to overflowing with crates
and boxes of various sizes, all neatly labeled as to contents.
Some held incense. Larger ones contained bolt upon bolt of
cloth. Some of these were rich silks and others velvet or
cotton. More and more his father's shops stocked foreign
goods, and these boxes were stenciled in the strange script,
with equivalent Chinese characters beneath. These were
the ones Fengmo now stood before, taking inventory. Normally this chore would have been performed by a clerk,
but of late Fengmo felt the need to fill his days with activity, thereby giving himself less time for troubling
thoughts. Since he truly found the many family enterprises of interest, he threw himself wholeheartedly into
them.

Hearing someone enter the room, he looked up to see his
father, whom he greeted with courtesy. The two of them
had spoken little since the night they had spent together
at the tea house on the Street of the Golden Bridge, and the
younger was beginning to wonder if his father had forgotten their conversation completely.

"I would see you in my office," Master Chang informed
him briskly.

Fengmo raised his eyebrows in a question, but his father's expression told him nothing. Following behind, he
went through a door at the back of the storeroom and entered
a small neat office. A large desk of unadorned teak dominated the room, and Master Chang took his place behind

it. After taking a letter from the pocket of his black silk robe, he bade Fengmo be seated. The two faced one another, and without preamble, the elder began to speak.

"I have given much thought to your request to go abroad," he said. "Do you still wish to do so?"

There was a pause. Fengmo was beginning to repent his earlier decision, made in such haste. If he were to go away, he might not see Golden Willow again for a year or even two. At least now he could peek at her, albeit guardedly, during the evening meals. Yet these times were as much torture as they were pleasure. His own emotions confused him.

"I am not certain, Father," came his hesitant reply. The inscrutable stare he received disconcerted him more than ever.

"Well, in any case, I have given it thought," Master Chang said. "I have a suggestion to make which seems a compromise." He tapped the letter with his forefinger. "This is correspondence from an associate of mine. Perhaps you will remember hearing me speak of him. His name is Wong Cho, a good friend."

Fengmo nodded, remembering snatches of conversation exchanged in years gone by. To his best recollection the gentleman referred to was a resident of the coastal city of Shanghai.

Master Chang continued. "Since he speaks their language, Wong Cho acts as intermediary in many of my dealings with foreign merchants. He has made a most generous offer, which I hope you will find pleasing. You are to go to him in Shanghai where your visit will serve a dual purpose. While there, you will be tutored in the foreign tongue until you speak it passably well, and at the same time learn that portion of my business. In the end you will be able to handle our foreign trade yourself." He sat back and waited for his son's reaction to this carefully laid plan.

As for Fengmo, he had the somewhat disquieting feeling that while all this seemed simply a suggestion, in reality it was more a command. He forced enthusiasm into his reply. "It sounds very interesting, Father. I thank you for your consideration."

When he made no further comment Master Chang explained in more detail. "Going across the sea does not seem a good idea just now. You are well aware of those Japanese vultures in Manchuria. Political affairs are very uneasy at present. In fact, Master Wong, who is well versed in such affairs, informs me there is trouble brewing abroad also. Better for you to stay closer to home, my son, though I realize you wish to do otherwise."

Fengmo could not quite meet his father's eyes. "I agree, sir."

"You wish to go then?"

Fleetingly, the younger man wondered what would happen if he were to answer in the negative, but he quickly put the thought aside. In his mind he knew he *should* go away. Only his wayward heart rebelled. "Yes, Father, I wish to go."

Master Chang beamed. "Good! Then it is settled. You should begin your preparations today for there is much to do. I would have you depart in three days' time."

He did not inform his son that he had already sent a letter of thanks and acceptance ahead to Master Wong.

Chapter Eight

Crystal was establishing her own place in the House of Chang. Her nature so uniquely combined sweetness with strength of character that in less than a single cycle of the moon she became a great favorite among her peers. The other servants knew, as had the old gardener, that she would one day hold power over them, but while this fact might force them to be outwardly courteous, it could never have demanded their private respect. Respect was a commodity Crystal won through sheer force of personality. She did not indulge in gossip, especially none that revolved around her mistress or other members of the Chang family. Yet she managed never to appear haughty or self-righteous either. For all her youth, she showed wisdom and a shrewd perceptiveness about those around her. Encouragement seemed to come from her without effort, and as a result, anyone with a problem wanted to share it with her.

There were few things that aroused anger in Crystal, but those few were soon known by all. After a while, no one would have dared cast the least aspersion against Golden Willow, for to do so was to bring the wrath of all the gods down upon oneself in the form of a tiny serving maid. The head cook in the kitchen learned this at his dire expense. This cook, Li Chi, was married to Madame Chang's female servant. Normally a boisterous fellow, he was given to a good, if often slightly loud, temperament. The grease-encrusted apron he so proudly wore was his badge of merit, accepted evidence of culinary genius. But where Crystal was concerned, Li Chi held a grudge. Firstly, he was very jealous for his own wife's authority, which he felt was threatened by the newcomer. Secondly, Crystal refused to pay his own First Son, whom he considered highly eligible, the least bit of attention, though it was obvious to anyone with eyes that the boy was besotted by her. Why, she would not even give this good son a sideways glance!

Mornings were not Li Chi's best time in any case. For the first two hours or so after he arose from bed he was cranky and out of sorts with everyone. Most of the staff took the precaution of tiptoeing around him during that period of the day—all except Crystal, who was not easily intimidated by anyone, least of all a man. The verbal barbs the cook tossed her way when she came to eat her morning meal disturbed her not a bit—at first.

"Oh, my," he would say in a honeyed voice. "Here is the queenly new one come to grace us with her presence. I best fetch a stool for her at once!" So saying, he would do exactly that, but with such exaggerated mannerisms that the act of courtesy could only be construed as an insult.

Crystal was not to be so easily baited, however, and with a gracious smile she would accept his offering as if the gesture were something other than sarcastic.

Seeing that this sort of ploy accomplished nothing, the man revised his tactics. He kept needling until he eventually found her weakness. Then, by continuing to make sly, thinly veiled innuendos about spoiled young ladies, the daughters of rich and well-named families, he could enjoy watching Crystal suddenly go all stiff and silent. Finally, one morning he carried this fun a bit too far, and unfortunately for him, there was many a witness to his humiliation.

"I hear tell there are *some* young women these days who are so pampered and spoiled they refuse to lift a finger for themselves," he said to no one in particular. "Oftentimes their servants are rotten too. Good-for-nothings who give themselves false airs." The spectators did not respond to this, but all covertly watched Crystal, who kept her attention tightly riveted on the bowl of *jok* she was eating.

"I suppose you cannot blame a mere servant for being lazy," Li Chi continued. "After all, why should a body do more than necessary? It is the rich ones I find disgusting, especially the rich women who do nothing but eat and play the whole day long, and grow fat as cows in their old age.

Why, I hear tell some of these women cannot even rouse themselves for the sake of their husbands!"

Spots of color appeared on both of Crystal's cheeks.

"Yes," prodded the cook, "these women are so worthless they even refuse their lords, so the poor young masters are forced to take what little pleasure they can with flower girls."

With quiet dignity, Crystal set her bowl aside and rose to leave. She was just passing by Li Chi when he chose to issue his next comment. "Now take the wife of our master's First Son. She is one of those—"

The closest weapon at hand was a plucked fowl. Crystal snatched the limp thing up from a nearby cooking block and, holding it by the legs, charged full force at the surprised Li Chi.

"You son of a turtle's turtle!" She swung her arm in a wide arc and the dead bird caught its target square in the face. "You will leave my mistress out of your loathsome conversations!"

This attack was more than the antagonist had bargained for. The blow caught him off-balance, causing him to fall to one knee. Still enraged, Crystal now gave her normally subdued temper full rein. With righteous fury she continued to pummel the man's head and shoulders. "Take that, you garden worm! And that! And that! You are not worthy to prepare broth for the one I serve!"

This was an insult beyond bearing, and with an injured bellow Li Chi almost got back on his feet, only to be beaten down again. Bits of bird skin adhered to his nose and forehead. Finally, in an effort to escape further pain and loss of face, he scurried on all fours to hide beneath the raised cooking block and covered his head. Crystal pounded him severely the whole way. When she could no longer reach the object of her wrath, she threw the fowl after him. It hit his large backside and fell to the floor with a resounding splat.

The kitchen was absolutely silent for a moment. The dozen or so servants who had been watching this spectacle held their breaths. Then, together, they began to laugh, poor Li Chi's own wife and eldest son loudest of all. Amidst this roar, Crystal came to herself and smiled in embarrassment. Straightening her shoulders, she gathered what remained of her dignity and left the kitchen with no small amount of aplomb. Only then did the cook creep from his refuge. The best he could do was wipe the grease from his red face and try to make a joke of the entire affair.

From that day on Li Chi gave Crystal a wide, silent, and highly respectful berth. In private, however, he counseled his unbelieving son, "I tell you, the last thing you need is such a spirited wife. A man could easily die by marrying such a one!"

Yes, Crystal managed very well in her new home and would have been completely happy except for the loathing and contempt she felt toward Chang Kao. For all her nimble mind and tongue, she could not think of a name or an oath vile enough to suit the man who had made her beloved mistress so thoroughly miserable.

There was another thing that constantly nagged at the edges of her mind too, and it was this. She became convinced that Golden Willow's sorrow was even more deeply rooted than it had first appeared to be. Crystal had served the other girl for as long as she could remember, until now they seemed almost two halves of the same whole. Before the wedding she had often come upon her mistress to find her gazing off into space, a dreamy expression on her features. It had seemed natural enough in those days. Now, however, the same moods were entirely at odds with circumstance. Yet they persisted.

At night, after the gross sounds emanating from the adjoining bedroom had subsided, Crystal would lay on her narrow cot in one corner of the sitting room, pondering. Perhaps, *if* she could unravel the mystery of Golden Willow, she could also find a way to make her happy. At last, though, since no key seemed forthcoming, she let her mind dwell upon her own life and plans.

Her general dislike of the male gender and disdain for the sex act were daily becoming more ingrained. It was certainly not because she lacked admirers, or because she feared spinsterhood. In fact, the eldest son of Li Chi was forever stumbling across her path, while the Second Son of the waterkeeper also vied for her attention. Neither was given the least encouragement. The more Crystal thought, the more she became convinced that marriage was not for her. That a match might be arranged for her without her prior knowledge or consent became her greatest fear.

Desperate that this should not happen, she finally decided she must broach the subject with her mistress. She chose that quiet time after Golden Willow had awakened and groomed, but before Kao had stirred.

Golden Willow sat at the table partaking of her morning meal of white rice and strips of salted pork, noodles in thin broth, and tiny winter apples. She was in one of her reflective moods again, quiet—listening to some voice or seeing some image apparent to no one but herself. And again Crystal wondered and worried.

Golden Willow laid her chopsticks aside and Crystal approached. "Would you care for more tea, Mistress? I have prepared Cloud Mist this morning."

The faraway look left Golden Willow's eyes and she smiled. "Only if you will join me. Sit down, Crystal. It has been a long time since we have had the opportunity to speak in any depth. Tell me now how you find life in the great House of Chang."

It seemed a perfect opening. Crystal took a seat, much as she used to do in the days before the wedding, and in no time she was telling her mistress of the other inhabitants, the ones who gave service to the rich. Each character she described in detail and truthfully, yet with such gestures, expressions, and examples that soon Golden Willow was wiping tears of mirth from her eyes. Crystal had a talent hidden to most. She was an uncanny mimic. By blowing her cheeks out and shifting her posture, she could become the rotund and oily Li Chi in a flash. Likewise, when she stooped, squinted, and let her lips droop slightly at the corners, one would almost swear they saw Li Ma in the flesh. Purposely, she saved her description of the eldest Li son for last.

"I tell you, Mistress, never have you seen such a bumpkin! Why, he stumbles every third step or so and he is constantly in the way. I no sooner turn a corner than there *he* is, tripping over his own big feet." She clicked her tongue in mock disgust. "It must be that right eye of his, the one which refused to look straight. It turns in just so." Slowly, in nearly incredible pantomime, she crossed not both eyes but only her right.

Golden Willow covered her mouth to soften a peal of laughter. "Shame, Crystal!" she chastised without conviction. "How unlike you to make fun of another's deformity. Has it not occurred to you that the poor boy might suffer another malady?"

Her face normal again, the serving girl was all innocence. "What malady, Mistress? The dolt seems sound enough to me, in spite of his crooked eye."

"Stir your brains, you silly thing! The fellow is blinded not by his eye but rather by his admiration for you!"

Crystal had the good grace *and* the acting ability to blush. "Oh, surely *not!*"

Golden Willow shook a prophetic finger. "Mark my words, I tell you his mother is probably already cooking a brew with the matchmaker. Any day there will be someone calling upon me to request your pledge."

Now was the propitious moment for Crystal to let her countenance fall. Her expression of dismay was not feigned either, for she knew she *must* make Golden Willow understand her plight. "Please, Mistress, do not say such a thing! Promise you will not pledge me or offer any dowry at all!"

Seeing this look and believing it to be—as it truly was—genuine, Golden Willow hastened to reassure. "Do not fret, Crystal; I will bid for time and come to you first. You shall not have to wed a man whom you cannot tolerate. Only with your permission will I guarantee your troth."

"I will *never* give permission." The words were spoken softly, without a trace of defiance, and yet they were very firm. Crystal lowered her eyes. "I wish never to wed, Mistress. I want no man in my bed or in my life. The marriages of others have shown me nothing I desire for myself."

Shaking her head, Golden Willow reached out and rested her hand on the other girl's arm. "Do not judge by what you have seen here, Crystal." Her voice was an intense whisper. "All men are not the same. Believe me."

Absorbed, neither of them realized that Chang Kao had awakened until a click sounded and his disheveled form filled the doorway leading from the bedchamber. The blue night-robe he wore gaped open in front, revealing an expanse of bare flesh. He yawned widely and scratched, blinking his eyes. "Crystal!" he barked. "Fetch me some tea at once. My mouth is dry."

There could not have been a less opportune time for him

to make an entrance. All the loathing Crystal felt boiled
up in her as she slowly stood. Normally, she kept her eyes
downcast and her face passive when he was about; but
now, caught unaware, her gaze fixed itself on him and contempt was clearly mirrored in her expression. It was all
she could do to force herself to move.

This disdain was not missed by Kao. His eyes narrowed
to slits as he watched her taking halting steps toward a
tray that sat atop a warming brazier. Just as she reached
for the bamboo handle of the teapot, he took four giant
steps and caught hold of her jacket. Lifting her nearly off
the floor, he shook her until her teeth rattled. "How dare
you look at me so!" he bellowed. "You are nothing in this
house, nothing but a female slave! Do you think I will
abide your insolence?"

The serving girl went limp beneath this assault, her
head wobbling back and forth like a cloth doll's.

There was a small fruit knife lying on the table next to
Golden Willow, and without taking time to consider the
possible consequences, she grabbed it and leapt up. Running, she threw her own body between Kao and Crystal,
shoving her husband back with all her might. Crystal
dropped to the floor in a heap.

Blotches of rage mottled Kao's face. His heavy jowls
quivered with indignation. "You!" he snarled. He took a
step back toward his wife. "I will teach you . . ."

His voice thinned to a shriek of pain, for in a swift movement Golden Willow buried the small knife hilt-deep in his
extended and threatening forearm. Just as quickly, she extracted the blade and blood gushed out, splattering his
robe and the floor. He stared at her in dumb shock.

She was crouched, with eyes glittering dangerously. "If
you dare lay a hand on my servant again, I will surely kill
you!" This warning was hissed from between clenched
teeth. There was something about her strength, a tigerlike
ferocity, which caused Kao to pale.

"My arm," he whined. "I am bleeding to death!"

Straightening herself, Golden Willow threw the knife
aside. All tension left her body and an expression of complete calm claimed her features. She unwrapped the sash
which girded her waist. With cool dexterity, she wrapped
the thing about her husband's wound, speaking quietly

the whole time. "If you accuse me of this, I will freely admit my misdeed. I will also tell the entire household exactly what life is like here in the apartment of Chang Kao. After I confess, even your own mother will know how I am used by you. I will gladly accept the shame of returning to my parents' home."

This warning, issued in a voice so tranquil, caused Kao to pale still further. Tears of self-pity pooled in his eyes as he cradled his arm and slunk silently back to the bedchamber, closing the door behind him.

When he had gone, Golden Willow turned back to Crystal. The neat braid the serving girl normally wore had become unraveled and the top three buttons of her cotton jacket were missing. She looked up at her mistress with adoring eyes, but when she spoke her voice was strangely choked.

"No, Mistress," she whispered, "I wish *never* to marry."

Heaven repented its fair mood, and once more it began to snow. Crystal awoke and hurriedly dressed, her teeth chattering loudly. The air in the apartment was so cold her breath came out in puffs of fog. With deft ability, she went quickly about fueling the four braziers, which would soon warm the sitting room. Once assured the coals had caught sufficiently, she donned a long coat of heavily padded cotton. It had become her habit to rise very early and, after seeing to this duty, go to the water shed to arrange for Golden Willow's bath. Only then would she allow herself to retire to the huge main kitchen and take her morning meal with the other servants.

Dawn was just beginning to pierce a leaden sky when she stepped outside. There was no wind, and huge snowflakes drifted down, a kaleidoscope of pristine beauty. She was halfway across the court when a latch rattled and the moon gate began to swing inward. For no reason she could imagine except that it was early and a little eerie in the half-light, Crystal stepped into the sheltering branches of a small pine. Concealed there, she watched to see who would enter.

The tall figure of a man appeared. Dressed as he was in a heavy jacket, leather boots, and gloves, it took several moments for her to recognize the intruder. Her eyes widened slightly at the sight of Chang Fengmo.

He took a couple of tentative steps into the court and then stopped. A fur hat covered his hair, but flakes of snow lit and caught on his dark brows and lashes. His eyes fixed themselves on the door of his brother's apartment, and the look of sorrow and longing stamped on his features caused the generous heart of Crystal to twist in sudden and painful understanding. His expression was not unknown to her, for she had often seen one similar.

Oh, Mistress, she silently cried. *This has been your burden all along! It has always been the Second Son!*

So Fengmo stood. He was statue-still, the only movement his breath clouding the air. He presented such a sight that Crystal was nearly overcome with the maternal desire to comfort him. For the first time the little maid experienced a tender rush of sympathy toward a member of the male gender. He whispered then, softly, but she heard each word.

"Goodbye, My Soul. Goodbye." He turned and abruptly left the court.

With the quick stealth of a winter fox, Crystal followed him, her mind racing. *He is leaving and my mistress does not know! Somehow I must find a way to tell her before she hears it unexpectedly from another. She must know too that he bade her farewell.* She traced his steps to the main gate, which stood open onto the street. To her surprise a small caravan was waiting.

The sight of an automobile was still an unusual one in Tanpo. Only a few of the most wealthy families owned one, and even so they were rarely to be seen on the narrow streets. The houses of Chang, Tse, Lung, and Lau boasted businesses large enough to justify trucks, but only for transporting cargo. The loud, gear-grinding contraptions rumbled to and from the warehouses, causing the residents in those poorer sections of town to swear aloud in fear.

Two trucks and a large automobile now stood outside the gate, their headlights aglow like the eyes of malevolent beasts, and the sight of them filled Crystal with trepidation. Chang Fengmo stood in the beams of these lights giving instructions to three men she had never seen before.

"Since we haul no cargo, we need not worry about robber bands," Fengmo explained. "I have been instructed by my father to hire a small cadre of armed men for our return trip, however. There are supposed to be many guards available in Shanghai if one only knows how to select them properly."

The words "Shanghai" and "return" did not go unremarked by Crystal, and she breathed a small sigh of relief from where she remained hidden beside the gate.

"I know of many such," offered one burly fellow, who then gestured toward the man next to him. "Lee here has a cousin in Shanghai who can be hired."

"Very well." Fengmo nodded. "You two get into the trucks now and follow, but not too closely. Fong Lu will lead the way."

The third man he indicated fairly leapt in his anxiety to open a back door of the automobile. "This way, Young Sir. I will have you on the streets of Shanghai in no time!"

Chang Fengmo allowed himself a rueful smile. "*If* you can find the way, you rascal."

The man named Fong Lu laughed loudly, a slightly nervous sound. "Never fear, Master. You are safe with me."

Crystal shivered as Fengmo bent and disappeared into the bowels of the frightening foreign machine. When the engines roared to life, she jumped and ran swiftly back into the safety of the compound, her heart hammering at top speed.

Chapter Nine

Kao faced a dilemma. After his mistreatment of Crystal and the subsequent confrontation with Golden Willow, he no longer felt any confidence or authority within the confines of his own apartment. On the night following the incident he did not retire at his usual hour. After the evening meal, he donned a heavy coat and went directly to that tea house on the Street of the Golden Bridge. The wound on his forearm still throbbed painfully, for he had not the nerve to go to his mother to have it attended. This discomfort and his private loss of self-esteem combined to put him in a very poor frame of mind indeed.

The proprietress of the tea house, Madame Ying, made men her business. She almost gloated aloud when she saw Kao, his face a mask of petulance, walk through the door. He was no stranger to her in any case. Many of his days were spent gambling and drinking in her establishment. But this was the first time she had seen him at night since the renowned wedding and she could only assume there had been a spat between the newlyweds, a fact which gratified her no end. Dissatisfied husbands were her stock-in-trade. They never failed to swell this lady's already bulging coffers. She greeted Kao with a warm smile.

"Ah, good evening to you, Young Chang. How pleasant to see you again. My little flowers have missed your illustrious presence."

Not to be placated, Kao scowled deeper. "Do not speak to me of women tonight. They are ever the undoing of a good, decent man."

Madame Ying allowed herself to look contrite. "Yes, yes, we are too often a burden, I am sure. It shames me no end to know how many of my own kind are worthless creatures." She sighed and shook her head. "It is a pity we cannot all have the soothing grace and even temper of Sweet Harmony."

They stood in the foyer, but at this mention of a new and unfamiliar flower girl, Kao let his eyes range over the occupants of the main tearoom. Several girls sat on a raised platform plucking instruments while three or four others moved about serving patrons. There were none, however, that he had not seen before, and he had bedded with most of them as well.

Madame Ying chuckled to herself at his obvious interest and disappointment. "You will not find Sweet Harmony *there,* sir. No, she is too highly prized to waste on average men. Her company is reserved for those special patrons who I know have finesse and taste. It takes a rare sensitivity to appreciate her unique talents." The woman shrewdly avoided any mention of hard cash.

Kao drew himself up with a look of supreme hauteur. "What am *I* then, some country clod?"

"Oh, indeed not! You have always been most welcomed by my flowers."

"Well, I am glad to hear you say so. Now, bring me this girl of yours."

Madame Ying was careful to look abashed. "I would if I could, sir. Perhaps on some other evening. Unfortunately, tonight she is especially reserved for a very influential man. I dare not . . ."

This settled the matter for Kao, who was just the sort to always insist upon having anything he believed to be exclusive or unavailable.

"I care not one bit about your patron, woman. I can pay twice as much, no, three times more than this other man you speak of. I demand you let me share the company of Sweet Harmony at once!"

With a great show of reluctant intimidation, Madame Ying escorted him to one of her private rooms. She was a little disappointed when he refused to order food dishes, but mentally tabulating the price she intended to charge for the girl and the strong sorghum wine he wanted, she felt compensated well enough.

The small chamber where Kao awaited his pleasure was one he had never been in before. There were no windows or

pictures, and the only furniture sitting on the thick carpet
was a low table surrounded by large, brightly colored cushions. The oil lamps in the corners burned brightly against
walls covered in dark green velvet draperies. He was just
beginning to grumble aloud at what he considered to be
poor accommodations when Sweet Harmony entered bearing a cup and a small bottle of wine upon a silver tray. She
kept her eyelids lowered modestly as she took small, minc-
ing steps to the table. The silk of her thin robe whispered,
and the scent wafting about her person was a kind Kao
had never smelled before—a light, intoxicating musk. Just
inhaling it caused an almost instantaneous physical response.

"Wine, My Lord."

Her voice was like honey, her gestures the most graceful
he had ever seen. The tempo of his breathing quickened as
she stood again, for the robe she wore was sheer enough for
him to glimpse the ripe curves of her body beneath. That
single flimsy garment was all that covered her.

Unknown to Kao, there were cords installed behind the
wall coverings. Sweet Harmony pulled each cord in turn
and he gasped as he realized they were in a room of mir-
rors. So spellbound was he, he still had not put the wine
cup to his lips when she returned and knelt across from
him, close but not quite within touching distance. Slowly,
she raised her glance and gazed straight into his eyes.

"Drink, My Lord. It is a special mixture. I hope you will
find it to your liking."

There was something about the way she said this that
made her words seem more a command than an invitation,
but Kao complied without hesitation. The normally fiery
wine was laced with another, undefinable tang, as much
aroma as taste. His tongue felt suddenly thick and unwieldy.

Reaching into the wide sleeve of her robe, Sweet Harmony extracted a long narrow feather, the former plumage
of a wild pheasant. Kao stared at the thing, transfixed, as
she began sliding it between the thumb and forefinger of
her left hand. It bent and shimmered in the light.

"Drink."

Again she managed to convey an irresistible command
and he gulped down what remained in his cup. The room

became warm and he loosened his robe. When the feather lightly touched his hand, he started involuntarily.

The flower girl appeared not to move at all, and yet the feather flickered from place to place over his body, lingering at one ear, trailing down his neck, tickling the top of his chest. He could no longer resist the impulse to reach for her.

"No!"

She held the feather at the cleft of his throat, and though he could hardly feel its touch, it stopped him as surely as if it were the blade of a knife. He looked at his tormentor in mute question.

Sweet Harmony smiled. "Pleasure is not a pastime to be rushed, My Lord. Recline now and take your leisure."

When he continued to stare, his mouth agape, she rose and gently pushed him back until he rested against the cushions. Her cool fingers deftly manipulated the sash of his robe and then the garments beneath. Within a very short time he was almost completely exposed and ready for her continued ministrations. Once more she plied the silky feather in a way that inflamed his senses. He began breathing in shallow, almost labored pants, but whenever he thought his pulsing body could stand no more and attempted to touch her, she managed to elude him.

At last she laid her titillating weapon aside and stood above him. Her lips parted just slightly and he could see the pink tip of her tongue dart from between small, even teeth. Unfastening her robe, she let it fall in a pool around her ankles.

The potion Kao had imbibed now took full effect. His limbs felt weighted and immobile, his mouth dry. Only certain parts of his body remained vibrantly alive. A groan escaped his lips as the flower girl walked around and around him, her eyes never leaving the shaft of his manhood. She stroked her own body intimately, and while Kao itched to fondle the smooth flesh himself, his hands remained strangely and infuriatingly inert.

Sweet Harmony chuckled, a low husky sound emanating from deep in her throat, and then she straddled his hips with her tiny feet. Her eyes looked boldly into his while she lowered herself, inch by slow, deliberate inch, onto his engorged erection.

Women were hardly new to Chang Kao. A common street whore had first introduced him to carnal pleasure at the tender age of thirteen. Since then his appetite had continued unabated. A veritable parade of flower girls, interspersed with an occasional unwilling female servant, had passed beneath his perusal. But nothing in the past had prepared him for the ecstacy, the sublimely exquisite art of Sweet Harmony; her hands, her feet and thighs all seemed to move at once while the muscles of her inner body tightened and loosened rhythmically. Just when he thought it would end, she withdrew to attack him anew. Everywhere he looked, their mirrored images were reflected back.

The pleasure was too much. Finally, he cried out in a rasping voice. "Please!"

Sweet Harmony laughed and allowed the floodgates of his passion to be released. Afterward, he lay in her arms, weeping and suckling her breasts like a newborn babe.

Many hours later, Chang Kao opened the door of his own dimly lit bedchamber. Standing above the sleeping form of his wife, he pouted.

What a fish she is, he thought spitefully. Even in sleep her fingers clutch her garments together. I am not the fool she thinks, either. I know very well she has always held me in contempt. Why, even when we were children she despised me and preferred my younger brother because he had such bold, winning ways.

Tears of self-pity filled his eyes. In a rare and fleeting moment of honesty, he acknowledged his own cowardice. Looking at the woman he had been given for a wife, he realized he feared her also, and he swore silently. *Pie-e-e-e! My parents have gone and married me to a she-devil!* I will not touch her again. Just as soon as possible, I will arrange to have my own separate court. Until then I am going to keep myself to myself and the farther away from this tigress the better!

Thus determined, he chose to sleep far on his own side of the high bed and turn his back on Golden Willow. Moreover, he wore a thick night-robe for once. Just before slumber claimed him he smiled. He decided he had no need of a wife anyhow. Not when he could avail himself of Sweet Harmony.

* * *

Li Ma stood behind the chair of her mistress and endeav-ored to remain as quiet and unobtrusive as possible. This was not a good time for an underling to draw attention to herself. The air in the room fairly crackled with tension as Madame Chang arranged and rearranged the papers which lay in front of her.

The two women were in one of the central rooms. Sitting at a large ebony table, Madame Chang had been examin-ing the household accounts, meticulously tabulating fig-ures, as she did each month. It was a chore she enjoyed, and until a short time before she had been happily ab-sorbed, her fingers flying over the beads of a small abacus. Li Ma was not certain what had brought about the change, but suddenly her mistress had stopped, snatched up one of the account sheets, and uttered an oath.

"By the gods, I will have that pup's hide," she had ex-claimed. "Li Ma, go fetch that eldest son of mine at once!"

Making all haste, Li Ma went to the court of Chang Kao. When the servant, Crystal, poked her head out of the apartment door, the older woman delivered Madame Chang's summons in her most officious voice. "The Re-vered Madame wishes to see her eldest son without delay."

Crystal looked over her shoulder and then turned back and spoke in a whisper. "The young sir is still abed, Old Mother, and my mistress is in her bath."

"Well then wake him, girl! His mother is in no mood to be kept waiting, I tell you. You'd best advise your master not to drag his feet!"

With this Li Ma turned and marched away, feeling no small amount of satisfaction. She was delighted to exercise her authority over Crystal, who she felt certain needed an occasional reminder about who was who in the House of Chang. Moreover, she was downright gleeful at the pros-pect of forcing Chang Kao to rouse his lazy self.

The serving woman hated the eldest Chang son passion-ately and with more than ample cause. That worthless, rich young man had besmirched her family name in the foulest possible way, a way that could never be forgiven. She would never forget the day, four years before, when her own sweet daughter had come to her all disheveled, battered and weeping. The evidence had been unmistakable. Chang Kao had come upon the poor girl cleaning a bedchamber. Stealthily, he had gone in and closed the door. Then, without pity or regard for her virgin state, he had forced himself upon her.

Li Ma's face still burned with shame and fury when she remembered the incident. It had been necessary for her to keep knowledge of the attack even from her own husband, for had the volatile Li Chi learned of it he would have gone wild and taken a meat cleaver to the man who dared defile his daughter.

And then where would we be? she wondered. No, I did the right thing by going to my mistress. My daughter now has a home and three fine children. No one except her husband and I know how she was dishonored. She can still walk with her head held proud.

Madame Chang had been very generous, as well she should have been. Anxious that Master Chang not learn of the misdeed, she had immediately secured a husband for Li Ma's distraught daughter. The man had been a poor tenant farmer until then, but Madame Chang offered him a large plot of land as dowry. Upon this land sat a stout four-room house, a mansion by peasant standards, and in addition he was given a goodly amount of silver to begin his life anew.

Li Ma sighed in contentment thinking about her beautiful grandchildren. Though her hatred of Kao continued unabated, she realized her daughter was probably far better off than she could have hoped to be in any other circumstance. The farmer turned out to be a kind and diligent man who prized his wife highly. Born in the great House of Chang, she seemed to him a queen, tarnished virtue notwithstanding. He worked hard and his small fortune had grown accordingly. Against all odds, heaven had smiled on the ill-begotten marriage.

There came one other tiny redeeming gratification for Li Ma as a result of all this, and that was Madame Chang's unsatisfied curiosity.

"So, you have a grandson," the mistress had remarked upon learning of Li Ma's first grandchild. "Was he a big boy at birth?"

There had been other such questions asked at wide intervals, all with the same cool subtlety: "Has your grandson a thick head of hair?" "Has he taken his first step yet?" "Let me see, on what day did you say your first grandson was born, Li Ma?"

Not in the least stupid, Li Ma knew exactly what bothered her mistress. Yet it gave her a perverse sort of pleasure, a kind of vengeance, to keep Madame Chang in the dark.

Yes, the servant often thought, let her wonder if she has a grandson by that vile Kao! Never will I let her be certain it is not true. After all, it is no more than fair that she should feel some obligation toward my daughter.

Now, standing behind her mistress, Li Ma anticipated Kao's entrance. She was anxious to learn what trouble was brewing and what retribution might be exacted. She most fervently hoped the eldest son was in for serious chastisement.

She did not have to wait long. Less than a quarter of an hour passed before Chang Kao came blundering in, robe crooked and hair on end. His narrow eyes were still puffy with sleep, and his red lips pouted as usual.

"That worthless servant of my wife's woke me from a sound sleep, M'ma," he grumbled. "If I were not so kindhearted I would have given her a good kick."

Madame Chang ignored this. "Pour my son a cup of tea, Li Ma. Perhaps it will help clear his head so that he can give me a few ready answers."

The serving woman obeyed immediately, never showing her pleasure at the expression of apprehension on Kao's face. Li Ma was well acquainted with the soft, controlled tone her mistress was now using. It was a sure sign of impending danger.

Kao took the cup and was about to take a seat when his mother stopped him. "Come look," she said. "I need you to shed a bit of light on a problem I find here in my accounts."

"Why, I know not what help *I* can be, Mother. I know nothing of such female matters."

"Oh, I agree. This business of household matters most certainly falls within a woman's domain, *my* domain, does it not?" She pinioned Kao with her eyes and he shifted from one foot to the other. Suspecting some kind of entrapment, he began to stutter slightly.

"Well, yes . . . I mean . . . of course, you have always . . . at least it would seem to me . . ."

Her response was cold as ice. "Since you seem to agree, perhaps you can explain why I have these."

She held up several sheets of flimsy rice paper and Kao strained to read the characters and figures printed on them. All at once his eyes widened and he flushed.

"They would seem to be receipts of some sort, Mother. But I . . ." His voice trailed away.

"I see you recognize your own *chop*. Then explain to me, if you please, why you are purchasing a new bed, wall hangings, three teakwood tables, and this." She rattled the papers for emphasis. "There must be enough silk here for a whole apartment and more! The list goes on and on. Your father's warehouses must surely be empty by now! Why, I have never seen such a greedy girl as that new wife of yours! How dare she be so demanding? And how dare *you* take it upon yourself to spend such amounts without first consulting me?"

It had never occurred to Kao that his mother would blame Golden Willow for his spending, and he was sorely tempted to let it remain so. In the end, however, the truth would come out and he would be in more trouble than ever.

"Speak up!" Madame Chang snapped. She sat straight as a pine, regal.

Wishing he had wine instead of only tea, Kao downed the contents of his cup in a single loud gulp. Then, after clearing his throat, he answered with false bravado.

"It is true enough that I purchased certain necessities, Mother. It is also true that there is enough to furnish an apartment. Indeed, that was exactly my intention." Seeing he was about to be interrupted by his stern parent, he rushed on. "I am going to have a court all to myself. There is one vacant, that one far to the rear of the compound."

Now it was Madame Chang's turn to be momentarily nonplussed. Encouraged by her apparent speechlessness, Kao gained confidence. He began to strut back and forth in front of her.

"Yes," he said, "I have decided to have a place of my own, just as my father does."

There was a loud crack as Madame Chang stood and

slapped the tabletop with the flat of her hand. The account sheets flew in all directions.

"Chang One!" she exploded. "Close your mouth this instant! You are not the head of this household, a man married for years, father of sons! You are a bridegroom with duties to fulfill. You may *not* have the rear court. I forbid it!"

After taking two very deep breaths, she sat down again and calmly motioned Li Ma to pour her fresh tea. Then, completely ignoring her eldest son, she began to put in order those sheets of paper which still remained on the table.

Kao stood rooted to the spot. Huge tears glistened in his eyes and he sniffed loudly. "No one treats me with respect in this house," he whined. "One day I will be lord here, yet all despise me."

His mother gave him a withering glance, distaste stamped plainly on her features, but she said nothing.

Wiping his nose on the sleeve of his robe, Kao continued. "Yes, even my own wife hates me thoroughly, and I do not know why."

This last complaint evidently piqued Madame Chang's interest, for she stopped shuffling the papers and looked at him closely. At the sight of his trembling lips and the hurt on his face, her own expression softened somewhat. Against her will she remembered the child he had been, the little boy with soft hair and laughing eyes whom she had been so proud of. Where had that little boy gone?

"What a thing to say, Kao," she responded in a mild voice. "Golden Willow seems a very dutiful wife to me. I do not understand all the nonsense of young people nowadays. Surely you two have not quarreled already."

He opened his mouth to answer and then promptly closed it again. For just a moment he had been tempted to tell his mother of how his wife had attacked him, but on second thought decided otherwise.

Madame Chang sighed deeply. "Oh, come now. Sit down, my son, and have more tea. I have no wish to bicker with you. Let us talk this all out and have done with it."

Li Ma nearly ground her few remaining teeth, but she served the tea nonetheless. Kao sipped it, dabbing his eyes from time to time. He peered over the rim of his cup and saw his mother's altered mood.

"What I say is true, M'ma," he ventured. "With all respect, I must tell you I have been done a grave injustice. That wife of mine, that esteemed daughter of Tse Liangmo, is a hard, cold woman. Not once have I seen her smile. She puts on an act before the family, but in private she constantly reviles me. Even before her servant she calls me names, until now that lowly creature looks upon me with contempt. I tell you I can hardly stand it!"

Though Madame Chang had grave doubts about the validity of this story, she made a show of indignation.

"Well," she huffed. "I will just have to talk with my daughter-in-law at once. Her mother will speak to her also. There is no reason you should not have respect in your own apartment, after all."

"Oh no, M'ma!"

Kao flushed a deep red. He had not meant to blurt out his protest. Quickly, he tried to recover. "I do not think you should have to solve my problems, M'ma. Even if Golden Willow could be persuaded to be more civil I would not want to live with her. A man such as myself needs a warm-blooded woman, a woman who can laugh and enjoy life. My wife will never be that kind. What else am I to do? Would you have me live day in and day out with a shrew?"

Madame Chang sat for several moments without answering. Though her face did not show it, her mind was in turmoil. When she finally did open her mouth to speak, she selected each word with care.

"Perhaps you are right, my son, at least in part. Sometimes a short separation will do a young couple a world of good. I will allow you to have your wish, but only for a while."

Some of the warmth left her tone, and there was no mistake about the fact that she meant what she said next. "Even so, you and your wife have a duty to the family. I command that you shall return to your wife each and every month for at least three days. I will send word to you concerning which days they are to be. Other than that you may have your own court—for a short time."

Kao smiled sweetly and again she thought of the little boy she had loved so much.

"I will do just as you say, M'ma. I am indeed lucky to

have been blessed with such an understanding mother. Not one son in a hundred has . . ."

Madame Chang held up her hands for silence. "I have much to do, Kao. Please leave me now."

It was all he could do to keep from skipping from the room. He could not believe that his mother had actually given in to his wishes. Of course, he would still have to lie beside that wife of his once in a while, but at least he need not look at her every day. Now, if only he could bring Sweet Harmony to the house as Second Wife, all would be perfect!

Master Chang ambled down the corridor toward his favorite room, the library. It was the one place he could go and expect to remain undisturbed for any length of time. Only rarely did even a servant accompany him, and everyone knew to scratch upon the door before entering if he was present there. He was, therefore, surprised to find his sanctuary already occupied.

Golden Willow stood before one shelf-lined wall, her hands clasped behind her back, looking wistfully up at the volumes arranged there. Engrossed, she had not heard him come in and he took this opportunity to observe her at close range.

He was struck anew by her beauty as she leaned slightly forward and tilted her head to one side in order to better examine titles. She wore a fitted jacket and wide-legged trousers of a dark plum-colored brocade that lent her fair skin an additional glow. Her hair, pulled back in a braided chignon, was thick and lustrous.

Her youth touched Master Chang. Suddenly he felt a pang of remorse knowing she was not happy in his house. Thankfully, he had found no evidence that she was physically mistreated by Kao, though he had carefully observed and asked cautious questions here and there. Still, seeing her now, it was not difficult to understand Tse Liangmo's love and concern. He himself was smitten by an almost overwhelming desire to protect and cherish this small, lovely girl.

Golden Willow chose that moment to turn toward him. Their eyes accidently met, and in that fleeting moment they were able to touch souls, however briefly. She lowered her eyes at once.

"Forgive my intrusion, Father Chang. I did not hear you enter."

He cleared his throat and waved a negligent hand. "No matter, child. Have you seen some book here which sparks your interest?"

"Oh, many, sir." Her enthusiasm was obvious. "You have even more books than my father. It would take a lifetime to enjoy them all."

Her use of the word "enjoy" rather than "read" did not escape his notice and he suddenly remembered Liangmo mentioning a scholar that had been hired to tutor his only daughter. An idea occurred to Master Chang. He turned and pretended great interest in selecting a book. When he spoke his voice was intentionally offhand. "You may feel free to select a book whenever you so choose, Daughter-In-Law."

In his peripheral vision he saw her smile and her shining eyes. "And you need not ask," he added.

To his delight, she clapped her hands like a youngster. "Oh, thank you, Revered Father! You cannot know how I have been longing for books. The few I brought with me from home have been read and read again until I fear they will fall apart."

She stopped in sudden embarrassment and peered at him shyly. "Do you think me terrible?"

"And why should I?"

Her color deepened. "My mother says too much knowledge is not good for a woman. It makes a female unattractive. She also counseled me to keep my love of learning to myself lest I displease you and Madame Chang. I am very disobedient."

Master Chang could not suppress an amused chuckle. "Your mother is no doubt wise, child, but in this particular instance she is quite mistaken, I assure you. My son's mother is very well educated and I find her quick mind stimulating indeed. No doubt my son has much the same taste."

At this mention of Kao her countenance lost all animation. She did not reply at first, and when she did it was in a low monotone. "I hope you are right, sir."

At that moment Madame Chang entered the library unannounced. She carried a platter full of winter melon and sweetmeats. When she saw Golden Willow there with the elder Chang, her face clearly mirrored her displeasure. She directed all her attention toward her husband, completely ignoring the presence of the girl. "I thought you might wish a bit of refreshment, Father of My Sons."

Golden Willow bowed deeply from the waist and made a hasty exit. When she had gone, Master Chang turned a frown on his spouse. "How unlike you, Peaceful Dawn. You did not even greet our little daughter-in-law. No doubt you have wounded her feelings."

"Perhaps she can use a wound or two," Madame Chang responded crisply. "I think Little Flower and Liangmo have raised a very rebellious girl. She is too bold by far. Had I known, I would not have let the marriage take place."

This obviously unfair statement surprised Master Chang still more. He was about to tell her so when he saw her set down the platter and furtively massage one temple. There were faint smudges beneath her eyes too, something he had not previously noticed. Upon giving it a moment's thought, it occurred to him how different his wife seemed of late. There was a restlessness about her, a sharpness of tongue and temper quite out of character.

"What is it, my little heart?" he inquired solicitously. "Sit down and tell me what troubles you, for troubled you certainly are."

Madame Chang moved gracefully to a chair. After artfully arranging herself, she expelled a very deep sigh and looked up at her husband with weary eyes.

"You are right, Hai-teh," she murmured. "I have much on my mind these days, not the least of which is our First Son and his wife. There is something very much amiss in that marriage."

Again Master Chang experienced that sinking feeling that often precedes bad news. Lately, any mention of his firstborn caused this reaction. His reply did not betray his apprehension, however, for he did not want to add to his wife's distress.

"Ah," he laughed. "You are ever the worrier, I swear.

All young couples have their highs and lows. Have you forgotten?"

At once the atmosphere in the room lightened. Husband
and wife smiled at each other in mutual recollection. Neither of them would ever forget the first days they had
spent together.

Peaceful Dawn had been a northern bride, proud and aristocratic. Her father and the father of Hai-teh had been
business associates, and through that connection the
match had been made.

The prospective bride had come to her new home with
several preconceived attitudes. In the first place she was
convinced, as were all those who lived in the far north,
that no one else quite matched the intelligence and good
breeding of those in her home province. She was doubly
unhappy to leave her mother, whom she knew she would
never see again. Combined with this was her general distaste for what she believed the marital state to be. Her
own father was a man of seemingly unquenchable appetite, with not only a First and Second Wife, but two concubines as well. Peaceful Dawn was second born of the First
Wife, and she could not forget the pain her mother suffered
on account of her father's philandering.

It had taken many days for her to travel by caravan,
complete with servants and household goods, from her
birthplace to mountainous Tanpo. There had been no automobiles then, and the entire journey had been endured in a
horse-drawn litter. She arrived at the House of Chang
sore, dusty, and completely out of sorts. Though her prospective mother-in-law was kind enough and endeavored
to install her comfortably, Peaceful Dawn remained quiet
and withdrawn. She was hatching a master plan.

All too soon the wedding took place. Amidst well-wishes
and merriment, she was led to her new apartment to await
the coming of the groom. Little did poor Hai-teh guess
what was in store for him. Eagerly, he entered the bedchamber to consummate his nuptials. His heart pounded
with excitement. The sight of Peaceful Dawn sitting so demurely on the edge of the bed, her hair all loose, her skin
glowing, made him dizzy with happiness. How lucky he
was—how beautiful she!

It was a shock, therefore, when he reached out a tentative hand to stroke her smooth shoulder, only to feel her teeth sink deep into the flesh of his wrist. Emitting a howl of surprised outrage and pain, he leapt back.

Meanwhile, Peaceful Dawn had scampered back into the center of the canopied bed. "Do not touch me!" she hissed.

At first Hai-teh only held his wounded limb and gaped, but soon enough a righteous indignation took hold of him. His face flushed an angry red.

"What is this, woman? Are you not my proper wife and I your husband?"

He took three steps toward the bed, but stopped when his bride reared up like a cat and made her tapered fingers into claws. Deciding it wise to use a different tactic, he tried a little gentle persuasion. "I do not intend to hurt you," he wheedled, still moving toward her. "Come now, My Lady, at least let us talk this thing over."

In what was to become a very characteristic action, Peaceful Dawn lowered her arms. Her face took on an unruffled serenity, while her body settled into graceful repose. Her voice, however, still carried an edge.

"Stop, My Lord. Do not take another step."

Hai-teh was more confused than ever. This enigmatic young woman seemed to change her shape, her very essence, as quickly as any chameleon. The physical desire he had been feeling receded somewhat with his perplexity. Looking at her lovely face and form, her dark, almost beckoning eyes, he was surprised to find himself wondering about the soul of her.

Still, his dignity was just a bit pricked by her earlier ferocity and present high-handedness. So, pulling himself up with as much pride as he could muster, he walked to the bed and sat bravely down almost within reach of her.

If he expected her to jump and skitter away, he was disappointed. She did not move an inch.

"This seems a very poor way to begin a marriage," he said, trying to sound more mature and self-assured than he felt. "Am I so rude-looking that you fear me, woman? Or perhaps I am too lowly and ugly for one such as you."

This last was unmistakably sarcastic, but Peaceful Dawn responded with galling magnanimity. She peered at him closely and rendered verdict in a clear voice. "No, My

Lord, you are not too terribly ugly, I suppose. As for fear—I fear no man."

Rubbing his wrist, Hai-teh smiled sardonically. "I am glad to hear it. I always thought that animals bite only when they are afraid."

To his surprise she smiled back. "I bit you for emphasis, My Lord, not from fear."

Such obvious disrespect should have angered him, but strangely it did not. Instead, her plain talk and spirit served to fascinate him in the extreme. His previous contact with women had been limited largely to his mother and two younger sisters. The few flower girls he had known seemed empty-headed things, especially when compared to this intelligent, ravishing young woman he had married but a few hours before.

He looked away, not wanting his admiration to show. "Perhaps this would be a propitious time for you to inform me of what you so desperately wish to emphasize, My Lady."

Peaceful Dawn grew very serious. She spoke in a low voice, so that he had to strain somewhat in order to hear her clearly. "I am only a female," she began. "As such I am your servant and completely at your mercy. We both know that a man can do what he pleases, while a woman must do what she must. Nor is it my place to question tradition. I only know what I can or cannot tolerate."

Here she paused to fix Hai-teh with a piercing gaze. "I will not tolerate another woman in my domain, sir. You must pledge to me now that you will never take another wife. Nor will you take a single concubine."

Hai-teh stared at her. This was unheard of! He was speechless at first, and when he finally found his voice it was nearly incredulous.

"You, who have not yet proven you can bear sons, ask this of me?"

Peaceful Dawn lowered her eyes and plucked at the folds of her sleeping garments. "I do."

Standing, he began to pace back and forth. After a few moments he stopped and looked at her, only to pace again. She watched him with veiled eyes. Beneath her calm exterior her heart fluttered in her breast. It was difficult for her to breathe. She knew that her entire future hinged on this moment. She kept her eyes lowered now, afraid that he would see her trepidation and think her less than totally resolved.

At last he stood still. "And what if you never give me sons? Is my house and my family name to disappear from the earth just for the sake of your pride?"

"I will give you sons, Young Sir."

"How can you know?"

"I will give you sons," she repeated. "A promise for a promise."

She met his eyes with her own. "If sons are the only things needed to insure your fidelity, then you will have them aplenty."

There was such conviction emanating from her that Hai-teh could almost believe she possessed a supernatural power. He stepped to the bed just as she came up on her knees. She was radiant! A goddess!

When he reached for her, she did not fight or pull away. "Your pledge, Husband," she whispered. "I would have your pledge!"

Her flesh was soft and warm beneath his fingers and his body once more pulsed with desire. "It will be as you say," he gruffly replied. "A promise for a promise!" With that he took her in his arms.

Peaceful Dawn conceived within the month.

The Chang marriage had not been without storms or pitfalls, but both promises had been strictly kept. Peaceful Dawn brought forth four robust sons, and in turn Hai-teh remained faithful. Not only did he keep his oath not to bring another woman into the house, he also refrained from even lying with an occasional flower girl, a fact which astounded his friends.

"Come, Hai-teh," one would tease. "Madame Ying has a new flower, the most delectable female on earth. Try her for an evening and see for yourself!"

But never once did Master Chang yield. The truth of the matter was that he never wished to. All others might think Peaceful Dawn a cool, aloof woman; he knew better. Fire smoldered within her soul. She was passionate without vulgarity, strong and proud. He loved her.

Not until their fourth son was born did Master Chang move out of his wife's court, and then only for the sake of her health. That last birth had been difficult and danger-ous. Had he continued to live with her day in and day out, the temptation would have proven too great for them both. As it was, he went to her only at certain intervals, warmly welcomed each time.

No, Madame Chang was not the calm, unruffled person she showed to the world. Hai-teh knew this and respected her all the more for her ability to exercise control. It hurt him to see her as she was now, nervous and unhappy over the plight of their son's marriage.

Walking to the chair where she sat, he patted her hand. "Do not worry about Kao and Golden Willow. Those young people will adjust soon enough. Wait and see. In no time there will be a child to set things right."

"A child," Madame Chang repeated. "A *child.*"

Never had her husband seen her look so forlorn.

SHANGHAI

Chapter Ten

*F*engmo sat in the plush back seat of his father's automobile, unable to relax, gripping his knees until he was sure they must be black-and-blue. Fong Lu, who had been assigned as his personal servant and chauffeur, drove like a wild man. He enjoyed nothing more than racing over the narrow roads, honking and scaring the peasants out of their apathy. It was all the two trucks could do to keep up the breakneck pace.

Unfortunately, this recklessness frightened Fengmo nearly as much as it did the poor country folk, though he was loath to admit it aloud. It had taken only a day for him to realize how much he preferred the gentle sway of an old-fashioned sedan chair or the bumping of a rickshaw to this heart-stopping speed. There was no help for it now, however. In just a few more days they would be in Shanghai.

Fengmo closed his eyes and rested his head on the back of the seat, trying to picture himself somewhere else.

It was impossible. Fong Lu pressed down on the horn and Fengmo's eyes flew open again just in time to see an old man crossing the road up ahead. Walking with the aid of a staff, the man wore the high, square hat of a scholar and carried a large book beneath one arm. To Fengmo's horror he made no attempt whatsoever to get out of the way. Instead, he stood in the center of the road and stared death straight in the face.

Brakes screamed as Fong Lu brought the huge car to a jarring halt just inches from the fellow. The chauffeur cursed and rolled down the window.

"Old Honored One," he called impatiently. "Can you not see that a rich man wishes to pass? And did you not hear the bark of this machine? Step aside now!"

103

The scholar held his head high, his sparse beard fluttering in the breeze. The tome he carried so tenderly was the I-Ching. His staff, a hewn branch, was worn smooth with age. He peered inside the car and then hawked and spit upon the ground.

"Is nothing good enough for the young nowadays unless it be foreign?" he called back in a cracked and grumpy voice. "They rush about in these metal beasts, frightening good citizens. I tell you they are all the same. They choose their own mates, ignoring good tradition and laughing at their elders who are wiser by far. It is shameful! Shameful!"

The recipients of this unsolicited lecture had no way of knowing the old man was thinking of his own son who had gone away to a coastal city to study foreign learning and then returned thinking he knew more than his sire. The scholar lived with this son, and his old age was bitter because he was shown no respect by either his son or the sharp-tongued wife his son had chosen for himself without benefit of matchmaker or parental approval. As a result, anything foreign seemed automatically hateful to this old man. He now stood resolutely in the way of the automobile and refused to budge.

"Move away," Fong Lu commanded. "Other men's sons are no concern of yours. If you do not move, I will be forced to run right over you!"

The chauffeur and the old man glared at one another. Then slowly a sly smile spread over the scholar's wrinkled face. He narrowed his eyes. In one smooth and surprisingly strong motion he raised his staff and struck a blow at the right headlamp of the car. Glass tinkled onto the roadway.

"Pi-e-e-e!" Fong Lu screamed. He was about to leap from the car and thrash the grinning old man when Fengmo stopped him.

"I will speak to the old gent," he said. "You stay here in your driving place and do not move."

Pushing the door open, Fengmo got out and stretched his long frame. He was taller and heavier by far than the scholar, but the fellow seemed not in the least intimidated. He stared off into space and picked his nose with a dirt-encrusted fingernail. There were broth stains on his faded satin robe, and his wide sleeves were frayed.

Fengmo approached him and bowed deeply from the waist. "Forgive my servant, Honored One. He is but overprotective of me and my property. No doubt you are right about the youths of today."

This confession took the scholar by surprise, causing him to raise his shaggy eyebrows.

Fengmo gave him a wry smile. "I must confess, I myself am a most ungrateful son. My good father purchased this traveling machine and the two following behind in order to increase business and thereby provide his sons a rich inheritance." He lowered his voice. "Yet I am ashamed to say I hate these foreign machines. They go so fast my insides get all disarranged."

His listener clucked a sympathetic tongue and nodded in agreement, casting a dubious glance at the automobile.

Leaning closer, Fengmo whispered. "You would be doing me a great favor to put out the other eye of this beast, Old Father. If you do so, it will not be able to make its way in the darkness. Then I can rest at some inn or another and put off my father's business a while longer."

"Shame!" the scholar scolded. "I understand your feelings, Young Sir, but you must not think of such disobedience. Even if it is a vexation to you, you must do as your father thinks best."

So, at last, the man became malleable. In fact, he showed a great deal of interest in the magic vehicle Fengmo invited him to examine. Fong Lu sat behind the wheel, fuming and anxious to be gone.

The old man lived in the next hamlet, which was just a mile or so down the road, and when Fengmo learned this he extended another invitation.

"Why not ride along with me, Old Father? I will be happy indeed for the company of a kindred spirit."

For just a second or two the gentleman looked almost frightened, but when he spoke his voice did not quiver. "I might just consider it, Young Sir. First, however, I would like to see the insides of this beast."

Obligingly, Fengmo opened the rear door of the car and motioned him closer. "See, there are cushions and even a carpet upon the floor."

The scholar poked his head inside, sniffed a time or two, and tested the seat with his hand. "Very well," he conceded. "I will ride as far as my home in the bowels of this monster, but only for the sake of becoming better acquainted with its evil."

So off they went together, old man and young. Both ignored Fong Lu, who sat in the front seat muttering something unintelligible under his breath. Within a matter of minutes they came to a very small town. The scholar directed them down a muddy street where they came to a stop before a shop. Though run down, it was not a bad establishment.

From inside his shop, the proprietor looked through a window and saw the automobile. Wreathing his face in a solicitous smile, he hurried out to greet a new and obviously affluent customer. When the rear door of the car opened and the old man emerged, the proprietor's mouth fell open.

"Father!" he sputtered. "Am I dreaming?"

At this the old man stood straight and proud. His voice carried not only to his son, but to the gathering townspeople as well.

"This friend has brought me home, and here I am. What is so unusual in that? I will have you know my insides are not in the least disarranged either, though this machine flies like the wind."

Sitting in the back seat, Fengmo had to smile, for in reality his passenger had been quite terrified, clinging to the hand strap the entire way. Still, it was warming to see the obvious merit he had achieved in his son's incredulous sight.

Fengmo was just about to instruct Fong Lu to drive on when the old man reached back into the car and shyly plucked his sleeve.

"Will you not stay for a meal, Young Sir? No doubt this shop and my son's home will seem very humble by your standards, but it is warm and comfortable inside."

Fengmo shook his head. "It is very kind of you to offer, sir, but I do not wish to impose upon you and your family. There is my servant here and those fellows in the trucks. We will seek an inn farther up the road."

"Why, your servants are also welcome, of course! We are not so poor that we cannot afford to feed a few people. Come now, you must all stay and sup."

This generosity caused the smile on the proprietor's face to slip just a little until it occurred to him that a profit might be made. Surely this rich man would want to purchase a few items from the shop, if only for the sake of courtesy. With this thought, his smile returned and all but gleamed.

"By all means, stay!" he said. "You have been kind to my good father. I will hear no more excuses now. I insist you linger for a while and refresh yourself!"

Fengmo heard Fong Lu groan, but there seemed no graceful way to refuse their hospitality now. Besides, the old man looked so anxious, no doubt wanting to prolong his brief moment of glory, that Fengmo had not the heart to disappoint him.

So amidst a crowd of onlookers, they all trouped into the shop. The proprietor pointed out one cluttered shelf after another, expounding on the contents of each, while his guest nodded and murmured polite appreciation. For the most part his merchandise was made up of such mundane items as any hamlet store might stock. There were bales of tea and sticks of incense, sacks of rice, cooking implements and clay dishes. The smell of salted pork mingled with that of camphor and cinnamon.

In the rear of the same building were the rooms used for living, four in all. The old scholar slept in one room with his grandchildren while another bedded the proprietor and his wife. There was a small lean-to kitchen attached to the main room, which served as dining room and general gathering place for the family.

The scholar's son had two servants as well, a wrinkled old crone and her granddaughter. The sight of the latter cheered Fong Lu considerably, for there was only one thing the chauffuer liked better than the sight of a pretty maid, and that was his master's shiny automobile. Tossing his shoulders back and posturing proudly, he spent his time casting long sideways glances at the serving girl. In return, the object of his attention flushed deeply, forgetting for the moment that she was betrothed. Fong Lu often had this effect upon women, old and young alike, for his self-assurance, combined with a handsome face and winning smile, served to dazzle most women of his own caste, a fact of which he was only too aware.

The lady of the house sat with her back to the door. She wore a thin, soiled robe and her hair was uncombed. Her two children scrambled about beneath the table, playing with a dog of doubtful breed.

"Get yourself up, woman!" the proprietor bawled. "Make yourself presentable. We have an important guest."

"Yes," echoed his father. "Make haste, Daughter-In-Law! A friend of mine is here!"

Now, this slovenly woman was not in the least accustomed to being ordered about, especially not by her husband's aged father. *That old Buddah Head,* she thought. *What friend could he have that I would wish to impress?*

She was just about to say this aloud when she turned and saw Fengmo. At the sight of this tall, handsome man, she put her hands up to hide her unkempt hair and ran from the room. This instant jump to obey surprised and pleased both father and son since they were used to hearing her complain anytime she was urged to stir herself.

"Come, Young Sir." The scholar motioned toward the highest chair in the crowded room. "Please sit down."

Seeing this was the place of honor, however, Fengmo courteously declined, and took a lower seat only after his host had settled himself.

Soon all were gathered around the table. Fong Lu and the two truck drivers sat clustered together, obviously embarrassed by this forced familiarity with their master. Doing his best to relieve the obvious tension, Fengmo began by making light conversation. He remarked favorably on each dish the servants put before him and complimented the fine, healthy looks of the little boy and girl. Of one thing he made especially certain; he directed all his conversation toward the scholar. The proprietor noted this, and with each moment his father gained stature in his sight.

As for the old man, he was eloquent. His eyes shone brightly and his voice was strong as he talked of his studies and of the few students he tutored. His tales were both interesting and amusing, and soon even the children grew quiet and crawled up onto their grandfather's lap to listen.

The midday meal was served and nearly finished before the proprietor's wife came back into the room. She had donned a bright flowered robe made of some cheap cloth that glittered when the light hit it. Her hair was neatly combed and she had applied paint to her eyes and lips.

Fengmo grew warm and acutely uneasy in her presence, for when no one was looking she favored him with bold glances and fluttered her lashes in a wanton manner. After a short time he could bare it no longer and asked the woman's husband if he might be allowed to reexamine the shop before taking his leave.

The proprietor was only too happy to oblige. Try as he might, he had not been able to keep from counting every gulp of tea and every bite eaten by Fengmo's servants, all men of hearty appetite. Moreover, it made him a little nervous to have this young man in the same room with his bedecked wife, whom he thought positively beautiful in spite of her shrewish tongue.

Everyone knows how rich young lords are, the man told himself. The rich have a way of taking whatever they want. What if this fellow takes a liking to my woman?

Thus, he rose without delay and led Fengmo and the others back through the shop. To his consternation his wife followed right behind and then ran about showing bits of merchandise.

"Look, Young Sir," she would say. "Is this not a fine piece of porcelain?" Or, "See this pretty wind chime, Young Master."

At one point she held up a bolt of cloth which held the same gaudy fabric from which her own robe had been cut. "This would make a lovely garment for your mother or sister," she suggested, and then gave him a sly smile. "Or perhaps there is *another* upon whom you wish to bestow a special gift."

The scholar and his son both flushed at her bluntness, and seeing their chagrin, Fengmo quickly spoke up.

"That is indeed good-looking, Madame. If you will allow me to purchase the entire lot, I am sure my mother will be delighted."

Standing beside the door leading to the street, ready to leave at a moment's notice, Fong Lu grinned from ear to ear trying to imagine the lofty Madame Chang garbed in such a thing. He was about to laugh aloud when he caught his master's warning glance and was forced to pretend he had been attacked by a fit of coughing.

The amenities were performed, of course. The scholar offered to give the bolt of cloth to his guest without charge, while his son stood by sweating. In return, Fengmo steadfastly refused this generosity and in the end insisted upon paying at least three times what it was actually worth. Afterward, he also bought several other items—a few toys, some tinned sweets, and tea.

Last, he came to a glass case which displayed a number of trinkets and a small selection of water pipes. One pipe was quite nice and he saw the old man cast a lingering glance on it.

"Let me see that silver pipe," Fengmo said. "The fine one there in the center."

The proprietor hurried to do so, rubbing his hands together the whole while. He had ordered that pipe long before, mostly for show. Only a relatively wealthy man could afford such a purchase and there were few of those in the village.

Fengmo held it up and admired it for several moments. The scholar looked wistfully on, but made no comment.

"I will definitely take this," Fengmo decided. "Please give me a pouch also, the best you have."

The proprietor took the pipe and wrapped it in a long pouch made of red silk, trimmed in black velvet. With a bow, he handed it back to his guest.

"This is a gift," Fengmo announced. "A gift for a friend who is old and very wise. Though I have not known him long, still I have benefited from his wisdom." With this he handed the pipe to the scholar.

Tears rushed into the old man's eyes and he quickly wiped at them with the corner of his ragged sleeve. His son hung his head a little, looking slightly abashed. The proprietor's wife opened her mouth to protest, but evidently reconsidered and snapped it shut again without speaking.

So it was that Fengmo left these people happier than he had found them. The shop would prosper because the townspeople had seen him enter; the proprietor's wife would brag for days about how she wore a robe just like that of a rich dowager. Most important was the regained pride of a nice old man.

Chang Fengmo did not analyze this, nor in fact did he even fully realize the good deed he had done. It had seemed to him only the best and most natural way to handle a potentially troublesome situation.

Later that afternoon he did purposefully commit an act of charity, however. He instructed Fong Lu to stop again, this time in a dilapidated, run-down village that boasted only four or five hovels. Arms laden, he got out of the car and walked up to the poorest house. An old grandmother sat sunning herself in the yard, while three children dressed in tattered clothes squatted nearby. The woman stared suspiciously at the tall stranger who approached.

"Old Mother." Fengmo bowed in greeting. "Here is some tea and a bit of cloth you might like and which I cannot use myself. Take them in good health."

So saying, he laid down the bolt and the tea he had purchased earlier that day. The grandmother blinked harder, sure she must actually have fallen asleep and be dreaming or having a vision. She watched as the children clustered around the apparition.

Fengmo looked down into the hungry faces of these waifs, and wished he had food, real food, to give them. There was one boy of about six and another still in late infancy. The girl was no more than four and her eyes were red and swollen with disease. His heart turned painfully.

"I have not forgotten you," he murmured gently as he handed each of them a toy and a handful of sweets. He saved the best toy, a little cloth bear, for last. This he gave to the nearly blind girl, and the tot cuddled it close.

Without waiting to observe the reaction solicited by his impulsive acts, Fengmo walked briskly back to the car and got in. Fong Lu, who had seen all this, shifted gears and accelerated away.

What sort of man is this Chang Two? the chauffeur wondered. I must watch and see, for I have been given as servant either to a saint or a fool—I know not which!

The last leg of his journey was the one Fengmo enjoyed most. It was necessary for him to board a small British ship and travel down the Yangtze River to Shanghai. There were the usual problems; bribes had to be paid right and left. Being Chinese made it difficult to get decent accommodations. Finally, however, a comfortable two-room cabin was secured below decks.

Both the car and trucks were to follow on large, motor-driven barges. Of the drivers, only Fong Lu accompanied the master, a fact which pleased him not at all. Without his beloved automobile he became just another servant. Furthermore, there were no pretty young girls aboard the vessel. Everywhere he looked he saw only other male servants, wrinkled old amahs, or those disgusting, pasty-faced foreigners. Consequently, the chauffeur stayed in the cabin whenever possible and waited for the trip to be over.

Chang Fengmo liked to walk along the deck and watch the land they passed. Something new was happening to him. Secluded in Tanpo as he had been, he had never before given much thought to his nation as a whole. Oh, he had studied history, of course, and knew the names and characteristics of each province. But this was different. For the first time he was seeing his fellow countrymen at close range. At home he had been pampered, and for the most part separated from the common folk, the farmers and petty merchants, beggars and sweating laborers. Now, suddenly, he wanted to know them all. It was as if his recent pain had given him new perception.

Golden Willow was still ever with him in spirit. At night his dreams were full of her. Against the black velvet of his sleeping mind he would see again the perfect oval of her face, her soft pliant mouth and liquid eyes. When he awakened to find himself miles from her, he experienced the feeling of a terrible void. There was an emptiness in his life and soul that cried out to be filled, and this longing made him somehow more sensitive to everything and everyone. In his emotional condition the misery of others reached out to him, a tangible thing.

One day he was leaning on the ship's rail, watching a little girl on shore. She was no more than a child herself, and yet she carried an infant tied to her back as she knelt along the bank pounding laundry. Her arms were stick-thin, and her face sore and chapped by the weather.

"Poor mite," he murmured, talking to himself.

"Yes," agreed a strange voice.

Turning, Fengmo met the candid eyes of a young Chinese about his own age. He was dressed in Western fashion, in a black suit. Around his neck he wore the white collar of the foreign god-men. The stranger smiled and introduced himself.

"Forgive me if I intruded upon your thoughts," he said. "I am Long Han. From your interest I surmise this is your first trip to Shanghai."

"It is," Fengmo confirmed, smiling also. "I am Fengmo, Second Son of Chang Hai-teh."

The other men allowed his glance to quickly take in Fengmo's attire and then come to rest on his face again. "You are from the high country?"

"Tanpo."

With each passing day Fengmo was becoming more acutely aware of his clothes, for he was still wearing long robes. His father had told him he would need to purchase Western suits when he reached Shanghai. Now he understood why. Of all the passengers aboard the ship, either foreign or Chinese, he was one of only a few in traditional dress.

The quick appraisal by Long Han had not been contemptuous, however, and Fengmo allowed himself a rueful smile. "No doubt I look like some back-hills bumpkin to you."

Long Han threw back his head and laughed. "No doubt!"

For a moment Fengmo was almost angry, but looking at the round, good-natured face and mischievously twinkling eyes of his companion, he also began to chuckle. Soon both men were slapping one another upon the shoulders and nearly crying with mirth.

It was the beginning of a friendship which was to last a very long time. The young men walked or sat on deck together during the day. At mealtimes they ate in the ship's segregated dining room, sharing a table in the section reserved for Chinese. Evenings were spent in Fengmo's cabin, which was the most roomy and comfortable.

A new world opened for Fengmo as a result of this relationship. He never tired of listening to Han talk about his years spent in the Christian school where he had been raised.

"My mother was widowed when I was six," he explained. "She had no family of her own and my father's parents had passed away. The foreign missionaries helped her when no one else could. They placed her as a servant in the well-to-do home of an American diplomat and gave her back her pride. In gratitude she gave them the only thing of value she possessed—me."

"How hard it must have been for you," Fengmo commiserated.

"Not at all." Han shrugged. "Actually, I was quite fortunate. I was able to see my mother from time to time. There were other children to play with. Most importantly, I learned to read and write, something I would have been denied otherwise. I was required to study hard and in addition to learn much of the foreign holy book. It did me no harm. The missionaries are good people, and I believe they care deeply for me."

"And now you, too, practice the foreign religion," Fengmo mused.

"In my own way," Han chuckled, "though I fear my mentors most heartily disapprove of my methods."

There were many questions Fengmo wished to ask, yet he did not wish to offend his new friend. He began tentatively. "I have heard much about this foreign religion, Han, and must admit some of the things I hear give me pause."

"I am not surprised." Long Han seemed not in the least perturbed.

"For instance," Fengmo probed, "it is said that godmen, such as yourself, are denied women."

"That is true only of a certain sect," the other replied. "Thankfully, it is not the one I practice. The missionaries I spoke of are husband and wife, in fact."

There seemed no delicate way to put the next question, but Fengmo could not contain his curiosity. "I also hear that you eat flesh and drink blood!"

To his shocked surprise, Han nodded in the affirmative. "This is true, though not in the way you imagine." He then went on in an attempt to explain the complicated symbolism of Christian Communion.

Many such discussions took place between them. Fengmo listened intently, but accepted none of the foreign ideologies. To him eternity was a never-ending wheel; a person left life only to enter it again forty days later in another form. The circle could not be complete until perfection was achieved. Fengmo could in no way reconcile this belief with the idea of a Christian paradise.

The strange thing was, Han could. He seemed to have no difficulty whatsoever intermingling many Chinese customs and beliefs with his own brand of Christianity. Fengmo guessed his charismatic new friend must make many converts because of this unique ability, even if it did indeed drive his adopted parents to distraction.

Long Han was an endless font of information, and Fengmo was grateful to have him close by to answer his own unceasing questions.

One day, near the end of the voyage, the two men had just emerged from the dining room when Fengmo violently rubbed his nose.

"Ai-e-e-e!" he exclaimed. "I swear those foreign devils have a terrible stink!"

Han laughed and pulled out the short-stemmed foreign pipe he smoked almost constantly. "Why do you suppose I am so fond of this thing? It helps fend off their odor."

Fengmo shook his head in puzzlement. "I do not understand it. These foreigners, with their strange hair and eyes, are certainly ugly, but they seem clean enough. I wonder what makes them smell so bad?"

"It is the things they eat. Did you not notice their plates? They consume great quantities of red meat which is not always cooked clear through. They like it that way— all bloody and dripping."

Fengmo paled, but the other man went on to elaborate. "That is not the worst, my friend. They are also very fond of milk. You will no doubt find it hard to credit, but they even pour it in their tea sometimes, along with a glob of sugar. There is also a dish called *cheese,* which they consider a great delicacy. It is cow's or goat's milk which has been allowed to sit and grow sour or even hard. They—"

"Say no more!" Fengmo begged, and shuddered convulsively. "What horrible barbarians they are!"

At this, Long Han grew more serious than Fengmo had previously seen him. "They are not *all* so," he murmured pensively. "Some of them seem almost Chinese. I know such a one. She is gentle and kind and smells as fresh as a spring breeze."

The lines of sadness etched on Han's face prevented Fengmo from commenting. Instead, he was quiet, thus giving his friend an opportunity to bare his soul if he felt so inclined.

"She is the daughter of my foster parents," Han continued in a faraway voice. "Her Christian name is Mary, but to me she will always be *Maeling*—the pretty one."

Shaking his head as if to clear it of unwanted recollections, Han resumed his normal joviality. "As I say, these foreigners are not all so ghastly. In fact, a few are almost acceptable."

Fengmo did not pry further. His heart overflowed with sympathy, however, for he rightly guessed his companion suffered an unrequited love. This knowledge served to forge the bond of their friendship closer still.

Each wrapped in his own reverie, they did not talk much more that afternoon, and the next morning the ship docked in the bustling port of Shanghai. Han and Fengmo clasped hands, bowed formally, and promised to meet again soon. Then they parted, both just a bit misty-eyed.

Fong Lu was nearly out of his mind with joy.

Chapter Eleven

Nothing in his past experience could possibly have prepared Fengmo for the city of Shanghai. His father had done his best to describe it; Long Han had spoken of the place at some length since he lived there. But no words or verbal pictures did justice to the reality. It was a different world, a step from one century into another. Try though he might, he could not prevent himself from gawking like a raw schoolboy.

The harbor and dock area alone was mind boggling. Foreign fleet ships, glistening white, were surrounded by junks, tugboats, barges, and sampans. Small fishing vessels wove merrily through this montage, and seamen unloaded their catches on the docks, seemingly unperturbed by the huge crane-driven cargo nets swinging precariously overhead.

Just the task of disembarking and seeing that the baggage was put safely ashore was no mean task, even for the resourceful Fong Lu.

Master and servant stood close together, surrounded by four medium-sized wicker trunks, feeling very much like disoriented aliens. All around them was a cacophony of sound. Languages and dialects they did not understand were being spoken, bawled, and cursed. Good manners seemed to have been blown by the wayside, for they were jostled and pushed from every direction. Fong Lu came to himself first, and quickly took charge as best he could.

"Stay here, Master," he instructed. "I will seek us conveyance at once. But under no circumstances take your eyes from your possessions. Sit upon them if you must; otherwise they will be stolen from beneath your very nose."

Fengmo nodded, not in the least put off by his servant's

new tone of command, which would have seemed high-handed less than an hour before. Suddenly the cloth money belt he wore strapped about his midsection felt as if it weighed a ton.

It seemed an eternity before a small automobile screeched to a stop in front of him, though in fact only minutes had passed. Smiling, Fong Lu was riding upon the running board with one arm hooked through an open rear window.

"Here I am, Master," he beamed. "This *taxi*"—his tongue stumbled over the word—"will take us to our destination. It was not easy to convince the driver to take us, either. I had to promise him a rich passenger."

The driver he mentioned was a wiry man with a pock-marked face and greedy little eyes. Moreover, he made no move to get out and assist Fong Lu in loading the luggage as one might have expected. Instead, he remained behind the wheel, picking his teeth and berating Fong Lu.

"Hurry up, you turtle head," he yelled. "I have no time to waste on the likes of you or this *illustrious* master of yours. Time is money to me and there are clients aplenty waiting for my service."

This impertinence made Chang Fengmo flush with anger, but under the circumstances he felt he had no choice but to crawl into the musty-smelling rear seat of the vehicle. To his surprise, Fong Lu only smiled strangely at the rude fellow and got into the front without a single retort.

If they had expected the streets they traveled through to be less hectic and congested, they expected wrongly. Shop butted against shop without an inch between, with only an occasional narrow, filth-littered alleyway to separate them. At first, most of the buildings were only two or three stories high. Shops sat beneath and apartments above. Strung overhead were cloth banners proclaiming the names and wares of these shops, all intermingled with fluttering laundry that had been hung out to dry by the apartment dwellers.

Fengmo gave Fong Lu a thin slip of paper listing the address of the House of Wong, and Fong Lu in turn read it aloud to the driver.

The streets were alive with pedestrians in all manner of dress, ever watchful of the many vehicles rushing past them. The taxi driver honked, weaving the car through the traffic, a mixture of cars, rickshaws, pedicabs, and bicycles. From time to time he would lean his head out the window and curse in a loud, raucous voice.

The streets did finally widen when they came into the business district. At the sight of the Bund, Fengmo's mouth actually fell open. The buildings were so tall they seemed to reach up and scratch the very sky. They literally took his breath away. In Tanpo only a few buildings, mostly tea houses and temples, boasted more than a single story. But this! The fact that the banks and other places of commerce stood there, sun reflecting off their myriad gleaming windows, seemed incredible!

Though traffic was still very heavy, the driver slowed and began to point out different points of interest. To Fengmo's surprise, Fong Lu now became the rude one.

"Drive on, you fish head. We will have time later to see the sights and acquaint ourselves with this stinking beehive. For now it is your job to get us where we wish to go—as quickly as possible."

The driver shrugged. "I was only trying to please your young lord," he said in an injured voice. "Surely he is interested—"

Fong Lu cut him off without so much as a glance back at Fengmo for approval. "He is interested in arriving at the Street of the Blue Roofs, I tell you. Now, drive on!"

Muttering beneath his breath, the driver complied by accelerating. In fact, he whipped his automobile through the traffic so recklessly that Fengmo had to suppress an urge to reach out and cuff Fong Lu for his lack of judgment in angering the fellow.

Leaving the circle of the Bund, the driver took several rapid turns, drove on, and then turned again, until Fengmo lost all sense of direction. Fong Lu, however, let out a wild yell and raised his fist at the driver. "You son of a foreign sailor! Do you think I am a fool? Stop this meandering or you will eat my knuckles and lose all your rotten teeth!"

The taxi driver lost his smug complacency at once. Turning the car as quickly as he could in the opposite direction, he continued on, this time in a much straighter line. Unbelievably soon, the scenery started to change. They began passing large private homes which were separated by high

walls and elaborate fences. They were on the outskirts of
the city when a final turn took them into a wide cul-de-sac.
There upon a slight rise sat a house of gargantuan proportions. Terraced grounds and gardens stretched out all
around it, and these in turn were protected by a very high,
thick wall. From that distance the most outstanding and
eye-catching feature of the house was its slanted roofs,
and they were indeed constructed of vivid blue tile, all
trimmed in gold. The House of Wong.

The taxi driver stared up at the house, and this time he
stirred himself to get out of the car and lend a hand. He
looked Fengmo up and down with new respect. Once the
baggage was set beside the gate, he bowed low.

"That will be two pieces of silver and three coppers,
Young Sir. I trust you will enjoy your stay in Shanghai."
His voice dripped solicitude.

Fengmo reached for his purse, but had no time to re-
trieve it before Fong Lu once more interceded.

"Two pieces of silver indeed!" he barked. "You cheating
weasel! You shall have three coppers and no more. My
master is generous in giving you even that much, seeing as
how you drove in circles and did your best to fleece him just
because he is a stranger to these parts."

The argument that ensued was enough to make Fengmo
wince and wish to cover his ears, but in the end the driver
did settle for a single silver piece and seemed delighted to
get it. When he had gone, Fengmo turned to his servant.
"You have never been to Shanghai in your life, you wily
rascal. How could you know we were not headed in the
right direction?"

Fong Lu smiled sheepishly, but not without a certain
pride. "The truck drivers warned me in advance this
might happen. Your friend, Long Han, also took me aside
for a lesson in city ways. I was not sure that turtle was
cheating. I only took a guess."

The two men looked at one another. At first they smiled,
and then they began to laugh uproariously. In their shared
hilarity they did not hear the huge iron grilled gate behind
them swing open. They started simultaneously when a
deep voice interrupted them. A giant man, obviously the
gatekeeper, stood there.

"Welcome to the House of Wong Cho," he said, and

bowed. "We have been expecting you, though on which day we could not be sure. Come in, please."

Fong Lu bent to fetch the wicker bags, but the gate-keeper stopped him.

"I will take care of those. I believe you are in need of a little rest." A broad smile split his face. "It would seem young Master Chang here is in very capable hands."

This comment let them know he had observed the entire incident with the taxi driver. Admiration for Fong Lu was very clearly written on his face.

He was not alone in his esteem. Walking up to the awe-inspiring house, Fengmo also whispered thanks to the gods and to his wise father. Fong Lu was going to be a very worthwhile soul to have around—very worthwhile indeed!

The next days flew by, for the arrival of Fengmo and Fong Lu just happened to coincide with the upcoming sixtieth birthday of Master Wong Cho. The entire household was in a whirl of activity. Laughing servants ran to and fro, chattering and buzzing about what new delicacy the cooks had decided to add to the feast menu.

A servant himself, Fong Lu could not help being caught up in this excitement. Since he was not a part of the regular staff, he had ample opportunity to observe the others while he went about his own duties. He was now Fengmo's personal body servant, a position quite new to him. Waiting upon a single individual, with all the expertise that entailed, had never before been within his scope of responsibility. He worried more than a little that he might appear unfit or unworthy to serve a rich young lord in this capacity. What he did not realize was that the Second Son of Chang Hai-teh had also never had a servant exclusively his own. So, luckily, the two of them were quite satisfied with each other.

Fong Lu was bright and sharp of wit in any case. He was not above asking questions, and since he was in a new place his queries did not seem unusual to the other servants. They gladly informed him of where this or that was, or what fixtures the house contained. A lively discussion took place over the morning meal one day, when he casually mentioned he must take his master out on the town and have him fitted for new clothes.

By the time the meal was finished he had an extensive list of the best clothiers in Shanghai. More important, he also had a very good idea of what prices should be charged and the most effective method of price haggling with each merchant. Armed with this knowledge, he was once again able to astound his master with his ingenuity.

Fengmo was becoming unshakably convinced that he possessed a rare and irreplaceable jewel in the person of his servant, a conviction which proved very valuable to Fong Lu when, a few days after their arrival, he needed to make a special request.

The two men were in the suite which had been given to Fengmo. It was surprisingly large and well furnished, boasting four rooms in all. There was a bedchamber for Fengmo and one of smaller proportions for Fong Lu. The sitting room had shelves of books, comfortable chairs, and shaded lamps powered magically by a thing called *electricity*. Wonder of wonders, however, was the fourth room. Neither master nor servant could believe their eyes when they first saw it. The room contained a privy. Unbelievable! In addition there was a built-in basin for washing. Both hot and cold water actually came into the room through hidden pipes. One had only to turn the brass dragonhead faucets in order to have the liquid come gushing out. Likewise, water was piped into a large tub designed for bathing. This gleaming fixture dominated the room, sitting upon iron feet shaped like lion's claws.

On the evening Fong Lu decided to make his request, he and Fengmo were in the main bedchamber. It was quite late. Fengmo was drinking a last cup of tea while Fong Lu carefully put away the new clothes, which had been delivered that afternoon. There were suits of linen or silk and some made of a fabric called sharkskin. There were also shirts cut with collars and tight-fitting sleeves, and strange thin scarves also make of silk, which were tucked beneath a shirt collar and then tied in a knot around the neck. Fong Lu put all these garments upon parallel wooden rods and hung them neatly in a large wardrobe. Last of all, he put away three pairs of tight-fitting Western shoes. One pair was made of snake skin that had been dyed black and white, while the others were of cow's hide, one pair brown and the other solid black.

Giving them one final flick with a buffing cloth, he closed the wardrobe door. Standing, he sighed deeply.

Mistaking this exhalation for resigned disgust, Fengmo looked at him. "Those Western shoes do look most uncomfortable, do they not? I am glad I can at least wear my own robes and slippers while here in the house."

"I think your new things look quite dashing," Fong Lu responded. "Though, of course, I cannot know how they feel." It was obvious he wanted to say more, but he was unsure how to begin.

"Young Sir," he finally ventured. "I have a favor to ask and yet I do not want to be a bother."

"You could hardly be that," Fengmo assured him. "Quite the contrary. I fear I would be adrift without your sensible brains to guide me here in this crazy place."

"But the favor I wish involves *cash*, Master."

Fengmo laughed. "I have never known a fellow so concerned with another's money! Ask what you will, man. If your request is reasonable, you shall certainly have it. I daresay you deserve a reward."

"It is not only myself I think of, sir. I know you would not want to be shamed before the other rich men of this city, nor before your host, Master Wong. All the other menservants here, the ones who drive automobiles, dress differently than I. They laugh at my trousers and quilted jacket and my round skullcap. Most of all they find my pigtail a source of great hilarity.

"They all wear coats of gray, Western in style, with tight breeches which are flared at the top. Moreover, they have fine black boots which come almost to their knees, and hats with visors in front."

He looked at Fengmo miserably. Tiny spots of color appeared on his cheeks. "I feel somewhat a fool, Master."

Hearing this plea, Fengmo did not laugh or even smile. He knew only too well the humiliation his proud servant had been suffering.

"It was thoughtless of me not to realize your dilemma, Fong Lu," he apologized, and when the other man started to protest, he held up a hand to stop him.

"No, do not make excuses for me. You will take some silver and go purchase all you need tomorrow. I will fend for myself while you attend your own needs for a change.

And do not purchase only your driving clothes either. You will no doubt need a few others—buy them also."

"Oh, I need only the one suit, Young Sir, honestly! You are being too kind."

Chang Fengmo forced himself to scowl and speak in a very stern way. "You will do exactly as I say. I will not have a servant of mine running about like some country clod. Do you understand?"

Fong Lu murmured in the affirmative and bowed deeply before retiring to his own room. That night he lay on the soft bed that was temporarily his and counted his blessings. He could almost see himself, hair shorn, all decked out in proper city style. Soon that haughty little serving girl, Jasmine, would be truly dazzled by him.

Yes, Fong Lu decided, life in Shanghai was going to suit him very well.

Chapter Twelve

The day of feasting arrived. To reach the age of sixty was an event worthy of celebration, and the Wong family set about it with relish. Master Wong, who looked more a man of forty-five than the age he actually was, submitted to all the fuss with indulgent equanimity.

Over a hundred guests were expected for the festivities. Every influential businessman in Shanghai had been invited. Amidst the bustle that had been going on, Fengmo felt singularly out of place. One thing was abundantly clear—he did not understand the customs and lifestyle of these city dwellers.

Master Wong noticed the discomfort of his young guest, but for the first few days left him alone to make his own first impressions. In the meantime, he gave a great deal of thought to the last letter he had received from his friend, Chang Hai-teh. After the normal, courteous salutations, it read:

> You have my unending gratitude for accepting the charge of my Second Son. Though a father should not compliment his own offspring, I tell you he is an intelligent and industrious boy. I send him into your keeping as a learning experience. While he is in Shanghai, I wish him to, conduct certain business on my behalf. He has been instructed to purchase some quality jade and ivory, and also some everyday foreign stuffs which will sell well here in Tanpo. I also wish him to apply himself to grasping at least a passable amount of language spoken by the *Ying Man.* I beg you to give him the benefit of your wisdom in these matters.
>
> There is another thing, however. This son of mine has

been sorely wounded, but his wound is of the soul and heart rather than the flesh. I send him away from his home for a spell in the hope he might be healed and forget. . . .

Before it closed, the letter went on to exchange family news, and views on the troubled political climate.

Master Wong had given that letter much thought, and consequently, he watched Fengmo closely. As for giving the lad a lesson in business acumen, he most heartily looked forward to the task. He loved bartering and any kind of transaction, large or small, in which he must use his brains and a bit of manipulative intrigue. Known for his shrewdness in such matters, he had made a vast fortune for himself, quadrupling the already healthy estate left to him by his own father.

Ah, but matters of the heart—now that was something else. He himself had been wed to a girl he had never seen before the wedding, a most satisfactory arrangement, even if his own sons *had* broken that particular tradition. Heaven saw fit to bless Master Wong in the person of his mate, Joyful Spirit. She was a most equitable and satisfying wife. Unlike many of his position and wealth, he cared not for womanizing. His First Wife was his only wife. Other females did not interest him. He never stopped to wonder if this was because he loved Joyful Spirit deeply, or simply because his life was busy and fulfilling in and of itself.

Early on the morning of his birthday he stood at the window of his second-story bedchamber and looked out over the small park which was a part of the grounds around his home. Morning mist hovered about the pines and white-barked birch trees. A pair of deer nibbled foliage in an open meadow. Just at the edge of the clearing, he glimpsed the silhouette of a tall youth.

"I see our guest is up and about," he said.

Behind him, sitting at her dressing table, his wife answered. "If you speak of Chang Fengmo, I believe he is always up with the dawn. The servants tell me he has made it a habit to go walking in the early light."

"A quiet lad," her husband mused.

"Yes, but I think perhaps he is also very shy. It would

not surprise me to learn those rowdy children of ours scare him. What a bunch they are!"

Joyful Spirit smiled as she made this comment, for her family was her life and no mother could have been more proud of her brood.

Master Wong stretched. "My blood could use a bit of stirring. I think I will join him."

This surprised Madame Wong since she knew he was not normally the sort of man given to leisurely constitutionals, but she said nothing. One thing she had learned over the years was that her lord did nothing without a purpose.

By the time Master Wong arrived at the park, Fengmo had walked on to the lake and was standing upon a red lacquered bridge, staring out over the water.

"Hello, Young Chang," Master Wong called from a distance, not wanting to startle the young man. "Might I join you for a breath of morning air?"

"By all means, sir," came the expected reply.

For a while the two stood together in companionable silence and then began to stroll casually along, first around the vast grounds and then slowly up through the garden paths that led to the house. It was a good opportunity for light social intercourse. Master Wong pointed out different areas and explained how and when they had been landscaped. The acquisition of certain flora, wild animals, and fowls had taken many years. Fengmo was impressed, not only with the fortune it must have cost, but with the creative and artful thought that had gone into the planning.

Coming from a family of wealth himself, he was not easily awed. But the House of Wong surpassed anything he might have imagined. Instead of being compact and divided into many courts as his own home was, it was a sprawling structure with the grounds serving as one giant court for the use of all. The main house was two stories high. Only the main hierarchy of servants resided there, while the others, who numbered at least fifty, lived in a separate building. In addition there was a beautiful gabled temple, complete with a pair of resident priests. It was all breathtaking.

Inside the house proper was a combination of old and new, all somehow blended harmoniously. Eastern decor met and complemented Western convenience and comfort.

The room that most amazed Fengmo was the one that dominated the house.

All rooms, upper and lower, surrounded a sort of inner court. An opening had been cut into the roof and covered with a glass dome. The air was fragrant with potted hothouse flowers and shrubbery. A fountain sat in the center, above a pool where gold and white speckled fish cavorted beneath perpetually blooming lotuses. There were brightly colored birds as well, free to roam as far as their clipped wings would allow. They sang almost constantly, as if every day were spring. Two servants were assigned the unending task of cleaning the droppings and cast-off plumage of these exotic creatures.

This aviary garden was the favored place of Master Wong, and it was here he and Fengmo relaxed in highbacked bamboo chairs to share morning tea.

After they were served, Master Wong held his cup in both hands and blew away the steam. "The day following tomorrow, once I have had a chance to recuperate from merrymaking tonight"—the older man grimaced comically—"you and I shall begin doing the business you came to conduct. I hope you will enjoy your stay with us."

"I am sure I will, sir," Fengmo answered, though it was not quite true. "I thank you for your hospitality."

Master Wong looked thoughtful. "I know it is your father's wish that you be tutored in English, but I have yet to secure an adequate teacher. I cannot instruct you, I am afraid, since I learned the language in a slapdash manner myself. Do not worry. I will ask about among my friends. No doubt one of them will be able to supply a good recommendation."

As if providence had been eavesdropping, a servant approached and cleared his throat. "There is a call, Master," he announced. "A gentleman wishes to speak with the young sir here."

Fengmo's brows shot up in surprise. He had heard the jingle of the ugly talking instrument, which hung upon a wall in the hallway, but he had never expected to speak into the thing himself. It was with a certain amount of trepidation that he took the proffered earphone and spoke his name into the receiver.

A crackling voice came booming into his head. "Good

morning, Chang Fengmo! How do you find life in the House of Wong?"

For a moment Fengmo was too startled to speak, and after a moment's silence the voice sounded again.

"It is I, Long Han. Speak up, man. I cannot hear you!"

Fengmo laughed self-consciously, but soon they were both immersed in animated conversation.

"Are you still determined to speak the foreign tongue?" Han asked. When his listener answered in the affirmative, he continued. "I have just the fellow for you then. He is a foreigner and a friend—another god-man, to use your term."

Not wanting to seem rude or ungrateful, Fengmo hesitated. He was not at all sure he wanted to get close to a foreign devil, even if he was the friend of a friend. Long Han seemed to read his mind.

"This man is not obtrusive, I assure you," he said. "Moreover, he is hard pressed for cash. You have my word that he does not even smell bad."

Fengmo smiled. "Have you already spoken to him?"

"Of course not. I would not presume so, not even upon a country boy like you. If you will allow me, I will come by for a visit tomorrow and bring him with me. You may judge for yourself before making a decision."

A time was set for the next afternoon and Fengmo hung the earphone slowly back in place. A lopsided grin tugged at the corners of his mouth as he stared at the telephone.

I do believe I like a few of these contraptions, he decided. Imagine talking to another man from miles away!

He had heard of telephones, of course, but to actually see and use one?

He was not sure he would ever accustom himself to modern life.

That evening Fengmo was subjected to more cultural shocks. The house was filled to overflowing with people, both male and female, some of them foreign. Automobiles of every shape and size crowded the street and circular driveway. This feast was like none Fengmo had ever experienced. For one thing, the guests did not gather in a single large banquet hall, neatly seated and separated by age and sex. Rather, long tables had been set up and the guests strolled by serving themselves helter-skelter. Had Madame Chang been able to see this, Fengmo was certain she would have fainted dead away.

Most alarming, however, was the way men and women mingled, casually drinking intoxicating beverages in long-stemmed glasses and smoking enough cigarettes to make the inside of the house appear shrouded in fog. All the men wore white Western jackets over black slacks. The women were attired in a mixture of modern and traditional gowns.

The only soul who seemed in the least normal was Madame Wong. This quietly cheerful woman sat in an elaborate chair and remained there the entire evening. When she was approached, she bowed her head graciously and uttered a few courtesies. Otherwise, she simply looked on and whispered occasional commands to the servants. Sensing a kindred spirit, Fengmo planted himself beside her reassuring presence, speaking and moving as little as possible.

Unfortunately, this self-imposed hermitage could not last forever. Shortly after midnight the older guests began to yawn, most following the example of their host, Master Wong. Watching the older man, Fengmo suspected he was not so much ready for sleep as he was tired of all the hubbub.

If the more mature guests were susceptible to a not-so-subtle hint, the young ones were not. There was quite a large group of young people, too, for the Wong children had a huge circle of intimates between them all. Fengmo had seen many of them coming and going from the house.

Wong Cho and Joyful Spirit had seven children. The six eldest were all sons, and each was called simply by the number that signified the order of his birth, though of course they had been given proper names as well. Wong One, Two, and Three were married men with children, while the younger ones remained free as the wind and seemed intent upon staying so. The last offspring was a daughter. She was called Bright Autumn and had been so named because she was conceived in her mother's last year of fertility.

These seven children and twenty or so of their remaining companions were still wide-eyed and ready for the real fun to begin after the older guests departed.

Madame Wong rose from her chair and groaned tiredly. "I am ready for a soft bed," she said to her husband. "My old bones are creaking in every joint. Let us retire and leave these rowdies to have their good time. I will instruct Sung Chow to keep a watchful eye on them."

"For all the good it will do," Master Wong grumbled under his breath.

This lax attitude and chaperoning procedure would have shocked Fengmo at the beginning of his visit, but by now he realized it was an accepted practice, at least in the Wong household, for men and women to congregate together, often with only a servant to watch over them. Even so, the idea made him acutely uncomfortable, and when his host and hostess started to leave, he moved to follow them. To his surprise it was Madame Wong who turned and stopped him.

Laying a gentle hand on his arm, she smiled. "Stay here with your peers, Chang Two. It is time you and my children become better acquainted. They are an interesting lot really—not nearly as fearsome and wild as they seem."

Fengmo colored, embarrassed that his emotions were so obvious. Since there was no way to decline politely, he lingered at the door looking wistfully after the retiring couple. No sooner had they gone than one of the girls in the remaining group called out loudly to the others.

"Thank the stars and moon! Let us all go into the other room, Bright Autumn. My two feet are just itching to dance!"

She had a bold jarring voice which made Fengmo wince, but the rest of the group laughed and clapped their approval of her suggestion.

Wong Three, a man in his late twenties, led the way. He spoke back over his shoulder to the servant, Sung Chow. "See that drinks and refreshments are brought to the music room, Chow. We do not need to see your face every second, either. We are not children, after all."

The hapless chaperon simply shrugged and headed toward the kitchen.

The youngest Wong son stopped and spoke to Fengmo as the others filed out the door and turned down the hallway.

"What a bunch of fools," he muttered. "If they would not badger me unmercifully, I would go to bed this instant.

Come, we will sit together. For myself I am going to drink nothing but tea. My poor head and stomach are in a turmoil!"

Fengmo, who had imbibed almost nothing, nonetheless agreed, and he and Wong Six straggled behind.

The room they entered was one Fengmo had not been in before. Smaller and more intimate, it contained several couches which lined the walls. The highly polished parquet floor was not covered by rugs of any kind. Upon a table in one corner sat another modern miracle, a radio. It squawked and screeched as one of the male guests, a foreigner with hair the color of straw, turned the knob and began rotating a large dial. A small window in the box glowed brightly. Suddenly music came blaring out, a discordant Western tune. Several of the girls began snapping their fingers. Soon most of the people in the room were dancing—male and female together. One tune stopped and a foreign voice made an announcement. Then the music began again.

Fengmo watched with a mixture of chagrin and appalled fascination. From time to time a couple would stop to rest, putting their heads together in intimate conversation, while the girl fanned herself prettily.

"Look at them," Wong Six hissed, his brows beetling. His disgust was apparent, and when he saw his sister walking toward them, his scowl deepened.

Bright Autumn made Fengmo extremely nervous. She smiled now, and all at once the room seemed to grow more crowded and unbearably warm.

She came to a halt directly in front of him. "Come, Chang Two," she invited. "Dance with me. I have been slow in bidding you welcome to our home."

He flushed deep red. "Thank you, but I cannot . . . I mean to say . . . I do not . . ."

Wong Six came to his rescue. "I think our guest is worn out by the evening's gaiety, Sister."

She made a face at her sibling and turned back to Fengmo. "Surely you are not tired already, a big fellow like you." Her voice was light and teasing. "If the steps are strange to you, I will be happy to give you a lesson."

"Do you not hear well?" Wong Six barked. "He does not

wish to make a display of himself as you and these other geese do! Can you not leave him be?"

The air fairly crackled with tension, and people were beginning to stop and pay attention to the argument brewing between the fiery-tempered brother and sister.

Face burning with humiliation, Fengmo stood, bowed stiffly, and all but ran from the room.

"See what you have done!" Wong Six accused. "Our parents would be very displeased with your poor manners, girl. You do not realize inland fellows are not like your other friends. No doubt he finds you a regular hussy, which is not far from the truth!"

He had more to say, but Bright Autumn was not listening. Thoughtfully, she looked at the door through which Chang Fengmo had disappeared.

In spite of the hour, it was a long time before Fengmo could sleep. His mind kept flitting back and forth between Tanpo and Shanghai—old traditions and new ways—Golden Willow and these modern girls—and most especially Bright Autumn.

Golden Willow was the essence of grace and gentility. Her every movement bespoke breeding, yet her eyes held the passion of a universe. There was nothing so tender as the curve of her lips, nor as enchanting as the gentle sway of her walk.

Fengmo loved her more than breath. Separated from her not only by distance but by fate, he was almost overwhelmed with misery. And for some reason his pain at this moment was more agonizing than ever before.

At home he had *belonged*, even in his unhappiness; but in this place he was alien, an extraneous soul struggling for approval he was not sure he really desired.

Preparations for the celebration of Master Wong's birthday had kept him from becoming well acquainted with the Wong progeny except for brief contacts. Yet, he sorely felt their curiosity and amused censorship.

Until tonight he had seen Bright Autumn only at mealtimes or on a rare evening when she was not out with one young man or another. During those times he had kept his distance. He found her disconcerting and would have avoided her at any cost had he been able. It would not have been difficult in a house less modern, a traditional home where families kept their unwed daughters safely hidden.

Not so in the House of Wong! Here sister and brothers were free and easy with each other, laughing and exchanging stories about their friends. If a guest came and he was young, he was thrown in among the rest as if no barriers existed.

Fengmo did not wish to keep away from Bright Autumn because she was unattractive. In truth she was quite pretty, small and fine boned like most women in Shanghai. She had great dark eyes, shaped like apricots, over a dainty, slightly upturned nose. Her lips were full and perfect as rosebuds.

There were other things about her, though, which made him uncomfortable in the extreme. She wore her hair cut short in the foreign fashion and it curled in tight ringlets about her face. Cosmetics accentuated her eyes, and she painted her lips and long fingernails cherry red. The gowns she wore were of a Chinese style, made of silk or brocade and with high collars, but they were pinched in at the waist and slit up one side to expose her legs. On her feet, instead of soft embroidered slippers she wore strange shoes which were elevated in back and balanced on very high, thin heels. Fengmo always expected her to fall down, but she moved regally, her hips swinging in a way that made him blush.

She was a happy creature, full of fun and chatter, and though she was not actually bold, she was teasing and mischievous. He was sure that she found his reticence and old-fashioned habits a source of mirth.

Bright Autumn was also spoiled. Fengmo had concluded this even in the short time he had been with the family. She was unbelievably pampered and petted for a female. Master Wong made much of her, not in the least discontent on account of her gender since he had six healthy sons. In fact, her father was the most guilty of giving in to her whims. On the rare occasions when her mother denied her something, she would run to him weeping great silver tears and have her own way in the end. The only member of the family who seemed impervious to her charm was Wong Six. With everyone else she had only to stamp her tiny, unbound feet to have her every wish fulfilled.

This house and this city are all topsy-turvy! Fengmo decided. Moreover, I do not like their customs one little bit!

Dancing! The very idea left him flabbergasted. How indecent to hold a woman close while strangers looked on, and to press yourself against her whether you loved her or not! Watching the escapades tonight, he had twisted and turned in his seat.

Thinking these things, he tossed and could not sleep. Finally he buried his face in his pillow and groaned aloud. How he wished he could just go home where his heart remained, where up was up and down down.

At last he fell into a fitful slumber. All that night his dreams were punctuated by the visage of Golden Willow. Her face kept shimmering and changing, so that when he awoke the next morning he was not certain if it had been she who had visited his sleep or the other—Bright Autumn.

Chapter Thirteen

Winter dealt gently with Shanghai. Consequently, during the month before the New Year the weather was fair and mild, with blossoming fruit trees, giant hibiscuses, and moss-covered ground providing a riot of color as Fengmo and his two guests sauntered through a garden area of the Wong estate.

"This place is magnificent!" Long Han exclaimed. "By all the gods that be, I swear I have never seen anything like it!"

This remark struck Fengmo as quite humorous since Han supposedly believed in only one deity. Evidently, the third member of their group was also amused, for he laughed aloud.

Long Han turned a frown on the youthful American. "Well," he defended himself, "perhaps I should have taken the name of our Heavenly Father in vain. No doubt that would please you better!"

Sean Duncan shook his head but continued to laugh. When he finally spoke, his deep voice was almost without accent. "No wonder Father and Mother despair of you, Han. You have a singularly unorthodox way of adhering to your beliefs."

Chang Fengmo smiled and listened as the pair continued to banter. The air was fragrant and without breeze. The buzz of insects was all around, and he felt a kind of lassitude after his restless night. Coming upon a small, open pagoda, he saw several of the Wong sons lounging there. Wong Two and Four were seated in wicker chairs while Wong Three lay stretched full length on a stone bench, his head resting atop a silk pillow. Wong Six reclined upon the

137

bamboo-matted floor, but when he saw Fengmo and the others, he sat up and called out to them.

"Chang Two, come join us. Bring your friends along and introduce them."

These amenities done, the seven young men settled themselves. It was a lazy day for everyone, especially the Wong offspring, who still had fuzzy heads from the evening before. The presence of a foreigner seemed to disturb no one except Fengmo, who was still making an evaluation. While a desultory sort of conversation ensued, he continued to observe Sean Duncan.

The man was not tall by foreign standards. Standing no more than five feet, seven inches, he was of medium build and well proportioned. When actually speaking, his face grew animated, but otherwise bore only an expression of quiet interest, slightly distant, as if he were listening for a word or sound not yet heard.

The variegated coloring of most foreigners distracted and repelled Fengmo, but in the case of Sean it did not. The short, sandy-colored hair and blue-gray eyes somehow blended with his tanned complexion in a way that was acceptable. Just as a forest subtly changed in the fall of a year, muting from vivid green to soft, hazy brown and gold, so did Sean's overall appearance seem natural and not jarring. His jaw was firm and his features bore the unmistakable stamp of honesty.

To his surprise, and for no reason he could clearly define, Fengmo was drawn to this young man who was separated from him by generations of breeding in diverse cultures. Still, he was not quite convinced he wanted to spend the countless hours it would take to learn a new language in such close proximity to this stranger. He watched Sean closely while the others talked. As if aware of this perusal and mutually curious, the foreigner met his eyes from time to time and smiled a faraway, listening smile.

"I think I will go out on the town tonight," Wong Three said, and yawned expansively. "That wife of mine is getting on my nerves. It will do her good to be left alone awhile."

Wong Four laughed. "What does my third sister-in-law want now?"

"You have it right, Little Brother," the other responded

with sour countenance. "That woman always *wants* something. I often wonder if she married me only for the sake of money. Last night she saw a bit of jewelry worn by another guest, and now she must have a trinket like it or die. I could hardly sleep for being pestered. I swear my ears were about to bleed from all her pecking!"

"It is your own fault," Wong Two expounded. "You should have taken a wife who contents herself with a flock of children. My good Little Mother was aptly named. She does not whine all the time for pretty baubles. No, she makes herself busy with our two children and cannot wait for the third to be born. Now that the days have finally come when a man can choose his own bride, he must show a bit of good sense."

This lecture caused Wong Three to bristle. He sat up on the bench and glared at his older brother. "I will take my wife to yours any day! Brilliant Jade is at least good to look at!"

Wong Four, by nature a peacemaker, interrupted them before this confrontation turned into full-scale war. "Stop, you two. Both of you have nice wives, each in her own way. But going out tonight does sound good. It is time we introduce Fengmo here to Shanghai."

The brothers looked at one another with gleaming eyes, all except Wong Six.

"No doubt you will do your best to corrupt him," he muttered in annoyance. "If you have your way, he will return to his home shot through with decadence."

"Oh-ho, listen to the Righteous One!" Wong Three hooted. "Little Lord Big Heart speaks again!"

The others laughed also, but Wong Six only turned his nose up disdainfully. "Go ahead and have your fun," he sniffed. "You think nothing of gorging your fat selves and prancing about the city spending gold as if it were water while others starve. You think it will go on forever, but you are mistaken."

"Now he plays the oracle," Wong Two whispered in mock fright. "Beware, the great seer of the future! Listen lest you die!"

"Tell me, Little Brother, if you care so much for the poor, why do you not give away your hefty allowance? If you are so ashamed of being rich, why not go out and give the poor all your fine robes and Western clothes? No doubt they will bow at your feet in gratitude. And while you are about it, be sure to give them a tenth of the food you consume from dawn to dusk."

The youngest Wong son sprang to his feet, his cheeks bright red. "You!" he hissed. "You all make my stomach churn. There will come a day when you'll despise your words. There will be no poor or rich then. Your filthy money will be worthless as wind!"

He turned malicious, glittering eyes on Sean Duncan and Long Han. "The people of this nation are going to rise up and throw every foreigner and every friend of a foreigner into the sea. Have fun while you may, all of you. But do not expect me to give you sympathy when the day of reckoning comes. I will not cry with you—I will laugh in your faces!"

With this he stalked from the pagoda, his words still ringing in the air. An uncomfortable silence lingered. His remark about foreigners left his brothers looking at Sean and Han in embarrassment.

"He is just a youngster," Wong Four apologized. "In his heart I do not believe he is really the firebrand he pretends. Perhaps in his last life he was a blind beggar child and that makes him too sensitive. Sight of the poor and maimed have always caused him pain, and so he hides his tenderness behind indignation. I hope you will forgive his rudeness."

Long Han waved a negligent hand. "Do not feel badly on our account. My friend and I have tough hides; otherwise, we could not do what we do."

Sean Duncan nodded agreement, but Fengmo noticed how he kept looking down the pathway Wong Six had taken.

"I wonder . . ." he said aloud. But he did not finish the sentence. Instead, he rose to leave and thanked the remaining Wong brothers for their hospitality.

Fengmo walked to the gate with his visitors. As they left, he shook their proffered hands in the Western way of greeting and farewell. Long Han gave him a questioning look and Fengmo nodded almost imperceptibly, thereby letting his friend know that he had decided to accept Sean Duncan as tutor.

* * *

That night Fengmo did indeed go out with Master Wong's five eldest boys. It was an experience he was never to forget. Shanghai was known as the city that did not sleep, and now he learned why. A special colored electricity called *neon* kept the place constantly lit. In Tanpo people slept at night, but here they seemed to continue their activity endlessly.

Fengmo looked out a window of the huge black car Wong One drove through crowded downtown streets, and he did not believe his eyes. Shopkeepers were still conducting business; vendors of every description hawked their wares in loud voices; men and women roamed the thoroughfares in droves!

"Do these folks never close their eyes?" he asked, incredulous.

Wong Four, who sat next to him, answered. "Perhaps in shifts. It is hard for a merchant to close his eyes when there is a profit to be made."

According to Fengmo's guides of the evening, Shanghai boasted every kind of entertainment imaginable. In addition to the clubs, race tracks, and casinos, there were theaters which were a wonder unto themselves. Fortunately for his peace of mind, Fengmo had already heard stories of these miraculous places where images of people, alive and talking, flickered on and off a large, flat screen. His own father carried a few magazines in one shop about these films, and Fengmo knew they had been the source of some heated family discussions. Evidently his little sister, Moon Shadow, avidly secreted these books against her mother's most strict disapproval.

The car moved slowly past a myriad clubs. Wong Five, a young man only slightly older than Fengmo, explained all the kinds of shows that could be seen inside them.

"Some have acrobats and jugglers, others musicians. But the place we are headed is the most gala of them all. Wait and see."

The others seemed to find this amusing, for they snickered and elbowed one another, a fact which Fengmo found a little alarming. The mild trepidation with which he had begun the evening increased.

Just moments later they came to a stop before a three-story structure. Unlike the surrounding buildings, it sat back from the street a short distance and boasted a small garden in front. The plants were set about with lights and torches, which cast the white walls and gold-tiled roof of the club in dazzling splendor.

Several servants stood waiting at the gates and one of them jumped to open the car doors. After Fengmo and the others had disembarked, the fellow got behind the wheel and drove away.

A sigh of relief escaped Fengmo's lips as he noticed that all the patrons entering the club were men. Perhaps this is just another glorified tea house, he thought hopefully. I could have a nice evening after all.

Once inside they were approached by a pretty girl in modern Chinese dress who greeted them and led the way to a large table in a room dominated by a curtained stage. The room was noisy, but to Fengmo's continued delight it also was full of men. The only females were those who moved about the tables serving drinks. These girls wore the same modern attire, but Fengmo accepted this as only natural. No doubt they were simply flower girls in updated costumes.

As soon as they were all comfortably seated, Wong One ordered a round of drinks, which arrived almost instantly. These were a delicious concoction of crushed ice and fruits of various kinds. They were also supposed to be laced with foreign liquor, though Fengmo decided the stuff must be very weak since he could hardly taste it.

Looking around the room, he found it strange that there appeared to be no gambling going on; nor were any of the patrons eating. Instead, the men talked to one another in subdued, expectant voices.

"Is there to be a performance or some such up on that stage?" he inquired innocently. "Everyone seems to be waiting for some momentous event."

Wong Four responded seriously. "Yes, a momentous event indeed. But it will not take place for awhile yet. Have another drink."

In fact they all had several more before the room slowly darkened and the curtain covering the stage went up. This stage was dimly lit, and the patrons hushed as soft music began to drift out to them from an unseen source.

For some reason, Fengmo felt light-headed and more happy than he had been for a very long time. When a traditionally clad flower girl minced out on stage, he settled back to relax and enjoy her song. For a fleeting moment he remembered the flower girl, Sweet Harmony, who had helped soothe him one terrible night.

The girl on stage knelt on a small cushion. Her hair was bedecked with tiny orchids, and her voice as sweet as her face promised. It rose and fell in delightful warbles. Then, almost imperceptibly, it began to change. Her song had been a tale of lost love and longing, but suddenly the words became slightly lewd. She stood just as the music took on a more modern tempo, and began to disrobe. The stage lights brightened.

Fengmo leaned forward in his chair, his eyes bulging in their sockets. He gasped as the girl unpinned her hair and shook it loose. It cascaded around her like a veil of midnight. Now he noticed the modern shoes she wore, those high, spiky things, and was amazed when she began to dance and kick up her legs. With each movement her words became more suggestive and one more piece of clothing was discarded. Finally, she was left with nothing covering her at all except three tiny imitation parasols pasted to her breasts and somehow affixed over her most private part.

"By the gods!" he whispered, unmindful of the muffled laughter at his table.

The girl quit singing, but the music played on. Fengmo doubted she had breath for anything but her dance in any case. She ran about, undulating in a manner most unseemly. Her hips ground to the beat of a drum in faster and faster circles. The men in the audience began to make rude noises and yell out to her as she pranced. She moved faster yet and gave them a vixen's smile.

All at once the music stopped. The patrons grew quiet again as the girl faced them, her feet planted wide apart, arms akimbo.

Fengmo nearly jumped out of his skin when the sound of firecrackers exploded into the room. The crowd hooted wildly as all three parasols began spinning in unison. At last the curtain lowered and the main room flooded with light and conversation.

Fengmo sat back in his chair with a giant exhalation. "This city is like none other on earth!" he said, and took several gulps from his glass. "I fear Wong Six was partially right. I will not be the same man when I return to Tanpo!"

The five Wong brothers watched him to see if he was going to grow angry at the prank they had perpetrated. In their silence he peered at them, one at a time, trying to decide if their jest had been one of malice or simply a bit of good-natured fun.

Holding his glass up to the light, he smacked his lips loudly. "This foreign drink is not bad. I do believe I will have another, even if the liquor *is* fit only for babies." He looked around the room with a bored expression. "This place is beginning to weary me. Is there nothing more exciting to do?"

The Wongs gawked at him in stunned surprise until he began to laugh.

"Well, well," Wong Four chuckled. "It would seem our guest is no dullard after all!"

By this time Fengmo was quite intoxicated. Normally, he would have politely refused to cavort any longer, but his defenses were down now and he went about the city with them, visiting other clubs and gambling establishments.

Furthermore, he imbibed far more than he ought. His reward came the following morning when he awoke with a head that felt as if it would drop from his shoulders if he so much as moved.

Chapter Fourteen

*F*ong Lu adapted to city life with a great deal more equanimity than his master. As servant and chauffeur to a rich man, he had his own social status, one not lacking advantage in a place like Shanghai. There were moving pictures, various sideshows, restaurants, and even dance halls for just such as he. He enjoyed them all to the fullest.

Many of the serving girls in the city, like their mistresses, were singularly lacking in shyness. They did not run away when a man looked at them, and some were even immodest enough to give a fellow a gaze for a gaze. In the evenings they could be seen in groups of two or three, walking arm in arm and laughing gaily as they made their way to a favorite club.

Unlike Fengmo, Fong Lu was not in the least appalled by either the idea or practice of mixed dancing. He thought it wonderful to be able to cling to a strange woman in public without fear of retribution.

Yes, Shanghai suited him very well indeed. There were more pretty girls in the place than he had formerly imagined on the entire earth. The House of Wong alone boasted more than a few, and one stood out among all the rest. Her name was Jasmine, a tiny, delicate creature with short hair and bangs cut straight across her forehead.

Jasmine kept all the unmarried male servants entranced with her smiles and twinkling eyes. She looked at everyone straight on with those lovely sloe eyes, and if she seemed a bit bold, still she could be had by no man. She came close and teased, only to turn elusive in the next instant. It was enough to drive them to distraction.

Fong Lu was taken by this girl also, but he perceived her nature almost at once. This Jasmine thinks she is above

all, he concluded, because she knows how much she is admired. Well then, the man to conquer her will certainly be
one she believes she cannot have. I am going to be exactly
that one!

It did not take long for this ploy to work. When Jasmine
saw she was not noticed by the handsome servant of Chang
Two, she was perturbed beyond telling. She began going
out of her way to flash Fong Lu winsome smiles, all to no
avail. He seemed to love his master's stupid automobile
more than he did anything.

One day while he was polishing this monstrosity, Jasmine made an excuse to walk past him. In her hands she
carried a small potted plant, and seeing he did not turn to
look at her, she dropped the thing.

"Oh no!" she cried in a helpless voice. "The master will
be quite vexed with me for not planting this in the garden."

Fong Lu did not turn.

Jasmine thrust out her lower lip and narrowed her eyes
at his back, but her voice was still sweet and imploring.
"No doubt I will cut my fingers to pieces on these shards,"
she said, bending down and pretending to pick up the
broken pot.

Even so the chauffeur did not turn. He continued rubbing a cloth in wide circular motions over an already
gleaming fender, stopping only to pick at an invisible resi-
due of lint. In the end she had no choice but to clean up the
mess she had made on the bricked driveway and then return to the house—enraged.

As if this were not vexation enough, she often came upon
Fong Lu lounging about the kitchen or in a central room of
the servants' quarters to find him in animated conversation with some other, less pretty maid. At these times she
would duck out of sight around a corner and clench her
fists. Stamping a dainty foot, it was all she could do not to
scream.

Meanwhile, Fong Lu made it his business to find out
what Jasmine did during her spare time. With very little
effort he learned the dance halls she was apt to frequent
and began haunting the places himself. He never asked
her to dance, however. Instead, he would saunter over,

looking at everyone and everything but Jasmine, and then choose as partner some girl sitting close beside her.

He had gauged his prey well. After a few weeks of this treatment, Jasmine was ready to throw her proud self at his feet. Thus, when he finally did ask her to dance, she was nearly ecstatic. She chattered vivaciously and pressed herself close against him.

So it was that these two became the talk of the Wong staff. Jasmine quit flirting and expended all her considerable energy on Fong Lu. As for Fong Lu, he forced himself always to remain just a little aloof for fear he might lose his enchantment.

If the chauffeur liked his new life, he also found something about Shanghai he hated with vehemence—it was overflowing with foreign devils!

Since the dance halls and other clubs he frequented were not the most expensive, they also attracted foreigners in uniform. Most of these men were bawdy, seafaring sorts, big of frame and rude in manner. If one of them consumed too much wine or other strong spirits, he grew even more obnoxious.

What was a simple Chinese man of dignity to do when some huge, hairy beast pushed him aside and took his woman? To kill a foreigner would bring swift and final retribution not only on one's self, but often on innocent bystanders as well.

Fong Lu had already been pushed and shoved by these foreigners just enough to severely damage his pride. He loathed them and could barely keep his face from betraying this fact when he was forced to wait upon Sean Duncan.

How can my good master stand being next to the likes of that god-man? he wondered. Those eyes of his give me the chills, even if he is not all covered with hair!

Sean Duncan, born and raised in China but educated in the United States of America, was neither fish nor fowl. The people he loved most were not his people. He was the son of the missionaries who had reared Long Han, and brother to the beloved Mary.

When sent "home" to college, Sean had been the most miserable of young men. Brought up as he had been, theology seemed a natural enough vocation. More important, however, it promised to be the quickest route back to China.

Returned to his surrogate country, he moved about the people, part of them but not one with them. Their concerns had always been his, and yet most of them refused to accept him. To them he would always be a foreign devil, a strange god-man.

The distant rumbling emanating from Manchuria was his most immediate worry. Imperial Japan sat perched there, behind-the-scenes manipulator of a weak puppet government, while casting a lascivious eye on the whole of China. No one believed the mockery of weak Pu-yi sitting on a pretend throne, but though the world cried its outrage, the Japanese stayed. Already they had attempted an attack on Shanghai and been repelled.

Sean felt certain the Japanese would return, for the political instability and technological backwardness of China made it appear an easy plum to pick. The people themselves knew not where to turn for leadership. Chiang Kai-shek held power at the moment, but his government lacked unity and was riddled with corruption. Another man, the son of a peasant, Mao Tse-tung, had pulled together quite a vast following, though his disciples were forced to conduct their doings in secret or face a firing squad.

Sean was not sure of all that Mao stood for, or whether his teachings were good or bad. He only knew the lack of unity in China was dangerous. If the country could not act with quick harmony, it would be even more defenseless. The one thing that encouraged the American and filled him with hope was the indomitable spirit of the people. The seething masses of China were a dauntless and enduring lot.

While tutoring Chang Fengmo, Sean was able to discuss these things to a certain degree, for his pupil was avid not only to learn English but to absorb all he could of his own country. The two often spent long hours after the main lesson was over talking of politics and even religion. Sean made not the least effort to convert Fengmo, a fact which both surprised and pleased the latter. It was more a time of sharing—and an exchange of ideas and feelings. Shortly, they became so close the barriers of race and physiological differences melted away of their own accord.

One day, not long after the first lunar month, Sean came to the House of Wong without his usual anticipatory vigor. Fengmo greeted him at the door and they retired to the library together. Once the sulky Fong Lu had been sent for tea and they were alone, Sean pulled a letter from his vest pocket.

"What is the matter, my friend?" Fengmo inquired. "Your face is three inches longer than the last time we met."

"I have just received this from my sister," Sean replied, turning the missive in restless fingers.

"Is she not well?"

Sean sighed deeply. "She is very well, I fear. It is not Mary I am concerned about."

"Your parents, then?"

Unable to sit still, Sean rose and began pacing back and forth. He spoke in a strained voice. "Oh, what to do!" he lamented. "I am a man torn in two! One side of my heart must rejoice for my sister, while the other cries out to . . ."

He turned and looked at Fengmo with miserable eyes. "Do you remember that I told you Mary had gone to America?"

"Of course. You said she was attending a college there. Lucky, these Western women."

"Yes, lucky!" Sean groaned. "Lucky for Mary. Lucky for Mother and Father. But how terrible for dear Long Han!"

Suddenly, Fengmo felt his stomach muscles tighten as he prepared himself for what he knew would come next.

"I did not tell you all," came the dreaded words. "My parents sent Mary away for more reason than just to see her educated. They hoped against hope that she would find a suitable husband—suitable by *their* standards."

"And she has done so," Fengmo confirmed, striving to keep his tone neutral.

Sean crumpled the letter angrily. His voice bitter with frustration, he cried, "How shall I ever tell Han?" Throwing himself into a nearby chair, he rested his elbows on his knees and ran trembling fingers through his hair.

Fong Lu entered with tea, but Fengmo quickly signaled him to set the tray down and leave again. The silence that followed was heavy, for there seemed no appropriate words to speak. Finally, Sean leaned back and wearily rubbed his eyes.

"You should have seen them as children," he reminisced. "Even I was jealous of their companionship. Long Han would never call her Mary as we did. No, for him she was always The Pretty One. When they were very small they romped together, Han forever the brave protector.

"My parents did not realize until nearly too late that at some point the friendship had taken a giant step forward. For Long Han it *was* too late. But Mary was younger, less sure of herself and her feelings. She was sent back to America. . . ."

His voice trailed away. When he looked up at Fengmo, there were unshed tears glistening in his smoky eyes. "I fear I have committed two grave wrongs today, Young Chang. In the same breath I have burdened you and broken confidence with Long Han."

"You have done neither, friend." Fengmo put a hand on his shoulder. "We have shared much that is good over these past weeks. If we cannot also unload a bit of sorrow, we are poor companions indeed. As for Han, he never told me all, but I guessed the truth."

The room grew quiet again. Texts were open upon a table. The tea sat unpoured and growing cold. At last, Sean rose and his shoulders slumped.

"There are not enough words in any language to help me soften the blow I must now inflict. I fear I will do you no good as a teacher."

Fengmo nodded his understanding. "Nor would I be an alert pupil. Do you wish me to come with you, Sean? Perhaps between us both . . ."

"Thank you, but no. This is something I must do alone. Who else could understand what Long Han is about to suffer? It is best his grief and shame be limited, at least in the viewing."

Fengmo almost spoke then, almost shared the most secret part of his soul. But at the last instant, he changed his mind. To do so would have been to add yet another concern to the gargantuan millstone of worry Sean already bore. So instead he walked quietly with the other man as far as the gates.

Sean paused before stepping out into the street. His head tilted slightly to one side, and once more Fengmo had the impression his friend listened for some sound as yet unheard.

"Would the world not be a better place if God had made us all the same?" Sean asked, almost as if he questioned himself. "How wonderful to have no barriers to separate mankind!"

With that he turned and walked slowly away.

Fengmo watched him go. "Sean Duncan," he said softly, "you are a man misplaced."

It was many days before Fengmo saw either Sean or Long Han again. Meanwhile, he made himself busy both with his English lessons and with taking care of his father's business. In his melancholy mood he found little pleasure in the company of the younger family members. The same was not true of Master Wong, however. The older man exuded a sort of natural comfort, and under his tutelage, Fengmo was fast learning the art of sharp dealing.

"Never let a man know what you are thinking," Wong Cho coached. "Moreover, it is always better if *he* thinks you are just a bit dim-witted. This is not hard to do, especially not with the white foreigners. Many of them seem to believe that if one cannot speak their language well, one is automatically stupid. It serves me to keep my bumbling accent and to stutter a great deal. I hem and haw, watching them the entire while. Observe closely and you will notice the white men, most particularly the Americans, cannot put on a mask. No, their big faces just hang out with all their thoughts stamped plainly upon them."

Fengmo quickly learned the truth of this counsel as he and Wong Cho went about business. Careful to keep his own countenance still and immobile, he watched the older man play the fool only to end up the fox. If Master Wong actually wanted the eighteen bales of cotton sitting in the corner of some warehouse, he would meander all around them and pretend great interest in some other worthless stock. He made sure to adjust his spectacles way down on his nose, and then sucked his teeth like some country clod.

It was all Fengmo could do to follow instructions and not smile—or worse, laugh aloud.

"You are learning, my boy," Wong Cho would say, and give him a hearty slap on the back. "Soon it will be your turn."

Fengmo did not know whether he looked forward to such opportunity or not. The idea of playing the clown before foreigners galled him, but Master Wong so enjoyed the sport himself, it could not help but hold a certain appeal.

An entirely different type of technique was needed when dealing with their own countrymen, or the wily merchants from Korea. Many of these men were equal in bargaining stature. To them, striking a deal was an art to be practiced with devoted finesse.

Fengmo thoroughly enjoyed going with his host to visit the wholesale merchants, jewel vendors, and different craftsmen. To do so was to watch a master at work. He never failed to be amazed at the difference between Wong Cho, the family man, and Master Wong, the businessman. At home his host was jovial and relaxed, always ready to smile and dole out an abundance of affection. His children thought him a regular tender heart, an image most incongruous with his reputed ruthlessness in financial concerns. Master Wong was a man very much respected by his peers.

One day Master Wong took Fengmo to the establishment of Yen Shu, a famous jade dealer. This man owned a tiny factory where superb craftsmen worked day and night producing some of the finest art objects to be found anywhere on earth. Hundreds, even thousands of hours might be spent on a single piece. A few of these priceless masterpieces were displayed in glass cases. Tiny electric lights had been installed to shine down on their gleaming perfection. They rested on beds of black velvet so that there would be nothing to distract the eye of a prospective customer from their minute detail. Fengmo stood entranced before one case. Inside sat the miniature of a three-tiered floating pleasure palace, all done to scale.

"My father would give his soul for this," Fengmo breathed.

Master Wong answered in a low monotone. "Let us hope you do not allow Yen Shu to exact so great a price."

Just then the proprietor entered the small showroom. He was a large man, immaculately groomed and clad in a dark Western suit with vest and white shirt beneath. He bowed formally from the waist, but when he raised his head a pleasant smile graced his features.

"A pleasure to see you, Wong Cho. Let me take this opportunity to thank you again for your hospitality. Your birthfeast was an occasion I will not soon forget. I trust your sixtieth year has proven prosperous thus far."

"It has indeed, Shu. Thank you. And how is the illustrious Madame Yen these days? My wife tells me that your lady is with child again. Congratulations!"

Fengmo was introduced, and such courtesies continued to be exchanged for quite a while before Yen Shu led his guests into a private office.

Though not large, this room was opulent. A rich white-and-red Peking carpet covered the floor. There was a fine chest, black lacquered and inlaid with a design done in mother-of-pearl. Ivory-based lamps were softly lit beneath silk shades. Most impressive was the huge teakwood desk. It gleamed with polish and on one corner sat a lone telephone. The only other object there was a jade Buddha. The god smiled benevolently, as if pleased with his solid gold loincloth and the gold loops dangling from his long earlobes.

A clap from Yen Shu quickly brought a servant who served tea and then retired again.

Master Wong cleared his throat. "I have brought my young friend here because his father is a great collector of jade. Perhaps you remember Chang Hai-teh. He did business with *your* father."

There was little more than a moment's hesitation. "Yes, of course. Is he not the gentleman who married Peaceful Dawn, the First Daughter of Ling Tou, that revered governor of the north?"

Fengmo was amazed at the man's phenomenal memory. His father had not been to Shanghai in over five years, and then only for a brief stay. It had to have been twice that amount of time since Master Chang had visited this shop.

"You are interested in selecting a purchase for your father?" Yen Shu asked.

Fengmo inclined his head slightly. "I have some interest

in one piece I saw, though I am not sure it is exactly what I desire. The pleasure palace you have on display is intriguing."

The proprietor leaned back in his chair, his face suddenly smooth and bland. All friendly solicitude was set aside as he prepared to do business.

The first price he quoted was so incredibly large that Fengmo could almost feel sweat form on his own forehead. It took all his concentrated effort to present a facade of cool experience and implement the lessons he had so recently received.

The two men bartered for over an hour before a bargain was finally struck at just under half the amount Yen Shu had originally quoted. Both men were satisfied, however, and they smiled at each other in mutual respect. Rice wine and sweetmeats were served and toasts offered all around.

Master Wong and Fengmo were just rising to leave when the telephone jangled. Yen Shu answered, listened, and motioned them to be reseated and wait. After a short, rapid conversation, he put the receiver back in its cradle.

"You may find this interesting, Chang Fengmo, and you also, Wong Cho, if either of you is interested in some really ancient artifacts. I have just learned there are a few to be had. Some crazy bone over on the Way of Heavenly Peace is up to his ears in debt. I am told he will sell his sons' inheritance in order to keep his bad habits."

The opportunity was too tempting to pass, and Master Wong and Fengmo readily agreed to drive with Yen Shu to the man's house.

The Way of Heavenly Peace was in an older section of the city proper, where the homes sat close together, separated only by thick courtyard walls. Yen Shu pulled the car to a stop before a set of massive but unpainted gates. A slovenly servant answered their knock and then led them through run-down courtyards filled with women and squalling children.

Inside this once-grand house there were dogs running loose to clean up crumbs and bits of food the inhabitants habitually tossed underneath tables and chairs. The floors and furnishings were all coated in a thick layer of dust.

The master of the house turned out to be little neater than his abode. Introducing himself, he rushed Yen Shu and the others to his storeroom without any of the usual courtesies. Though this room was a hopeless jumble, it held many beautiful things. There were wall hangings and inlaid chests of every hue. All were chock-full of ivory and jade pieces, the treasures of many generations.

Master Wong was the first to find something he desired, a tiny statue, and it was indeed breathtaking to behold. Carved from ivory, it was done in the likeness of a peasant who sat upon a stone fishing. The fishing line was a thread of gold, and on its end dangled a plump fish fashioned from a blue enamel the shade of lapis lazuli. So intricate were the scales on this fish that each moved individually.

The master of the house wrung his hands and whined about hard times, but he was not convincing. Moreover, he was no match for Master Wong, who drove a very hard bargain. If there was one thing Fengmo's host could not abide, it was a fool.

When this business was finished, Fengmo walked about examining things. On top of one chest he spotted a red lacquered trinket box sitting sideways and covered with grime, its lustrous beauty barely visible. When its owner saw his interest, he rushed over and showed him how to open all the tiny compartments. There were earrings, hair ornaments, and bracelets in the drawers, but one object in particular captured and held Fengmo's eyes. It was a small ring of apple green jade, cut in a solid circular piece and mounted in gold. Delicate lotus blossoms had been woven in gold filigree and set into the flint-hard stone so that its surface remained smooth and even. As he picked the ring up and laid it in his palm, it seemed to glow and grow warm.

"A fine little piece!" the owner proclaimed. "There is a story behind it too, if you care to hear it."

Never taking his gaze from the ring, Fengmo slowly nodded.

The man hawked and spat carelessly on the floor. "Some female ancestor of mine received this ring as a gift. They say she was a woman of honor, though somehow she managed to fall in love with a man forbidden to her. The man returned her affection. They could not show their love openly, of course, and yet they refused to defile it by acting unseemly in secret. This ring, given by the man, was a pledge between them. It was to pass from hand to hand until their souls united again in another incarnation."

Listening, Wong Cho saw Fengmo's face and grew alarmed at the grief he saw so plainly stamped there. "It is a pretty story," he said abruptly, "but a story nonetheless. A heap of superstitious nonsense."

"Maybe so," the man replied. "I must admit it has been of no use to me. I once gave it to a pretty little flower girl who had cast a spell over me. Fool that I was, I had hoped she and I were the incarnate lovers. It seemed remotely possible at least. After all, would not a soul wish to stay in its rightful family? Surely it would get too lonely wandering the world over."

The fellow's debauched eyes turned dreamy for a second. "Oh, how she squealed with delight when it was given to her, and swore she would wear it forever!"

Spitting on the floor again, he shrugged. "I was wrong about that nasty little baggage, however, for the very next week she threw the ring in my face. She said it held an evil magic. 'It bites my finger,' she screamed, 'and brings me bad luck!' "

Suddenly, the owner of the ring realized he might be killing a sale and quickly amended his tale. "I did not believe a word she said, of course. She had simply found some other, *richer* man and needed an excuse to be rid of me. I know what women are!"

Fengmo's heart had quickened and now it thudded within his chest. The ring grew warmer and he closed his fingers possessively around it. "I will have this ring," he said in a hoarse voice. "How much do you ask?"

Yen Shu and Master Wong looked at one another aghast. Had the boy suddenly lost his wits? One *never* let a seller know of his determination in advance!

The two rolled their eyes in unison as the master of the house quoted a ridiculously exorbitant price. Likewise, they both muffled a gasp when Fengmo refused to barter, but instantly succumbed.

"Done," he agreed, his tone subdued and distant.

The room was absolutely quiet, with both the seller and the two older businessmen in a near state of shock.

Fengmo noticed none of this. Nor was he aware of how he had taken the joy from a potentially enjoyable afternoon. Almost meekly, he followed them out and back through the filthy courts.

Silence reigned supreme as Yen Shu drove the other two back to the shop and left them at their own automobile. Fengmo and Master Wong were halfway home when the elder exploded.

"Damn all the gods, boy! I cannot believe all my lessons have been for naught! You have lost a great deal this day. Let us pray you need never do business with Yen Shu again!"

But his words might as well have been spoken to the wind.

That ring must indeed be enchanted! Master Wong exclaimed to himself. *It has captured the lad's soul!*

In this he was mistaken, however, for Fengmo's soul was not captured. It flew up the river and on into the high country where it joined his heart. The ring, still clutched tightly in his hand, warmed his palm, and for once he did not try to push away the face and form that came to him. Instead, he gave free rein to his love, if only for that brief moment in time.

Chapter Fifteen

"Will you not stop playing with that thing for a single second?"

Fong Lu turned and looked over his shoulder. "This is not play, Jasmine. The rain last night has left spots on my master's automobile. They must come off at once or ruin the paint."

So saying, he bent down and gave himself vigorously to the task. The weather was warm and sultry and he had put aside his shirt in order to move more freely.

Jasmine stood holding a lacquered tray on which rested a pot of tea, cups, and a small platter of confections she had made with her own two hands. She did not speak again for a moment. Instead, she let her eyes travel over the chauffeur's broad rippling back and flushed at the thrill of pleasure such a sight gave her. His bare flesh was the color of bronze and ridges of muscles fanned out beneath his well-developed arms. There was not another male servant in the entire Wong household to compare with him for strength and beauty.

"Can you not stop for just a short while?" she sweetly implored. "I have put together a small feast for you. I would say that machine is clean enough in any case, for I can see my face reflected in it already."

Standing, he gave one door a final loving caress before wiping his hands on the buffing cloth. "It does fairly gleam, does it not?"

"You have labored hard," she said, hating the car with a passion. "Come now and rest a bit."

Together they walked down the circular driveway to the edge of a garden area, where Fong Lu settled himself on the edge of a large boulder. He watched as Jasmine put the

tray down and knelt beside it to pour tea. Though two cups
were obviously there, she filled only one and handed it up
to him.

"Will you not join me then?" he invited.

He still marveled that a man and maid could feel such
freedom in one another's company—not like in the high
country.

"Thank you," she said, lashes fluttering. "First try one
of these dainties I have baked for you."

Knowing full well she sought his approval, Fong Lu
spent a moment admiring the small cake she gave him.
Made of dates and dark sugar and covered with a sprinkling of sesame seeds, it was indeed tempting. He emitted
a grunt of appreciation as he bit into it, and enjoyed seeing
her eyes sparkle.

They ate in silence for several minutes before she asked
him a question. On the surface her query seemed casual
enough. "What sort of place do you come from, Fong Lu? Is
it like Shanghai?"

"Very different," he replied. "It is high in the mountains, closer to the heavens. There are trees aplenty but
less foliage."

"Is it more beautiful then?" There was a slight catch in
her voice.

Fong Lu thought for a moment. "I would not say *more*
beautiful necessarily, for there is no comparison. Here
there is beauty of one sort, and there another."

Jasmine sat below him with the afternoon sun shining
on her jet-colored hair. The surrounding ferns and flowers
seemed to provide a frame for her pretty, upturned face.

"Tell me of your home and the differences," she murmured softly. "I would like to know of your roots and
where they are put down."

Fong Lu did not notice the predatory glint in her eyes.

"Well," he began, "here in Shanghai the beauty is of
bright lights and a strong energy. There is no such excitement in Tanpo. Yet, there is beauty of another sort. It is a
place of peace and quietude. Crops are grown on the hills
all around. The seasons in my province are clear-cut and
individual. In the winter it is very cold, but dazzling with
snow and icicles. There is a park there, too, with a small

pond which freezes over, and the little children skate upon it."

Speaking thus, he began to realize for the first time that he was indeed just a bit homesick. His voice grew slightly dreamy. "This time of year, the snow is just beginning to melt. The streams fill and fish frolic. A bit of green will be showing here and there. It would not be so vivid a hue as here in Shanghai, I suppose, but after the blight of winter the colors seem brighter. The sky is a startling blue and laced with fluffy clouds. In Tanpo the air is fresh and clean."

Jasmine grew restive. "It sounds lovely, but what of maids and men? Is that inland province not very old-fashioned? I would wager there is not even lighting on the streets there, and no clubs or dance halls either."

Fong Lu looked down at her and suddenly viewed her with new perspective. He had planned to approach Fengmo shortly and request that Jasmine be secured as his wife. Seeing her now, however, he felt a surge of relief that he was not so committed. This lovely, modern girl was not in the least suited to his normal lifestyle. She would be unhappy trying to conform to the old traditions; nor, he decided, would he want her to try. Such a pretty thing, she was perfectly suited to the gaiety of Shanghai.

By the gods, he asked himself, how could I present such a one to my old mother and father? They are but peasants, people of the land. This Jasmine would sniff at their humble, earthen-floored home where the ox and chickens sleep indoors at night. Moreover, my parents would be disdainful of her in return. They would be scandalized by her bold Western ways and her cropped hair!"

With these thoughts racing through his mind, Fong Lu set his cup firmly down and stood. He liked the modern idea of being able to choose his own bride, but this maid was not for him. Abruptly, he bid Jasmine good day and went zealously back to work while she stared after him in mild confusion.

Over the next few days, he was cool in the extreme and avoided her whenever possible. When he went out with his friends at night, it was to clubs he knew she did not attend.

Of course, confrontation could not be put off forever, and inevitably Jasmine met him in a corridor as he came out of the library one afternoon. They were alone, and she put a hand on his arm. Tears glittered in her eyes, and when she spoke her voice quivered. "Why are you angry with me, Lu? What have I done to displease you?"

Fong Lu attempted to ease away from her, but her grip was firm. Finally he hid behind a facade of indifference he did not actually feel. "Turn me loose, woman! I have no time for quibbling with silly females right now. My master and the foreign scholar await their tea."

Pettishly, he jerked his arm free.

A sudden fury boiled up in Jasmine at this high-handed treatment—a fury born of hurt and frustration. "You are a stiff-necked mule," she hissed. "I have been a fool to waste my time on the likes of you. I will bother you not one moment longer, bumpkin! You are nothing to me now, do you hear? Nothing!"

Turning away from him, she ran down the corridor, but it was some time before the sound of her sobs quit ringing in his ears. He went on to fetch the tea, feeling very much like a worm.

Two evenings later, while out on the town with his fellows, Fong Lu was surprised to look across the dance floor and see Jasmine there also. Two girls had come with her and they looked around in trepidation. It was not a very nice club they were in, and most of the women in attendance were paid to dance with the male customers, many of whom were foreign sailors.

Seeing him take notice of her, Jasmine laughed gaily and pretended she hadn't seen him. There was paint on her face, and the dress she wore clung to her tiny but curvaceous figure.

Fong Lu bent sullenly over his drink and tried to ignore the fact that she danced by with other men, always making sure he saw and heard her. She appeared to be having a wonderful time.

In fact, Jasmine was totally miserable. During a lull in the music, she sat fanning herself and one of her companions leaned close. "Let us leave this place," the other girl whispered. "These men are liable to mistake us for prostitutes if we linger!"

But Jasmine refused to listen. She was determined to attract Fong Lu and win him back at any price. She had not meant a single word she had hurled at him in the deserted corridor, and had been weeping almost constantly ever since.

A shadow fell across her face and she paled as she looked up to see a foreigner looming over her. He was dressed in the white uniform of a seaman and his face was florid. A thatch of short gray hair covered his head like a brush, and another growth sprouted from just beneath his bulbous nose. His eyes were bright blue and glazed. The few words he spoke were nearly unintelligible, but there was no mistaking the beefy hand he extended in invitation.

Jasmine suppressed a shudder of revulsion. But standing, she forced herself to smile, for she could feel the angry, piercing gaze of Fong Lu upon her. In that instant she decided she had found the perfect way to make him jealous and thereby bring him to heel.

The music resumed. Trembling just a little, Jasmine allowed the sailor to embrace her and sweep her out onto the dance floor. She could not see over his shoulder, but each time she suspected they were close to the place where Fong Lu stood at the bar she laughed and pressed herself against the delighted man.

Fong Lu gripped his glass in both hands. Disgust and shame contorted his features. He could hardly believe that this girl, with whom he had been so infatuated, who he had thought so wonderful, was conducting herself in such a flagrant manner. She was a disgrace to all Chinese womanhood!

Just then she whirled by again and was able to glimpse his expression. Mistaking what she saw, she pressed herself closer yet and let out a giggle of pure pleasure.

Fong Lu *was* jealous! He *did* care!

The dance finished and breathlessly she took a seat, sure that he would approach momentarily. When he did not, and in fact turned his back toward her, her rage and determination knew no bounds. Again and again she accepted the drunken seaman as partner, and each time she made sure to cuddle up to him. Soon the foreigner began to openly caress her waist and bury his face in her hair. But desperate to accomplish her end, she allowed and even appeared to return his ardor. From time to time she would quickly peek at Fong Lu to gauge his reaction. To her chagrin, he refused to look in her direction at all.

The foreigner kissed the nape of her neck with wet lips and she laughed loudly, shaking away the tears which scalded her eyes.

With a shattering blow, Fong Lu slammed his drink on the bar and stalked from the club alone. A warm breeze ruffled his hair as he came out onto the crowded street, but it was not refreshing. It was pungent with the smell of city filth and compressed humanity.

Stumbling into an alleyway, he clutched his sides and began to vomit.

Chapter Sixteen

Wong Six adjusted the spectacles he wore further up on his almost bridgeless nose. "The foreign devils *must* be driven out!" he insisted. "I know you have an American friend, and still I tell you this. Even if the people of that nation are not so bad as others, they are bad nonetheless. They all grow fat by the sweat of our brow!"

He and Fengmo sat across the table from one another in the private room of a large tea house. His elder brothers, Wong Four and Five, were there also, but they lolled on cushions nearby, listening while two flower girls played zither and lute.

Fengmo did not answer immediately. Over the past weeks and months he had discovered that he liked this sixth Wong son in spite of his intensity. Between the diverse personalities of Wong Six and Sean Duncan he was getting quite an extensive education.

"Did you know," Six continued, "that there still exists a park in this very city that bears a sign written plainly, in both English *and* Chinese, 'No Dogs or Chinese Allowed'?"

Fengmo's brows shot up in indignation. "Why is such a thing tolerated then? Is this not *our* country?"

"Perhaps the British do not think so," Six answered blandly. "The park belongs to them and to the other white foreigners, after all."

"They may own the topsoil, or at least believe they do, but you and I know that underneath the land is all Chinese!" Fengmo's outrage grew. "Yes, the land is ours all the way down! It has been so for untold generations!"

"You speak truly, friend, but I think the foreigners are ignorant of the fact. Moreover, our present leaders will not put them in their place. Chiang is weak, as all Chinese rulers have been weak since the time of the Boxers. Those Nationalists are cowards. The foreign devils have ships equipped with cannon. They have might and technology over and above our own."

Wong Six clenched one fist for emphasis. "I tell you they take advantage of our peace-loving natures! We have always been, and still are, a nation of farmers—people of the land. Worse, our leaders stand by and turn their heads while China is raped by opium-dealing foreigners! It is time for a *new China!*"

This political fervor was highly contagious and Fengmo was stirred, but at the same time part of his mind remained cautious and contemplative.

"Our people are slow to change," he finally said. "They take great pride in the ancient wisdoms and accept new things, new ideas, only with grave reservations. Indeed, where I come from all is ordered and peaceful. Few can read or write. The peasant is upon the land—just as he always has been. He cares not who rules or does not rule. If the harvest is good, he is happy. If it is bad, he curses heaven and hopes for better. For the most part, I believe these peasants to be a contented lot."

Wong Six leaned back in his seat and his lower lip curled contemptuously. "Forgive my bluntness, friend, but how would *you,* the son of a rich landowner, know if they are content or not? Do you go out upon your father's lands and look into the homes of the poor? Have you seen their big-eyed, hungry children during times of famine? I will wager not."

Fengmo winced under this inquisition, for it was true that he had no direct or personal knowledge about such things. Still, the implied criticism of his father sorely chafed and he could not help but be defensive.

"I know this, Six. My father is a good, righteous man. If a tenant farmer upon our lands feels abused by a steward, he has redress. He is always given fair audience. Once every month, just after the full of the moon, my father holds court."

"A rich man will dispense a rich man's justice," Six scornfully replied. "I tell you the poor must rise up and overthrow the evil rich! If the rich will not climb down of their own accord, then we must force them, even unto bloodshed if necessary!"

"We?" It was Fengmo's turn to be disdainful. "You can hardly be counted among the poor, my friend. What of your own kind father? Is he not also one of the filthy rich? Yet, I am sure you love him and would not want him brought low."

The youngest Wong son picked at a sliver of duck with the end of his ivory chopsticks. "You are right and wrong. My father has always been kind and gentle with all his children. But I have seen his hardness too. He gives no leeway in the pursuit of wealth, and he has no real sympathy toward the poor, for all his pet charities. He works with our corrupt officials and pays them off when their rules do not suit him. He can do this because he is rich. It is true I love him—how could I not?—but he too must be brought down for the sake of the masses."

The face of Wong Six glowed, but Fengmo was appalled. "You would really allow your comrades to destroy the house of your ancestors?"

"It *will* happen whether I allow it or not. But to answer your question, I will not only allow it, I will help do it with my own hands if necessary!"

Fengmo was shocked into silence, but his companion took the lack of comment for approval of his own dedication. Leaning forward, he whispered conspiratorially. "Come to a meeting with me, Fengmo. I am sure that once you hear our leaders speak, you too will want to be one of us!"

Wong Five picked that propitious moment to approach the table and Wong Six stopped speaking immediately.

"Is this young pup bending your ear again?" the elder brother asked. "Pay him no heed, Fengmo. He is almost a fanatic with those high ideas of his. Come now, bring your wine and listen to the pretty flower girls we paid good money for."

Once more Wong Six allowed his ire to surface. He looked at his brother with contempt. "You care for nothing except betting on animals, eating, and tickling your manhood, Brother. You are a disgrace!"

The older man threw back his head and laughed. "You have it exactly right! I am not in the least like you. I enjoy

my life and feel no weight of guilt for my father's wealth.
The taking of pleasure seems good and right to me—
natural!"

"This room is beginning to smell bad," Six retorted. "It
is time I leave, lest the noxious vapors overcome me."

He rose, but gave Fengmo a last, deep look before leaving. "You and I will talk again soon. But for now, go and
play so you can make these fools happy."

Wong Five only laughed again after he had gone. Then,
guiding Fengmo by one shoulder, he led him to a soft cushion and attempted to draw him into the gay spirit of the
evening.

Fengmo listened to the flower girls with only half an
ear, however. The things Wong Six had said kept going
around and around in his mind. He might even have been
tempted to go to one of the underground meetings except
for one thing.

How can a son turn against his own father? he wondered. There is something decidedly wrong with an idea
that will do that to a young man!

So, not without worry, Chang Fengmo hardened his
heart somewhat against the teachings of the man called
Mao.

Chapter Seventeen

The library was quiet save for the ticking of an ancient foreign clock which hung upon one wall, a piece much treasured by Master Wong. Fengmo sat hunched over his books and scowled. He had read the scramble of words before him a dozen times, and still they made no sense. Restive and moody, he slammed the text shut and rubbed his eyes.

A window stood open and a breeze heavy with the scent of lotus and honeysuckle wafted through the room. Not for the first time, he wished to inhale the cool, crisp air and the piney essence he associated with home.

Home!

Fengmo sighed deeply. He was not scheduled to return to Tanpo until after the seventh lunar month, and this was but the second!

He was not ungrateful for all he had been able to absorb in Shanghai. His host had taught him well the convoluted ways of the world marketplace. Sean Duncan and Long Han had become true and edifying friends. From the five eldest Wong sons he had learned the true art of pleasure. Those gregarious and energetic young men had introduced him to every kind of entertainment the city had to offer. In addition to an enlightening taste of the rather unsavory night life, he had seen excellent plays and attended concerts. He had enjoyed it all.

Only his encounters with the sixth son had left him troubled and uneasy, but even those he believed would inevitably prove beneficial. He was convinced that the best way to learn the timbre of his nation was to listen and then compare different ideologies and schools of thought.

There was also that tiny ring of jade, which he had acquired and now kept always on his person. It gave him much comfort.

Yes, in just a few months the bustling city of Shanghai, with its hodge podge of peoples and ideas, had undoubtedly changed his life. But how he longed to flee it nonetheless!

He was a man who loved seasonal change: a first, clean snow; leaves that turned color and withered; green shoots peeking up through dark soil; the dry rustle of summer. Here the weather was less distinct. There was something disenchanting about a place that was hot so often, even when it rained. Moreover, he did not look forward to the violent monsoons which he knew would soon be whipping the coast.

Fengmo looked up as the door of the library creaked slightly and then swung open. He nearly cringed when Bright Autumn entered. This daughter of Wong, with her laughing ways, represented all he found most distasteful about modern women. She and her kind provided yet more reason for him to get himself back home!

At first Bright Autumn seemed not to notice him. Oddly enough, she was not wearing one of her modern dresses on this occasion. Instead, her body was draped in a flowing blue robe with wide sleeves and high collar. Her fluffy hair had grown a little and was feathered behind her ears.

She turned toward him and her eyes widened slightly. "Oh, excuse me, Chang Two. I do not mean to intrude."

He shuffled the papers that lay scattered on the table. "It does not matter. I am about to leave in any case. This *English* will be my death!"

"You do not care for your studies?" Her question was spoken in a soft, clear voice, quite unlike her usual chatter.

Fengmo stood and at the same time expelled another weary breath. "The language I am learning will no doubt prove useful in the future. This is simply not a good day for bending my brains, I fear. I seem unable to concentrate."

Bright Autumn walked to the open window. "It is the coming spring. I believe it is affecting us all."

Suddenly aware of their close proximity, Fengmo stood and gathered his books. It was disconcerting to realize he had just spoken more words to her in a span of moments than he had during his entire stay in the Wong household.

Turning, she saw his discomfort and smiled. "Perhaps in your case, you are only a bit homesick."

He flushed deeply, thinking that she once more saw him as a fool. "Perhaps," he answered crisply, and then left the room without a backward glance.

Moving to stand behind the chair he had occupied but a moment before, Bright Autumn ran her hand over its carved back. His body heat lingered in the polished surface of the wood.

"He hates me," she whispered, her lower lip trembling. "He hates me!"

Her brothers were the first to notice the slow and subtle changes taking place in Bright Autumn. And for once, divining the source of this transformation, they did not tease her. Nor was this pretty young woman the empty-headed creature Fengmo assumed her to be. In the beginning, smiles and banter had simply been her way of attempting to put him at ease—a way which had failed miserably. Once she perceived his reaction, however, she ceased cajoling and observed him instead. She also listened closely to the anecdotes her brothers exchanged about him in private.

Slowly, almost without conscious awareness, Bright Autumn fell in love with the quiet boy from Tanpo. In the process she became more subdued and reflective. Each dress she had designed for herself was less flamboyant than the one before. As her hair grew, she had the curls snipped away a little at a time, until her serving girl swore she would look just like a boy.

Once she realized that Fengmo truly did not care for most Western ways, she too came to dislike them. Upon giving it thought, she suspected that perhaps she always had. I am Chinese, she told herself, and so now I will become Chinese instead of some bastard mixture.

Her many friends, of course, soon noticed the changes taking place and, unlike her siblings, they teased her unmercifully.

"Before you know it," one girl taunted, "you will be allowing your old parents to select a husband for you."

"And what of it!" was her quick retort. "I do not care so long as they pick wisely!"

These same friends were gradually becoming abhorrent to her. How terrible the boys, with their sweating palms and clumsy embraces, and how sad the girls, who painted their faces and spoke in high, chichi voices. She came to hate that half-Chinese, half-English slang with a passion. Finally, she refused to speak anything but the pure, cultured Mandarin used by the educated.

Bright Autumn took on a new form, neither completely traditional nor modern, but uniquely her own. It was not until she quit going out in the evenings, however, that the truth dawned on Madame Wong. Positively delighted, this illustrious lady could not wait to inform her unsuspecting mate.

The two oldsters were lying side by side one night in the high bed they had shared throughout all their married years. Master Wong had already closed his eyes and was nearly asleep when his wife accosted him.

"Our only daughter is ready to wed, Husband," she stated in a matter-of-fact tone.

"M-m-m?" came the drowsy reply.

"I say our daughter is ready to *wed.*"

There was a snort, a brief silence, and then Wong Cho bolted upright in bed. "What! Did you say what I think, woman? Why, Bright Autumn is only a child yet! I do not believe in these early betrothals!"

He turned a scowl on his wife even though it was dark and she could not see. "No, and I will not have you conniving with a matchmaker behind my back, either!" A sudden thought occurred to him and he flopped back down on his pillow, cackling with relief. "I daresay you will have a war on your hands if you pursue this nonsense," he hooted. "Since when could either of us force our daughter to do a single thing she wished not to do? Furthermore, she will have no man except one she selects for herself. She is a very modern girl, our Bright Autumn."

Joyful Spirit let him enjoy his laugh awhile. When she spoke again, however, her voice was serious. "She is two years older than I was when you and I wed, Cho. But I agree she would strongly oppose any match I might try to suggest. It is almost sad in a way. Long ago I had hoped that the nice Second Son of Chiu . . . Ah, well."

Wong Cho pulled the white silk sheet up around his

chin. "Now that the matter is settled, my little heart and liver, let us get some sleep. The future of our daughter will take care of itself, and perhaps that is as it should be. Who is to say that luck alone does not see *us* happily wed?"

"She has already chosen," Joyful Spirit bluntly said.

Her husband flew up again. "Who is it? Oh heaven, I hope not that oldest son of Tung who is always moping about our gates!"

"No, My Lord, it is not Tung Ho. She loves Chang Fengmo, our houseguest."

For a moment they were both silent, and then Cho smiled into the darkness. "Chang Two," he mused. "Well, I swear. Thank all the gods it is not one of her fast friends, or worse yet, a foreign devil. That, I would not abide!"

"You are pleased then?"

Slowly, Wong Cho lay down again. "I think so. The Second Son of Chang Hai-teh is a fine lad. It should be a good match, but . . ."

Now it was his wife's turn to leave the comfort of her pillow. "But what?" she demanded. "Is there something I do not know?"

Easing her back, Cho offered reassurance. "Do not worry yourself, Mother of My Sons. I will write Fengmo's father in the morning. We shall see what we shall see."

His wife was not pacified. "I do not think that wise, Cho. Bright Autumn would want her prospective groom to make his own decision, I am sure. For once she is being patient and so must we. If Fengmo does not decide for himself, how can she be sure of his love?"

"I *will* write Hai-teh," he repeated in a voice which did not encourage argument. "In this instance, the *old* way is the *best* way."

"Oh, how I hate it when you are mysterious!" she grumbled, but said no more.

Neither spoke for a long time. Finally Wong Cho rolled onto his side facing her. "Joyful Spirit?"

"Yes?"

"Our parents matched us in the old way, without our ever having seen one another. Are you not sure of *my* love?"

Joyful Spirit sighed, a deep contented sound. Putting one plump arm around his waist, she rested her head against his shoulder. "I am sure," she replied, "but I am lucky."

The letter came early one afternoon, but Fengmo was too busy to read it. Glancing only at the rice paper envelope and seeing his father's bold calligraphy, he smiled and set it aside until he could give it a more leisurely perusal. It was just after dawn the next morning when he finally retrieved the missive and settled down in the sitting room of his own suite to fully enjoy its contents.

Fong Lu, grumpy of visage and withdrawn, poured tea and set about selecting his master's attire for the day. Around them, the house was quiet and still. It was, therefore, a shock when Fengmo uttered a loud and violent oath. Startled, Fong Lu dropped the shoes he had just lifted from the wardrobe and rushed from the bedchamber in alarm.

Fengmo was standing in the middle of the room. "By the invisible beard of Buddha!" he exclaimed. "It is not to be believed! My father sent me to Shanghai for modernization and then does this!"

Fong Lu looked his confusion. "Is it bad news, Master?"

Fengmo stared at him. "Bad news? It is worse!" He began pacing back and forth, his feet pounding against the carpeted floor with resounding thuds.

"Please, Young Sir," Fong Lu implored, "sit down and calm yourself. I will fetch you some heated wine from the kitchen."

"Calm . . ." Fengmo nodded. "Yes, I must be calm and think out a solution to this dilemma!"

With a groan, he threw himself into a chair while Fong Lu made haste to get on with his errand.

Three more times Fengmo let his eyes scan the pages of the letter he held. In part it read:

Honorable Second Son,
 The last report from my friend, Wong Cho, informs me that you continue to do very well in Shanghai. My old eyes can hardly wait to feast themselves on the jade treasure I understand you have secured. . . .
 . . . It seems to me only appropriate and right that the great houses of Wong and Chang should be thus united

in wedlock. Your mother and I are both pleased, and can
only assume the maid, Bright Autumn, is a respectful
and dutiful girl. . . .

. . . Wong Cho makes one very strange request,
though I suppose it is to be expected from so modern-
minded a man. He asks that you come to him personally
with your consent. Like all good fathers, he is concerned
with the happiness and welfare of his children. He would
be sure in his own heart that you are indeed a willing
and anxious groom.

The final sentences of the missive seemed strangely intuitive, and Fengmo's vision blurred slightly each time he
read them.

. . . Remember, my son, life is not always perfect, and
so it also is with the marriage state. To love is no doubt
grand, but simple contentment is not to be scorned
either. In fact, I am not at all sure it is not preferable to
chasing the elusive bird of romance.

"My dear old father does not know the spot he has put
me in," Fengmo groaned. "If I refuse to marry Bright Autumn, which I most certainly must, I will wound the feelings of my kind host. Yet, how can I do otherwise? Even if
my heart were free, I could not abide life with one of these
'new' females!"

Fong Lu poked his head into the room and looked
around. His concern mounted as he realized the young sir
had been babbling aloud to himself. Nevertheless, the servant entered with a jolly, forced smile.

"I have your wine, Master," he said brightly. "A swallow or two and all will be well!"

"I do not need wine, Fong Lu. A brisk walk will do more
to clear my head of troublesome thoughts. I will dress
now."

Morning mists wove in and out of the bamboo groves and
towering eucalyptus trees. A songbird called to its mate as
Fengmo drew near the small meadow and paused to watch
the deer feed. A doe raised her head at the familiar sight of

him, but still sniffed the air cautiously, ready to take flight with her new speckled fawn should the need arise.

In spite of his problems, Fengmo once again found a measure of peace amidst the beauty surrounding him. The moss-covered stones, meandering streams, and lush undergrowth all bespoke an almost celestial promise.

Moving on, he approached the red lacquered bridge, only to stop in his tracks. There upon it stood the lone and unexpected figure of Bright Autumn. Fengmo stood staring at her for several dazed moments, unable to credit what he saw.

Could this be the same teasing, modern girl he constantly avoided? It seemed impossible. Her hair was Chinese again, falling straight and even to her shoulders and ornamented with fluttering pins of pearl and jade. She wore a short, high-collared jacket of pale yellow silk over matching trousers. Most amazing were her shoes. Gone were the Western monstrosities, replaced by daintily embroidered slippers and white stockings.

Fengmo was nearly overcome with wonder at this transformation which he had failed to notice in the making. Purposefully, he trod upon a large twig, making it snap, so as not to startle the girl who stood gazing out over the lake.

Bright Autumn faced him as he came onto the bridge, and the sight of her face caused the breath to catch in his throat. She wore no cosmetics whatsoever, and yet her lips were berry-bright and full. Her brows were two perfectly arched half-moons above soft brown eyes. Just as with the doe, these eyes too held a certain caution. Her skin was smooth and lustrous over high cheekbones touched with the subtle hue of ripe apricots.

"Good morning," she greeted without sign of smile or laughter.

Fengmo found his voice. "Do I disturb you, Lady?"

"Not at all." She turned back to the rail. "Come look at these fuzzy little swans. See how they rush to keep up with their mother."

They stood thus awhile, young man and maid, both a strange combination of old and new. It was a sign of their times that they could be alone together and relate almost as equals. Oddly enough, for once Fengmo did not feel threatened.

Now, watching the mother swan chastise a wandering chick, Bright Autumn did laugh a little. The sound was low for a woman, and sweet. "Is a female ever content without young ones about her?" she asked.

She said no more but turned and looked at Fengmo, the love shining like a beacon from her face. In that instant, realization struck him like a thunderbolt.

Almost immediately her expression resumed its placid calm and they turned in unison to look out over the water once more. Fengmo, however, was shaken to the quick. It seemed incredible that this situation could have transpired without his being aware of it. Moreover, the sudden knowledge of her love caused him sharp, almost agonizing pain.

Why, he wondered, is fate so cruel? This beguiling creature would be easy to love if my heart were not already so completely bound!

Bright Autumn held a small enamel bowl, and from time to time she tossed a few of the bread crumbs it contained out over the water. Her hands were narrow and soft, with tapered fingers and beautiful crescent nails.

Giving her a long sideways glance, Fengmo contemplated his father's letter. His mind raced over and over its contents. Then, all at once, he knew what he must do. He would not be a fool! The powers of heaven had chosen to deny him the mate of his soul, but if he could not have the woman he loved, at least here was one he could adore and cherish. It was more than most men could claim!

Abruptly, he bowed and murmured a quick and seemingly distracted farewell. Taking giant strides, he turned toward the house, determined to speak to Master Wong before he lost his courage.

Chapter Eighteen

Joyful Spirit reclined on a couch in the sitting room of the suite she shared with her husband and wept great silver tears.

"Hush," scolded Wong Cho, struggling to swallow the lump in his own throat. "Our daughter will be here momentarily. Do you want her to see you like this?"

Joyful Spirit shook her head but could not prevent another sniff or two. She dabbed at her eyes one last time before a soft knock sounded on the door.

"Enter," called Wong Cho.

Bright Autumn peeked in. "You wish to see me, Father?"

"Yes, child. Come in, please, and be seated."

Watching her comply, Master Wong could hardly keep from smiling. His daughter might be reformed—all traditionally clad, with shy, downcast countenance—but her stride was still free and long for a girl. She carried herself with a modern self-assurance he could not help but admire. Once she was perched demurely on a low stool, he cleared his throat.

"Your mother and I have news for you," he announced. "I hope you will prove worthy and dutiful."

Bright Autumn looked from one parent to the other in sudden trepidation. Surely they had not . . .

Master Wong spoke sternly. "You have long been finished with your education, girl, and I find all your gallivanting most unseemly."

"But Father! I have not been—"

"Do not interrupt!" Master Wong turned to his amazed spouse. "You see what manners she lacks, Mother of My Sons? I thought you had trained her better!"

This false rebuke gave credence to Madame Wong's tears. Both mother and daughter flushed deeply, though for different reasons.

"I believe it is time for you to show proper deportment," he went on, suppressing a twinkle. "The matchmaker and astrologers have been busy. It is time for you to wed."

Bright Autumn felt her heart quiver and plummet. She paled, but within an instant color came rushing back into her cheeks. A flint spark of her old rebellion kindled in her eyes.

If they have gone and betrothed me to that odious Second Son of Chiu, I will refuse to have him! I will refuse to have anyone they select!

Her thoughts were plainly mirrored on her face, but her father gave her no opportunity to give them voice. Deciding his game had gone far enough, however, he quickly attempted to put her mind at ease.

"Six moons from now, you are to become the wife of Chang Fengmo, Daughter. What have you to say?"

Her face went blank and Master Wong leaned forward in alarm as her lips moved without emitting a single sound.

Throwing her husband an accusing look, Madame Wong rushed to her daughter and briskly chafed the girl's wrists. "See now, you old bone! Look what you have done! Her soul is escaping!"

She gently shook Bright Autumn and crooned. "Come back, dear soul, come back! We need you still!"

Suddenly Bright Autumn slumped in her mother's arms and began to weep. "Oh, M'ma," she cried. "I am so happy!"

Madame Wong chuckled and rocked her back and forth while her husband sat back in his chair, feeling like a weasle.

"Females!" he muttered in his own defense. "They have no sense of humor at all!"

Bright Autumn lay in her modern bed and wished for the private comfort of an old-fashioned canopy. A full, bright moon shone through her open window and a cacophony of insects serenaded the night. Restless and unable to sleep, she finally threw aside her light coverlet and got up.

Moving to the window, she looked out at the distant glimmer of city lights.

"I will miss you, Shanghai," she whispered, "but I must follow my heart."

How she loved Fengmo! Yet how little she really knew of him. She still did not understand what it was about him that so compelled her. He was handsome, yes, but there was something else as well, something that drew her as surely as a moth to flame. She saw nobility in every plane of his face, in his very bearing. Though he had spoken no more than a few words to her, she was convinced beyond any doubt that he was the most honorable and courageous of men.

Even laughing at herself had not helped. He brought out every ancient feminine instinct she possessed. She wanted to wait upon him, bear his children, worship him. The thought of sharing his bed made the blood course rapidly through her veins in a way she had never before experienced.

A soft breeze caressed her cheek and she sighed, wishing she could put aside her doubt. The same niggling worry had plagued her all day. Once her father had finally informed her of the betrothal, and she had come to her wits a bit, the terrible unwelcomed question had leapt into her mind.

What if he does not love me?

Sitting alone in her room, Bright Autumn buried her face in her hands. "I will *make* him love me," she promised herself.

I must go to him, she decided. He must know how I feel. Surely he would not have agreed to our match if he did not care for me! He is shy, but when I tell him of my own love, I will be able to look into his eyes and thereby know he feels the same!

Having at least chosen a course of action, she returned to her bed. Even so, it was a long time before she fell into a light, fitful slumber.

Somehow Fengmo knew she would be there waiting. There was no reason to think so since he had seen her in the park only one time before. Still, he knew and hastened his steps, half expecting, half dreading their next encounter.

She stood upon the bridge, more beautiful than ever, tendrils of fog swirling about her. Slowly he approached, and when she turned to him with those soft doe eyes, he did not turn away, but met them straight on. To his surprise, Bright Autumn was the first to lower her glance.

"My parents have informed me," she said.

"I hope you are not displeased."

It seemed unbelievable to him that he, Chang Fengmo, was actually speaking openly, not only to a female, but to his own betrothed. More incredible was the fact that for some unknown reason he did not feel ill at ease.

"I am not displeased, My Lord. Now that we are intended I should not be here, but . . ." She hesitated. "Even if you think me bold, I would have you know a thing."

He smiled at the modest flush he observed on her cheeks. "Speak then."

She looked up and bravely met his eyes again. "I would have you know from the beginning that I love you." Her voice was resolute and clear.

These words, and her direct way of speaking, startled Fengmo somewhat, though he already knew her heart. He did not know how to respond.

She searched his face for only a moment, and then her head drooped as she expelled a quivering, crestfallen sigh. She turned to leave.

"Bright Autumn." He reached out and gently touched her arm. When she refused to look at him, he spoke to her softly. "I will be a good husband. I am no good at giving speeches, but you will not regret giving your pledge. I promise."

Her response was so low he had to lean close in order to hear. "For now it is enough," she breathed.

Standing on tiptoe, eyes squeezed tightly shut, she brushed his lips with her own. Then, in a flash, she was gone. He glimpsed her back as she darted through the trees and then disappeared behind a giant mass of ferns.

Fengmo stood statue-still for several moments before putting a finger to his lips. The Western custom of kissing was new to him and he tried to unscramble his own emotions. Then, unbidden and undesired, came the memory of other lips. He could see clearly the gentle outline of a mouth he held most dear. Suddenly he felt a pain of remorse so sharp that it bent him nearly in two. To his horror he began to weep. The tears came in a rush, and deep sobs shook him to the depths of his very soul.

Standing there, shamed by his own weakness, Chang Fengmo once more cursed fate.

There was rejoicing in the House of Wong. Word of the betrothal spread like wildfire, first among the family members, and almost as quickly throughout the servants' quarters.

The intended couple did not meet alone again and in fact returned almost completely to the ways of their ancestors. Bright Autumn stayed close to her mother and out of sight, appearing only at mealtimes or for walks, which were attended by a sister-in-law or serving girl. To her siblings' surprise, she blushed furiously whenever Fengmo's name was even mentioned in her presence. This was not the sister they knew, but they loved her the more.

Madame Wong was the most delighted of all. "See," she would say to her husband, "I have raised a modest maid after all. She will make Chang Fengmo a very good wife!"

To this Master Wong could only agree. He too thought Bright Autumn would make the best of mates. Nor did he believe that she would ever completely return to her modern ways. Young Fengmo would never allow it, even if she were to try. But he knew also that the fire and temper he secretly loved in his daughter had not been altogether extinguished. They had only been muted by love. Woe unto the Second Son of Chang if he should prove *too* old-fashioned! Bright Autumn would never tolerate concubines —of that he was sure! Neither would she countenance heavy drinking or gambling. Pity the poor boy should he turn into a no-good, for under such circumstances he would likely lose his ears!

Ah, but Fengmo is not a louse, Master Wong assured himself. He is strong and full of good intent.

And if he has loved another? And if he still does a little?

Master Wong shrugged. He will not be able to resist my Bright Autumn for long. Moreover, that girl of mine shines with enough love for them both!

Chapter Nineteen

*F*ong Lu sat in a wicker chair in the inner courtyard, while all around him the House of Wong slept. His only illumination was a small oil torch, which flickered and cast eerie shadows against the walls. Even the birds were quiet, with heads nestled beneath their wings.

He was so weary! Weary of this house and the lush gardens—the scent of forced lotus blossoms. Quite simply, the chauffeur wanted to go home. He longed for the sight of his parents and older brothers who lived in the Tanpo countryside upon Chang farmlands.

As he sat thus, thinking morose thoughts, he heard a soft rustling just behind him. Startled, he came to his feet and turned to see the round face of Jasmine peeking from between the foilage of a large potted palm.

"What are you doing hiding there?" His voice cut through the gloom like a knife.

Jasmine slowly stepped forward. One glance told him she was naked beneath the scarlet robe she wore. Her lips were painted berry pink, and black kohl ringed her luminous eyes.

"I came hoping to find *you,*" she said, making no pretense. "I know your master came in late."

She shifted slightly and her robe came down over one shoulder, exposing her left breast. She made no attempt to right the garment, and against his will, Fong Lu felt himself becoming aroused. The cloying aroma of night-blooming hibiscus seemed to press all around him.

"If you have something to say to me, then say it and be gone," he said. "There is no need for stealth."

She stepped closer and the clean, female musk of her mingled with that of the flowers. Saying nothing, she unfastened the sash of her robe and let it fall open. Her body was the shade of rich cream, its perfection only heightened by the dark brown of her delicate nipples and the midnight thatch of her pubes.

For all his winning ways, Fong Lu had not had a woman in a very long time. Furthermore, he had never lain with a woman he knew. No, he shared the forbidden intimacies of clandestine sex only with occasional prostitutes, albeit ones of clean repute. Now, looking at Jasmine, his body pulsed and he began to perspire.

She came closer still and wrapped her soft arms around his neck. "Do you not desire me?" she whispered against his lips. "Feel the heat of my body, Lu. It cries out to you!"

When he groaned but made no move to embrace her, she trailed her hands back down and unfastened the buttons of his white shirt one at a time. This done, she pressed against him. The firm roundness of her breasts scorched his chest and he could feel her grind against the rising mound at his crotch. Almost of its own accord, his body began to rock back and forth, matching the tempo she set.

"Take me," she moaned from deep in her throat. "Take me!"

In that moment any small restraint he might still have felt fled completely. Crushing her in his arms, he lowered her to the cool tile floor and buried his face in the sweetness of her neck. Between them, his hands struggled to loosen the belt buckle of his tight-fitting gray trousers. Finally, his manhood sprang free. He plunged into her waiting body without preamble. So crazed was he, he did not even feel her long nails rake his back, ripping the shirt he still wore.

When it was over he slumped against her, spent—revolted at himself and more so at Jasmine. The moment his senses stopped jangling and he could breathe, he raised himself up and began putting his clothing in order.

Below him, Jasmine stretched like a kitten and yawned prettily. "When will you go to the young sir?" she asked. "We should be wed now, I would say, and the sooner the better."

For a moment Fong Lu simply stared at her with a blank expression. But then, as her meaning took root, he began to chuckle. It was not a pleasant sound as it rose and became full-fledged laughter.

Jasmine scrambled to her feet and clamped a hand over his mouth. "Hush! You will wake the entire house!"

He jerked her hand away and gripped her wrist so tightly she winced. "Let them wake," he hissed. "Let them all come down so they too can enjoy this little comedy!"

"Fong Lu," she pleaded.

His eyes narrowed to glittering slits. "No doubt you think me a regular fool, a grasshopper just come down from the country. Well, perhaps you are right, vixen. I *am* a peasant, and proud to be one. But even an ignorant peasant knows when he has been with a virgin. You were no such thing! I would not wed a harlot! Never!"

Jasmine swung her free arm and pummeled him until he released her. Her wrath was quickly spent, however, and she crumpled back to the floor, covering her face with both hands. Sobs shook her body.

"Please, Fong Lu," she wept. "I love you. Do not use me harshly!"

Looking at her, his flesh crawled with mingled disgust and self-loathing. "Never come near me again, woman. You are vile and a shame to your sex. I want to see you no more!"

So saying, he spit on her and then turned on his heels and stalked away.

The House of Wong was in the midst of domestic chaos. Red-eyed servants went about making all manner of superstitious signs to ward off evil, and priests were called in to chant incantations over the corpse of Jasmine.

After Fong Lu left her, the serving girl had gone into the kitchen and taken down a knife used for gutting small game animals and fowls. She then went to her own room to clean herself and put on her finest robe. All alone, she had reclined on her cot and pulled the knife blade across her own tender throat.

Her mother, a favored family servant, found Jasmine just so the following morning, lying in a congealed pool of blood. The old woman raised a hue and cry that threw the entire household into instant turmoil.

According to the customs and religious beliefs of her

family, three days passed before Jasmine was cremated.
Things gradually resumed a semblance of normality, except for the servants' being a bit more hushed and subdued
than usual. Some were affected to a greater degree and
others less, depending upon how close each had been to the
deceased.

Fong Lu was one of those greatly affected. *Why was I so
cruel?* he asked himself over and over again. It is true I did
not love her and that she acted like a wanton, but would a
little kindness have been so hard?

At night he tossed and turned. The sound of her weeping
haunted him until he slept hardly at all. During the day he
imagined the other servants were casting him furtive
glances of accusation.

All joy went out of life for the once-gay chauffeur. He
wanted desperately to go home. Unmindful of his peers'
laughter, he once again donned his quilted jacket and
round, old-fashioned skullcap.

Fengmo, of course, saw this drastic change in his servant, but did not realize its cause. Worried, he tried to cajole Fong Lu into better humor.

"Such a long face!" he teased. "What happened to that
spry, laughing fellow who delivered me to Shanghai? You
remember, the one so lively and anxious for city excitement?"

Fong Lu only looked at him dully with dark-smudged
eyes. "Perhaps he is tired now and only wishes to go
home."

Not knowing how to comfort him, Fengmo could only pat
him on the back. "Cheer up, man. It will not be too much
longer."

But Fong Lu did not cheer up.

About two weeks after the funeral, there came a soft
scratching on the door of Fengmo's suite. It was quite late,
but the young master was still out feasting with friends
and Fong Lu was alone. A black fog of depression still
hung over him, and his smile had been completely lost in a
sea of guilt. No matter what he did, the face of Jasmine
stayed with him.

When he opened the door, he recognized the servant who
greeted him as one of the many kitchen helpers, an older

man who was not given to boasting or putting himself forward. In fact, Fong Lu could not remember having spoken to him at all before.

The servant motioned to him. "Come with me, Fong Lu, Servant to the House of Chang. Someone would speak with you."

Fong Lu made no move. Lately he imagined there had been a subtle change in his fellow servants. Since the tragic death of Jasmine, none seemed as friendly or open as they once had been.

"Who would speak to me, Old Father? I am tending my duties and have no time for idle chatter."

"It is not only one, but many—all of us who serve this house," the old man replied. "It is a matter of some importance."

Fong Lu was now more apprehensive than ever. The old man saw this and hastened to reassure him. "It is no mob," he said. "You are in no danger. Though you seem to think so, you are not despised by the servants here."

Fong Lu nodded and followed the man downstairs, knowing it would be futile to refuse. After all, if they meant him harm, would they not come for him in any case?

Moving through the indoor courtyard, he shivered. The vast room seemed to leap with the ghost of a small, pretty girl. By comparison the well-lit kitchen was nearly blinding. Moreover, it was filled to overflowing with servants, both male and female. Only children were conspicuously absent.

A large chair had been brought in, and seated upon it was an old gray-haired woman who Fong Lu recognized at once as being Jasmine's mother.

The others had been speaking in low voices, but when they saw Fong Lu enter, a hush fell over the assembly. The old man who had been his guide melted into the crowd, leaving him to stand before the seated woman alone. After looking him up and down she spoke.

"I have a matter to discuss, Fong Lu. This is a court of sorts and you will listen carefully."

Fong Lu looked back at her, his posture straight and a little defiant. "Speak then and I will listen, but I am not one of you and you have no power over me."

The old woman ignored this. Tears came to her eyes and she wiped them away with the corner of her sleeve.

Merciful Heaven! thought the chauffeur. *Here is an ancient mother weeping and she will surely accuse me. My life is worthless!*

"Fong Lu," she said, "you have been chosen to serve justice. As you know, my daughter did away with herself. Indeed, I should have expected it. She had been shamed beyond all redemption."

Someone saw us in the inner court! What excuse can I possibly make?

Fong Lu hung his head, for he knew there was no excuse. He *had* taken an unmarried maid. That she had enticed him did not matter, nor that he had not been the first. The blame was his and he would no longer deny it—not to himself or to these others.

The old woman continued in her cracked and quavering voice. "My little maid was not always witty. She did not always show wisdom. One night, a month or so before she joined her ancestors, she went out dancing with her friends."

Here she stopped to cast a disparaging glance around at the younger folk in the room. "Have I not said that all such modern customs are evil? Yes, and now I am proven right!"

Fresh tears squeezed from her eyes. "But my little Jasmine would not listen to me. She was sometimes a willful child. Not bad, however; not wicked as so many city girls are nowadays. Friends went with her to this vile place, and while she was there a big foreign devil asked her to dance. He asked her many times, and many times she accepted."

She looked pathetically from face to face. "What was she to do? Can one refuse foreigners anything? No, I tell you!

"My girl came to me that night weeping. Her clothing was all ripped and she was covered with grime. At first she could not tell me what had happened. She only wept and wept. 'It is my own fault, M'ma,' she said."

An angry flush crept up the woman's face. "It was many hours before I learned the truth. That wicked devil took my Jasmine by the arm and led her outside, pretending they both needed a breath of air. She did not want to go, but he was strong and she could not pull away as he took her through a side door into an alleyway."

The old mother was now sobbing in earnest and Fong Lu had to strain to understand her.

"That hairy beast had his way with my Jasmine," she cried. "Her flesh was all bruised and torn. Even so she might have recovered had it not been for the wild seed which sprouted in her womb. Oh, she was shamed! Shamed! I was going to send her away, but . . ."

Fong Lu looked with pity on the woman as she sat weeping hysterically. It was all clear to him now. He finally understood why Jasmine had come to him like a wanton. He could not even blame her for her attempted deception, for she could not have been in her right mind. He also knew that none of these terrible things would have happened if she had not been so determined to make him jealous.

With this new understanding, some of the guilt he had been feeling lifted, but not all. What remained mingled with his white-hot hatred of the foreigner who had perpetrated the foul and unthinkable deed upon poor Jasmine.

The old serving woman had calmed herself enough to go on. "You have been chosen to do justice, Fong Lu. I have heard that you cared for my girl. There must be a retribution! You have someplace else to go, and perchance you might succeed and escape. The rest of us are tied to Shanghai."

She looked him in the eye. "Will you do justice, Fong Lu?"

His face was white and he answered in a tone of deadly calm. "I will."

WAR

Chapter Twenty

*F*engmo was just mounting the last garden terrace when angry shouts pierced the morning air. Looking out over the grounds and finally down the driveway, he spied the brawny figure of the gateman leaping up and down. Though the fellow's actual words could not be deciphered, it was obvious he was cursing while he shook one beefy fist for emphasis. To Fengmo's surprise, the recipient of this wrath was a foreigner, dressed in military white, who stood outside the gate and looked from between the iron bars with a flushed, angry countenance. There were gold epaulets on his shoulders, which signified him as an officer of some rank.

The racket had evidently not disturbed the house yet, for it sat quiet and peaceful as ever in the early light, with not even a servant in sight. Curious, and thinking to be of assistance, Fengmo quickened his steps and descended.

"What is the problem here?" he called once he was within hearing distance.

The gateman quit his agitated dance and turned toward him with an expression of relief. "Thank heaven you are here, Young Sir! I can make this rude barbarian understand nothing! He is stupid, just as they all are!"

Fengmo winced at this insult, for the officer had become even more florid and appeared to be grinding his teeth.

"He would have me summon the master at this despicable hour," the gateman ranted on. "Can you imagine? I told him to go away with his odious troops and come back this afternoon, but he babbles on and will not listen a bit! Oh, what terrible, ignorant Chinese he speaks too. Why, my own Little Three makes more sense, and him not even nine months old yet!"

It was then that Fengmo realized there were others, perhaps twenty uniformed seamen. They were also clad in white, but were without epaulets, and wearing different, smaller caps. His heart began to race when he saw they were heavily armed with rifles in their hands and revolvers on their hips. With difficulty, he forced himself to remain calm.

"I will speak to this gentleman," he said. "In the meantime, you do as he says. Go and rouse your master at once."

But the gatemen had taken only three or four steps when the officer yelled, "Halt!"

Fengmo turned to the man and raised his brows slightly. "Did I not understand correctly, sir?" he asked. "Do you not wish to speak to the master of this house?"

The officer was growing more flustered by the minute. He opened his mouth several times without speaking, obviously unsure of which words he wished to use.

"I come," he finally managed with a heavy accent. He pointed at the locked gate. "Open!"

Fengmo heard the gateman snort derisively and turned a scowl on him. "Control yourself, man! Your linguistic superiority will not ward off bullets!"

He then smiled at the officer. When he spoke, he pronounced each word slowly and with care. "You wish to come in?"

The man nodded and repeated himself. "I come—now!"

Fengmo looked from him to the armed seamen and back again. "You may come in," he agreed. "Alone."

At first the officer only frowned, but then shook his head violently. "No! *All* come! All!"

A deafening bang followed by a series of loud rattles and the roar of an engine interrupted this strained discourse. Fengmo nearly laughed with relief at the sight of Sean Duncan perched behind the wheel of an old, dilapidated automobile. The contraption was covered with dents and its paint was peeling off in several places. It screeched to a stop and the American gracefully emerged, an engaging smile upon his face. After giving the officer a nod, he approached the gate and spoke to Fengmo.

"Well, friend," he said heartily, "you invite me for morning tea and I come to find this hullabaloo. What seems to be the matter?"

In fact, Fengmo was not expecting Sean until late that afternoon, and it was all he could do not to gawk in surprise and thereby betray them both. A few seconds lapsed before he was able to answer.

"This illustrious gentleman," he explained, "appears to be somewhat upset. We are having no small difficulty communicating."

"It is a shame *you* understand *no* English," Sean enunciated, the smile not quite reaching his gray eyes. "Have I not encouraged you over and over again to study the foreign tongue? Now perhaps you will pay attention. Meanwhile, let me offer my humble assistance."

He turned his full attention on the naval officer and began speaking in rapid sentences while Fengmo looked on in confusion and struggled to make sense of what was being said. All he was able to gather was that the officer wished to speak to Master Wong at once and that he had no intention of entering the estate without his detachment. Other words passed between the two, but Fengmo was able to make out only a few, for the officer's dialect was peppered with idioms and slang. A heated discussion seemed to be taking place about some sailor who had been attacked.

When Sean finally turned back, his face was dead serious. "I think it wise you go and rouse your host immediately," he said. He looked at the gateman with feigned disdain. "While you are doing so, perhaps this great, lazy bump will unlock the gate and let us in. I myself will escort the captain and his men to the house."

After bowing courteously, Fengmo so instructed the gatekeeper and turned his own steps toward the house, careful to walk as briskly as possible but without breaking into a full-fledged run. Once he was indoors, however, he showed no such restraint. With a bound he was off and flying up the stairs three at a time. He banged loudly on the door of the elder Wong's suite and then burst in without decorum.

"By the gods, boy!" exclaimed his host. "What is it?"

Master Wong stood at the door of his bedchamber, his sparse gray hair in disarray. He wore only his nightclothes and was barefooted. Madame Wong called nervously from behind him.

"Forgive me, sir." Fengmo was breathless. "There are armed foreigners coming up the drive and they will be here momentarily. I will admit only their leader, but you must hurry!"

"What has happened?" the old gentleman asked. "I have offended no foreigners."

"I know not, sir. Sean Duncan arrived but a few minutes ago and I am sure he will inform us in time. The leader is unable to speak our language, though I believe he understands well enough. So take care what you say. Hurry, sir!"

With that Fengmo started back downstairs. Behind him he could hear Master Wong muttering to himself. "Where *is* that manservant of mine? Servants can never be found when they are most needed!"

Fengmo opened the front door just as Sean and the commanding officer arrived. The detachment of seamen remained in the driveway shuffling their polished black boots and shifting their rifles restively.

Inside the foyer, the captain's eyes opened wide, for he was able to see into the breathtaking indoor court. He swept the hat from his head and allowed his glance to dart nervously from place to place. Envy was clearly stamped on his features.

Sean remained more relaxed than Fengmo had ever seen him. His face was unperturbed and he paused to light his pipe. Only his eyes remained grave.

"This gentleman has come on urgent business," he said, "though I have assured him there must be some mistake. One of his men was attacked and killed last night and he believes the culprit to be here."

"He is mad!" Fengmo said without thinking. His suspicion was justified by the look of chagrin on the captain's face.

Master Wong arrived just then. His hair was combed neatly in place and he had covered his sleeping garments with a robe of heavy wine-colored brocade. After greeting Sean, he spoke directly to the captain in very stilted English. "Good day, Illustrious Sir. Welcome." He peeked over the top of his spectacles in that foolish way he had cultivated. "You have trouble?"

The naval officer was obviously relieved to be able to return to his own language. When he answered, his voice was not rude, but certainly not courteous either.

"Yes," he said, "but you have trouble also. One of my men was murdered last night. Murdered. You un-der-stand?"

Master Wong bobbed his head up and down and smiled a silly smile. "Man die, yes, yes. Too bad!"

The captain turned to Sean. "Does this old fool really understand me? He seems awfully damned chipper."

Sean puffed deeply on his pipe. The barest smile tugged at one corner of his mouth. "He understands well enough," he answered.

Shrugging, the captain resumed speaking to the master of the house. "As I said, Master Wong, my man was killed last night, stabbed through the heart by one of your houseboys."

The smile left Master Wong's face, but he continued to affect his accent. "No, no! My servants no kill! No kill!"

The captain scowled. "The man has been identified," he insisted. "You understand i-den-ti-fy? There was a witness who saw the whole thing from a doorway. He knows your houseboy!" His voice rose, as if by volume he might compensate for what he lacked in clarity. He was nearly shouting in Master Wong's face. "Your houseboy, Fong Lu—*Fong Lu!* He murdered my man! Un-der-stand?"

Fengmo gasped, forgetting for the moment that he was not supposed to comprehend English, but Sean neatly compensated for this lapse by dropping his pipe. It clattered against the tiles.

"Drat!" he exclaimed, stamping his feet all around to kill any stray sparks. When he had finished with this pantomime, he looked guilelessly at Fengmo.

"Fong Lu," he muttered in Chinese. "Is that not the worthless fellow who used to wait upon you?"

"I . . ." Fengmo stuttered slightly. "Yes, that is the man, but I find it hard to believe he would—"

"Well, I do not," Sean interrupted. "Did he not run off several days ago and leave you without a chauffeur? That servant had no loyalty at all!"

Master Wong managed to keep all his expressions in check, but this farce was beginning to wear on Fengmo's nerves. He could only nod his agreement to the statement

Sean had just made while the listening naval officer peered from face to face.

"Is the man no longer here?" the captain asked Sean.

"No, sir. He was a most unreliable sort. I believe the lure of city life became too much, for he ran away. Perhaps there was a woman. In any case, he obviously did not wish to return home with his master here."

The captain eyed Fengmo with deep suspicion. "Is this Chinaman leaving Shanghai?"

"In just a day or so," Sean answered without a waver.

"Well," the officer drawled, uncertain just how next to proceed. "We should search the house regardless, but if *you* say the devil is gone . . ."

Again he looked closely at Fengmo and seemed to come to a decision.

"Still," he stated, "I'm going to leave a detachment—just in case that murdering *chink* comes back. We'll find him sooner or later, even if we have to turn Shanghai inside out. These yellow monkeys can't be allowed to go around killing our people."

"Do as you think best, Captain, of course." Sean began to repack his pipe. Two spots of color had appeared on his cheeks, but his voice remained steady. "I am sure Master Wong will be most happy to cooperate." He turned to Wong Cho, unable to suppress a twinkle. "You understand? Co-op-er-ate!"

"Yes! Yes!" Master Wong bowed several times. "Most happy! Most happy!"

He and Fengmo bowed again, together, and wreathed their faces in smiles as Sean led the naval officer back outside. After the door snapped closed they looked at each other, all expressions of solicitude gone.

"Where is your man?" Master Wong asked urgently.

"I do not know!"

It was the truth. Fengmo had not been concerned by the fact that his servant had not returned the night before. Fong Lu had requested the evening off and Fengmo had been more than happy to grant the wish, hoping that a bit of relaxation might bring the chauffeur up out of the doldrums. But regardless of these facts, Fengmo did not believe Fong Lu capable of killing anyone—not even a foreigner. He was just about to say so when Sean Duncan came back through the door.

"Come," said Master Wong in perfect English, "we will take tea in the library." He gave Sean a stern look. "You understand? *Libe-elli!*"

They all three laughed, their mirth exaggerated by the overwhelming relief they felt.

Once they were settled in the library, Master Wong had to pull the bell rope several times before a servant arrived. It was Jasmine's mother who appeared, and she wore an expression of calm serenity.

There were armed guards posted all around the estate. The uniformed men were not obtrusive for the most part, but they were vigilant. In groups of two they patrolled the gardens and outlying areas of the grounds, in addition to keeping a constant watch on the main gate. Moreover, they stood at the front and back doors of the house and servants' quarters. Any vehicle coming in or out of the Street of Blue Roofs was thoroughly searched—any, that is, except the miserable-looking vintage automobile driven by Sean Duncan.

Fengmo still found Sean's story hard to credit. According to the American, Fong Lu had appeared at the gates of the mission compound that fateful night, breathless and splattered with blood, hoping to find Long Han. When he learned the Chinese convert was gone on a short sabbatical, he pleaded refuge of Sean personally. Much against his parents' wishes, the forthright young man had provided shelter for the fugitive.

"But why would he have killed the seaman?" Fengmo had asked, incredulous. "Fong Lu is not the violent sort at all."

This query Sean would not answer. He simply replied, "He had cause."

Life in the Wong household was sharply curtailed by the presence of armed white men everywhere. The brothers, not privy to all the details, complained loudly, especially Wong Six, who could not feel easy going to his secret meetings.

One thing was certain, Fong Lu must be smuggled out of Shanghai. Again, it was Sean who laid plans and expedited preparations. Without telling anyone exactly how it would be accomplished, he simply instructed Chang Fengmo to make ready for the return trip to Tanpo.

The day before the journey was to begin he made a startling announcement.

"I will go with you, Fengmo," he said. "Long Han has returned and will be happy to stay and help my parents, for that way he can at least torture himself with news of Mary. As for me, I have always wanted to get a better look at this great nation of yours. Shanghai is not the whole of China, after all, and I have seen little else."

Fengmo could only nod polite acquiescence. In fact, he was not dismayed at the idea, for Sean had become an integral part of his life. He was loath to leave this young man who seemed so different from the rest of his race.

That evening the two walked to the old automobile together, trying to ignore the guards who leaned against one fender, smoking and talking in low, guttural voices.

"It will be less conspicuous if I meet you aboard ship tomorrow," Sean said in quick, fluent Mandarin. "Long Han will come and see us off."

Smiling, Fengmo tapped the hood of the car. "I hope you do not intend to drag this thing with you. Its coughs and moans would scare the peasants to death."

"Have no fear," laughed Sean. "My father would be lost without it. I doubt it could withstand the journey in any case."

Looking into the candid eyes of his friend, Fengmo wondered how his own parents would react to the presence of the American.

Sean seemed to read his mind. "Tell your father you can now continue your English lessons," he said. "Free of charge."

The next morning saw the household a virtual beehive of activity. There were inventory lists to check and recheck against the already loaded trucks. The drivers had hired eight rough-looking fellows to ride guard, and these men swaggered about, eyeing their white counterparts with blatant hostility.

Last, of course, there were farewells to be said. The five elder Wong brothers were jolly and teasing, telling

Fengmo he must return someday and bring with him a nephew—or two or three.

"Watch when you get home," Wong Six told him privately. "Keep your eyes open and you will see I have spoken the truth, comrade. Prepare for a new day in China!"

The emotional Madame Wong wept copious tears and embraced Fengmo. "I will miss you, my boy, though I will see you soon again. My lord has decided I can accompany him and Bright Autumn to Tanpo four months from now. Until then, keep yourself well."

Just before he was to leave, Fengmo stood in the driveway with his host. Only Bright Autumn had not come to see him off, and he searched for her face at each window.

"My daughter is at the bridge," Master Wong quietly informed him. "Go to her."

She was indeed there waiting, but not alone. An old serving woman stood a distance away, keeping a watchful eye on the couple as they said goodbye.

"May the gods be with you until we meet again, My Lord," Bright Autumn said, her glance shyly lowered.

"And you also take care," he replied.

Strangely, he chafed under these formal banalities. For just one more moment he wished to see her smile. Instead, he noted a silver tear, perfect as a drop of morning dew, trickle down her cheek.

Reaching into the pocket of his slacks, he felt for the small jade ring. It grew instantly warm when he touched it, and again he was comforted.

I should give this expensive trinket to Bright Autumn, he thought. She is to be my wife. It is more than time for me to grow up and put childhood foolishness behind me.

But he could not do it. The ring remained tightly clasped in his hand, and he knew he would give it to only one. Bowing, he bid his betrothed a final farewell and walked away.

Bright Autumn lifted her head and watched him until he disappeared from view.

She whispered a promise. "Soon, my love."

Chapter Twenty-one

They had been traveling inland aboard the British vessel for several hours before Sean finally put Fengmo's mind at ease concerning the fate of Fong Lu. Both men had been rather quiet and downcast since leaving in any case, for their farewells with Long Han had been sad all around.

Changed indeed was that young man, once so full of wit and good humor. The Long Han whom Fengmo had met on his coast-bound journey seemed to have disappeared. The love Mary Duncan had scorned, the worship and devotion, the Chinese convert now attempted to pour into his vocation.

According to Sean, Long Han spent hours on end reading the Sacred Scriptures or upon his knees in prayer. Having lost his hearty appetite, he was also terribly thin and drawn. Dark circles ringed his once-laughing eyes and his smile was a mere shadow of its former self.

It struck Fengmo painfully that even he had not suffered so from his lost love. With all the anguish of seeing his beloved Golden Willow bound in marriage to his own brother, he still had not put aside his interest in life. But Long Han, it now appeared, cared for nothing but his foreign god and what he called "the Lord's work."

"He will become a fanatic if he continues so," Sean had remarked. "And if he does he will do more harm than good as an evangelist."

To Fengmo this had seemed a singularly strange remark, coming as it did from another man also supposedly of the cloth. But then, Sean Duncan never failed to amaze Fengmo with contradictions of personality. Why, he was no longer even wearing the dark suit and white collar which denoted his calling. Rather, he had appeared at the

Shanghai docks wearing a pair of light khaki-colored slacks and matching shirt. Then, completely ignoring the curious and disapproving stares of his fellow passengers, he chose to eat with Fengmo in the Chinese section of the ship's dining hall. The foods he selected were also native. In addition, he seemed to Fengmo more at peace than ever before.

"Perhaps," Fengmo wryly suggested, "your god accidentally thrust you into the wrong skin, my friend, for you are like no white man I have ever heard of!"

Sean only smiled. "And how many white men do you know?"

"None except you," Fengmo admitted. "But I still maintain you are unique. I swear, man, you are even becoming inscrutable, and is that not reported to be an Asian characteristic? For instance, how long must I be expected to wait before I learn of my manservant? Have you tucked him away in a trunk below decks or what?"

Even though they were alone in the cabin they shared, Sean lowered his voice. "He is *not* aboard, but ahead of us on one of the barges."

"How can that be?" Fengmo asked in surprise. "I saw those trucks and the automobile loaded with my own two eyes. They were also thoroughly searched before being allowed to leave the House of Wong."

Sean then went on to explain how Fong Lu had been secreted in a narrow space behind a front seat in one of the trucks and been given food and water by the drivers while preparations were made to get under way.

"He was cramped, to say the least," Sean said. "I fear it is luck alone that helped him escape in the end, however, for we could not be sure the seamen would not force the drivers to get down out of the cabs while the searches were being conducted. Woe unto poor Fong Lu if they had, for his feet were protruding and pressed tightly against the door."

"But how did he get inside the truck to begin with?" Fengmo wanted to know. "There were guards everywhere!"

"Not until after the captain left the House of Wong. Before then, you will remember, the seamen remained only at the gate and later in the driveway. As for your chauffeur, well, he was in the trunk of my father's automobile all the time. While you and I were talking to the diligent captain, Fong Lu let himself out and climbed over the estate fence. It was not difficult for him to then cut through the grounds and slip into the servants' quarters."

"But those quarters were guarded night and day!" Fengmo still protested. "It is a miracle he was ever able to get out again!"

"Well, a minor miracle, perhaps," Sean conceded, a smile playing about his lips. "But those vigilant sailors were not on the lookout for a sweet, retiring maid."

Fengmo spent only a moment trying to picture Fong Lu in such a disguise before he began to guffaw. It was impossible for him to believe that his broad-shouldered, strutting chauffeur could have fooled anyone by being dressed in feminine attire. For hours after he learned of this charade, Fengmo would conjure up pictures of his servant thus decked out and begin to laugh anew.

They were off the ship and two days upon dry land, however, before the fugitive finally appeared in person. Prior to that time there had still been a noteworthy sprinkling of foreigners about and, consequently, great caution had to be exercised.

Their motor caravan stopped that night at a small wayside inn, and Sean and Fengmo were sharing a small bottle of heated wine in the privacy of their room when a soft scratching sounded at the door. An instant later, a smiling Fong Lu walked in and casually bowed.

"Do you wish anything else before you retire, Master?" he asked, just as if he had been serving them all along.

To the profound relief of Fengmo there was now bounce back in his chauffeur's steps. During the following days, Fong Lu also exhibited the ability to laugh and joke again, though perhaps a bit less often than he once had. There remained a certain reticence about him which discouraged any questions regarding his alleged crime. In the end, Fengmo decided it best not to pry, for in his own mind he was convinced that some very compelling reason must indeed have existed for his servant to take the life of another. It suddenly seemed enough that Fong Lu was safe and sound and in relatively good spirits.

* * *

In just hours they would be home!

Fong Lu pressed down on the clutch and shifted gears, wishing he could accelerate and fly up over the hills, rather than creep as he was now forced to do. The sight of each tree and cloud, each jutting boulder, made his heart sing with joy. Never had a land looked more fair to him.

He could hear his master and the American deep in earnest conversation in the back seat. They were still discussing a topic which they had been belaboring for days on end.

"My father *does* care for the peasants," Fengmo was saying in an agitated voice. "Regardless of what Wong and his comrades seem to believe, the Honorable Chang Hai-teh is no tyrant. You will see, Sean. The people of the land are quite a happy lot. True, famines do come, but it has always been so, and this is hardly a landowner's fault. My own father demands the utmost frugality of his family at such times. He cannot, of course, feed the entire population, but neither does he allow us to flaunt our prosperity."

So the conversation went and Fong Lu continued to listen. Mentally he wagged his head at what he perceived to be ignorance on the part of his well-meaning young master.

What can he know of us? the chauffeur thought. His sisters are alive and well, not dead or being raised in some foundling home because his parents could not afford to feed them. He has seen only the best of Tanpo and never really looked at the rest.

These thoughts did not indicate the least bit of hatred on the part of Fong Lu, however. He simply accepted Fengmo's lack of knowledge as very representative of all rich folk. This apparent indifference to the suffering of the poor had been a fact for generations. Moreover, he had no hope that it would ever change.

In truth, the chauffeur considered himself quite fortunate. As the lowly third son of a tenant farmer, he had not been needed to help work the tiny plot of land his family leased. His father had therefore sent him to the House of Chang at a very tender age, hoping a place might be found for him within the household staff. Thus, there was one less mouth to feed.

Luckily, Fong Lu had proved to be both talented and resourceful. He was only ten when given the unadmirable job of apprentice to the animal keeper. His hands soon became raw from shoveling dung into carts, which were then driven up into the farmlands. But no job seemed too menial for him, nor did he ever shirk his responsibilities or complain. The plain food he was given tasted wonderful to a little boy who had never before had enough to eat.

Then came the great and glorious day when Master Chang began to purchase foreign motor vehicles!

Drivers had finally been recruited, but in those days no one knew how to work on the metal beasts when they broke down. The jumble of engine parts was a fearful mystery to all—all except the curious Fong Lu. That quick-witted sixteen-year-old had almost instantly shown a natural aptitude for tinkering. Within months his services became indispensable.

The last vehicle to be purchased was the automobile, and that long, gleaming dream of a machine soon became the most loved thing in Fong Lu's life. He nearly worshiped the high, rounded fenders and bright strips of chrome. The fact that Master Chang rarely used the car dampened his young spirits not at all. With almost filial tenderness, he polished it and drove it over the narrow dirt roads of the countryside to keep it running smoothly. When the long journey to Shanghai was proposed, therefore, the Third Son of Farmer Fong seemed the only logical choice to be selected as chauffeur.

Yes, Fong Lu believed himself to be a lucky man indeed. Over the past months he had even grown to feel a fierce loyalty toward his young master, who he felt to be good and kind despite his obvious lack of worldly wisdom.

Now, listening to Fengmo's discourse, he was startled and a little dismayed to find himself drawn into the conversation.

"Fong Lu," Fengmo said. "Your people are of the land. Tell me, when things go amiss, do the peasants curse the rich men or heaven?"

Both! the chauffeur thought, but did not say so aloud. Instead, he kept his eyes glued to the road and gave the expected response. "Why, that Old Man in the Sky, of course, Master."

Not so easily pacified, Fengmo persisted. "Well then,

are you not angry when you see what the rich have, and even what they waste? It would seem natural enough since your own folk must occasionally suffer hardship."

"Has it not always been so, Young Sir?" Fong Lu was very careful to answer the question with other questions. "Must it not be the will of heaven that there are both rich and poor? Should all men suffer because most do?"

This ended the discussion for the time being. However, Fong Lu looked into the rearview mirror just a few minutes later and saw the eyes of Sean Duncan meet his own in mutual understanding and knowledge. For some reason, this contact and unspoken communication warmed him.

The American had definitely become the man Fong Lu respected and adored most on all the earth.

The sound of bursting firecrackers exploded in the afternoon air, and shouts rang through the many courtyards. "The Second Son has returned! The young lord is home!"

The House of Chang was suddenly charged with life. Adults and children alike rushed out of the gates to crowd around the motor caravan. Though a bit intimidated by the cadre of armed men, they still could not contain their curiosity.

Fengmo emerged from the automobile and stood looking at all the faces pressed in around him. He smiled broadly, for to him these faces seemed the best and dearest he had ever seen. They were ruddy and just a bit chapped by the cold spring winds, but they glowed with good health. In more than a few, he could discern the characteristics of his clan. One fellow had the full lower lip of the Chang family, and yet another the unusual bridged nose. A little girl, not more than three, gazed up at him with delicately curved eyes very much like his own. It was all he could do to maintain decorum and not shout out his joy at the top of his lungs. He wanted to embrace them one and all.

A gasp went up from the crowd as Sean Duncan also came out of the car, and everyone stepped back a few paces.

"Oh!" they murmured. "A foreign devil! What has the young sir gone and done? What will the old sir say?"

"Ai-e-e-e!" exclaimed one little boy, and nudged his

awestriken sibling. "I can see right through that fellow's eyes into his brains!"

This inaccurate observation had been made by Tan, Fengmo's next-to-youngest brother. A bit braver and more outspoken than the rest, he now stepped forward and examined the American more closely.

"Does the light scald his brains?" he asked Fengmo, playing the clown and thinking the other man could not understand a word he said.

"It does not," Sean answered.

The intrepid Tan leapt backward and nearly fell, while the crowd tittered nervously at first, and then began to laugh in earnest.

Master Chang chose that moment to come out of the compound gates. He had evidently heard this exchange, for he hesitated slightly before coming forward, and he frowned at his young son.

The crowd grew silent and expectant as the master bowed toward Sean. "Welcome," he said. "I hope you will forgive the rudeness of my boy. He is worthless and of no account whatsoever."

He turned his attention to Fengmo. "Your arrival is much earlier than expected, my son, but it is good to see you nonetheless. Your mother will be pleased. She is all aflutter with preparations for your wedding."

It was all Fengmo could do to adhere to the formalities and not weep at the sight of his father's calm, dignified countenance. Quickly, he introduced Sean Duncan and explained that this was the same individual whom he had previously written home about, his American tutor.

"He has done a very brave deed, Father," Fengmo said. "When this commotion is over and we have settled in, I will tell you the whole wondrous tale." This last he said with just a bit of anxiety, for he still could not tell for certain how his father felt about the presence of Sean, or whether he was, in truth, angry or not.

He sighed with relief when Master Chang answered in all sincerity, "Your friend is more than welcome, my son, brave deed or not. Come now, you must both be weary. Let us go inside and enjoy some refreshment. Instruct your man to guide these trucks and the automobile to the warehouse on Bantam Street."

"Oh no!" cried the impertinent Tan. "Father, we have all been waiting here patiently, hoping to see your latest jade treasure! Can you not show it now?"

The boy squealed in alarm as his father quickly snatched him up off the ground and applied several raps on his head with sharp knuckles.

"What a disrespectful one you are!" berated Master Chang, setting the tyke back on his feet again. "Tomorrow I shall instruct your scholar to give you an extra heap of lessons in proper courtesy."

The crowd nodded approval, but at the same time clucked their sympathy for the little boy, for everyone in the house was tenderhearted toward the charming and lively rascal. Then too, they had also hoped to glimpse the renowned artifact of which they had heard so much. The expressions of family and servants alike mirrored their disappointment.

Master Chang saw this and was touched.

"You are all invited to assemble in the central courtyard tomorrow evening," he said. "I will unveil the treasure then, and you can all admire it to your hearts' delight."

This promise satisfied everyone and the crowd began to disperse as he led Fengmo and Sean inside. Soon, the only ones left in the street were Tan and his elder brother, Hsu.

"Grrr," growled the youngest boy. "Someday they will be sorry! I am going to become a great general and rule over them all!"

Chapter Twenty-two

Golden Willow struggled to control the rapid beating of her heart. Fengmo had been home for an entire day and still she had not seen him. The evening before he and the American, who was his guest, had not appeared in the family dining hall. Instead, exhausted from their long journey, they had taken a light meal in Fengmo's apartment and then retired early.

But tonight she *would* see him!

I must calm myself, she thought, or I will surely give myself away! I cannot continue to blush and fluster like some unmarried serving girl!

These past months had brought a degree of serenity to her life, and until the day before she had believed there might be a chance at least for contentment, if not true happiness. Her loathing for Kao had not abated, but New Moon and Moon Shadow remained her beloved companions. Indeed, those two were like her own sisters. Little Tan and Hsu had also taken to visiting her court of late. She loved them dearly, even if they did have a tendency to wear on her nerves from time to time. Most important was the relationship she had developed with her father-in-law.

Ever since their first encounter in the library, Master Chang had begun to show a most surprising and solicitous interest in her welfare. Against all tradition, he had put aside the barriers of age and sex. Now it was his habit to meet her in that same room perhaps three or four times a month and discuss with her the books she had read, or even the current political situation as he viewed it. She had come to look forward to these quiet exchanges with utmost anticipation. On only one occasion could she recall being sorry for the companionship they shared.

She had come into the library about a month before and felt her usual gladness at finding Master Chang already there. After reading several articles to her from the latest newspapers he had received from Canton and Shanghai, they discussed the distressing turn of events at some length. As always, the threat of Imperial Japan was ever on their minds.

Once this conversation was ended, however, the older man became somewhat restive. Getting up from the table, he walked along the bookshelves and scanned the volumes in a desultory sort of way. Golden Willow was just about to excuse herself when he spoke.

"I have received a missive from Shanghai," he said in a rather distracted tone. "It contained glad tidings concerning my Second Son."

Golden Willow sat very still then, careful to keep her expression only mildly interested, even though his back was turned toward her.

"Chang Fengmo is to be betrothed," he quietly announced. "Soon I shall have two daughters-in-law to enjoy. I pray his intended will prove half so delightful as you."

What a terrible moment that had been!

Even now, remembering, Golden Willow could feel her heart wrench. Only good fortune had saved her from humiliating herself that afternoon, for Master Chang had suddenly remembered some forgotten errand and rushed from the library without looking back. Had he done otherwise, he would have seen the tears in her eyes.

For several days thereafter she had remained in her own apartment and not gone to the family meals or even allowed anyone to visit her. Crystal had let everyone know that her mistress suffered a severe head cold and might be contagious. Only Madame Chang could not be deterred by such warning. That cool, aloof lady had insisted upon coming into the apartment regardless. But once having seen the red, swollen eyes of her daughter-in-law, and perceiving that the girl did indeed have congested sinuses, she had simply prescribed a foul-tasting herb broth and then left again.

So it had been that Golden Willow was able to wash her sorrow in cleansing tears, and thereby reconcile herself somewhat. She had always known her beloved must one day wed, and she did not think it should be otherwise. Her sorrow was born not of jealousy, but despair. She even attempted to convince herself that it would be better if Fengmo no longer loved her. In this, however, she failed miserably, for she knew she wanted his love desperately.

Now, months before expected, he had returned.

Golden Willow rebuked herself for wondering if his soul reached out toward her own. At the same time, she longed to be able to look at him, to see him and know if his heart remained constant.

Crystal, that perceptive little maid, chattered constantly, and in that way kept her mistress well informed. At this very moment she was busy giving great consideration to selecting an outfit for Golden Willow to wear to dinner and the following festivities. She pulled one beautiful robe after another from the bedchamber chest, only to discount each in turn. Finally she held up one, a brocade of a more modern cut than the rest, and gave it her undivided scrutiny.

"Ah yes," she decided, "I think this is exactly the right one, Mistress. It is heavy enough to protect you from the chill, and with these long fitted sleeves you will not even need to wear a jacket. Moreover, it is your best color—orchid!"

Golden Willow passively submitted to being bathed in scented water and having her hair styled in a braided chignon.

While Crystal's nimble fingers worked the silky strands of hair, she talked as usual. "The house is simply abuzz with news of the Second Son," she said. "They say he is much changed by his Shanghai adventures. For one thing, he sometimes babbles in a strange tongue with that foreigner he dragged home."

Golden Willow smiled. "I believe that language is called *English*, Crystal, and it is very difficult to comprehend. It says much for the young sir that he has been able to master such tongue twisting."

"Perhaps," the serving girl conceded, and then rushed on to another topic. "They also say he has brought a new servant into the household for his personal use, a fellow who used to work in the barns. Imagine! I hope I do not have to get close to this Fong Lu, for he probably reeks to the sky of manure! A girl in the kitchen told me he is the very lofty sort, quite taken with himself. He will not even give the maids a glance. No doubt he thinks himself too good for the rest of us just because he has been to Shanghai with the Second Son."

Thus Crystal spoke, imparting what scraps of information she possessed. After helping Golden Willow to dress, she produced a perfect lotus blossom and nestled it in the hairdo she had finished.

"There!" she firmly pronounced. "You are a vision of loveliness, Mistress. No woman on earth can compare with you, not even one from Shanghai."

Golden Willow flushed at this bit of flattery, but also scowled. "Do not speak so again, Crystal. I have no interest in competing with anyone—most especially not anyone from Shanghai. You should be ashamed for saying such a thing!"

From this gentle rebuke, Crystal knew her mistress did not wish to hear gossip concerning the upcoming wedding, and so kept silent on the subject.

The main courtyard was ethereal. A full April moon hung in the sky, smiling down like a benevolent goddess upon the congregation below. Colorful paper lanterns had been strung around the perimeters, and oil torches flickered in an uncommonly gentle breeze, casting dancing reflections off the huge fishpond. Seated in chairs and upon stones and on the brick-tiled courtyard floor, the House of Chang was gathered. Everyone was hushed. Even the children were quiet and expectant. Upon a high table next to the pond sat an object all draped in silk cloth. Staff and family alike patiently awaited an unveiling of the treasure. Meanwhile, they were content to listen as Madame Chang played the zither. Sitting on a thick bamboo pallet, she caressed and plucked the strings of her favorite instrument in a way that brought tears to the eyes of her audience. Nearby, the old gardener accompanied her on his lute.

Sitting between his father and Kao, Fengmo surveyed this almost celestial scene and realized anew how much he had missed his home. He let his glance wander from face to well-remembered face, saving the one he cherished most of all for last. On the opposite side of the courtyard, among the women, his eyes sought and found Golden Willow. Her hands rested gently in her lap and the flicker of torchlight played across her face.

All at once, Fengmo feared the thunder of his heart would drown out the music. He drank in the sight of her. And then, as if she felt the touch of his perusal, she turned toward him and their eyes locked. Fengmo started slightly as he felt a rough tug on his sleeve.

"It is good to have you back, my son," his father whispered. "You have done very well and I am proud of you."

Rather than feeling complimented by this praise, Fengmo felt somehow chastised. From then on he made a concentrated effort to look only at the graceful figure of his mother—and nowhere else.

Not so Moon Shadow!

That headstrong young lady, now almost sixteen years of age, never took her eyes off the handsome American who stood leaning against a far courtyard wall. Every now and again he would draw deeply on his short-stemmed pipe and then blow out a great cloud of blue smoke. Moon Shadow could smell the sweet tobacco fragrance even from where she sat.

I am going to learn English, she decided. There is no reason why I should not, either. After all, we now have a teacher right here in the house!

The music stopped. Madame Chang put aside her pluck and nodded in her husband's direction to signify that she was done playing. The rest of the gathering also gave him their full and undivided attention.

Master Chang stood and cleared his throat. "This is a very special night," he said. "My good Second Son here has returned from afar and in so doing provided us a rare opportunity. While in Shanghai, he was able to acquire an object most unparalleled in beauty and craftsmanship. The treasure I am about to unveil should not be hoarded, however, for beauty is a thing to be shared. I choose, on this delightful spring's eve, to share it first with you, my family. Come now, let us enjoy it together."

At this invitation the entire assembly got up and clustered around the high table. Once they were settled and quiet again, Master Chang gently pulled aside the silk drape. An awed gasp of wonder rippled from the crowd as, in reverence, they let their eyes feast upon the convoluted intricacies of the sparkling jade pleasure palace.

It was upon this scene of peace, then, that calamity abruptly intruded.

When a loud cry sounded from without the main gates, it took those in the House of Chang several moments to bring their minds back into focus and realize something was sorely amiss. Even so, they could hardly believe their ears when Tse Liangmo, Golden Willow's father, burst into the courtyard.

"War!" he cried. "It is now really and truly *war!*"

Chapter Twenty-three

Bright Autumn opened her eyes and lay very still. She could not remember dreaming, and yet her heart was pumping and her breath came in small gasps. It was very early, dawn was just peeking through her window. Her drowsy mind struggled to sort itself out.

Then she heard the sound and knew what had awakened her so abruptly. Throwing her coverlet aside, she leapt out of bed and ran to the window. There, against an orange and silver painted sky, she beheld a sight that sent thrills of terror to the marrow of her bones. Above her head, coming in a fast and deadly drove, were warplanes, Japanese Kates and Zeros, the emblem of the Rising Sun glittering scarlet on their wings.

"M'ma, P'pa!" she was finally able to scream, but her voice was lost, devoured by the angry swarm overhead.

Fear-induced adrenaline gave her legs impetus and she moved. Bare feet slapping against the tile floor, she bolted into the corridor and ran toward the suite of her parents. Vaguely she heard the cries of servants from below and the frightened squawking of birds as they fluttered and beat themselves against the walls of the inner court.

Her mother and father emerged from their rooms just as she rounded the last corridor. They, as she, were dressed only in their bedclothes. Madame Wong's thin gray hair hung down past her waist in total disarray. Her bound feet were wrapped but unslippered, and she looked near to fainting. The rest of the family converged from every direction. Bright Autumn's brothers and their wives appeared with sleepy-faced children in their arms and clinging to their legs. All looked toward Master Wong.

The older man wasted not a moment. For the first time,

he regretted the bright blue tiles that magnificently covered his house and the servants' quarters, for he knew that when viewed from the sky they must provide a most enticing target.

"Pick up the children and run for your lives!" he ordered. "Go out into the park!" There was no hysteria in his commanding voice, only authority. "Come, Bright Autumn. Help me with your mother!"

Immediately the younger sons began scooping up the children who were not being held by their own parents. Bright Autumn rushed to her parents. She supported one of her mother's arms while her father took the other. It was a torturous trip toward the staircase, and all the while the house shook. Windows rattled as the noise overhead became more deafening. They had almost reached the first landing when Master Wong looked back over his shoulder and cursed. Lagging behind was Brilliant Jade, the wife of his Third Son. She, who had no children of her own, had not picked up the little son of Wong Two. The lad, no more than three years of age, clung to her leg, his lips trembling, while his supposed protector stumbled along, her arms full to overflowing with jewel boxes, robes, and dresses.

"Drop those!" Master Wong bellowed. "Take the child and run!"

But Brilliant Jade took no notice, if indeed she heard him at all. She continued to stagger beneath her burdens, unmindful of the child. Master Wong looked from her and his grandchild back to his beloved wife, his face a mask of indecision.

"I will get them, Father," Bright Autumn shouted over the din. "Take our mother to safety. I cannot support her alone."

Madame Wong was weeping now. "These feet! These worthless feet!"

Bright Autumn turned and started back down the corridor. "Take care and hurry, Daughter!" She heard the command her father called after her.

When she approached, Brilliant Jade did not appear to see her. Neither did she seem aware of the terrified child who was now beginning to moan and hiccup.

"Brilliant Jade!" Bright Autumn could not keep the anger from her voice. "Put down those worthless things at once! We must go!"

Still, the other girl continued to move slowly forward. Her arms tightly gripped her precious possessions and her face was stark. Every step or two she tripped over a long golden gown, which hung down from the rest.

Bright Autumn began tearing at the pile she held, and at the same time yelled at her nephew. "Run, Leinpo, run after Grandfather and Grandmother! Go, little one, go!"

The tot wasted no more than a fraction of a second after staring up at her stern and frightened face. On sturdy legs he ran down the corridor. His blue night-robe fanned out behind him like iridescent wings as he disappeared down the stairs.

Under Bright Autumn's continued determined assault, Brilliant Jade's tightly held treasures spilled over the floor. Earrings and bracelets, golden hair ornaments and brocade dresses flew in every direction.

"No! No!" Brilliant Jade pushed Bright Autumn roughly away and got down on her hands and knees to regather those things which were more dear than her own life.

"You fool!" Bright Autumn became a bundle of fury. The world around her roared. In her rush and vexation, she spared no sympathy for her sister-in-law. With a banshee cry she attacked the other girl and pulled her up by the hair. When Brilliant Jade struggled against this rough treatment, Bright Autumn slapped her viciously across the face.

The other girl staggered back and stared. Her face was bloodless white except for the vivid welt outlined on her cheek. Her eyes rolled in shock. "We are going to die!" she screeched. "We are all going to die!"

Bright Autumn wasted neither time nor breath on persuasion. Locking Brilliant Jade's wrist in an iron grip, she began dragging her toward the stairs.

Master Wong thought his lungs would burst. His wife was heavy in his arms, and his little grandson, Leinpo, held fast to the edge of his garments as he took a final, staggering step into the thick copse of eucalyptus which stood deep within the estate grounds. The rest of his family and a few of the servants were already there, all except his daughter and Brilliant Jade.

Laying Madame Wong down upon a pile of fallen leaves, he heard her cry. "Bright Autumn! Oh, my Bright Autumn!" Her lamentation seemed to drown out the thunder of war.

Wheezing with exertion, Master Wong turned back. His heart thudded painfully against his ribs. His knees were weak and trembling. Looking toward the house, he suddenly thought of the distance to be retraced as hundreds of miles. The muscles of his calves were in agony, but worse than his physical pain was the horrible vision of his beloved daughter being shredded by the bombs which were even now falling on the city. He forced himself to run.

All at once he felt the presence of Wong Six running beside him, and though he could say nothing, this support gave him a new burst of energy. Together father and son neared the meadow, when suddenly a huge peacock broke from the surrounding foilage and bolted across the pathway. Master Wong stumbled and fell. His sides ached and, unbeknownst to him, he was weeping.

Wong Six pulled him up, and they went on over the labyrinth of trails which had once provided such pleasant leisure. Along the horizon behind them, the sky was mottled with black, billowing clouds. The screams of the populace became an unending wail. Wong Six lifted an arm and pointed toward the house.

Coming out of the door was Bright Autumn, but she was struggling violently, tugging at someone or something.

The heavy thud of running feet sounded and Master Wong and his youngest son turned in unison to see Wong Three behind them. His eyes were darting and terrified. "Brilliant Jade," he panted. "I must help to find her!"

Then he also looked toward the house and saw his wife being pulled by Bright Autumn, clawing and screaming, through the main door. The three men moved forward at the same time, but they had covered only a few yards when the world became a nightmare. A single fighter plane swooped down and with ear-splitting cacophony spewed fire and death from beneath its tilted wings. The men sprawled face forward on the ground, covering their heads as a shower of bullets riddled the earth and trees around them. Almost instantly there was an explosion. Chunks of plaster and shards of tile rained down. Wong Three screamed as a large splinter of wood impaled his leg. The plane, skimming the treetops, lifted and sped away.

"By all the gods," Master Wong wept, coming up on all fours, "let her be alive!"

It took every ounce of willpower he possessed to force himself to raise his eyes and look toward the house again. At first he saw only smoking debris, but then, as he wildly searched the rubble, he saw a patch of white silk fluttering in the faint breeze—Bright Autumn's pajamas! She lay halfway down the circular driveway.

The angry rumble of powerful engines droned overhead once more as the airplanes came back into group formation and fled the scene of their carnage. This din and the cry of Shanghai were punctuated by the screams of Wong Three. The fallen man writhed and clutched his torn leg. Splintered bone jutted out of the limb, and though it was not bleeding heavily, muscle and gristle were ripped and exposed. Wong Six bent over his brother while Master Wong forged ahead.

He could still detect no movement from the small heap which he knew to be his only daughter, his youngest and most beloved child. Nearly blinded by tears, breathing in labored gasps, praying incoherently, Wong Cho came over the final terrace. He could see her body clearly now. Her unbound hair fanned out over the red bricks. Her face was turned away from him and she did not move.

Brilliant Jade was nowhere to be seen, and at that moment he could not force himself to care. Gently, he knelt beside Bright Autumn and touched her shoulder. He thought his heart would stop when she moaned. "P'pa?"

Though her voice was faint, Master Wong was overcome. No amount of masculine pride or generations of tradition could hold back the floodgate of his emotions. He wept unashamedly and with rejoicing.

Nothing could have induced Master Wong to take his family back to the partially destroyed house, for he feared the end of terror had not yet come. Within hours, his worst fears were more than realized. The planes did indeed return. For days the air raids continued almost constantly. On the second night, during a brief lull, Master Wong took his sons—all except Wong Three—and crept through the grounds and on to the house in order to forage food for the family. They passed the meadow, where a fallen doe gazed at them with vacant eyes while her fawn bleated softly and nudged her dried and stiffened teats. The small lake was now surrounded by ripped and broken trees; the lacquered bridge was gone and the waters of the lake muddied. The body of a swan lay on a far bank, its once-graceful neck broken in two.

"They will pay for this!" Wong Six hissed from between clenched teeth. "I swear they will pay!"

"We are safe," Master Wong murmured, refusing to concentrate on the wanton destruction of that which he so deeply loved. "Let us be thankful."

His elder sons nodded morosely and walked on. They did not see the mask of hatred which contorted the face of Wong Six. His features were washed in moonglow, and he raised a fist as he uttered an oath to the cold, unfeeling night. "Yes, the Japanese *will* pay, but so shall the *Kuomintang*, those deserting Nationalist dogs who have abandoned us to follow the traitor Chiang Kai-shek."

The sights they viewed that night were grisly. The servants' quarters were completely destroyed. The house proper had been scorched and there were broken windows, but except for one outer wall, which was crumbled away, the structure appeared miraculously intact.

For all their modern education, the sons of Wong Cho remained a surprisingly superstitious lot. Their eyes were wide and frightened as they picked their way through the rubble. The uncommon quietude immediately around them was only heightened by the distant sounds of lamentation going up from the city. Wong Four, that peaceful and gregarious soul, began to shiver, and when his foot inadvertently struck the disembodied head of an old manservant, he screamed and then began to vomit.

There were many such mementos to be found along the way. Arms, legs, fingers could be glimpsed at sundry spots among the wreckage of the servants' quarters. But the men could not turn back. Food had to be obtained, and blankets and medical supplies.

While Master Wong and his two eldest sons went into the kitchens and cellars for food, the three younger were sent upstairs to gather blankets and pillows. Both children and adults also needed shoes and clothing, for none knew how long they might be forced to remain out of doors. Once they reached the top of the stairs, the young men separated to comb different areas. The house no longer seemed familiar, but rather a place of shadows and strange sounds.

Wong Six went into the large nursery and began filling a sack with bare necessities for his nieces and nephews. This was one of the several rooms which no longer had an outer wall, and the moonlight spilled in. Never before had he given the six children he lived with much thought or attention, but now he was strangely affected by their topsy-turvy beds, mangled furniture, and the toys scattered about. The light threw the room into eerie relief. Though he knew it was ridiculous, he felt as if he were being spied upon. He cursed himself for a fool as chills played up and down his spine, and he quickly stuffed little trousers and shoes into his sack. He stood and was almost to the door leading to the corridor when he heard a sound.

"Four? Five?" he softly queried.

A giggle answered him, and a second later the ghostly figure of Brilliant Jade appeared in the doorway. Her hands were extended straight out, and in her palms she held a mound of glittering jewels.

"Ah, Little Brother," she laughed. "See what I have? You need not worry. My jewels are perfectly safe!" She was dressed in a beautiful red gown and her face was garishly painted.

Wong Six felt his stomach turn. The eyes that looked into his were glazed and more than a little mad. Brilliant Jade's scarlet lips were pulled back from her teeth in a death's-head grin.

When the familiar faces of Wong Four and Five appeared behind her, Wong Six breathed an audible sigh of relief. The demented girl kicked her feet and screamed as the two took hold of her, but she did not release the treasure she held. Even so, it was no easy task for all of them to carry both her thrashing body and their burdens to the lower level of the house where Master Wong and the others, alerted by the commotion, met them.

Planes buzzed in the distance, a swarm of angry, vengeful hornets, and by the time the group of men managed to

get their unwilling captive back to the eucalyptus grove,
Shanghai was once more under attack. The horror began
anew and yet more of the city perished. Master Wong
knew that sooner or later he must go out into the city to see
for himself the terrible damage being wrought and the
state of affairs in general. In addition to the screams of div-
ing Zeros, the rattle of machine guns, and the explosions,
the thunder of anti-aircraft cannons could be heard. The
din was horrific.

But his family must come first. Joyful Spirit had made a
valiant recovery once their daughter—bruised and dirty,
but safe—had been carried to the grove. Little Mother,
Wong Two's wife, and White Peony showed themselves to
be of much stouter stuff than he would ever have imagined
they might. Alas, it was the men, his five eldest sons, who
caused him the most worry. Wong Three, of course, was
gravely injured, but still his loud moans were more piteous
and constant than need be for a man of courage. In his condition, he could in no way help his wife, who now clung
constantly to Bright Autumn for comfort. Wong One and
Two held their wives and kept their children close, but at
the same time they seemed incapable of definite or inde-
pendent action and looked constantly to him, their father,
for solace and guidance. The unmarried men stayed to
themselves and offered no suggestions, though they were
quick to obey any command. Strangely enough it was the
seven or eight servants who lent the most support. As ever,
they helped soothe the children, prepared cold meals, and
kept themselves generally busy when an attack was not
actually taking place.

Master Wong looked at his family and suddenly realized
he could not afford to become weary or depressed, or give
in to the occasional sharp pains which now plagued him
and rendered him breathless. He must remain resolute
lest his children and the future generations of the House of
Wong perish.

For six days and more the warplanes of covetous Imperial Japan circled and dove down upon the panic-stricken
populace of Shanghai. Thousands were slaughtered as
they tried to escape by train or rivercraft and on foot. Cars,
rickshaws, and pedestrians crowded the streets, sorely
hampering the Kuomintang in its final retreat. The cries

of wounded and dying citizens filled the air and rose to mingle with the acrid stench of fire and destruction.

Then suddenly, it was over. The Chinese army was gone. Every railroad and highway leading out of the city was cut off, obliterated. The mouth of the Yangtze was clogged with corpses, capsized vessels, and floating debris. The only haven of safety which remained was the unscathed International Settlement. Even the arrogant Japanese had not had enough audacity to weather the wrath of the Western world by destroying the foreign community, a community which could now offer protection to few Chinese. Shanghai was finally and unquestionably defeated. The click of soldiers' boots and the rumble of war machinery sounded through the narrow streets once more as the Imperial Japanese Forces took possession of its trophy.

On the seventh day, Master Wong did leave his family and go out on foot into the city. Only his youngest son volunteered to accompany him, and in his wounded pride and disappointment he would not press the others.

The horror that met his eyes beyond the estate gates, the carnage of fire and death, the weeping orphans, the dogs sniffing and then devouring stiffened corpses, tore at his soul. With bleeding hearts, he and Wong Six let their lamentations rise with thousands of others. Nearly as demoralizing as the destruction were the brothels and gambling establishments already preparing to cater to new masters.

Sick at heart, father and son returned to the estate and barred the gates. The ravaged expressions imprinted on their faces as they joined the others smothered all questions.

Master Wong gazed around at the destruction of his own property and then knelt before a small garden shrine and offered up a prayer of thanksgiving. His home, though damaged, was standing and habitable. His family was still drawing in and out the sweet breath of life. Heaven had seen fit to spare the House of Wong, and its master was abundantly grateful.

A fine powdering of plaster dust and slivers of broken glass coated much of the house interior, and for once everyone worked to clean it. Many of the servants had fled the grounds altogether when the city was first attacked, and few had returned. Those of the staff who did remain stared in wonder as Madame Wong briskly put Bright Autumn and her two eldest daughters-in-law to work. Only Brilliant Jade was excused, for she was still addled and not herself. She sat in a daze and only laughed from time to time. Always she clasped a small bauble in one hand.

Madame Wong shook her head in dismay. "I never *did* think that girl was altogether sound," she confided to Bright Autumn. "Her mother also was skittish and too high-strung. I tried to tell your brother, but of course he would not listen!"

The wife of the eldest son, White Peony, was a placid young woman. Moreover, she had come from a much less prestigious and wealthy home than the House of Wong. She needed little encouragement to roll up her sleeves and begin setting the house in order. The other daughter-in-law, Little Mother, was also industrious, but her special gift seemed to be with the children. She distracted them by telling stories and playing games, and thereby calmed them. She also proved an excellent nurse to Wong Three, who could not yet stand on his shattered leg.

Everyone was busy. Madame Wong bustled about as best she could on her tiny bound feet, giving orders and seeing that everything was properly done, while her husband instructed his sons.

"We do not know what will happen next," he told them. "Of one thing we can be sure, however: we can expect no good of the Japanese invaders. Already horrid tales of their atrocities are rampant. For the most part, their planes attacked only strategic targets, but their foot soldiers show no such restraint. We must look carefully after our womenfolk and hide all we can of our valuables.

"Five, you and your youngest brother are to go immediately and dig small trenches here and there around the estate. Map them carefully so we can locate them later. Into these holes you are to put the most precious of our jade and ivory pieces, as well as most of the jewelry and other treasures. Leave only enough in the house to alleviate suspicion. When you have finished, cover the holes up and spread loam carefully over them again."

While this was being done, he and Wong One and Two went down into the cellar and chipped away some of the bricks so that the gold and silver could be secreted behind the walls. This disturbance was also hidden from possible detection behind large casks of rice wine.

On the evening of the eighth day, the family sat gathered, along with the servants, in the large inner court. Electricity had not yet been restored, so torches and oil lamps had been lighted and placed around. Everyone was eating simple food, drinking tea, and enjoying together the first leisure they had known in many, many hours.

Bright Autumn glanced around at the gathering and reflected upon the great equalizer this disaster had proven to be. The servants no longer seemed servants, but simply people, each with a name and individual fears and talents. Looking from face to face, she could almost smile at how similar they all appeared. Her own hair was pulled back and covered with a cotton scarf. Her hands were blistered and her nails split and broken. The day had been extremely humid and she longed to wash the sweat and grime from her flesh.

She let her mind dwell on these simple things in as much depth as possible, for she did not want her greatest fear to surface. During the time the bombs had fallen, she had been tortured by a single thought: *I am going to die without ever seeing Fengmo again! I will never know his love or bear his sons!*

In the hours since, she had been too busy to allow herself the luxury of personal sadness, but now it threatened to grip her again.

Her eldest nephew, a boy of seven, yawned and cuddled against her arm. "Are we slaves now, Aunt?"

"No, dumpling," she murmured, and nuzzled the top of his head.

Wong Four was the first to be alerted to a distant noise. He set his bowl down and leaned forward in a listening attitude. "Shush!" he whispered. "I think vehicles approach!"

Every face in the room grew pale, almost waxen as the sound suddenly became more audible. Large, obviously military vehicles were indeed coming up the drive.

Master Wong came to his feet in a rush. "All you women get yourselves down into the cellar at once! Take the children with you! Go now!"

"I will stay," said Madame Wong flatly. "Who is going to believe a house with no women at all in it, huh? I am old now, and ugly. That will keep me safe enough."

Master Wong gave her a fierce scowl but knew it would accomplish nothing to try and persuade her once she had folded her plump arms across her chest as she had just done.

"I too will stay," said an old female servant, and Master Wong cursed in exasperation. The younger women had no sooner disappeared down the corridor when there came a loud and persistent banging at the front door.

Master Wong went to answer, and this time he did not put on his stupid face, for he knew that the callers who waited would not likely be fooled by his usual charade. Nor did he have any desire to appear humble before the conquerors of Shanghai.

Opening the door, he stood erect and looked into the face of a man perhaps ten years his junior. This man's crisp tan uniform displayed the insignia of a captain of Imperial Japan. All around him were soldiers with raised rifles and fixed bayonets.

"I am Captain Inaka," the man said, "servant of the Great and Immortal Hirohito, Emperor of Japan. This sector of your city is now under my command!"

The captain then clicked his heels and dipped his head in the quickest and least courteous of bows. "Stand aside, Grandfather! I wish to inspect your home as a possible headquarters!"

Master Wong held the door wide and did not even wince as the black boots of the soldiers marched loudly past and across the beautiful tiles of the foyer, leaving rude scuff marks as they went. Nor did his face betray the fearful pounding of his aged heart. Softly, he closed the door and followed them to the inner court.

The other men in the Wong household stood facing Captain Inaka and his men. Even Wong Three had been raised up and leaned against his eldest brother. All maintained resolute expressions. Wong Six alone could not control his features to any great degree. The hatred and contempt were plainly visible in the curl of his lower lip and in the set of his jaw.

The captain stood with his feet planted wide apart and

his arms akimbo as he let his eyes take in the luxurious surroundings. His face registered little emotion, but he could not quite eliminate the awe from his voice. "Wong Cho, the rumors I have heard are true. You do indeed have a worthy home."

Master Wong felt his heart plummet. If this Japanese officer knew his name, then he must also know of the women!

As if reading the other man's mind, Captain Inaka gave his men a rapid series of commands, which sent them fanning out in every direction. He then turned toward Madame Wong and bowed deeply. When he raised his head again, he was wearing a smile that did not reach his snapping black eyes. "You will forgive my troops, Grandmother. They are but courageous fighting men and are not trained in niceties. Do not worry about your litter. They will be safe enough."

Madame Wong did not speak, but inclined her head majestically. In truth, she could not have uttered a word, for she was nearly eaten alive with fear for her children.

"It pains me to expel you and your family from your ancestral home," the captain continued in the same smooth tone, "but you no doubt realize that my men must be quartered somewhere. You cannot expect the victorious to sleep in the streets."

Just then there came the sound of screams and crying from the rear of the house and a few moments later the women and children were herded into the court. White Peony and Little Mother ran weeping to their respective husbands while Bright Autumn stood with her arm protectively about the shoulders of a blank-faced Brilliant Jade.

Master Wong could remain silent no longer. "I protest!" he said with vehemence. "Can you not see all these helpless folk who are under my care? How am I to feed and shelter them if you take my home?"

His belligerent tone alerted the soldiers and they quickly aimed their rifles and glittering bayonets in his direction. Captain Inaka began to walk casually around the room. He looked at each of the Wong sons with cool, contemptuous appraisal.

"These men do not appear helpless to me," he said, as he gently tapped his foot against the bandaged leg of Wong

Three. "I daresay this one can get work readily enough. Perhaps he can hire himself out as a rickshaw driver, or . . ." He paused and smiled. "Come to think, I myself will put him to work on the blockades."

Wong Three stared straight ahead, never flinching, until the captain moved on to the women. He passed each female in turn, stopping to scrutinize only when one was young. Lastly, he planted himself before the place where Bright Autumn stood with Brilliant Jade, who opened her eyes wide and began to whimper.

Captain Inaka gave the frightened girl only a brief glance before turning his full attention on Bright Autumn.

"And to which son do *you* belong?" he asked softly.

"To none," she answered in a clear voice. "I am Bright Autumn, daughter of Wong Cho and betrothed to Chang Fengmo."

The captain put his hand up and caressed his lower lip while his gaze raked the girl before him from head to toe. Then he slowly reached out and plucked away the scarf she wore. Her hair cascaded around her like a blue-black veil and his eyes kindled.

The sudden silence in the room was broken when two of the soldiers laughed in rude anticipation.

The captain turned on them furiously, and the spew of words which issued from his mouth caused both men to pale. However, he did not look at Bright Autumn again. Instead, he stalked officiously back to the center of the room. "I am not heartless," he announced loudly. "A victor is not above showing mercy. Therefore, you may remain, Wong Cho, since you are in your dotage, and your wife and daughter also. But the others, all but the servants, must be gone by dawn tomorrow. In the meantime, my men and I will make camp outside."

He was just about to leave when Brilliant Jade let out an ear-piercing scream. The startled soldiers turned guns on her as she broke away from Bright Autumn and danced wildly toward her mate.

"Wife!" Wong Three cried, and threw out his arms toward her.

But it was too late. The sound of an explosion shattered the air and Brilliant Jade dropped to the floor with a soft thud.

For a heartbeat, the room was silent as the Wong family stared at their fallen member in horror. Then, in mindless rage, Wong Three stumbled toward the soldier who had fired the deadly shot. Chaos ensued.

Bright Autumn stood paralyzed while the life she had known and taken for granted crashed down around her. Amidst the roar of gunfire, she watched her three eldest brothers shot down. White Peony too, and the baby son she held, were pinned by bullets and crumpled into small, motionless heaps.

Bright Autumn's heart fluttered in her breast as Wong Six, that most volatile brother, grappled with one enemy soldier and finally managed to wrench the rifle from his grasp. With a wild cry, he then turned the weapon upon its owner and fired. In the confusion that followed, he leapt across the room and disappeared into a darkened corridor.

Captain Inaka shouted an order that sent his men in immediate pursuit. There were distant yells, several shots, and then an almost deafening silence.

The only sound Bright Autumn heard, and one she was never to forget, was that of her mother weeping.

Chapter Twenty-four

The war had not yet crawled far enough inland for Tanpo to be greatly victimized. Still, the citizens in and around the mountain community could not help but feel the thudding reverberations of China's distress. Communications with the coastal areas had all been eliminated, so that now the most dependable information to be garnered was from the occasional refugees who were just beginning to trickle through on their way farther north. Spring had passed, and summer arrived without any word from Shanghai. There was nothing to do but wait, hope, and offer up prayers to the deities.

Heaven, in its capriciousness, had chosen to compound the tension of current events by visiting upon the province an unusually hot season. As ever happens when the air is hot and sultry, tempers and emotions flared high, especially among the folk who were forced to work for their sustenance. This was true of the peasants upon the land as well as the servants in the great houses of town. While the rich were able to lounge about in cool baths or duck into the inviting recesses of a tea house, the lowborn were forced to toil on.

Crystal was more fortunate than most, for her mistress was mild of temper and undemanding. Nonetheless, the serving girl preferred to be up before dawn's light as usual, and complete as many tasks as possible before the sun reached its sweltering zenith. In this she was not alone. Now, unlike the winter months, the water shed, kitchens, and grounds were beehives of activity in the early hours, with everyone anxious to do what they must and be finished quickly.

On one particular morning toward the end of the sixth

solar month, Crystal, much to her dismay, slept later than was her habit. Opening her eyes and seeing daylight already beginning to filter through the window, she leapt up and quickly threw on her light cotton clothing. Without so much as combing her long braid, she grabbed a large kettle and bolted for the door.

Knowing she would be hard put to get water and have the morning tea prepared before her mistress also rose, Crystal groaned aloud when she saw the group of servants already awaiting their turn before the caldron. Her eyes were still puffy and her mouth dry, and it was all she could do to stand patiently in the steam-filled shed. The other servants seemed a bit out of sorts also, for there was none of the normal jostling and good-natured banter this morning. Everyone simply waited and stepped forward, one at a time, to have their kettles filled and make any special requests they might have for water during the day. Finally, Crystal approached the waterkeeper.

Now, this old gentleman was quite fond of the serving girl, and for her alone he had a bright, toothless smile. "Ah, good morning to you, Crystal!" he beamed. "I wondered where you were. The water for your mistress's bath is all set aside. My sons here will tote it for you straight away if you so desire."

Crystal bowed politely in spite of being harassed. "Thank you, Old Father. You are too kind. Give me perhaps a measure of time and then bid your sons come to the court of my lady."

The keeper nodded and smiled again, thinking not for the first time how much indeed he would like to have this little maid for a daughter-in-law.

Crystal was just about to put her kettle forward and have it filled when she felt herself nudged aside. Her brows beetled in a fierce scowl as she turned and saw the manservant of the Second Son standing there with his own small brass kettle. Without the least hesitation, she bounced back to her original position, thus knocking the surprised Fong Lu back two paces.

"Can you not see I am here?" she asked irritably. "In this house, we servants show a bit of courtesy—not like in the barnyards."

Now this scathing remark seemed totally unnecessary

to Fong Lu, who was also in a rush. Moreover, he had no
intention of being put down by an impudent female, especially not before the waterkeeper and his two grinning
sons. So, pulling himself up with as much dignity as he
could muster, he stepped forward yet again.

"Move aside, woman," he said. "Think you that I am
here on my own account? I serve the Second Son and he is
even now up awaiting some refreshment. He comes first
before *your* mistress, or any female save his own mother!"

Crystal turned her pert nose up and only extended her
kettle toward the waterkeeper. "I will move when I am
done here, bumpkin."

This was too much for Fong Lu who, though not usually
overbearing for his own sake, was nonetheless very demanding on the part of his master. His face flushed. "Do
you not hear well?" he barked. "The young lord is waiting.
Move back I say!"

The old waterkeeper could hardly contain his merriment at this unexpected scene. A low chuckle escaped his
puckered lips, and his face glowed with mirth as he waited
to see who would emerge victorious in this contest of wills.
Crystal slowly lowered her kettle and narrowed her eyes.
Then she did indeed step smartly back, and in so doing
trod heavily—and with malice aforethought—upon Fong
Lu's foot.

"*Pie-e-e-e!*" the manservant exclaimed. "Watch your
step!"

Suddenly, Crystal was all sweetness and light. "Pardon
me," she said in the nicest possible voice. "Did you not bid
me make haste?"

It was Fong Lu who now made his eyes slits. He looked
at her, trying to decide if she was in fact as innocent as she
sounded, or just continuing to be sarcastic. In the end he
decided he must accept her apology, even though he seriously doubted its sincerity. He could do little else before
the cool amusement of the spectators when the maid stood
there as she did with such demure patience.

"Well," he grumbled, his foot throbbing, "there is no
reason you cannot rush without being so clumsy, but I will
forget it this once. You may have your turn in just a moment here."

So saying, he now moved forward and held out his kettle

to the waterkeeper. Unfortunately, this put his back to the smiling Crystal.

A little disappointed at this anticlimax, the waterkeeper was just dipping up his steaming ladle when his eyes fell on Crystal and opened wide. His two sons also smothered simultaneous gasps at what they saw, for that tiny maid had raised up one foot, and she now placed it with some strength against Fong Lu's exposed backside and pushed.

"There, you haughty dog!" she snapped. "Take that for your rudeness!"

Fong Lu pitched forward, kettle in hand, and sprawled face down, barely missing the earthen stove upon which the caldron sat. He lay very still for a moment, and then, gradually, he sat up and finally stood. With no small amount of dignity, he set his little kettle down.

"Never before have I slapped the ears of a female," he said in a deadly quiet tone, "but this will surely be the day."

He reached out swiftly to snatch at Crystal, but even so he was a split second too late. With a wild cry, she threw her empty kettle at his head, barely missing him. Her face a bright and florid red, she then followed with a full-fledged assault. In the storm of flailing arms and doubled fists she began to pummel him about the head and shoulders.

"Take that, you son of a pig!" she screamed. "So you will strike *me*, will you? Take that! And that, you who ought to die! *Ha,* and *ha* again!"

Fong Lu threw up his arms to protect his head from this barrage, but all the while he inched closer to his assailant. Soon,. he found himself exactly where he wished to be.

"Ha, to *you!"* he bellowed, and then grabbed hold of the shrieking maid.

In a single motion, he tossed her over his shoulder like a protesting sack of grain and carried her to a corner of the shed in which reposed a huge barrel of unheated water. He eyed the thing while Crystal continued to kick her legs and beat upon his back.

"You son of a dog!" she squealed. "Son of a turtle! Son of a pig!"

"Cease insulting my ancestors at once, vixen!"

"Put me down, you son of a foul—"

Her sentence was cut in two as he swung her down and, with great dexterity, plunged her into the barrel of cold water. Forcing her head beneath the surface, he held it there for several seconds before he turned and walked away.

Casually, he retrieved his kettle and extended it one final time. "Please, Old Father," he said courteously, "might I now have that water? My young sir awaits his morning tea."

So saying, he was indeed given his water. Ignoring the sputtering and cursing emanating from the corner of the shed, he left.

The night was hot, but less so on the lake upon whose bank sat the tea house on the Street of the Golden Bridge. Around the lake were colored lanterns, and upon its surface flat boats. Aboard one of these pleasure crafts were Master Chang, his two eldest sons, and Sean Duncan. There was also a cook, preparing delicacies over a small brazier, and two flower girls, Sweet Harmony and a girl named Orange Blossom. These beautiful young women served wine and food while the men reclined upon large cushions and talked.

"So far we have been most fortunate," said Master Chang. "I hear the army is a little to the east of our mountains but not yet inclined to move up through the passes. For this I thank the gods. We need no soldiers in Tanpo!"

"You cannot fight a war without soldiers, Father," Fengmo reminded him. "If the Japanese continue to swarm inland, you will no doubt be glad to have troops nearby."

The older man snorted. "You say! Where the army is, there is fighting also. Tanpo needs none of it. When soldiers are about, no woman can be safe. They are not honorable men, even if they *are* needed. Moreover, there is nothing strategic here in this isolated place to interest generals. Perhaps we will remain at peace."

"There are crops in Tanpo," interjected the reserved Sean. "No army can exist for long without food. Forgive my saying so, sir, but I fear the peace we enjoy cannot last long, not with three armies on the loose."

To this Master Chang reluctantly nodded. Over the past

weeks he had learned to like the young American very much. He also respected his guest's opinions, which seemed always to be based on sound knowledge, regardless of their quiet expression.

"I too fear," said the older man, "though I cannot help but hope. Which army, I wonder, will first appear at our gates? Pray it not be the Japanese, but who is to say our own are much better? I do not know whom I dread more, the Kuomintang or those brave and wily bastards who follow Mao. They are said to hit and then run like thieves in the night. Courageous they may be against the enemy, but I hear too that they stir up the peasants wherever they go."

Thus far Kao had spoken hardly at all, for he had been too busy feeding his voracious appetite and tickling the sole of Sweet Harmony's shoe. But at the mention of peasants, he perked up and smiled disdainfully. "If you need to know anything about the peasants, be sure to ask Little Brother here," he scoffed. "He is forever out upon the land these days, poking his long nose around and stirring things up himself."

"I do not stir up the peasants, Kao," said Fengmo mildly. "I only wish to see how they fare. It is pleasant sometimes to walk along the fields and see our own people busily tending the soil."

"Well, our father has land stewards to attend to such tasks, and they do not need your help, I am sure. No doubt they, and the farmers too, think you are a spy."

Fengmo's brow furrowed and he was about to retort when Master Chang motioned them both to be silent. He looked from one son to the other. Lately, he was becoming very concerned about his eldest son, and this seemed as good a time as any to bring him down a notch.

"It would not hurt you to also stir yourself a bit, Kao," he said. "As eldest you should be taking more interest in our family enterprises."

This rebuke, administered before his younger brother and the despicable foreigner, caused Kao to flush with annoyance. His resentment increased as his father continued.

"Not only that," said the elder Chang. "Of late I perceive you spend far too much time in tea houses." He cast a quick but pointed look at the flower girls. "You would do better to expend your time and vital juices at home where you belong. I daresay if you do not get me a grandson soon, you will lose the privacy and freedom you now seem to enjoy so much."

His meaning could not but be clear to all those present. And seeing the sudden pallor of his Second Son's face, Master Chang would have retrieved his last words had he been able.

"You are unfair to me, Father," Kao whined. "I believe you favor Fengmo over me. Here I am, stuck with a cold, hateful wife, while you give my brother a modern, warm-blooded wench from Shanghai. It is not fair to me at all!"

Looking sideways at Sweet Harmony, Kao pouted and did not see the angry and piercing eyes his brother turned in his direction. But Master Chang saw, and so did Sean Duncan.

Sean was nothing if not an astute observer, and he now knew the truth of what he had suspected for weeks. He had not found it surprising that, since arriving home, Fengmo had become more withdrawn and restive, for everyone was worried about the Wong family. Neither was there any doubt in his mind that Fengmo felt overwhelming and genuine concern for the safety of his betrothed. Without any solid news from Shanghai there was great question about the welfare of Bright Autumn. Sean fretted too for the safety of his own family.

But all the same, in Fengmo's case, Sean soon came to realize there was something more, some unspoken sorrow troubling the other man. Watching the Chang family interrelate, he soon began to speculate about his friend and the wife of Kao. Now, studying the unhappy face of Fengmo, he knew he had speculated correctly.

My two best friends, he sadly thought, have both been wounded to the soul by love. Yet here sit I, also wounded, because I know nothing of love at all!

Golden Willow searched along the teakwood shelves of the library for a book which might hold her interest through the long, sultry afternoon. Though she had bathed but a short time before, she could feel the trickle of perspiration behind her ears and on her forehead. Her clothes were already damp and uncomfortable.

Seeing nothing on the lower shelves that intrigued her, she stood back and let her eyes scan those farther up. One at a time, she read the titles of classics and historicals, but none suited her mood on this occasion. She sought some lighter diversion, something that could be read in a short time for simple entertainment, a book of spirit tales perhaps, or a foreign picture book. Then, in the corner of a very high shelf, she saw a tome bound in red silk. It appeared very old, and no title showed along its binding. Not having noticed this book before, she was curious. So, pulling a stool over, she climbed upon it and stretched. Even then she had to stand on tiptoes before she finally managed to extract the volume from its neighbors. After blowing a thin layer of dust away, she proceeded to open it without bothering to come down from her perch.

The first page, done in delicate watercolors, met her eyes and she gasped, for there in perfect detail was the likeness of a man and woman entwined in the act of passion. Though both figures were clothed, the woman's breasts were bared and the man was lapping one delicate nipple with the tip of his tongue.

Golden Willow blushed, but at the same time she was stirred in a way she had never been before. She knew without a doubt that the book she held was forbidden, and yet she could not prevent her fingers turning the next page, and the next.

Her eyes took in every nuance of the paintings, and the blood began coursing rapidly through her veins. Her body tingled strangely. She did not connect this erotic art in any way with what she knew of Kao. No, the man who still came and slavered on her each month bore no resemblance to the men she saw displayed on these pages. The women they held wore expressions of rapture, as if they were being transported by delight to some unearthly paradise. Nor did they look like courtesans or harlots. Rather, they were dressed and coiffured as ancient women of wealth and breeding must have been.

She had no idea of how long she had been standing there transfixed when the sound of approaching footsteps brought her back to reality. With trembling hands, she quickly put the book back on the shelf, but she still had not come down off the stool when a tall, masculine figure appeared at the door.

So it was that when Fengmo entered the library, he saw Golden Willow, all flushed and trembling. When their eyes met, he was taken aback by the fever of her gaze, and in a rush his own vigorous body responded. His heart was like thunder in his ears as the agony of his desire became almost insurmountable. His knees threatened to give way as he took several steps toward her.

"My son . . ." The voice of Master Chang drifted to them from the corridor, and a moment later that illustrious gentleman walked in. His eyes widened in surprise as he looked from Golden Willow to Fengmo. The air about him was so charged with tension, it was all he could do not to shout out his alarm.

Golden Willow was the first to regain a semblance of composure. "Excuse me, Father Chang." She came down from the stool and bowed deeply. Her cheeks were scarlet. "I came to return a book and will be gone now." So saying, she nearly ran from the room.

Master Chang turned to his son and spoke with a mildness he in no way felt. "I have been going over the inventory list of our largest warehouse, my son, and I have no idea of what we are going to do with all those boar bristles we normally ship to Shanghai. Do you think . . ." His voice trailed away, for looking at the miserable countenance of his son, he could not go on. The pain of that young man was palpable.

"Father." Fengmo murmured only that single word, but it held a world of pleading. Shoulders slumped and defeated, he also left the room.

Master Chang remained standing there for a long time. *I must rectify this situation*, he decided vehemently, *for it cannot continue as it is for a moment longer!*

Having made a decision, he stalked out of the library and through the courts with resolute strides. The servants and children who saw him pass were almost frightened by the stern expression on his face.

He did not pause to knock upon the door of his eldest son's apartment, but instead threw it open and entered unannounced. A male servant nervously approached, a fel-

low with a sallow complexion and quick darting eyes.
"May I help you, Master?" he said. "The young sir was out
until the wee hours and he is still abed."

The face of Master Chang grew even more thunderous.
"Well, bid him rise at once!"

After the servant had scurried away, the older man
paced back and forth in the sitting room, his restless irritation only increased by the loud complaining he soon heard
emanating from the bedchamber.

A few moments later Kao appeared at the door. "What
emergency is this, Father?" he asked, yawning. "I was
having the sweetest dream when this nasty lout ended it
all!"

By this time, the servant Kao indicated was busy making tea, but his thin, furtive face was alert and listening.
Master Chang saw this and turned a malevolent gaze on
him. "Be gone," he said. "I would have private words with
my eldest son."

Immediately the servant rushed out the front door, no
doubt anxious to spread a morsel of gossip to the rest of the
household.

Master Chang took a seat and turned his full attention
on his son.

Still unconcerned, Kao yawned again and began to
scratch himself. His large, soft body was slowly turning to
fat and there were lines of debauchery around his mouth
and eyes.

Master Chang felt sick with disgust, but forced himself
to speak quietly. "It is time for you to put some meaning in
your life, Kao," he said. "I can no longer tolerate your lax
habits."

Kao blinked several times and shook his head. "What do
you mean, Father? I have done nothing."

"Nothing is right!" retorted his father. "You are lazy in
the extreme these days, and I will have no more. You are
fullgrown, and it is time you played the part."

Kao rubbed his scalp in confusion and tried to make his
drowsy mind come to terms with what he was hearing. Finally, he decided it best to employ a tactic which often
worked when he was forced to deal with his mother. Almost without effort, he allowed his lower lip to quiver
slightly.

"I can see you are mightily upset, Father. But what have I done wrong? There I was, sleeping in my bed, all peaceful and quiet, and now you pounce upon me as if I had committed some terribly wicked deed!"

Master Chang's brows knitted in vexation. "Kao, there will be no discussion. You are going to do as I command without argument or question."

He cleared his throat. "Firstly, you will return to the court of your wife without further delay."

Kao's eyes opened wide. "But, Father, you do not know—"

"Quiet!"

Kao sniffed and two great tears squeezed from his eyes.

"Secondly," Master Chang continued, "you will begin at once to make yourself useful. I will expect you to appear in my office on Bantam Street in the morning—*early!*"

Taking no notice of his son's ignoble tears, the master of the House of Chang then rose and walked out of the apartment.

Chapter Twenty-five

Captain Masaru Inaka considered himself a civilized man. Now, standing before a mirror in the suite that had once belonged to Wong Cho and Joyful Spirit, he gazed at his reflection critically. His dark hair showed only a few silver strands along forehead and temples; his face was still smooth except for a single deep crease between his heavy jet-colored brows. The whites of his eyes were pure and clear. Only his mouth seemed unsatisfactory, for when he smiled, the corners of his lips turned down instead of upward.

"Why, you look like a fierce tiger when you smile," a geisha girl had once told him, thinking to please him with a compliment.

Indeed, in those days he had been content to look like a leering tiger, but now his fearsome countenance was a burden and an irritation to him.

Not that he wanted to look like a lamb, mind you. No, his men would never respond to a sweetly smiling simpleton. But how was he to convince the desirable Wong daughter that he was at least human if his very smile was threatening?

Slowly, Masaru turned and admired the muscles of his arms and bare upper torso. It was a passionate body he scrutinized, with blood still roaring through its veins. Few men of thirty could have boasted such a trim physique. Women from Tokyo to New York City had sprawled beneath it and sighed their pleasure. Only Bright Autumn, that ravishing and stubborn Chinese enchantress, seemed immune.

Masaru Inaka cursed himself for a fool. *Why do I not just take her and be done with it?*

But he knew he would not—not unless it became absolutely necessary. He was a warrior and a patriot, not an animal! He liked to bed a willing female who thrashed only in *genuine* throes of ecstasy. So had he imagined Bright Autumn doing hundreds of times over the past weeks, and each time his body had nearly exploded with desire. In all his fifty-one years he could not recall wanting a woman more than he did this girl in the House of Wong. He ground his teeth in frustration just thinking about it.

Giving his flat belly a soft slap, he turned away from the mirror and walked into the bedchamber, with its large canopied bed. He hated that bed and, in fact, refused to sleep in it. Instead, each night he rolled out a futon and rested peacefully on the floor.

His uniform hung neatly in the wardrobe, and as he leisurely put it on, he continued to think of Bright Autumn. Yes, he decided, sooner or later I must have her, but if not tonight—well, I still have my small pleasures!

Wong Cho looked furtively to the right and left before lifting the large brass knocker on the mission compound gate. There was no one in sight except a lone beggar sleeping against one wall. It was several minutes before the gate opened. The wizened face of an old woman peeked out through a narrow crack. Her hooded eyes were alert and suspicious.

"What do you want?" she asked. "The foreigners are gone from here and will not be back for a very long time—if ever."

"I do not seek the white people," Wong Cho informed her haughtily. "Let me in, woman. I wish to speak with the Chinese god-man, Long Han."

Hearing his exalted way of speaking and seeing the fine suit he wore, the old woman reluctantly swung the gate open just far enough to admit him. Once he had squeezed through, she quickly closed it again.

"You will find him in the last building on your left," she grumbled. "He still teaches school, though I do not know why. It is a waste of time for these tykes to cram their heads with learning when the world is coming to an end!"

Wong Cho ignored this fatalism and pointed his steps immediately in the direction she had indicated. He passed several small and apparently deserted buildings, but as he neared the last he could hear the voices of children reciting mathematical equations. Looking through an open window, he saw a small classroom with no more than eight young students gathered around the thin figure of Long Han.

"Very good," Long Han said to them as he spied the face of his visitor. He motioned to a boy of about ten. "Now, Chen, you will take over, please. Have your classmates repeat each problem three times. I must be gone for a few minutes." So saying, he handed the boy a text and made his way out the door.

"Good day, Master Wong," he greeted. There was a bright smile on his face. "I am glad to see you are safe in these troublesome times."

Master Wong was a bit surprised, if pleased, to note the healthy color in Long Han's cheeks, for the last time he had seen him, the young man had looked quite ghastly and sick.

"Come," Han invited, "let us sit over in the shade. I am sorry there is no tea to offer you. Our supplies are quite limited here, as you might well imagine."

Once they were settled on a wooden bench, the older man looked around at the dusty yard and unkept buildings. "Are those little ones the only students you have left?"

Han nodded. "There are no others whose parents can afford to pay now. The ones here have no kin and so I care for them." He frowned with worry. "How much longer I can do so I do not know, for there is little money to feed and clothe them now that the American sir and his wife have gone."

"And what happened to Sean's parents?"

Han looked even more downcast. "After the bombings they went to the International Settlement and have now left for their homeland. They were very distraught at leaving without Sean."

"Was there no way for them to contact him? Surely foreigners are not cut off so completely as we are." Wong Cho awaited an answer to his query with the utmost trepidation, for it concerned his very reason for calling.

"Perhaps they could have," Han replied, "but they chose not to try. You see, they are very disappointed in their son right now. They believe he has no real interest in the ministry. Indeed, they are right. Sean cares not for the *work* as they do—or as I do."

Han continued without any implied criticism in his voice. "Sean has not found his true calling yet, but when he does, I strongly suspect it will not be in the Christian ministry."

The smile returned to his face as he looked closely at Wong Cho. "Now then, sir, why have you come? Can I help you in some way? You look more than a little worried."

Long Han was right; the face of his guest, which was usually so composed, was now creased with an anxiety even the wily Wong Cho was unable to hide.

In brief terms, the older man brought his companion up to date on the tragedy and present dilemma of his own family.

"And now," he finished, "I have those vultures in my own home! After my elder sons were killed, and my daughters-in-law, and my baby grandson"—tears formed in Wong Cho's eyes—"their captain relented and let us all remain in certain damaged rooms of the house. My sons are forced to do hard labor but allowed to sleep with the rest of us—all except my sixth. I know not his fate. Only my daughter, Bright Autumn, has rooms to herself."

Long Han flushed. "I am truly sorry, sir."

Wong Cho saw at once what the other man was thinking and hastened to correct the misconception. "No, no, Han! My daughter has not been shamed, and that is exactly why I am here. I need to know if you are able to send messages by way of the foreign community. I can only hope your collar helps get you in to them, for I myself dare not try to contact those acquaintances I used to have. It is urgent I get a message to Tanpo."

"It might be done," said Han thoughtfully. "I have been thinking of trying to send a letter to Sean and Fengmo for some time." He looked up and smiled. "Yes, I am quite sure it can be arranged through an old friend of mine who still remains in Shanghai—if I use care. What message do you wish me to send?"

Wong Cho stood up feeling many pounds lighter than when he had first come. "Tell Chang Fengmo only this when you write to him: say that Bright Autumn is leaving Shanghai within a fortnight and will be enroute to Tanpo."

Long Han stood also. "There is nothing else you wish to say?"

"No. I do not want you to put anything on paper that might endanger you more than necessary. Tell him only that she comes to him for safekeeping."

For several moments Long Han looked into the troubled eyes of his companion. "Be of good cheer, sir," he encouraged. "I will do all for you that is in my power."

Wong Cho put a hand deep into his jacket and pulled out a leather pouch. "Here is some money in the event you need it."

But Long Han pushed the offering aside. "My friend in the settlement is a man of the cloth," he said. "His is also an honorable soul. No bribe will be needed in order to convince him to do a good deed."

"Perhaps not," Wong Cho said. "Nonetheless, I think your little ones could use a few tea leaves and some wholesome meat. Keep this as my contribution to their welfare. The future of our nation will depend upon those young lives."

That evening, as Bright Autumn went in to bid her parents a good night, her father drew her aside. The two of them then had a hurried and whispered conversation. At first she shook her head violently, but finally, pale of face, she nodded and bowed in acquiescence. Her steps were slow and thoughtful as she walked down the corridor to her own rooms. As usual, she ignored the soldiers who stood on duty outside the captain's door.

Later, as she lay soaking in a tub of soapy water, rubbing a fragrant sponge over her glistening body, she did not feel the hungry eyes which were devouring her flesh.

High above her head, secreted in the rafters, lay Masaru Inaka, captain of the Imperial Japanese Forces. His bold black eyes stared lasciviously down through a tiny aperture that had been cut through the decorative ceiling, and fixed themselves, unblinking, upon the beautiful vision below. It was almost suffocating, and even though he reclined naked over the rough beams, sweat poured from his body. Saliva puddled at the corners of his thin lips as he watched Bright Autumn bathe. And, as she finally came up out of the water, he had to bite his own hand to keep from crying out in ecstasy.

Chapter Twenty-six

While war raged along the coast and the Japanese nudged inland, finding a fiercer and more obstinate resistance than ever they had anticipated, Tanpo continued in relative peace. Weekly, the number of refugees increased, but few seemed disposed to linger in the mountain valley. They all talked of the "North" and the "Caves."

But if war had not yet come to Tanpo, neither was there peace in the House of Chang. No, the great ancestral home was chock-full of dissension and minor skirmishes that brought the illustrious lord and master of that habitation near to pulling his hair out in vexation. The domestic strife among the servants alone was enough to make a man gnash his teeth to powder.

Gradually, even under the stern eyes of Madame Chang, the battle between Crystal and Fong Lu became contagious. The female servants sided with Crystal, while the men, ever mindful of their superiority, took a firm stance in favor of Fong Lu. This situation eventually got quite out of hand. The female half of the staff refused to cooperate with their counterparts. Husbands were sullen and received nothing but hostility from their wives. Each faction retaliated with the utmost lack of courtesy. At one point, Madame Chang called the entire group together and castigated them soundly.

"What nonsense," she had said from her high chair in the audience hall. "I know not the source of this contention, but it must not continue, for the whole house suffers."

She had gone on to harangue them in her imperious way about duty and loyalty, but the set of their jaws and belligerent expressions told her the lecture was all but wasted. Finally, in a state of great frustration, she had gone to her husband. Together they dissected the situation.

"It would appear to be a battle of the sexes," Master Chang mused. "Therefore, let us each approach one half of a couple. You speak to Li Ma, and I will call that fat cook of ours and see what I can wheedle from him."

At first this ploy did not work, for by then the issues were clouded. Li Chi, the cook, ranted on at length about the females getting "above themselves," while Li Ma spoke of all the men as "tyrants." It took a great deal of convoluted probing on the part of both master and mistress to get at the kernel of truth they sought. Once the meat of rumor and high emotions had been stripped away, however, and the bone of the matter clearly revealed, a second strategy was immediately implemented.

Both Madame Chang and her husband chose trustworthy emissaries to carry out their intrigues. Li Ma was cajoled and at last convinced to go to the feminine champion as a peacemaker.

"That Fong Lu," the old woman remarked to Crystal, "what a caution he is! He told my old man that he is miserably sorry for what he did to you in the water shed."

Crystal was attentive. "Is this true? Then why has he not told me so? I am the one he abused. A dozen times and more I have seen him, and he is always the same—just like a barnyard rooster! His haughty nose is always in the air!"

"What!" Li Ma opened her eyes wide. "Surely you do not expect a *man* to apologize! You know what males are, just like little boys. Still, my old man tells me that this servant to the Second Son is quite miserable indeed. His eyes are all bloodshot when he comes to breakfast of a morning. He can hardly forgive his loathsome self for putting hands upon an innocent and weak woman, particularly one as little and pretty as you—*especially* when you were right all along!"

Crystal sniffed in agreement.

For Master Chang's part, he did not pick Li Chi as his ambassador, for he knew the cook was too volatile and not nearly subtle enough. Instead, he chose the ancient gardener, who agreed without protest and swore himself to secrecy.

The old man, who loved harmony above anything, sought out Fong Lu one evening and offered to share a bit of gossip.

"I can hardly credit what I heard this morning," the gardener confided. "It concerns that little maid who serves in the court of the eldest son."

"Crystal," grunted Fong Lu disgustedly.

"Yes, yes," said the oldster. "I hear the girl is all aflutter and upset these days on account of what she did to you in the water shed."

Fong Lu looked at the guileless old man closely and then snorted. "Well now, I find *that* more than hard to believe. Crystal is no true female, she is a fox in disguise. I would not be in the least surprised to learn she is plotting a murder."

"Oh!" gasped the gardener. "Surely you must be wrong about her character. Why, I heard that she weeps of a night and tells anyone who will listen how ashamed she is for being so bad tempered. After her display in the shed, she fears no man will ever have her and that she will die a spinster for sure."

The old man sighed deeply. "Oh me, she is probably right. I certainly would not want a wife who could scald my hide off simply by speaking. No, I would not want such a one, no matter how fair she might be. Still, it is a shame that she will probably never get a husband. She certainly is lamenting the poor judgment she displayed on that day. I hear she told one of the other maids that she is especially sorry because she can see now how right you were on that occasion."

Fong Lu gave this some thought before answering. "Well, in that she is at least correct! It serves her right to suffer for her rash personality."

Even so his tone was less vehement.

So it was that domestic tranquility was restored to the staff. From that time on, whenever Fong Lu and Crystal happened to find themselves in the same place at the same time, which proved to be surprisingly often, they looked at each other shyly. Crystal began to make a great show of

feminine reticence, while Fong Lu proudly and magnani-
mously played the role of solicitous male.

It was not very surprising then that Golden Willow
called to Crystal one day and put forth a question. "I know
how you feel about marriage, Crystal," she began, "and I
would not have you think I would ever break my promise.
You shall never be forced to marry anyone who displeases
you, nor anyone at all if you choose not. But since you have
had an offer, it is my obligation to put it to you and return
an answer to the matchmaker."

"Of course, Mistress." Crystal kept her head lowered
and Golden Willow could not see her face.

"Very well then. I have been asked to give you in marriage to one Fong Lu, servant to the Second Son. I know he
used to work in the barnyard and that you think him quite
uncouth. I, therefore, assume you wish me to return a negative answer at once."

"No, Mistress." Crystal looked up with tears in her eyes.
"No, Mistress, I will allow you to give my troth."

Golden Willow grew alarmed at the tears and the quivering voice of her servant. "Oh, Crystal! You need not cry
and you need not accept the lout!"

Wiping her eyes, Crystal began to laugh in a high, sweet
voice. "Mistress, I accept Fong Lu freely."

Golden Willow sat back in surprise, causing the serving
girl to laugh harder still. "Do not look so!" Crystal said.
"We women are changeable creatures, after all. And Fong
Lu is no more a lout than most men. In fact, Mistress, I
think he might be a bit better than most."

So it was quickly arranged. There was great festivity
among the staff. Fong Lu's aged parents and elder brothers came in out of their fields and witnessed the brief but
gay ceremony. Delighted to see his servant so happy,
Fengmo gave the couple a tiny rear room and court within
the compound as their own special abode. No wedding gift
could have been more appreciated.

On their wedding night, the couple lay side by side on a
soft pallet, fulfilled and content. Fong Lu could not believe
his good fortune. He knew he would never be able to completely forget the terrible ordeal that had occurred in
Shanghai, but with Crystal to share his life, he could at
least bury the past and put it far from him.

Crystal snuggled beneath the arm of her new husband and sighed. "How I wish my dear mistress could know such joy." She laughed softly. "And to *think* I believed the doings of all men with women were totally vile!"

Fong Lu held her tighter and with his free hand stroked the silky smoothness of her breasts. "Is your mistress so unhappy then?"

"More than unhappy!" Crystal's voice was suddenly harsh. "That eldest son is a monster! Do not speak of it, but he used to be quite violent with my lady, though not any longer. He does not usually come home until very late these days, and then he is falling down from intoxication."

Thinking of his new happiness and how it had come about, Fong Lu chuckled. "It would seem to me violence is not always so bad. Did you not beat me soundly? And look where it has brought us!"

"Humph! What a barbarian you were, Lu. It is very fortunate that you had the good sense to be contrite."

Fong Lu's eyes had been half-shut, but now they flew open and he sat upright, releasing his embrace. "Indeed, woman, I was not contrite one bit! And why should I have been, seeing how righteous I was? It was you who sought and needed forgiveness."

Crystal sat up now too. Her uncoiled hair fell about her shoulders and down her back in disarray. She spoke softly. "There is no need for you to be so proud now, My Lord. A good man is no less so for humility. It was wrong on my part to remind you of your shame."

Fong Lu ground his teeth. "Hear me, Wife of Mine, I was never a bit sorry! That old gardener told me of your weeping, and it seemed only right to forgive you. I married you too, so you would not continue to suffer."

Crystal stared at him through the gloom and narrowed her eyes. "Why, you turtle's egg. I—"

But Fong Lu clapped a hand over her mouth and smiled down into her face. "I believe we have been the victims of a hoax," he said. "But let us forgive each other truly now. I like a little temper in a woman, and as long as you do not insult my ancestors I promise not to beat you."

She looked long at him and then gently bit the palm he held against her lips. "Nor I you," she replied.

They reclined again, and when they had finished laughing, they came together once more.

"No, Moon Shadow!" The voice of Madame Chang was very firm. "I have told you no, and no again. You are an unmarried maid and you cannot be alone with that foreign devil! No!"

"But M'ma, I would not be alone. New Moon can also learn the foreign tongue. Besides, *Shawn Dooncan* is not a devil! He is simply an American. My father and Second Brother think him very fine. In fact, I heard Fengmo tell Kao this white man is *almost* Chinese!"

Madame Chang rubbed her temples. "Moon Shadow, you are a very headstrong and disrespectful girl. Your elder sister is wiser than you and she does not wish to study the English. Moreover, she too is unwed. It would not be seemly. Go now and interest yourself in sewing or painting pretty flowers. Be gone, child. *Shooo!*"

Moon Shadow did not move. She wanted very much to stamp her feet in frustration. Then suddenly her face lighted in a half-smile. "There is my sister-in-law, M'ma. Golden Willow is a great one for books and acquiring knowledge. She is safely wed and therefore would be a chaperon of merit. No doubt she will leap at the opportunity to gain more wisdom."

Madame Chang looked closely at the countenance of her youngest daughter, but all she saw was the sweet and innocent visage of a child.

"Well, perhaps," she conceded. "That foreigner should work a bit harder for his keep in any case. We shall see what we shall see."

Not daring to wait, Moon Shadow bowed deeply. "Thank you, M'ma. I am sure you will do what is best and wise."

She walked from the room with great aplomb, but the very instant she left her mother's courtyard, she lifted the hem of her robe and flew. A happy giggle bubbled up out of her as she hurried to put forth her idea to Golden Willow.

"Shawn Dooncan," she sang to herself, over and over
again. *"Shawn Dooncan!"*

The letters, both in a single, very soiled package, had
been handed from hand to hand enroute to the House of
Chang. But for all its crumpled appearance and faded
calligraphy, no parcel could have been received with
more relief and anticipation than that one from war-torn
Shanghai. Long Han's message to Fengmo was read aloud
to the family after the evening meal, and its contents
brought tears to the eyes of the listeners. In plain words,
the author described the horror of the enemy bombing and
the oppression which followed. The Chang family wept for
their countrymen and for the nation itself as the true nature of war and what it entailed came home to them. A
heavy sense of mingled guilt and gratitude affected them
all when they thought of the comparative peace they were
still able to enjoy. At the same time, each tremulously
wondered how long that peace could possibly last. Only the
brief and hopeful message that Bright Autumn, Fengmo's
intended, was alive and would soon be escaping provided
them a moment of rejoicing.

That night, after most had gone to their beds and fallen
into fretful and uneasy slumbers, Fengmo and Sean sat together in the small courtyard they now shared. By the
light of an oil lantern, they digested the contents of Han's
private letter to Sean as he read it aloud:

Is it wicked to think that some good can come even
from a thing as evil and vile as war? I hope not, for a
strange and unexpected good has come to me. The Lord
God does indeed work in mysterious ways, my friend, for
He has seen fit to give me, amidst all this misfortune, a
new direction for my life.

Looking into the faces of my little flock, I can hardly
hold fast to my own personal woe. Though I shall never
forget the face and soft voice of your sister, the needs
of these children bring me up out of myself. Their hearts
are tender and bruised and they would surely be lost
without me.

Sean looked up from the letter with misted eyes.

"He is finally healed," Fengmo said. "It is good."

To this Sean made no reply. As he smoked his pipe, his head tilted in the peculiar way Fengmo had grown accustomed to. He looked with unfathomable eyes at the star-studded sky. Several minutes passed before he shook himself a little and spoke. "I sometimes wonder why I am here."

The faraway tone of voice and the expression on his friend's face caused Fengmo alarm. "You are welcome here always, Sean. Your presence is a great source of comfort and enjoyment to me."

"I did not mean here, in this particular place." The American fleetingly smiled. "I was speaking of my life in general. There seems no meaning to it at times, no substance. I want something, and yet I do not know what it is."

"You have a worthwhile work," Fengmo said in an attempt to give comfort. "It is more than many men can boast."

Sean looked at him. "I do not intend to pursue the ministry, Fengmo. It would appear I have sorely mischosen my vocation, for to me it seems gross and presumptuous, even egotistical, for an alien like myself to go about telling an ancient people they are damned unless they forsake the ways of their ancestors. No, I must set my feet on a different path."

"You are a gifted teacher and a scholar," Fengmo offered. "Even my mother, who hates all foreigners, must be impressed or she would never have allowed you to tutor my sister and the wife of my brother."

Sean chuckled, and now his eyes shone with his usual enthusiasm. "The latter is a very adept pupil indeed. As for your sister, Moon Shadow, I often wonder why she has taken on so difficult a project as the study of English."

"She has a penchant for *all* things foreign, I fear," Fengmo said, and he also smiled. "An attitude which has always vexed my parents sorely."

Later, lying in bed and unable to sleep, Sean thought of the youngest Chang daughter and at the same time sternly rebuked himself for the direction those thoughts took.

"She is only a child," he grumbled. "Only a very young and pretty child."

Chapter Twenty-seven

Bright Autumn was simply and plainly clad in a robe of plum-colored silk. The dark hue of the fabric was not her best color, for her complexion was more suited to light shades—yellows and leafy spring greens, or purest white. Neither was the robe cut in modern form-fitting fashion. From the high neck it hung straight down and had wide concealing sleeves, with no ornamentation of buttons or trim whatsoever. There were no bracelets upon her wrists, nor rings on her fingers, nor bobs in her shell-like ears. Her long, lustrous hair was pulled severely back from her oval face and wound into a large knot at her nape.

Even so, she was beautiful.

Her exquisite eyes were always softly aglow and the shape of her head was noble. Though untouched by paint, her clearly defined lips were full and dark pink. The graceful and free stride with which she carried herself could not be confined or hidden beneath any amount of flowing cloth. Her young breasts tilted upward, ever drawing the masculine eye.

Captain Inaka approached her as she stood looking out a window. They were in the room that had once been used to entertain her friends. At that moment, she was remembering the time she had first tried to convince the shy boy from Tanpo to dance. No music came from the radio these days, however. It was even now broadcasting war news and propaganda of Japanese victories. A small group of petty officers stood talking in one corner of the room, and every now and again one would laugh or gesture and then continue talking in the language Bright Autumn did not understand, yet hated. Her own parents were in the room also. They seemed to have aged years over the past weeks.

Her fourth and fifth brothers sat on either side of the couple, dressed in the rough cotton clothing they toiled in all day long. None of her family smiled. They conversed in quiet, unobtrusive tones among themselves, glancing furtively from time to time at the men who had taken over their home, their eyes unreadable.

"The monsoon has finally abated," Captain Inaka said. She could feel his breath against her neck. "Soon the sun will shine again."

Bright Autumn made no comment. Keeping her eyes forward, she tried to concentrate on the rivulets of rain streaming down the windowpane. Outside, the wind still howled, though with less force than it had during the preceding week. The presence beside her was odious and she suppressed a shiver.

Captain Inaka ignored her silence. Lifting his booted foot and propping it carelessly on the arm of an ebony chair, he too looked out at the stormy night. Every now and again the sky would flicker with distant lightning, casting eerie shadows over the face of the girl standing next to him.

"In three days, I am having a gathering here," he said. "Many of my fellow officers have accepted my invitation to come and dine. Some will be escorting women, of course, ladies they have selected from among your own country-women."

Bright Autumn turned cold eyes upon him. "Flower girls and whores."

The captain smiled his fierce smile. "Not all. More than a few come from illustrious families like your own. My general resides with a daughter from the House of Sung. I believe you are acquainted with her."

Her stomach tightened and turned sick. Hibiscus had been one of her closest friends. She wanted to turn and walk away from this man whom she hated above all, but her father's words kept echoing in her mind. "You must lure him, daughter," Master Wong had said, "but slowly, so that he does not suspect. Play the fisherman, and at exactly the right instant we shall *all* set the hook."

Captain Inaka cleared his throat. "I wish you to be my hostess on the important occasion. I have been very generous with your family—on your account. Is it asking too much that you reciprocate? I have not pressed you, as you well know I could."

There it was again, the threat against her family. Lately those threats, thinly veiled, had become more and more blatant. In the beginning Bright Autumn had been nearly paralyzed with fear, at every moment expecting the captain to force himself upon her, at gunpoint if necessary. Had he done so, she had silently vowed in advance to take her own life. If she could not go to her beloved pure and chaste, her life would mean nothing to her in any case.

But the captain had not forced himself, a fact which surprised her greatly. Finally, the character of this enemy began to dawn upon her, or at least she thought so. Though Captain Masaru Inaka was the murderer of her family and completely vile to her, he was apparently not a rapist. She suspected that his ego had helped keep him at bay this long—and something else too; there was a smoothness about him, an almost savage delicacy that hinted of sinister appetites. When he spoke to her, though it was in nearly perfect Chinese, his cadence was twisting and coated with hidden innuendo. The way he looked at her left her feeling vulnerable, nude, much like a butterfly pinned live in a display case. Never had Bright Autumn feared any man like she did the one now standing beside her. The only thing greater than her fear was her revulsion.

"I am waiting," he said impatiently. "I wish you to be my hostess for an evening."

"How can you expect me to pretend to enjoy your festivities when my brothers wear rags and work like peasants? Is it not enough that you slaughter us and defile our home?" She looked pointedly at his boot and the marks it was making upon the fine dark wood of the chair. "Must you shame us as well?"

Slowly, Masaru removed his foot. In his own home, he knew, he would not have been wearing shoes at all. But here, upon these cold tile floors . . . *Paw!* For all their ancient claims to civilization, he still thought the Chinese an uncouth and barbarous race.

"Your brothers need not labor," he said in a low, caressing tone. *"If* you could let yourself relax, be a little more amiable, I am sure their services on the blockades might no longer be required."

Bright Autumn allowed her eyes to meet his timorously. "Should I agree, for this once only, to play hostess to your companions, will my brothers be brought back in from the streets?" Her voice quivered with hope.

Masaru nodded and convinced himself that he had not needed to bribe this female for her favors. The girl wanted him—he knew she did!

Bright Autumn lowered her glance and pressed for just a little more. "And might my parents and the children and my sister-in-law be excused from attending your dinner, along with my brothers?"

This gave Masaru a moment's pause, for up to the present, he had forced the entire family to dine with him and his junior officers. There could be no better protection against poison.

A tear escaped Bright Autumn's eyes and her cheeks flushed. "It would shame my loved ones to see me play the traitor," she said from between pursed lips.

He studied her face intently. "Very well. For that single night your family can be excused to sup in their private rooms. But my men will be posted in the kitchen from tonight on. Think not that I am a fool, Daughter of China, for I am not. Nor would I be lenient if I suspected foul intent on your part."

She bowed and was turning to leave when he stopped her by placing a hand on her arm. Her flesh crawled. He smiled, and it was all she could do not to jerk away from his hot grasp.

"Wear your finest gown," he said, "and for that evening, at least, call me by my given name."

During the following days Bright Autumn was forced to employ every ounce of skill she possessed as an actress. Her brothers were indeed brought in off the streets, and she went personally to thank the captain. Slightly stammering, she had played the role of humility so well she nearly sickened herself. Had Master Wong been present and able to observe her charade, he would have been proud indeed. From that moment on, she made sure to be seen often by her enemy, and at the same time managed to

make such meetings appear accidental. While sitting
at the table in the large dining hall, partaking of meals
with the despised soldiers, she cast shy and covetous
glances at the captain. If his eyes met hers, she blushed
and turned away. In the evenings he would often look up to
see her gaze upon him, seemingly full of coy confusion and
indecision. Each time this happened the captain expanded
his broad chest and flushed with pleasure. His walk became even more swaggering and he was in rare and mag-
nanimous humor.

On the morning of the scheduled merrymaking, Bright
Autumn almost faltered. "I cannot do it, Father!" she said
tearfully. "When he puts his hands upon me, which is
more and more often now, I want to be sick. More than
that, I am frightened! If things should go amiss . . ."

Master Wong lowered his voice even though they were
in the damaged rooms the captain had allowed them to oc-
cupy. The children were gathered around Little Mother,
and over their games and laughter little else could be
heard.

"You *must* do it," he whispered desperately. "It is your
only hope, your only possible salvation. How long do you
think that animal will wait to claim you? It is too late to
change your mind in any case, my dumpling, for the plans
are firm and we dare not turn back now."

"But what of you and Mother and Little Mother and the
children?" Bright Autumn wept. "How will I know you are
safe?"

"We will be safe. Trust me." His eyes misted. "Someday
we will all be together and our nation will be whole again.
Until that day, however, you must have faith and hope.
You are part of the future, Daughter. Remember, Fengmo
awaits you."

These last words gave her more courage than all the
others combined. That afternoon, as she prepared herself,
she kept repeating over and over in her mind, *Fengmo
waits!*

Never had she taken more care with her appearance
than she did now. After she had bathed, a servant washed
and perfumed her hair. She sat in the sun for hours in order to dry the luxuriant mass before it was plaited atop her
head like a midnight crown. With art, she sparingly ap-

plied thickness to her lashes and a touch of rouge to her pale cheeks. Her perfect lips she outlined and colored vermilion. The most valuable and prized of her jewels had been buried, but there remained one pair of pearls, shaped like perfect dew drops, and these she hung from her ears. Her undergarments were of the sheerest silk and lace, and once more she slipped her feet into the high-heeled pumps, which gave her height and majesty. Last, she donned a long dress of Chinese style. It was modern in cut, with a deep slit that shot midway up her left thigh. The short sleeves and high collar only accentuated the roundness of her arms and breasts. A dazzling white brocade, the dress made her skin glow the color of rich cream.

When she had finished this painstaking toilet, she could already hear the sound of music and laughter drifting up from the inner court. Her knees quivered as she walked slowly down the corridor. Pausing at the top of the stairs, she took several deep breaths and then began her descent.

Masaru was laughing with another officer. The room grew suddenly hushed. When he looked up to see Bright Autumn coming down the stairs, the laughter caught in his throat and died.

Even his mistress, Kazuko, who awaited him in Nagasaki, could not compare to the vision he now gazed upon. His wife had also been considered an elite beauty in her youth. Again, no comparison could be made. Bright Autumn shimmered. She seemed no less than a breathtaking apparition. Smiling shyly at the upturned faces, her cheeks dimpled. As she came to the bottom of the stairs, she extended both hands toward the startled girl who had once been her dearest friend, that traitorous daughter from the House of Sung.

"Ah, Hibiscus." She smiled still more warmly. "How good it is to see you again at last!"

The murmur of voices resumed, but Masaru noticed with pride how all the men let their eyes slide in Bright Autumn's direction as she stood in animated conversation with the general's concubine. The old general himself was quite florid and his mouth was agape.

Masaru worked his way through the guests and approached the trio. Bright Autumn turned the full strength of her smile upon him. "Masaru," her voice teased, "forgive my tardiness. I am ever a slowpoke, as you well know." She laughed at herself in a sweet, silvery tone and slipped her arm through his.

Possessively, he took her from one cluster of guests to the next. He spoke of many things, but all the while caressed her shoulder or ran a lingering hand down her back with the proprietary touch of ownership. It gave him a thrill of pride to know that each man there was convinced that the daughter of Wong Cho was his private and willing chattel.

All through dinner he watched her—as she poured his wine and that of his male guests, as she leaned over and talked with her friend, as she cast him incredibly intimate glances. At one point he was sure he felt her hand brush his knee beneath the table, but when he looked at her, she lowered her eyes and blushed. For weeks he had planned and looked forward to having this dinner. It was just one step in his plans for future promotion. Now he only wished to see everyone leave. As he sat playing the genial and witty host, his manhood swelled in anticipation.

At long last the final guests, the general and Hibiscus, congratulated him on a splendid evening and bid a regretful farewell—not without the general casting Bright Autumn a sly and inviting look. Once they were finally out of the house, Masaru quickly shut the door and faced the woman who had inspired his dreams and given him many moments of deep clandestine pleasure. His eyes were alight.

"Did I do well, *Master?*" Bright Autumn asked in her soft, laughing voice.

He knew she had given him the title only in jest, and yet he responded to it in all seriousness. He closed the gap that separated them and embraced her. "It has been a good beginning," he said huskily.

He half expected her to pull away from him, to see the personality she had so delightfully displayed through the evening crumble away. But this did not happen. In his intoxicated and aroused state he did not stop to question his good fortune. She rested against the length of his body, pliant and unresisting. He inhaled the sweet fragrance of her hair and neck. "How I have waited," he whispered.

Slowly he led her up the staircase and then down the corridor. She did not pull back until they arrived at his suite. Her cheeks turned scarlet. As usual, two stalwart guards flanked his door. She looked from one to the other and then buried her face against his chest. When she spoke, her voice was quavering and inaudible to all but him. "Please do not hurt me, My Lord."

Over her bowed head, Masaru Inaka smiled, and his men were reminded of a tiger.

Bright Autumn thought her heart would stop when she heard the click of the bedchamber door closing behind her. Suddenly she imagined how an animal, a fox or a rabbit, must feel the instant before the deadly jaws of a trap close down upon it. When the captain pulled her to him, there was no playacting involved in her trembling. Her knees felt weak and she sagged against him.

"Ah, you are frightened, my China rose." His voice was like honey. "Let us not rush this momentous deflowering. There is some of that foreign brandy your father favored so in yonder cabinet. I will pour a small glass for you to drink while I prepare."

With terrified eyes Bright Autumn watched him do this. When he put the glass into her hands, she shook so violently she had difficulty bringing it to her lips.

"Drink," he urged. "It will heighten the pleasure which is to come."

The liquid burned her throat and brought tears to her eyes. She watched as her captor opened the wardrobe and extracted a rolled bundle, which appeared to be a small mattress. Meticulously, he began spreading it out on the floor. He then sat on the edge of the bed, which had once belonged to her parents, and beckoned. Her eyes darted toward the closed door and his muscles tightened slightly. "Do not be foolish," he whispered. "Come here."

It was not his soft and deadly command which restrained her. She knew that no matter what might come, she dared not take flight. The seconds now ticking past were crucial. To deviate from the prearranged plan would jeopardize the precious lives of her family. There was nothing for her now but to play out her part and pray salvation would not come too late. Her future life literally depended upon that salvation, for she was more determined than ever to keep herself pure. If this could not be done, she would die by her own hand.

"Do not make me wait, little lotus." His voice was still soft. "Assist me with my boots."

Keeping her ears keenly tuned to any muffled noise that might come from beyond the door, Bright Autumn set down her glass and moved toward Captain Inaka. When she was close, he extended his leg. Her hands shook as she knelt and struggled to remove his high-topped boots. She could feel his fingers unfastening the pins that held her hair in place. To her surprise, when she was about to rise again he put his hands on her shoulders and forced her to remain in a kneeling position. She kept her glance down, but she could hear and feel him unhooking the buttons of his formal military jacket. His chest was bare beneath and she could smell the odor of his body.

"You may stand now," he said in a strange voice, "and move back."

Bright Autumn wasted no time doing this, for she could now see that he was loosening his trousers. Her eyes flitted from left to right, everywhere but at him. The sound of her own heart thundered in her ears.

"Look at me!" His voice was suddenly harsh.

She stared into his perspiring face.

"Look at *me*, I say!" His trousers and undergarments dropped around his thick ankles and he kicked them aside. "See what pleasure awaits you, Daughter of China."

Bright Autumn gasped and turned away in horror as he began to rock back and forth on his heels. With his own hands, he began fondling his genitals. His eyes were glazed, and he seemed to be humming. Then he grimaced. The muscles of his neck stood out in cords and he released the grip he had on himself. His breath came in labored pants. He looked at her and a cruel smile stretched on his thin lips as he stepped forward.

She jumped back and stumbled, but he caught her wrist before she could fall and pulled her tightly against his burning flesh. "You will thank the gods for this night," he promised.

Without further preamble his fingers pulled down the zipper that held her dress together. His touch was light, lethal. Masaru Inaka stood back and let the garment fall away.

"Take off these others." He pointed a blunt finger at her sheer undergarments.

Slowly, Bright Autumn complied, but all the time her lips were faintly moving. Tears blinded her as she silently prayed. *Let them come! Merciful Heaven, help me now! Let them come!*

Heaven seemed not to hear. She stood naked before the man she loathed, shivering, trying to cover her body with hands and hair. She allowed herself a fleeting moment of hope when she saw he made no move to approach her. He stood gazing, a thin line of spittle drooling from his parted lips.

"You are exquisite!" His voice was little more than a croak. "But *that* I have always known. So many nights . . . So many nights . . ."

Bright Autumn neither realized nor cared that his words made no sense, for he suddenly came forward and gripped both her wrists. He was oblivious to the sobs which shook her body, and to her white, panic-stricken face.

Like the victim of a trance, she allowed herself to be led to the futon he had spread on the floor. It was not until she saw the two silken cords he brought from beneath that pallet that she came to life again.

Unmindful of any consequence, she screamed. The sound reverberated off the walls. Evidently, the captain had anticipated her terror, for almost instantly he brought forth a wad of silk and forced it into her opened mouth.

Bright Autumn began to see spots before her eyes. Her lungs struggled for oxygen. She thrashed her head wildly while her assailant forced her down and straddled her. His muscular legs held her writhing body in a vice grip. She could feel him trussing her hands above her head, and though the ropes were made of silk, they bit cruelly into her wrists.

Her vision was now mottled and blurred, but fate chose to leave her hearing unimpaired. The wooing voice of Masaru Inaka sounded above her. "If you will but relax, little lotus, you will thank me for the ecstasy I am about to give you."

He worked his buttocks further down her body without

releasing his iron hold. A moment later, she felt her ankles also bound. Then suddenly, his crushing weight lifted away. The gag in her mouth was loosened slightly. She gulped in a draft of air and looked up to see him gazing down at her. His eyes kindled brightly.

"So long," he murmured. "I have waited so, so long."

He knelt beside her as if in prayer. She began thrashing again, more violently, which only seemed to increase his pleasure. Slowly, he put out his hands and laid them upon her body. His fingers probed and pinched, gently at first, and then with more and more force. Bright Autumn felt her legs being viciously pried apart. The burning body of Masaru stretched itself on top of her. She could feel his manhood pressing, seeking entrance when, without warning, his entire body arched and stiffened. Wildly, he clawed at his back as his face went slack. His eyes opened wide in surprise and he slumped against her. She could feel the warm, thick oozing of his blood drip down her sides and between her thighs.

Her complexion was stark white as she looked up at the two men above her. One wore the uniform of a Japanese general and the other that of a corporal. The general gently pulled the gag from her torn and bleeding mouth.

Bright Autumn sobbed in relief and shame as she recognized the averted faces of her fourth and fifth brothers.

Now, lying atop a pile of straw, covered with a warm blanket, it seemed impossible to Bright Autumn that the rest of the night could ever have taken place. She looked up at the fading stars. Water lapped against the sides of the small junk as it creaked and strained against the current. The voices of her brothers and the vessel's captain drifted up from the dimly lit cabin below. The individual words they spoke were not discernible, but their tones were grave and subdued. She knew the danger was still omnipresent, for Japanese patrol boats were notorious for stopping and boarding rivercrafts, regardless of how innocuous one might appear.

Until this time, Bright Autumn, raised amidst leisure and affluence, had not given her father's vast wealth much heed. To be able to purchase whatever she desired, to wear the finest silks and eat the most dainty of foods had

seemed only natural. Even after the enemy occupied
Shanghai and her own home, the deprivations had been
more emotional than physical in nature. She now took a
moment to thank Heaven and all the gods for the wealth
that belonged to the family of Wong, and also for the wisdom of her father. Were it not for his ability to lay hard
cash on outstretched palms, she knew she would not be
here, in spite of her brothers' courage.

How those two brothers of hers had changed! Gone were
the soft, lackadaisical youths who cared only for having
fun. They had been replaced by hard, muscled men with
somber faces. She had seen with her own eyes the dead
bodies of the guards Four and Five had slain and then
dragged into the sitting room of her parents' former suite.
Those soldiers had had no opportunity to raise a hue and
cry before their mouths had been covered and daggers
thrust repeatedly between their ribs. She knew too that
the Japanese general was dead, and his driver, and the
guards at the gate—all dead, all killed without remorse by
her once laughing, tenderhearted brothers.

"And what of Hibiscus?" she had asked as they sped
through the streets toward the Shanghai docks in the general's car. "Is she also . . ."

Driving the bannered automobile, Wong Four had spoken over his shoulder in a cold, pitiless voice. "She de-
serves to be! I struck her on the head and then bound and
gagged her and threw her over the ledge of a terrace. If she
wakes with the dawn, she can thank the stars. If not—" He
shrugged.

Wong Five made no comment, and Bright Autumn remembered that he had once loved the Sung girl.

Near the docks a sampan had been waiting to take them
to the junk, which was piloted by a former outlaw. That
man was now hired by the Japanese to transport light military supplies up the Yangtze as the main enemy force
pushed inland. Still, he had felt no qualms about taking
the gold of Master Wong.

"He is a bandit and a pirate," Wong Five had informed
her. "He has neither scruples nor loyalty, but like all lowborn, he is greedy. He will not risk his life, however, or
that of his motley crew, beyond the coming of dawn's light.
By then the alarm will surely be out. We must disembark

soon and continue on foot." He had smiled wryly. "And disguised as peasants, no less. It will be the safest way to reach Tanpo."

Bright Autumn felt a sudden chill and pulled the coarse blanket close about her, wondering if the body of Masaru Inaka had already been discovered. Never would she forget the still, white face that had stared at her as she rolled the horrid body away from her. It would also be a long time before she recovered from the shame of having her own brothers see her all bound and naked. The questions had been plain upon their faces, but they had not asked a single one.

Footsteps sounded on deck and she saw the silhouette of a man coming up out of the cabin toward her. She hated herself for cowering.

"Are you asleep?" It was the soft voice of Four.

She expelled a shaking breath. "No, Brother. My brains and body are beyond sleep. Come, sit beside me."

His face showed briefly in the glow each time he drew on a cigarette. Bright Autumn could see the bitter creases at the corners of his eyes and down around his mouth. In just a few weeks, it seemed he had aged years.

"Our parents," she asked, "do you think they will be well?"

Wong Four nodded wearily and looked up into the sky, which was already beginning to bronze with the coming dawn. "They will stay in the mission compound with Little Mother and the children for a time. Long Han is no political activist and it is unlikely he would be suspected of harboring dangerous fugitives. They will be safe enough, I think."

He turned and fixed his attention upon Bright Autumn. She could tell his next words came with great difficulty. "And you, my sister, are you well?"

She put a hand on his arm. "I could not live if it were not true, Four. Except for the bruises, I remain as ever I have been."

They were both quiet for a time, and then the gentle rocking of the junk made Bright Autumn drowsy. Her eyelids were half-closed when he spoke again.

"I am thinking of our wild little brother," he said. "I miss his presence, and even his hot temper."

"Perhaps he yet lives," she murmured. "His body was never found, after all, only that trail of blood the soldiers followed into the park."

Four laid back on the straw beside her. "Yes," he replied with the hope of youth. A moment later she heard his breathing settle into a light, steady rhythm. In the light of approaching dawn, his face once more softened and regained a portion of its vulnerability.

Bright Autumn closed her own eyes, and just before sleep claimed her, another face filled her semiconsciousness. A smile touched her lips and she sighed as her dreams leapt forward, beyond the arduous days and weeks which lay ahead.

FATE

Chapter Twenty-eight

Until recently Fengmo had very much enjoyed the rigorous walks he took up over the terraced hills and through the tiny farming villages surrounding Tanpo. To protect his head from the relentless summer sun, he wore a wide, conical straw hat, and he always dressed without pretension. Occasionally, he took Fong Lu or Sean with him on these excursions, but most often not. He much preferred to go out alone to see how the people fared and how they were treated by the land stewards. At first, he knew, he had been viewed with deep suspicion by the peasants, for they all knew he was the Second Son of Chang Hai-teh. But a little at a time they had come to be less cautious. If they still did not talk to him much, or bring him their woes, well, at least they lifted calloused hands in greeting and called out good wishes.

Now, however, everything was changed. The peasants were silent and withdrawn again. Beside the tall figure of Fengmo, a donkey trotted, and atop its back sat the elegantly clad Chang Kao. The eldest son straddled the poor little beast, fanning himself and holding a parasol over his brow. He cast the peasants contemptuous looks and then turned his nose in the air.

"Oh me," he sighed on this particular morning. "I see no reason at all why I should be forced to get up at cock's crow and trouble myself with this foul-smelling business. What good does it do to pay stewards if the sons of a great house must come out here on the land?"

"Our father wisely feels that in these troubled times we should take a more personal interest in the land," Fengmo retorted. "There are gangs of bandits about, as you know, and troublemakers aplenty. There have always been those

279

who wished to stir up the simple folk and encourage them to revolt. Besides, Elder Brother, I should think it would do your heart good to see all this." He spread his arms to indicate the fields of wheat and long rows of radishes and beans and turnips. "This land is a grand inheritance to leave your sons."

"Sons!" Kao snorted. "I will never get sons from that dry stick my parents wed me to. Her womb is shriveled, I swear! And you can believe she is not barren for my lack of cooperation either!"

Fengmo turned his face away and looked out over the land to hide the angry flush he felt creeping up his neck. In the nearest field, he saw an old man busily hoeing a row of turnips. Though the man was not more than a few yards away, he kept his head down and refused to look at the passersby.

"Old Father," Fengmo called, "how *are* you today?"

The farmer straightened and bowed deeply several times. His wrinkled and leathered brow was dripping with perspiration and he wiped at it with his sleeves. "Heaven has not been kind this year, Young Sir," he called back. "We need rain. Still, I am well enough. My family has not starved yet."

"Fear not, my father will see you do not starve!" Fengmo declared.

The farmer opened his eyes in surprise, obviously believing not a word he heard, and went back to work, chuckling and wagging his head.

"Shhhh!" hissed Kao. "Why did you say such a rash thing? What can our father do against heaven, you stupid? Can he call down the rain?"

Fengmo looked at his brother with disdain. "We have granaries and they are well stocked. The poor on *our* lands need not starve during a short drought!"

Kao threw back his head and laughed. "I am no man of business," he admitted, "but even I know that in hard times the price of grain goes up and not down. *Never* is it given away. Grow up, Little Brother. If our father heard you, he would accuse you of still wearing swaddling clothes!"

Fengmo did not reply, for he very much feared Kao spoke the truth. Yet, he thought, it should not be so, and I will make my promise good if the need should arise. The family of this farmer, at least, will not starve!

Lately, he had found himself often vexed and unhappy because of what he observed upon his father's lands. He suspected the stewards of extortion and petty thievery. The people *did* suffer, and now he suffered with them. He was also beginning to understand how a man like Wong Six could have been drawn to certain ideologies. Fengmo could see no immediate solution to the problems, and this was what upset him most. To go to his father would be a step in the right direction, but even the wealthy Chang Hai-teh could not erase the misery of the poor, and his son knew it. So far, Fengmo had only watched and said nothing to anyone save Sean, the great listener.

He walked beside Kao with a brooding frown upon his face.

The two men arrived at a small village a short time later and went into its humble inn to cool off and refresh themselves before returning to the city. Kao looked around at the rough wooden benches and refused to sit down until the placating proprietor brushed them off with a cloth. And even then he lifted his robes and grimaced disdainfully.

A young girl came out to serve them. Though not pretty, she was handsome in the big-boned, healthy way country girls often are. Her lips were wide and firm and her cheeks ruddy. When Kao looked at her with bright eyes, she turned her face away.

Her father, the innkeeper, saw this exchange and called out to her. "You, worthless thing! I swear I hear your mother calling. Go now and see what it is she wants."

At first the girl just looked at him blankly, but then her eyes met his in understanding. Quickly, she made an exit through the rear door of the shop, her wide feet kicking up dust from the earthen floor. Inwardly seething, Fengmo watched his brother and saw also the little drama enacted between the innkeeper and his daughter. For the first time it occurred to him what the simple people, the servants and land tenants, could expect when Kao became head of the House of Chang. In that instant, he decided he could no longer put off speaking to his father. Some plan must be laid in advance to forestall his elder brother becoming a cruel tyrant. This must be done first for the people, but also for the sake of the Chang family name.

After drinking several cups of tea and eating a few stale sweetmeats, the brothers began their return trip. They had not gone far when Kao slapped his forehead with an open palm.

"Take me for a fool," he groaned. "I have gone and left my fan in that hovel! This heat will suffocate me if I cannot cool myself."

"It is not far back," said Fengmo with ill-disguised disgust. "We will return."

"Oh, do not trouble yourself, Younger Brother. The fault is all mine. Why should you walk the extra steps, seeing I have this sturdy beast to ride? Go on ahead and I will catch up with you in no time." With this he turned the donkey around, switched it smartly on the rump, and trotted away.

Kao did not ride all the way to the inn. Once it was within sight, he dismounted and tethered the donkey behind a chinko tree. Looking both right and left, he walked to the door of the establishment. He then peeked inside and saw the proprietor alone there. The fellow had his feet propped upon a table and was snoring loudly, oblivious of the flies hovering about his mouth and nose.

Kao smiled with satisfaction and, like a great, oily snake, slithered around the corner of the lime-washed building. Behind the inn he found what he sought. There, sitting in the rear dooryard, beneath the shade of the thatched roof, was the country maid. She was also alone and industriously weaving straw into a pair of sandals. Between strong white teeth she held the hemp, while her hands deftly and swiftly braided the stuff. In the heat she had unfastened the blue cotton jacket she wore. Kao could see her plump breasts swaying as she worked. Spittle formed at the corners of his mouth and his smile broadened. His eyelids drooped as he rubbed the swelling between his legs.

It was already too late when the girl looked up and saw him coming at her. The screams she would normally have sounded were muffled by the hemp in her mouth, and before she could spit it out, Kao clapped a rough hand over the lower half of her face. She kicked out her legs and thrashed, her eyes wide with terror. The thin trousers she wore gave way beneath a single mighty tug from her assailant.

Kao now wasted no time in pulling his own clothing aside. Dust flew up around their struggling bodies as he mounted her. But the girl was stronger than he had supposed. She arched her back and bucked, holding her ample thighs tightly together. Enraged and maddened by lust, he took her hand away from her mouth and viciously struck her with his fist. Her head snapped back and she fainted. Blood oozed from between her lips.

Kao now became like an unreasoning animal. He chewed the tender flesh of her neck and breasts and, grunting, forced her legs apart. So intent was he on his evil purpose that he did not see the shadow which fell across him and his victim.

"You dog!" The voice of Fengmo cut through the still, hot air.

Kao jerked back and looked up into a face twisted with rage, almost unrecognizable. His own fear suddenly became so great that his manhood instantly shriveled and he rolled off the girl. Hampered by his disarranged clothing, he tried to crawl away.

Emitting a terrible cry, Fengmo leapt upon him.

This cry brought the innkeeper running, and he in turn, seeing the condition of his daughter, raised such a racket that farmers came rushing in from the fields, and women from nearby huts.

The farmer, Fong, who was father to Fong Lu, was among those who arrived and saw Fengmo beating Kao. Over and over again the younger brother rammed his fist into the face of the elder.

"Stop him!" Farmer Fong cried. "If there is a death here, *we* will bear the blame!"

His words rang out and pierced the stunned brains of his fellows, who realized at once that he spoke a grave truth. If one of these rich young lords were to kill the other, regardless of the reason, the whole village would undoubtedly suffer. In unison the group rushed to pull Fengmo from Kao and then held him tightly by the arms.

"You *carrion!*" Fengmo spit and yelled at his brother,

struggling against the work-worn hands which restrained
him.

Kao came onto all fours. His nose was a pulp and his
swollen lips were already purple and bleeding. His two
front teeth were missing. He stood and held his side where
a rib had been broken. Weeping, looking from one hostile
face to another, he limped off and disappeared back the
way he had come.

"Calm yourself," Farmer Fong said to the still-thrash-
ing Fengmo. But neither he nor the others were inclined to
loosen their captive and let him go chasing after the
fleeing villain.

The attacked girl had come to herself and she now sat up
and began to weep, covering her face with her hands. The
women soothed her and pulled her tattered clothing together. The men solemnly watched as the same women
then formed a tight circle about the girl. After what
seemed an eternity, an old grandmother separated herself
from the others. She stood on tiptoe to whisper into the
innkeeper's ear.

That man had been wailing and tearing his hair, but
now he straightened his shoulders and spoke in a voice
loud enough for all to hear. "My daughter is a virgin still!
Hear me! Though she has been beaten and abused, her pu-
rity is intact. This ancient here will so testify!"

"It is true." The old woman nodded. "Thanks to the Second Son of Chang the maid is still a maid and fit to be the
wife of any man."

The men slowly released their grip on Fengmo and the
entire crowd turned toward him.

The innkeeper came and threw himself in the dust at
Fengmo's feet. "My gratitude knows no bounds, Master,"
he said, knocking his head against the earth. "I am a poor
man with nothing for a reward. My daughter is less than
worthless, but she is mine, and the only child I ever had
from my departed wife. The fact that my girl is still whole
is thanks to you and you alone. I am your slave if you will
have me!"

Fengmo ground his teeth in shame. It pained him to see
this man prostrated in humility after his innocent daughter had been so sorely used by a member of the House of
Chang.

Taking hold of the innkeeper, Fengmo lifted him up. There was a gigantic lump of mortification in his throat—and a hot ball of hatred in the pit of his stomach for Kao.

"Do not bow before me, please," he said. "You are good and honest men here, who work hard every day for the likes of me and my family. Would that I could wipe away this foul stain from the honor of our name!"

Though the villagers murmured polite consolations, Fengmo was not comforted. He could not bear to look into their honest, sympathetic faces. Bowing low himself, he turned and went hurriedly away.

The people of the village watched his tall, retreating figure. "That one is not a bad man," the innkeeper said. "It is a shame under Heaven that *he* is not the eldest son."

"Woe unto us," said the old woman who had examined the girl. "Woe unto us to have such a wicked man over us when the old Chang dies!"

"Woe unto us," they all repeated together, and silently cursed the power of the rich.

Yet, they had already heard good tales of a single rich man—a young man. And in their hearts they made a place for the Second Son.

Fengmo took huge strides all the way back to the city. He cursed aloud and shook his fists at the sky. He half wept and groaned. Still, his rage was unabated when he arrived home. Without hesitation, he stalked through the courts and burst into the courtyard of his brother.

Golden Willow sat there in the shade of her courtyard, painting. When she unexpectedly looked up and saw her beloved all covered with dust, his face an agony of emotion, she dropped her brush and parchment on the ground. Her first impulse was to run to him, and she might have done so had he not spoken. His voice was like thunder and hard as iron. His eyes glinted dangerously. "Where is that one who is called my brother?" he demanded. "Tell him to quit hiding and come out here at once!"

Golden Willow stared at him. Until this moment she would not have believed she could be frightened of this man whom she so loved, but the expression now on his face and the threat emanating from him gave her chills.

"He is not here," she stammered. "I tell you the truth. I have not seen him since before the morning meal."

Fengmo looked at her long and deeply. Some of his rage fled and his gaze softened. He suddenly realized how hard it must be for her to remain married to a man like Kao. Until now, Fengmo had tried to quell the animosity he felt toward his brother, knowing full well the root of his dislike was envy. He had been tortured by visions of Kao laying his hands upon this woman he loved. How much worse it was to learn that Golden Willow had not only been possessed, but very likely abused.

The disgust and hatred, the love and pity all combined in him and swelled until he felt he would die of pain. He shook so violently that he had to put his hand against the tree and steady himself. His face was drawn and pale and his lips quivered.

Golden Willow could no longer be still. Though Crystal stood in the doorway of the apartment watching, she walked to Fengmo and put her palm to his cheek. She said nothing.

He looked down at her and smelled the sweetness of her hand. "Oh, my heart," he whispered. He continued to gaze into her face for many moments, his eyes searching, and then turned and left the courtyard.

Golden Willow stood for a long time, her hand still raised. She was not sorry she had touched him, not sorry she had let her love show. At that moment she knew true joy.

Master Chang stared at the set features of his Second Son. The words Fengmo had just spoken were so reprehensible to the older man that he could not force his mind to function properly.

He had been sitting quietly in his library with Sean when Fengmo burst into the room, disheveled and fiery eyed. It had been very pleasant up to that point, for in the person of the young American, Chang Hai-teh had found a truly enlightening and different sort of companion. Now, however, he wished Sean Duncan was anyplace but there in the room to witness the ultimate humiliation of his family.

"Well, Father?" Fengmo demanded a response.

Master Chang moaned and put his head into his hands. Had anyone else come to him and related such a story, he would have denied and denied again that his eldest offspring was capable of the described monstrosities. But he could not doubt the word of this honorable Second Son standing before him.

Fengmo saw his father's pain and it twisted his heart. Still, his anger was stronger and would not subside. He knew he would never relent a single ounce of the hatred he now bore Kao. His heart was full of vengeance.

"Something must be done!" He spoke without remorse. "I must speak, Father, and you must listen! The crime my brother has perpetrated will be the undoing of this house. In these turbulent times the people will not tolerate a master like Kao."

"I need no lecture from you!" Master Chang tried to sound stern, but his voice came out only pained and weary. "The people upon the lands are of importance to me, of course. I have no desire to be murdered in my bed. But more than that, Fengmo, is the shame we must all feel."

The older man looked miserably at Sean. "Forgive us, friend. I wish to Heaven you could have been spared these grisly details. You must think me a poor father indeed to have raised such a one as my eldest. I swear I do not know how such a wild seed could have sprouted up between my good woman and myself."

Sean also wished he were somewhere else, but he spoke kindly. "Think not of me, sir. All the parents on earth are sometimes given to woe. It is unfortunate children are not born with a guarantee, but Heaven has not seen fit to give promises in advance." He floundered for some other words of comfort. "Perhaps it is Kao's Karma to be so. You cannot be blamed for his last incarnation."

Fengmo stared at his friend with an open mouth.

Slowly, Master Chang got up from his chair. His posture, which was normally so erect, was now stooped. "Yes," he muttered, "Kao is wicked to his bones, but I must take part of the blame, regardless of his last life. I have spoiled the boy and so has his mother." His shoulders straightened a fraction and his face became hard. "But no more! This is the end!"

Master Chang looked at the two younger men. He tried

not to see the pity emanating from Sean, but worse was the shame and anger of Fengmo, whom he loved above all. Why could *he* not have been the eldest? he wondered. My house and the future of my clan would be secure with one such as Fengmo to lead the way.

His shoulders straightened still more with the resolution coming over him. Fengmo shall lead the family! He shall! Under the law I can take the life of my firstborn for the shame he has brought upon us all. Kao must die!

The anger boiled up in him now and he would not allow a shred of mercy to invade his soul. Forcing himself to move, he bowed stiffly to Sean and Fengmo and set out for the courts of his one and only wife.

Li Ma lay curled upon a pallet in the corner of her mistress's sitting room taking a nap. The easiest way to escape a sweltering afternoon was to sleep it away. She had no duties to perform in any case, for Madame Chang chose the same respite during the hot summer afternoons.

Sweet dreams of retirement and laughing grandchildren were dancing through the mind of the old servant when she was awakened by a not-too-gentle hand shaking her shoulder. She blinked her eyes awake to see Master Chang standing above her. Her aged heart fluttered a bit upon seeing his thunderous expression.

"Rise, Li Ma," said the master in a tone almost *too* quiet. "Your mistress will have need of you soon."

Rubbing her eyes and groaning at the sudden disturbance of her bones, Li Ma sat and stared up at him. "What is the matter, Master? Is my lady ill?"

"Rise," Master Chang repeated, "and keep yourself ready!" His voice was still soft, but she dared not question further. Obviously, trouble was afoot, and since the master chose not to enlighten her, Li Ma crept to the door of the bedchamber through which he had just disappeared, and she listened.

Madame Chang had removed her outer garments and was lying atop the silk coverlet of her bed. A light net had been pulled around to keep off the pesky flies and other insects.

Her husband stood looking at her. Surrounded by the

gauzy film of the net, the lines of her face were softened. She appeared many years younger than he knew her to be, almost a bride again, all decked out in her white silken undergarments. In a flash, he remembered the many days and nights he had spent with her. He had come into this very room to see his eldest son for the first time.

How proud Peaceful Dawn had been! A glow had seemed to emanate from her that night. It had been a moment of beauty for them both as they looked down into the tiny red face of Kao together.

Master Chang stepped closer to the bed. "Wife?"

As always she opened her eyes immediately, for she was the lightest of sleepers. She smiled gently. "Is that you, Father of My Sons?"

"It is I."

"Shame, shame, Hai-teh, for a man of your ancient years to come sneaking in here during the day." She giggled softly and smothered a yawn. "Do not look so offended, you old bone. I am more than happy to see you."

She pulled aside the netting which surrounded her, a mischievous twinkle in her eyes. But when she saw that he made no move and that his face remained grave, a premonition began to steal over her. She cast the net further back and sat up in the center of the high bed, tucking her knees beneath her body. "What is it, Hai-teh? Has some disaster come?"

She said this with a smile, but her eyes were growing more frightened by the moment. When he still made no answer but continued to look at her with an unreadable expression, she grew truly alarmed and her voice came out sharper than she had intended. "Speak to me! Do not just stand there looking like a whipped dog! If you have awakened me from a sound sleep, it must be for some cause!"

Chang Hai-teh knew of no way to lessen the blow he was about to inflict. "It is our eldest son . . ."

She did not allow him to finish, for her feeling of impending doom was almost overwhelming now. "Oh, Merciful Heaven!" she exclaimed loudly. "My dumpling is injured! Did I not tell you something bad would happen if you sent him out to work like a peasant? Where is he? I must go to him this instant!"

Master Chang's face was like stone. "He was not injured. At least not in the way you seem to think."

His wife looked up at him and began to wail. *"Dead!* My baby is dead!"

Li Ma came running in from the other room, but Master Chang stopped her with a scathing glance and she backed out again. He then approached his wife and laid his hands upon her shoulders to keep her from thrashing about. She was already beginning to tear at her hair and rend her garments.

"Stop this!" he said from between clenched teeth. "Kao is *not* dead, though by all justice he should be!"

She suddenly became very still. Her tears dried and her face grew splotched. "What then? You come in here and frighten me half out of my wits! I am about to become very angry with you, Father of My Sons!"

Her husband sat on the edge of the bed and took her hand. "Our son has shamed us beyond all redemption, Wife, before the entire populace of Tanpo. And yes, even before our most grubby inferiors. He has laid his hands upon an innocent village girl in an abominable fashion."

Now she truly was angry and she jerked her hand away from him. *"Pie-e,* old man! You come in here on a peaceful afternoon and frighten me out of several years of growth only because some lumpish girl has lost her maidenhead? What has that to do with oldsters like us? Our son, I agree, should be more discreet and not conduct himself like a peasant. Indeed, I do not know why he would even wish to bother with some female grasshopper. But I must remind you, it would not have happened if you had not sent him out into the fields and villages like some lowborn. Still, he is not the first son of a rich house to romp with a country girl, nor will he be the last such to be lured by a hot-blooded lass." Her vexation showed plainly as she cast her husband a final disgusted look and prepared to lie back down.

It is exactly this kind of leniency which has brought us to such a sad state of affairs, Master Chang thought, and now he began to lose what sympathy he had for the delicate feelings of his wife. The rage boiled up in him anew as he clutched her wrist and jerked her upright. "Listen to me now," he hissed, his face so fierce that she drew in a

breath of fright. "This is no light matter! Kao did not be-
guile the girl, nor she him. In full light of day, on her father's very doorstep, he attacked her like a dog! He sav-
aged the girl brutally!"

Madame Chang began to quiver. "Who says such a vile
thing? It is a lie, I tell you. I will have the tongue of this
nasty gossip!"

In his wrath Hai-teh would spare her nothing. "It is no
lie!" he yelled into her face. "It is truth and you had better
believe it! Our Second Son witnessed the whole thing with
his own eyes. Kao had beaten the girl unconscious and
Fengmo caught him chewing on her body like a beast!"

Madame Chang's face paled and she bent over as if she
would be sick. Master Chang released his hold on her, and
though the blinding wrath he felt toward his son remained, he was suddenly remorseful for causing this wife
he loved such terrible and unexpected pain.

"Peaceful Dawn," he whispered. "Forgive me, my
sweet, for telling you these things in such stark terms, but
you must be made to see what our son has become. Perhaps
he has always been so and we have been blinded by our
pride and love. Now, however, we must accept the fact that
we have harbored and reared a devil in our midst."

His wife moaned. "It is a thing I wish *not* to know," she
sobbed. "He is my own beloved son, my very own. How
beautiful he was when I first handed him into your arms.
Oh, Hai-teh . . ."

Master Chang straightened and once more his face became like granite. "He is a son no more to me, nor to you."
He turned and walked to the door.

Peaceful Dawn lifted her head to watch him go, but before he could leave altogether, she leapt from the bed and
flew to him and fell down upon her knees. She clasped her
arms about his legs. "Do not harm him, Hai-teh, I beg you!
Do not harm our firstborn!"

Without a word he firmly pushed her from him and she
wilted into a sobbing heap.

As he left the room, he turned to Li Ma. "Go now and
tend your mistress. She has great need of your loving
care."

Li Ma bowed low and hastened into the bedchamber. She
was not gleeful at the pain her mistress now suffered, but

she was not sad either. Gently, she lifted Madame Chang
up off the floor and helped her back to bed. All the while
her soul sang in triumph.

*That loathsome, vile reprobate who defiled my daughter
is at last going to pay some terrible price. Thank you,
Heaven! Thank you!*

Kao, of course, had not gone home. Torn though he was,
his eyes swollen almost completely shut, he knew better.
By taking one alleyway and then another, he made his
way to the tea house that had become his favorite haunt.
After falling off the donkey, he banged upon the small rear
gate. A little girl servant came to answer. She screamed
and ran away in fright when she saw his battered countenance, leaving the gate ajar. Kao groaned as he entered a
rear courtyard, and a moment later Madame Ying came
rushing out, her hair all a mess. Without the paint she normally wore, she was very much a crone. The little girl who
had answered the gate ran beside her.

After taking one look at the nearly unrecognizable Kao,
Madame Ying turned to the child. "You wait here with the
young sir while I fetch Sweet Harmony!"

"But, Mistress!" the little girl cried in alarm. "He is
so . . ."

Her voice turned into a wail as Madame Ying viciously
pinched her cheek. "You will get used to all kinds of men
in time, you little stupid! Do as you are told now! Stay with
him until I return, or I will flay your skin off!"

When Madame Ying reached the room Sweet Harmony
occupied alone, a privilege reserved only for her finest
girls, she was huffing and puffing. She entered without
preamble and went straight to the small bed in which the
flower girl peacefully slept.

"Get up, you lazy thing!" the older woman said, shaking
the sleeping girl. "That rich young lord who craves you so
often is in the rear court. And what a sight he is! Someone
has nearly beaten him to death! He is weeping and crying
for you."

Sweet Harmony yawned and pulled the sheet up around
her chin. "Tell him to get his comfort elsewhere. It is early
yet and I am tired. He was here just last night."

Sparks flew from Madame Ying's rheumy eyes. "Get up,

I say! This is your chance to become more to him than ever you have been. Never is a man so easily manipulated as when he needs sympathy."

Sweet Harmony blinked her beautiful eyes, stretched, and yawned again. "I am not so sure I want to become any more special to that one. There is much about him I do not admire. Now, if it were that younger brother of his . . ."

Madame Ying slapped her hard across the face. "Get up! Do you suppose you are the only one here who stands to gain from this situation? Go to him this moment, you worthless wench, or you will find yourself on the streets!"

Sweet Harmony came wide awake then and made the utmost haste. She put on a light silk wrapper, smoothed her hair back just a little, and flew down the stairs behind her procuress. Once she actually saw Kao, it was not difficult to show dismay and sympathy. She ran to the bamboo chair where he was sitting and knelt beside him.

"Oh, My Lord! Who has beaten you so? Tell us and we will send for the magistrate at once!"

Kao groaned and spoke through his shredded lips. "I do not know who it was," he lied. *"Please!* Bring me some wine for my pain!"

Madame Ying, who stood beside the couple, immediately bid the frightened little girl to fetch wine from the kitchen. The child skittered away and returned almost instantly with hot rice wine. She handed it to Madame Ying to give to Sweet Harmony, who in turn helped Kao drink.

"I will send word to his father at once," said Madame Ying.

Kao heard this and cried out. "No! Send for no one!"

Both women stared at him in surprise. Kao hung his head down and wept piteously. "I do not want my father to see me like this. Only let me stay here with you, Sweet Harmony, until I am better."

He clutched the sleeve of her dressing gown and with the other hand fumbled into his dusty girdle and brought out a handful of silver.

The eyes of Madame Ying and the flower girl furtively met.

"Do not trouble yourself with money right now," Madame Ying crooned. "Come, let Sweet Harmony and me help you up to her room. There you can rest and allow your body to heal somewhat. I have an opium pipe. It will help more than anything to ease your terrible suffering."

So saying, she and her chattel, Sweet Harmony, did indeed each offer a shoulder of support, and led Kao into the tea house.

Master Chang did not have to guess the whereabouts of his son. He walked into the tea house on the Street of the Golden Bridge, trying to maintain a semblance of calm. It was only midafternoon and Madame Ying was not there to greet him in the foyer. The main tearoom was lightly sprinkled with customers during this time of day and many called out greetings to him, among them Tse Liangmo.

"Ah, Hai-teh!" the other beckoned. "Come join me for some refreshment."

Master Chang hesitated. He could think of no one he would less rather socialize with at the moment. Still, he went forward and greeted the man who had been his friend for so many years, and whose close companionship he had sorely missed since their disagreement over Golden Willow and Kao. All the while they talked, however, he looked about the room for a certain male servant he knew better than the rest.

"I am glad to see you," said Liangmo. "I have always enjoyed your company above others."

Master Chang smiled weakly, grateful there was no one else at the table. The wrath and shame he felt—and was forced to keep hidden—caused him to pale and perspire while his friend talked on about the weather and the crops, obviously trying to find new ground on which to reestablish their former camaraderie.

"I see this heat also causes you distress," Liangmo said. "I have ever hated these overlong summers. That Old Man in Heaven is fickle indeed. Perhaps we shall be fortunate. I see there is a large bank of dark clouds gathering to the west of us. We may have rain yet."

"It would be welcome," came the unenthusiastic reply.

Liangmo struggled on against this seeming indifference, for he had sorely missed the friendship of Hai-teh. "My poor Little Flower will hate the rain. Even in this weather she suffers terribly. The pains in her feet and legs give her no rest. Half of the time now she must stay abed. If it were not for our dutiful Golden Willow I am sure she would be out of her mind. That daughter-in-law of yours comes at least once a week for visits." He looked at Hai-teh contritely. "I must admit she looks well and happy too." *But not pregnant,* he wanted to add, and then decided this was a most unpropitious moment for complaints.

Master Chang wanted to cry. Instead he forced his unwieldy tongue to answer. "She is indeed a fine girl, Liangmo. Tell your good woman I said so. As for her suffering, I will send my own wife to her. She is great with cures."

All the while he spoke, his cold fingers fondled the hilt of the dagger he had secreted in his pocket. The beads of perspiration stood out even more on his forehead.

Liangmo looked at him closely. "Are *you* ill, Hai-teh? Your face is suddenly the most putrid color."

Just then Master Chang saw the servant he sought and rose. "Indeed, Liangmo. I am feeling a bit sluggish this afternoon. But no doubt I will be better soon. If you will excuse me?"

Liangmo nodded and frowned to himself as he watched Master Chang hurry up to a servant who stood in the foyer and begin to carry on an urgent and whispered conversation.

Master Chang snatched the servant by the sleeve and spoke in a low, harsh voice. "I seek my eldest son."

The fellow tried to pull away, but could not.

"I know he is here," Master Chang insisted. "I believe he has fallen on some misfortune and is on the upper floor seeking comfort from a certain flower girl who resides here. Take me to him and I will make it more than worth your while."

The manservant demurred and at the same time held his palm out. Soon he and the renowned father of Chang Kao were moving up the stairs and down a dark corridor.

The servant spoke in a whisper over his shoulder. "Your son is injured indeed, sir. But I would not have you think the accident occurred here. It did not. Sweet Harmony is only nursing him until he is able to return home." He looked behind him and chills ran the length of his spine at the expression he saw on Master Chang's face.

They paused before the curtained door of Sweet Harmony's room, and again Master Chang grasped the arm of the servant, this time with more force. His fingers bit painfully into the man's flesh. "You will *not* fetch your old mistress. This is a private family matter. Do you understand?"

White of face, the servant nodded and literally ran away.

The room where Kao lay with Sweet Harmony was small, but simple. There were erotic scrolls hung upon one wall, and in addition to the bed there was a small wooden table. On that table was a long-stemmed pipe. The air was thick with pungent opium smoke. Kao himself was beyond knowing anything. He lay nude upon the bed while Sweet Harmony, also unclothed, was stretched out beside him fanning his brow. Both their bodies glistened with sweat in the heat of the afternoon. It was thus that Master Chang found them.

When he entered, Sweet Harmony jerked her head around and then dropped her fan. Scrambling off the bed, she threw herself at the older man's feet. "This is no doing of mine, Master, believe me! He came here today just as you see him now, only in very great pain. I am only trying to give him release and comfort. Do not punish me, for I am guiltless in the affair!"

Master Chang ignored her pleading and stared at Kao. *This lump,* he thought, *this slack-faced scum was issued from my very own loins!* The bile rose in his throat until he felt he would choke.

Sweet Harmony lifted her head just enough to see the terrible expression on his face, and the moment he stepped around her, moving toward the bed where his son reclined, she leapt up and ran from the room.

Master Chang stood over his first-begotten son and slowly pulled the dagger from his pocket. *The law allows me to take his life, and take it I shall!*

He raised the weapon above his head and at just that moment Kao moaned softly and half opened his glazed, unseeing eyes. A gaping smile flitted across his features.

The dagger shook violently, suspended in air, flashing in the dim light which spilled through a small window. Master Chang lowered his hand without striking. His shoulders slumped forward and he sat down heavily on the edge of the bed.

He could not do murder.

While he sat thus Madame Ying came bustling in. She stopped abruptly when she saw the thing that Master Chang held. Her mind worked with the speed of an abacus.

"Illustrious Sir," she said in the most quiet of voices. "You cannot do this thing. There must be another solution, no matter the crime."

Kao's father looked up at her but said nothing, and she went on. "I know not what your eldest has done to anger you, but I can only imagine it must be grave indeed."

This was not true, for Madame Ying had a pipeline throughout the valley which compared to none, and by now she knew the exact nature of Kao's misdeed.

"Would, perhaps, it not be better to show prudence and mercy? Confine your son, sir. Put him safely away where he can do no more harm."

Her words began to break through the misery of Master Chang. He looked up at her shrewd face with questioning eyes. "And what do you suggest, Madame?"

She chose her words carefully. "With the right woman . . . and that"—she pointed a finger at the opium pipe—"he could be kept from all mischief. It is an extreme measure, I grant you, but is there another?"

Master Chang stood. The sigh he expelled was weary beyond belief. "I leave it to you then. Arrange for that girl who was just here. Provide the . . ." He could not utter the name of the insidious drug he so despised. "Fix your price and have your servants cart my *former* son home under cover of darkness. By then, I will have a court prepared."

He stared at her with hard eyes. "As you well know, Madame, I am not without power in this city. It would behoove you, therefore, to select those servants to assist you who have very closed mouths and no tendency for gossip whatsoever. Is my meaning clear?"

Madame Ying nodded.

When Master Chang left the room, he did not turn aside

and see the lovely girl who stood shivering and terrified in the corridor.

The voice of Madame Ying barked out for Sweet Harmony, and the flower girl knew her life was all but over. She would now wither and grow old, caged in the mighty House of Chang.

Golden Willow had just combed her hair and was preparing for the evening meal when Crystal came rushing into the bedchamber. Her little face mirrored alarm and confusion.

"Excuse me, Mistress, but you have a most unexpected visitor. Your father-in-law awaits you in the sitting room."

The two looked at each other in mutual surprise. It was breaking all tradition for Master Chang to come privately like this, unescorted by his wife, especially when Kao was not present. Even to meet in the quiet of the library, as he and Golden Willow had done so many times, was an unheard-of breach, but this . . .

Golden Willow stood and smoothed her gown. "Perhaps you should remain here, Crystal. I know the father of my lord. He would not be here without ample and pressing cause." With a premonition of doom, she then went into the sitting room.

Master Chang stood there looking like a very old man. He would not sit when invited but insisted she do so. In a low voice, he then told her the unadorned truth of what had transpired that day. All the time he was speaking he stared at the floor. When he had finished, the atmosphere of the room was heavy with his agony.

Golden Willow rose and went to him and bowed her head. "Forgive me, Father Chang. I have been an undutiful and most unwilling wife to your son."

A groan tore from him. "Oh gods, do not speak so! I know now what you must have suffered and I cannot bear it!"

He still could not look at her, but continued. "It is your right to return to the home of your parents if you so choose. I am sure you will do so, but I wish you to know this: I am proud to have had you as part of my family. Never would I have believed I could care so much for a daughter-in-law. My one overwhelming regret is that I have no grandchild for you and I both to love as a result of this mistaken union."

For several moments Golden Willow stood, filled with indecision. She knew that if she were to return to her parents, both the family of Chang and the family of Tse would suffer humiliation. And too, she could not put aside the fact that if she were to leave she would never see Fengmo again. When she finally spoke, her words were halting.

"Father Chang, I beg your forbearance. This has all been a shock to me and to you. Let neither of us act in haste. After a moon has passed, and I am sure there is yet no happiness in my womb, I will make my final decision."

She reached out a timid hand and gently touched his arm. "Even *then* I think it would be difficult to leave you."

Master Chang could only nod, for he knew if he tried to speak again he would surely weep.

The night that Kao, still in a stupor, was brought home, the House of Chang slept restlessly. Master Chang lay beside his weeping, inconsolable wife trying to soothe her, and yet remaining adamant in regard to his decision.

"All on account of a *country maid*," she kept wailing. "Please, Husband, pay her family off and let it be over. *Please!*"

"Her father will be compensated," came his relentless reply, "but that does not clear our name. Nor does it eliminate the guilt and menace of that one now in the rear court."

On went the weeping of Peaceful Dawn, but while her husband gave sympathy, he turned a deaf ear to her pleas.

Of all in the house that night, only one enjoyed a full and satisfying rest, and that was old Li Ma. Even in her sleep she smiled and chuckled.

Crystal and Fong Lu snuggled close and thanked the gods for their own good fortune. The night was sultry and more than usually humid, for threatening black clouds hung low in the sky, pressing the terrible heat down rather than offering relief. Most of the servants slept out of doors, and a few of the family also, to escape their suffocating rooms.

"At least my mistress will no longer have to be humiliated by that terrible beast," Crystal told her husband.

"My great sorrow is that she has no child to give her comfort. She will be alone. How awful it will be for her to be wed and yet not wed for the rest of her days. She cannot even claim to be a widow."

Fong Lu pulled her close. He hated to see her so upset about things she could not make better. "Try to rest, dumpling," he said, smoothing her forehead. "Perhaps heaven knows best. If your Golden Willow were to give birth, who is to say it would not be to another deviate like the eldest son? No, better to have no child than one which will inevitably break its parents' hearts."

"*Our* First Son will not be such a one, I promise." Crystal cuddled against him, sure she spoke the truth. She did not tell him then, in that somber hour, that she had already missed her first menstrual flow. Instead, she caressed her own still-flat belly protectively and thought of her mistress with sadness.

Both Crystal and her pragmatic mate happened to be right about Golden Willow's barren state. At that very moment she lay upon a thick, soft pallet in her courtyard. A protective net was spread all around where she rested. She too was thinking of what her life would become, and also of the children she would never know. Had she been asked prior to this night if she wanted a child by Kao, she would have vehemently replied in the negative. She had truly not wanted his seed to take root for fear a son born of such union might be marred, or worse, depraved. Now, however, looking out over the lonely years ahead, she felt hollow. A yearning took hold of her, a violent longing the likes of which she had never experienced before. She wrapped her arms around her own body and tears stung her eyes.

As if it were an omen, the clouds separated and the moon showed its face, surrounded by a sparkling canopy of stars. Golden Willow gazed at the beauty and wonder of it through misted eyes, but her soul was bitter. She would never hold a babe of her own in her arms! The fact hit her with unbelievable force. Why, on this night of all nights, did her womb cry out to be filled with life?

She turned her face into the pillow and beat her fists against it. "Better to have no son at all than to bring forth a demon!"

The hours passed, but she tossed and turned. The sound of crickets chirped all around her. The insects abruptly stopped their singing when the moon gate of the courtyard swung inward, creaking slightly on its hinges. A figure stood there for an instant and then the gate closed again.

Golden Willow thought she heard someone come in, but she had not seen the silhouette. She lay very still, trying to mock her own fear. Those ornery boys, Hsu and Tan, had best stop sneaking up upon me, she told herself sternly. I am growing overfanciful.

She relaxed a little as the crickets resumed their melody. The first breeze that had blown in many days wafted through the courtyard.

There came another stealthy noise, and again she stiffened, sure now that she was not alone. "Who is there?" she called softly. "Crystal?"

A tall masculine form stepped from the shadows. In an instant she knew who it was towering there and her breath caught in her throat.

Fengmo came closer. His face was dappled in moonlight. To Golden Willow he appeared like a god, visiting her in a dream. So tall he stood, his thick hair the color of polished ebony. He knelt beside her mattress and she could see the square line of his jaw. Again she marveled at his lips, so strong and firm. The strength she felt emanating from him at that moment was overpowering.

"My Lord," she whispered.

Fengmo heard those words of submission with wonder. He had come only to gaze upon her, he convinced himself. He had risen from his sleepless bed and walked through one court after another, not admitting to himself where he was actually bound. When he had finally opened her gate, he had been sure she would not be in the court, or if she were, that she would be fast asleep. And at first, he had believed she was indeed indoors. Then she had called out.

How beautiful she looked! Her raven tresses were unbound and fanned out around her, stark white against the pillow. Even in the intermittent moonlight her skin glowed like ivory. The silk shift she wore had worked down, exposing one round shoulder. Her ripe, pomegranate lips were parted slightly and he heard the quick intake of her breath.

He knelt beside the netted canopy which surrounded her, and drank in every line and curve of her face. The sight of her was like cool spring water to a man dying of thirst. He cast about in his mind for something, *anything* to say, just so he might hear the music of her voice.

"Will you leave us now?"

She did not answer, but sat up and looked full into his eyes.

A sudden fear came over him. "Do not leave! Do not go from here! Promise me you will not!"

She still did not answer.

"Make me a pledge!" His voice was in anguish now.

"I did not know for certain what I would do until this moment," she slowly replied. "Now it is clear. I cannot go from here, or from you, Fengmo, my love. I cannot go!"

Fengmo leaned forward and lifted one side of the net. His hand shook. He inhaled the clean womanly scent of her, mingled with the essence of jasmine she always wore. "I would claim you for my own if I could," he murmured.

"Speak not so," she cried. "For you cannot. Yet, my heart has always been yours—without claims."

Fengmo moved closer, drawn by the exotic aroma of her, the sheer charismatic beauty. "May heaven and all the gods forgive me, but I would have *more* now. I am near dying of want!"

She reached out her hand, just as she had that afternoon, and laid it upon his cheek. "May the gods forgive us both then, for I, too, long to be possessed by you."

Without further words, she withdrew her hand and loosened the ties of her night garments, pulling them off and laying them neatly to one side. It was strange to both of them that her shyness was less than his. Fleetingly, she wondered if it was the strange book she had glimpsed in the library that day that allowed her, who had always been shy and modest, to be otherwise now. Whether it was the knowledge she had happened upon in that forbidden book, or just her full, unsatisfied womanhood finally manifest, she did not know. She was only aware that at this moment her whole being yearned for fulfillment with this man whom she had loved her whole life long. Unashamed, eager, she stretched out again on her mattress and held out her arms. Then he too removed his clothing and soon they were side by side, pressed together in breathless anticipation.

Fengmo's healthy body rose to meet her passion. Still, he resisted the impulse to rush. He vowed to hold himself tightly in check. More than that, he was intent that she should enjoy fully what happened between them. Her passion must reach the same peaks of ecstasy he allowed himself.

He explored every crevice of her body with his hands, unable to credit that human hair and skin could be so soft, and as he did this, he watched her face.

Golden Willow closed her eyes and a soft moan escaped her throat. Her body shuddered.

He placed his mouth over hers and gently parted her lips that he might sample the sweetness within. At first she stiffened in surprise, and then her arms came up around his neck and she returned the probing of his tongue with fervor, clinging to him. It was he who pulled away first and began methodically trailing soft kisses down the length of her torso, stopping at each breast to trace circles there, and then traveling on.

She arched her back and whimpered. Her body was on fire with sensations far beyond anything she had ever dreamed or imagined existed. But when he rose above her, she would not allow him entrance. She pushed him onto his back with a gentle forcefulness that both surprised and delighted him.

Now, all those things that she had seen in the book came to her, and she gloried in the fact that she had accidentally been given such knowledge. There was no part of his body, not from his feet to his head, that she did not minister to with minute deliberation. And all the while, her own passion grew until it knew no bounds.

Finally, he was able to bear no more. With a groan he pulled her to him and claimed all of her. Their bodies rose and fell in unison, until Golden Willow had to cover her own mouth to smother the screams of delight which broke from her. She reached fulfillment again and again before Fengmo, at last, released his manly flood. The long moment was an agonizing bliss for them both.

They lay locked together for many minutes afterward, their minds coming together and then going in different directions. He held her close, smelling her hair, kissing her ears gently from time to time.

"We must go away from here," he whispered. "We must go away and make a life for ourselves, even if I am forced to become a common laborer. You are mine now and I will not give you up!"

A cool breeze rippled over their naked flesh. She did not answer and suddenly he became frightened. "Why are you silent, my heart?"

Golden Willow was quiet for a moment more. When she did finally speak, her voice was gentle and filled with sadness. "I hear you, my beloved, and your words pierce me through and through, for what you suggest can never be. What shame your father already suffers! Are you and I to now compound it by sneaking off like thieves in the night? And what of your mother and your sisters, and Hsu and Tan? What of my own parents? Can we forget that they too must have dignity?"

Her pain instantly transmitted itself to Fengmo and he bled inside. Yet he could not answer her queries in the way he wished. His soul was one of those few which were too noble, as was her own.

Fengmo and Golden Willow could not think only of themselves, however badly they wished to be together.

He rolled to one side but still held her tightly. "How can we continue to live so?"

Her voice was nearly inaudible. "We *cannot* be as we are tonight ever again. I feel no shame—only joy for what we have shared. But we must content ourselves with less. We dare not do otherwise."

He started to protest, but she placed a finger over his lips. "Hush, my love. Hear me. If I can see you walk through a court, or see you across the dining hall of an evening; if I can see your smile from time to time—these will be tiny joys for me. Each time I gaze upon you at a distance, I will remember the sweetness we have shared!"

She hesitated slightly. Her next words came out in a hoarse whisper. "You have *another* coming to you. With the trouble abroad, would she do so if she did not deeply care?" Golden Willow's throat constricted yet more. "You and she *must* wed and give sons to this house. Healthy sons are greatly needed."

Fengmo groaned and buried his face in her hair. "How can I? How can I now?"

She pulled away from him and sat upright. Her voice was full of pain but more stern than he could have imagined. "You *can* and you *must,*" she repeated. "Let not my love be the cause of your ultimate unhappiness, or the destruction of this honorable house. If I believed I had caused such a thing, I could not live!"

She began to sob and he pulled her back down and held her against his chest, knowing he would never hold her so again. The dawn was almost upon them and the sky was leaden, heavy with rain long overdue. Another breeze blew through the courtyard, colder this time, and he pulled the sheet up over them.

"You must go, my heart," she whispered.

Slowly, Fengmo sat and lifted Golden Willow with him. He placed a final lingering kiss on her lips. Pushing aside the net, he stood and, shivering in the chill air, put on his clothes. He reached deep into the pocket of his robe and brought his hand out again.

"I have kept this with me day and night since I purchased it in Shanghai," he said, kneeling beside her. The jade ring lay on his open palm. "I purchased it because of a legend its former owner told me."

He took her hand and slipped it on her finger. Her eyes widened, and in the light of dawn her face took on the hue of alabaster. She stared at the ring, transfixed, as he related the story of the tragic lovers of olden times.

"I knew at once that it was meant for us," he finished. "The ring glowed before my very eyes like a tiny beacon of hope. I knew then you and I were the incarnation of those poor souls! Though jade is known for its cold texture, this one is warm to my touch. When I hold it, I am comforted. I now pass it to you with the same promise."

He embraced her. "Our souls will meet yet again, dearest, and yet again, until we are able to spend our lives together honorably as man and wife. This ring is our troth and pledge throughout eternity."

"Yes," she echoed. "A promise for eternity."

After Fengmo left her, she fell down upon her pillow and

wept, and so it was that Crystal found her a short time
later. The rain had already begun to fall from the sky in
huge, dust-laden drops.

Crystal ran to Golden Willow, her face a mask of alarm.
"Come, Mistress! Get indoors at once, lest you be drenched
clear through! You will take your death lying out here. A
storm is coming!"

When Golden Willow sat up and the serving girl saw
that she was naked and her face all swollen with weeping,
she knew not what to think. Her concern grew. She hurried to wrap the soiled sheet about her mistress's shoulders. "Let us make for the apartment at once. You are ill!"

Still sobbing, Golden Willow could make no answer. She
stumbled and nearly fell several times before Crystal managed to get her indoors and tuck her beneath the quilts of
her bed.

For days afterward she stayed in that bed, while outside
the storm howled. She would confide nothing to Crystal.
Everyone else in the house was convinced they knew the
reason for her prostrated and overwrought condition. After all, had Golden Willow's husband not shamed her? Was
she not now a lone and barren woman?

The servants and lower members of the family spoke of
the tragedy in hushed voices, but only among themselves.
Not one maligned the House of Chang to an outsider.

Chapter Twenty-nine

The Tanpo Valley lay ankle-deep in mud. The crops, rather than being helped by the violent deluge, were severely damaged. The overworked soil eroded; invaluable silt washed away; wheat was beaten down and the hoped-for harvest was scant indeed. The faces of the country folk were drawn and bitter with the sure knowledge that they and their children must prepare for a harsh and meager winter. The situation was made worse by the increasing flood of refugees—most hungry, all in desperate need. The horde, in a rush to press northward while the weather held, gleaned what little remained in the fields.

As Kao had predicted, the price of grain shot sky-high.

This last fact was a great source of contention between Fengmo and his father. Master Chang considered himself a fair and just man, but he was one who saved his philanthropies for the city temples and foundling homes.

"Am I to feed the entire valley?" he asked his son angrily. "If I were to try, my granaries would be empty within a week and still people would starve. Moreover, a free gift of grain for only our own people would cause a clamor, a riot the likes of which has never been seen. Use your head, my son!"

"So instead, you make a profit!" Fengmo retorted in frustration.

"And since when is it wrong to make a profit? This house would not be standing now if your forefathers, and theirs before them, had been squeamish about making a profit!"

Master Chang struggled to remain calm and reason with his Second Son, who would one day take leadership of the entire clan. "In the nobleness of your heart, you be-

lieve the people would thank you for your kindness.
Fengmo, I tell you they would not. They would take the
helping hand you offer and chew it off to the elbow! I have
a few years on you; will you not listen and learn?"

But Fengmo would not listen. No words, nor rich man's
logic, could convince him it was right *or* reasonable to
squeeze the peasants dry—not even when that man was his
father, whom he had always loved and respected. A wall
began to grow up between the two of them, and each day
the wall grew higher because both were stubborn and each
refused to compromise.

During these autumn days, there were many things that
weighed heavily upon Fengmo. Now that communication
with his father was altered and all but broken, he turned
more and more often to Sean.

"You must be patient," his friend told him. "Change
cannot come overnight. Centuries of tradition—and, I will
admit, callousness—have molded men like your father. Do
not think I lack respect for the Honorable Hai-teh, for I do
not. He simply follows the teachings of your ancestors. He
wears blinders. Only time and a new kind of education will
remold him."

"I fear his education will prove too hard, or worse, too
late!" exclaimed Fengmo. "Our race is known for its caution, Sean. You know this is true, but there is a movement
afoot. Change is in the very air we breathe."

"There is a more immediate war to be fought," Sean replied, with just an edge of impatience. "The upheaval you
fear will surely come, but not yet, not until this other is
over and done. It is Japan we need fear most right now. Put
your heart and soul into survival, Fengmo. Your family
will need all the strength and stability you possess. Hold
fast to your dreams, but give them the place they deserve—
the future. Bad days, many bad days, lie ahead. Mend the
breach with your father. Find some middle ground and
come to terms with him. For the sake of yourself and all in
this house, let any conflicts be those you can face and fight
together. It is an old but true adage that a divided house
will fall. Let it not be so for the House of Chang!"

This lecture, and the vehemence with which it had been
spoken, surprised Fengmo. He realized that in his own
unique and indomitable way, Sean Duncan was adminis-

tering a rebuke. Yet Fengmo could not be angry, for he knew beyond a doubt that the American loved the people upon the land as well as the family of Chang. More important, everything Sean had said was true.

"I will try to find that middle ground you speak of, friend," Fengmo slowly replied. "I know my father is not without wisdom. I will go and attempt to talk to him in a more cool-headed manner."

He looked at Sean with a furrowed brow. "Do you truly believe that war will actually come even to Tanpo?"

"Yes," Sean said, and he also frowned deeply. "How long, I wonder, will the rest of the world stand by and watch the rape of China? My own homeland cries its horror and yet does nothing!"

Fengmo was tempted to suggest that Sean forget the great United States of America, a country which Wong Six had once told him "roared like a leopard" but was, in reality, "only a paper tiger."

"The symbol of that nation is an eagle," Six had said many times, "but its heart beats like that of a humming-bird!"

At first, Fengmo said none of these things, knowing how deeply he himself loved and cared for his own country. Still, he thought of the fair-haired American as an incongruous Chinese and not a foreigner, and in the end he decided to speak to him as such.

"The nation of your people is a babe yet," he stated, "still cutting its milk teeth. There is much your leaders have to learn."

It was the wrong thing to say. The normally imperturbable Sean bristled defensively. "Babes we might be, Fengmo, but my countrymen do not and have never lacked for courage. No, the people are only wearied now, drained by the Great Depression. They are leery of the conflicts of other nations, seeing how many they have of their own. But they *will* rally and hear the cries of China soon. I am sure of it!"

Fengmo commented no further. It suddenly occurred to him how, worried about his own affairs, he had failed to attune himself to the recently altered personality of his best friend and closest companion. Sean was unusually restless of late. His times of reflection seemed more frequent and exclusive.

Perhaps it is his plan to leave us soon, thought Fengmo, not without pain. It has been foolish on my part to take his presence here for granted. I will hate it if he does go, for he has become like my older brother . . .

Thinking of an older brother made him wince inwardly. Never could he remember Kao without also thinking of his beloved, and such thought was almost unbearably painful now. Having once known Golden Willow so completely, Fengmo was haunted by the memory of her skin and hair, lips and eyes. Strangely, he felt not a bit of guilt, neither for the physical act of love they had shared, nor for his almost torturous recollections. At times it was all he could do not to recant his high-mindedness and stride into her court. When sleeping he dreamed of defying the world, claiming her once and for all. Only with dawn's light did his more noble and sensible self return to acknowledge the hard truths of reality.

For several days after they had shared that beautiful and unforgettable night, he had not seen her at all. Through Fong Lu, who was kept informed by Crystal, he learned only that Golden Willow, chilled by the first sudden storm, had been taken ill. No amount of cautious probing had elicited further information. There had been nothing for him to do but wait and worry. How he longed to see her and know she was well!

Finally, pale of face and extremely passive, she had appeared at the evening meal. Pain ripped through Fengmo at the sight of her. He had to look down at his food lest someone see his private agony. Yet, as the meal progressed, a measure of peace came to him. The love they shared, the bittersweet secret, seemed to fill the room, passing back and forth between them without benefit of word or even a glance.

Ever so cautiously, he looked up and searched her fingers for the jade ring, knowing the sight would bring him comfort. A small frown creased his brow when he realized she wore it not. Just then she leaned forward and he was able to glimpse the tiny jade circle suspended from a gold chain which hung about her neck.

Ah, he had breathed, *she keeps it close to heart!* The

thought had given him temporary pleasure and peace of mind.

Since that night, hardly a glance had passed between them. But every now and again, Fengmo would enter a room or a courtyard and catch the essence of her still wafting through the air. So, during his waking hours, he kept busy and found a kind of solace. Only his sleep remained troubled and filled with unattainable fantasies.

Moon Shadow was growing desperate. No matter what she did to impress the man who held her affections, she failed miserably. He was a stern and relentless teacher, and she, Moon Shadow, felt like a dodo bird. It seemed impossible for her to grasp the slurs and flat, guttural cadences of the English language. Her small, oval face grew positively red with the effort. Moreover, the very presence of Sean Duncan hovering over her made the task more rigorous than it might otherwise have been. She much preferred the sight of him to the horrible books he pushed beneath her nose.

The fact that Golden Willow was able to do the same lessons with such quick avidity only made matters worse. Moon Shadow nearly died of humiliation each time Sean paid the older girl a compliment and then turned a cold, disparaging eye upon his youngest pupil. Her dreams echoed with his clucking disapproval.

Today it had happened again, and Moon Shadow acted more the fool than ever. She was thoroughly convinced he must view her as a complete idiot.

After a particularly lengthy, if gentle, admonishment from her tutor, she had jumped up from the library table, knocking back her chair in the process, and ran from the room in tears.

Now she lay on a bed in the room she shared with New Moon and wept in deep earnest. For once, her elder sister was not critical. Instead, she sat next to Moon Shadow and stroked her heaving shoulders. "Do not be sad, little cuckoo," she crooned.

Moon Shadow bolted upright and cried out her frustration. "Oh! Oh! See, you *too* think I am nothing but a stupid! Not one person in this whole house thinks me in the least intelligent or worthwhile!" Again she flopped down and wept louder, kicking her little feet.

"Do not carry on so!" New Moon said. "Who cares about the *English* anyhow? Certainly not I! It is a barbarous tongue, to say the very least."

Moon Shadow succumbed to violent hiccups. She sat and dabbed at her eyes with a crumpled silk kerchief. The tip of her nose was red. "Y-you understand no-nothing," she said. *"Hick!* It is that—that *S-S-Shawn Dooncan!"*

New Moon nodded in sudden understanding. "Aha! You hate him! I do not blame you a bit, Little Sister. He seems very polite, but he is so-o-o-o-o *ugly!"*

At these words, Moon Shadow broke into a long, loud wail and threw herself down with such violence that New Moon became frightened and ran to fetch their mother.

A few moments later, Madame Chang came rushing into the bedchamber. Right behind her came Li Ma, toting a tray laden with a pot of some foul-smelling brew and a giant cup. Moon Shadow spent the rest of the afternoon gagging and having her system purged. Her mother stayed by her side and nursed her with loving but suspicious care.

Sean sat alone in the twilight and smoked his pipe. He had chosen his favorite spot in the compound for this respite, the most deserted and quiet, a place he had discovered quite by accident while on one of his frequent meanderings. It was the small temple courtyard. The old priest who resided in the temple itself, preferring the company of his gods, seemed but rarely to avail himself of the pleasant garden. The place suited Sean to perfection. He came here often lately to enjoy the peace and solitude it provided.

I will miss this house, he thought. It is all a settled man could desire. Yes, a home, a thriving family, a wife . . . But I am not a settled man. I have been adrift since the moment of my birth.

He pulled a soiled scrap of paper from the pocket of his shirt and studied it for perhaps the hundredth time. Written in Chinese, it was an article from a Nationalist newspaper.

Sean often sought out the refugees and listened to their tales of what was happening in the war zones. It was by way of one of these conversations that he had learned of a group of American pilots who were fighting the Japanese invaders on China's behalf. The people had already branded them with the complimentary title of Flying Tigers. The article he now scanned enumerated many deeds of valor on the part of these men. Their courage, their support of the Chinese cause, beckoned to Sean Duncan as nothing ever had before. He knew that finally, at long last, he could seek and find a place where he belonged. He would contact these fighting men who were of his own race and strive to become one of them. They were no doubt violent sorts, rough and rowdy fellows who preferred the roar of aircraft cannons to the soft incantations of prayer.

Sean tilted his head to one side and could almost hear the thunder of those cannons. His soul leapt with new vitality, and suddenly he knew that he too was a man of violent emotions. He wanted to *fight*, give vent to his suppressed rage and frustration. He wanted no more of platitudes.

The shock of discovery, this unveiling of his own secret character, left him breathless and dizzy. I am not a low or mean person, he told himself with assurance. I am, quite simply, sick to death of this life of wandering lassitude. I love China with a vengeance, and now I will express that devotion!

He sat very still on the stone bench he occupied. His face was aglow with new determination as he dreamed his glorious dreams. He did not hear the warning snap of a twig. Therefore, when the figure of Moon Shadow appeared before him he was so startled that he dropped his pipe.

"I come to you, Shawn Dooncan," she said in a soft, timid voice, "to apologize for my stupidity."

It took him several moments to pull his soul back from the clouds. He bent and picked up his pipe, tamped it with fresh tobacco, and relighted it. He then gave his full attention to Moon Shadow, who remained exactly as she had been, standing with her head bowed, exhibiting an uncommon patience. Sean cleared his throat. "You are not stupid," he said mildly, and exhaled a wisp of aromatic smoke. "You are only inattentive."

"I am stupid."

He stood and looked down at the top of her head. "You should not be here, child."

She turned her face upward and gazed at him. Her eyes were brimming with unshed tears. "I am stupid, Shawn Dooncan, but I am no child. I love you."

"You are a child," he repeated. The words came with difficulty, for he was thinking how very lovely she appeared at that moment. "And by comparison I am an ancient."

Her face settled into stubborn lines. "You are my heart."

"God help me!" It was the first prayer he had uttered in a long, long time, and he automatically spoke the words in English.

"Why do you call upon your god? Is my presence so threatening that you need divine protection?" The tears were gone and she smiled mischievously.

Sean threw back his head and laughed. Obviously, his tutoring had taken deeper root than he had ever suspected. Her tinkling laughter joined his before they both grew serious again. Sean searched her eyes.

"I will speak to your father in the morning," he said gravely.

Her face beamed like a New Year's lantern, but she only nodded and bowed. She had gone as far as the courtyard gate when he called to her in a soft voice.

"It will be a prolonged betrothal, little one."

Moon Shadow turned and dipped her head in a bow. "Long or short, I am content to wait."

Chapter Thirty

The leaves on the birch trees were beginning to turn a mottled orange and brown. The winds blew almost constantly and often carried with them ominous clouds which inundated the valley with cold, pelting rains. The peasants kept indoors and fueled their braziers sparingly with dried grass. Wives mended and patched cotton clothing they could not afford to replace. The children gathered around oldsters and listened to spirit tales, while family men congregated in the small tea houses to compare their bad luck and mumble against the rich. In short, all pursued cold-weather pastimes.

The refugees once more became a trickle of perhaps fifty a day, but these, finding the fields fallow and plucked clean, came into the city. Many of them were hungry and resorted to begging. The shopkeepers and other petty merchants complained long and loudly about these people, who seemed always to have disturbingly ravaged faces and extended palms. Since they themselves had not been bombed, nor yet heard the true rumble and thunder of war, they had come to believe they would remain virtually unscathed. The rumors of war, the wild talk and occasional newspapers, still held their interest. However, they were fast tiring of the influx of ragged folk who sludged through the muddy streets with their sparse goods and squalling children.

A group of these small businessmen came collectively to complain and seek guidance from Master Chang. They were shown into the vast audience hall to await the pleasure of their acknowledged leader. All of them looked up to the Honorable Hai-teh, whose wisdom and business acu-

men was renowned. In fact, that respected gentleman had
been a lender and patron to quite a few of them.

So they waited, more than a little surprised to find they
were not served hot tea as had always been the case before.
An hour passed and almost another. The group was growing extremely restive and beginning to murmur in discontent when the large wooden doors swung open.

A servant entered to announce the arrival of not only
the Honorable Hai-teh, Master of the House of Chang, but
also Chang Fengmo, Illustrious Second Son.

The waiting men, having already noticed and commented upon the dual chairs sitting side by side upon the
dais, had automatically assumed the slightly lower one
was reserved for the eldest son. It was traditional that, at
any given time, the master of a great house might begin to
include his heir in the important doings which took place
in an audience hall. After all, it was inevitable that one
generation must slowly relinquish authority to the next.
But to the *Second Son?*

They fastened curious and speculative eyes on the tall
figure of Fengmo as he followed closely behind his father.
The young man bowed deeply toward his elder as the two
reached the dais, and, according to custom, did not seat
himself until Master Chang was comfortably settled. The
crowd became hushed and attentive.

Master Chang looked out over the group and cleared his
throat. His manner was far more imperious and officious
than usual. "My worthy fellow citizens," he began, "you
have called upon me and I am here to listen and to serve
your needs." He swept an arm in Fengmo's direction. "You
will note that my Second Son sits here as heir and cohort."

The crowd began to murmur again and he stopped them
with a raised hand. "You ask yourselves why my eldest is
not here instead and I will explain, though I need not. I am
free under the laws of this province or any other to choose
whom I will as my successor, but in respect, I give you full
explanation.

"My firstborn, Kao, has been stricken with a lingering
disease."

Both Fengmo and Hai-teh kept their chins up and their
eyes straight forward.

"He is ill and unable to take command of the numerous

and complicated family affairs," Master Chang continued. "But you will find that this one who sits beside me now is honest and has the innate ability needed to take his brother's place. I give you my word he will not be pompous or overbearing. He will lend an ear to your woes and administer justice fairly.

"Hear me. His tutelage and gradual accession begins now. I pray that, for your part, you will lend him the same attention and courtesy you have afforded me down through the years."

This said and apparently accepted, the formalities began. One man, a silk merchant who had been chosen as spokesman, stepped forward and dropped to his knees. After touching his forehead to the floor nine times in a traditional kowtow, he rose and looked from father to son. He respectfully addressed his loquacious preambles to both and then came to the heart of the business for which he and his colleagues had come.

"We are being hindered, Illustrious Sir," the spokesman began, "by the hordes of people coming at us from the southward and coastal regions. They are a wild-eyed and hungry lot who have no homes or hopes. Though we are not without pity, neither can we continue giving them of our sustenance."

Master Chang looked at the man and then down at his own fingernails. "Are those people still a horde then?" he asked in a mild tone. "I realize that, living here at this end of town, I do not see every little thing that happens. It seems to me, however, that they are fewer and fewer in number since the summer has passed."

The spokesman looked pained and wagged his head. Before answering he took a moment to smooth down over a very large belly the fine silk robe he wore. "To a degree you are right, of course, sir. But over the summer months they stayed primarily on the outskirts and moved along the valley roads. Now they come boldly into the city. Their feet are all muddy and they walk right through the doors of the shops. Hardly ever do they enter to make a purchase, either—certainly not in my own good store. No, they come inside to beg, or almost as bad, they linger out on the stoop to waylay and pester my customers. I am not the only one. We here are all in the same predicament. How on earth are we to make a living? We know that you have wisdom above such as us, Honorable One, and we seek your solution."

Master Chang still seemed intent on his nails. He sat thoughtfully for some time before looking up. His face was passive and his eyes unreadable. "Let me understand your problem. According to you men, the war refugees have become an abominable nuisance."

Most men in the room nodded and buzzed their assent, but a few hung their heads and did not look up.

"And," continued the Honorable Hai-teh, "during the summer, when they came by the hundreds upon hundreds, they restrained themselves, for the most part, by only plucking food from the mouths of the peasants."

His brows were beginning to beetle now, and there was just enough dangerous intonation in his voice to make his listeners shuffle their feet.

He fixed the spokesman with a baleful eye and called him by name. "You, Po Chuk, have you and these other good men thought of *any* solution you wish me to consider?"

Of a sudden, the silk merchant began to perspire. "We have thought of one possibility, Master," he mumbled.

"Speak up, man! I must be going deaf, for I cannot hear you."

Po Chuk looked up. His glance wavered and shifted. "We feel," he said, taking his courage in hand, "that it would be wise to bar the city gates at all times, instead of only at night as we have always done before. Refugees are easy to spot since they most often look like beggars and vagrants. The city gatemen could refuse them entrance."

To the surprise and trepidation of his audience, Master Chang stood and began pacing back and forth on the dais. Though not loud, his voice reached every ear. "Yes, I suppose that could be one solution. We *could* close out those folks who have been bombed and have lost their loved ones and their homes. We *could* complacently turn our backs on those crushed beneath the boot of Imperial Japan."

He stopped suddenly and faced the crowd. His eyes were angry and bright. The corners of his mouth turned down grimly. "I have not been as insensitive to your plight as you might think. My peers from the houses of Tung and

Tse and Ling have met with me, and we have discussed this troublesome issue at some length. We are all in agreement that there is indeed a problem."

His voice rose. "Think not that you men here must bear the guilt alone. *All* in this prosperous, well-fed city are culpable. But we shall be so no longer! Tanpo will support the people of this nation in their time of trial and woe!"

The vehemence of his last words made the entire crowd step back a few paces, thus leaving the quivering silk merchant standing very much alone.

Master Chang went on. "Every great and small house in this city will dip into its coffers and give, each according to his income, an amount for the temporary relief of the refugees. Makeshift shelters and a kitchen will be set up for them that they might rest and be fed a simple meal or two before they press on."

He cast the audience another look. "You need not worry much longer in any case. The snow will soon come and put an end to your hardships and long suffering."

A premature sigh of mollification went up from many of those gathered, but Master Chang had by no means finished. He paused only long enough to let his eyes meet those of his son.

"But," he continued, and the listeners stiffened again, "that kitchen I speak of will remain on Bantam Street throughout the cold and desolate months. Our own people, the peasants who toil for us, will be in dire need. If we combine our resources, they too can be fed. Everyone here, and all in the great houses, will tighten their belts just a bit so these aims can be accomplished. Let the poor at least be assured their children will be kept from starvation."

He sat back down again and looked upon the pale-faced men in the audience hall. "That is *my* solution, and I have faith you will agree it is one well thought out and worthy of consideration."

The crowd nodded silently. They knew very well that the houses of Chang and Tse and the others of wealth had combined and now presented a united front. To complain or refuse to comply would be disastrous. Loans could too easily be called in with the coming of the New Year and they need not necessarily be renewed or extended. Yes, the power of Tanpo now faced these citizens as never before.

Many there were ashamed of their own selfishness and lack of patriotism, but others were bitter. The latter group, however, had the good sense to keep that bitterness to themselves.

Suddenly weary, Master Chang adjourned the meeting and motioned to Fengmo. Following his sire out of the hall, the young man almost smiled, for his heart was near bursting with pride.

Two days later Master Chang was passing by an open gate that led into the small courtyard inhabited by his two youngest offspring and heard terrible screams emanating from there. Upon rushing in to see what the matter was, he was taken staggeringly aback to witness his own wife, her face a mask of rage, thrashing Hsu and Tan with a willow switch. Without mercy she whipped them the entire length of their writhing bodies, while they lay on the ground and screeched. She was breathing in harsh and labored pants.

Master Chang ran to her and caught hold of her flailing arm. "Wife! What is the meaning of this? Have you gone mad? Stop at once!"

He looked down on the prostrated, shivering bodies of his fourth and fifth sons and then, incredulously, at the bloodless face of his wife. Madame Chang jerked from his grasp and threw the switch violently aside. She spoke from between compressed lips. "Ever have my children been a vexation to me!"

She looked back at him with undisguised accusation. "And *you* are no comfort either! With your own wagging tongue, you have betrothed my little Moon Shadow to that—that *foreigner!* No, and you do not care that I disapprove most heartily!"

The pent-up bitterness spewed out of her mouth, leaving her astounded mate absolutely speechless. "I cannot mention my own firstborn, whom I loved, before you! There is a vile concubine residing in our back court!"

She turned a glittering and malevolent gaze on the cowering figures at her feet. "These two, they are *wicked* and will break my heart! It is not enough that they fill the drinking water with tadpoles and put snakes and lizards into the servants' beds. No, such mischief is not enough for this pair!"

She bent down and snatched a large, crooked stick up off the courtyard tiles. "These monsters, thinking I was only a small cousin, jumped out from behind their gate waving this weapon in the air. Moreover, they were screaming at the top of their putrid little lungs, '*Kill the rich! Down with the wicked rich!*' " Madame Chang's eyes thinned to slits. She shook the stick in her husband's face. "That is not all, Father of My Sons! When I had recovered from my heart failure, this one"—she prodded a whimpering Tan with her foot—"had the audacity to tell me, in the snotty little way he has, that he and Hsu have very noble ambitions. These two think it would be wonderful indeed, when they are old enough, to become *comrade generals!* They have been eavesdropping in the court of *your* precious Second Son, listening to the endless talks he carries on with that despicable round-eyes . . . your future son-in-law!"

"But our son and Sean do not believe in—" Master Chang tried to interrupt her tirade, but she would not allow him another word.

"Do not tell me of *beliefs!*" she yelled. Her face was now mottled. "There is no one in Tanpo who does not know you have become a champion of the wretched. Why, you are spending half our fortune, and care nothing for your own good heritage." Again she turned malevolent eyes on her two youngest. "Perhaps it is best after all. These children are ever like a thorn to me. Yes, and I see no reason why they should inherit one piece of silver between them!"

Madame Chang pulled at her hair. "Oh, it is more than I can bear! I must go to the temple and seek a measure of peace from our Goddess of Mercy! Only she can understand my bleeding soul!"

With that she threw down the gnarled stick and then marched from the court without a backward glance.

The boys had quit sobbing and now they lay very still, feeling the stern eyes of their father upon them. An eternity seemed to pass before they heard the quiet tone they had learned to dread most.

"I should beat you again and yet again, and so will I if ever I hear of such games being played again by you small, worthless persons. You will go to your room and remain indoors for the next week. Meals will be brought to you, but on no account will you speak to anyone except to each other. For those few days, you are no part of this family."

Master Chang's soul was in more turmoil than his young sons could possibly have guessed. *What have I done?* he wondered. *I no longer know what is good and what is bad. The world is upside down!*

Nothing seemed clear in his mind these days. Ever since the incident with Kao, his own Peaceful Dawn had turned into a shrew. Every little thing seemed to upset her. It seemed no matter what he decided, someone would be displeased. On one side there was his wife, whom he dearly loved, and on the other Fengmo, whom he also loved.

Master Chang expelled a long, weary sigh. *I can only do what I think right and best,* he told himself. *No man can do more!*

Suddenly, he felt old, old, old. With wagging head and shuffling gait, he walked away from the two quivering figures still lying face down on the ground.

After he had gone, the two little boys cautiously raised their tear-swollen faces. Groaning in misery, they stood up and limped indoors—but not before they broke the stick they had played with into very small twigs.

Once they had entered their own room, Hsu turned to his younger brother. "Do not speak to me either, you troublemaker! I will hear no word from you until all my bruises disappear!"

Chapter Thirty-one

*T*he air was like ice, so chill it hurt the lungs. Bright Autumn and her two brothers ascended the last rise and looked out over the valley. Tanpo sparkled like a perfect jewel in the near twilight.

"It will be warmer below," said Wong Four, slapping his sides. His breath came out in puffs of fog and he shivered.

All three of the travelers had chapped faces. Their clothing was suitable only for the lower regions—quilted jackets of blue cotton and light trousers. Their feet were shod in straw sandals and they carried crude cloth bundles. No one observing them would ever have taken them for the offspring of a very wealthy family, nor suspected for an instant that the three young people now standing upon the huge, pitted boulder had spent their lives amidst opulence and had never turned their soft hands to a task until recently. No, they looked like a trio of unsmiling peasants. With lean faces and weary eyes, they looked down upon the Tanpo Valley.

"It is beautiful," breathed Bright Autumn.

Her brothers said nothing for a time. A few weeks ago, either of them might have been apt to grumble at the sight of such a rural panorama, but no longer. The past now seemed almost like a dream, a fantasy which never really existed. Their feet were calloused, their muscles hard, and they knew the meaning of death and deprivation. The days and weeks spent traveling inland on foot, mingling with simple folk, most often sleeping out-of-doors, had given them a new and unexpectedly different view of life.

Wong Five shook himself. "We are lucky to beat the winter snow. I have never seen the stuff, but I swear I can feel it in the air! Let us go!"

Bright Autumn had gained much physical strength during her arduous journey, and something more as well—she had found herself enjoying the conversations she had with the other women she met along the way. All were refugees like she was, though in most cases they did not come from backgrounds of wealth or breeding. It soon became apparent, however, that the loss of a home was no less traumatic if that home happened to be humble. A bomb was just as devastating, death as real, soldiers as terrifying to the poor as to the rich.

"My brother was murdered by a great silver egg which fell from the sky," one young woman had told her. "He was working in our field and it dropped upon him without warning. We went out to see and could only find bits and pieces of him."

The girl's broad face was pale with shock. Her thick lips quivered. On that evening she had grown very dear to Bright Autumn. The two had wept softly together and shared their grief.

Bright Autumn knew she would never forget that girl, who she might have considered homely and uncouth at one time. Likewise, there had been old women, wives, and children—a veritable world of faces and tragedies that would stay with her until the day she died.

Yet at this moment, scrambling down steep slopes, her heart sang. The weariness of the preceding weeks fell away from her and her feet were sure and steady. Her muscles felt supple and vibrant as she made her way ever downward. Never could she remember seeing anything as breathtakingly beautiful as the sight her eyes now beheld. The valley was washed in puce beneath an orange and golden sky. The terraced fields, with their intermittent clusters of huts, seemed to roll and dip in purple shadow. And the city itself, sitting behind ancient walls, shimmered like an alluring, iridescent mirage.

Home!

The thought leapt into her mind unbidden, and suddenly she knew it was true. The vast estate in Shanghai, the city itself, was the place of her birth, the heritage of her forefathers and her parents. But Tanpo was to become, and would be forever more, her true home. Her sons and daughters would be born in this valley. As she moved along, she could almost feel herself taking root in the soil, which was becoming less rocky with each step.

It was dark by the time they finally began to weave along the paths which separated the fields. The smell of cook fires hung in the air and autumn mists were closing in around them. Hampered by the mists, they were forced to move slowly and with care.

"My stomach rumbles," said Wong Five. "I hope we will find a meal awaiting us. It seems an eternity since I have had more than rice and hot water!"

Bright Autumn could not help but smile a little at this remark. Oh, it was true enough that none of them had eaten lavishly on their journey, but it had been as much a matter of caution as necessity. Within their bundles, each of them carried a considerable amount of cash. However, they could hardly have moved with the refugees, that seething mass of poor, and eaten like potentates. There had been so many times when Bright Autumn wished she could buy spiced pork and dumplings, bowls of noodles, mounds of fruit and tender vegetables, not only for herself, but for all those around her. Even had she owned the wealth of the world it would have been impossible, for there was little to purchase along the wide swathe cut by the refugees. Only after she and her brothers began to ascend the range of craggy mountains had their fellow wayfarers fallen away. Few were now willing to chance being snowbound. It had seemed wiser for the refugees to wait out the coming season and pray the Japanese did not arrive too soon.

The trio arrived at Tanpo, only to find the massive, iron-studded gates tightly shut. Wong Four banged loudly and long.

"Who goes there?" called the keeper in a gruff voice. All that could be seen of him were his two rheumy eyes peeking through a small hinged door cut into the gate itself.

"We seek entrance, sir," Wong Four called back. "We three have business in the House of Chang."

"Step closer," ordered the keeper.

They came up to the gate and crowded around the peephole. The keeper lifted an oil lantern beside his face and peered at them with narrowed eyes. "Oh, no doubt!" he scoffed. "Every day of the week such as you have business with the Honorable Hai-teh. Go away!"

He was just about to close the little door when Wong Four spoke again. "Wait, Old Father! We may appear riff-raff to you, but we are not. Moreover, I do not blame you for your vigilance. Still, just to put your mind at ease, I will give you three pieces of silver toward your retirement. Could a beggar do that?"

The old man's eyes widened and his lids fluttered. "You could if you were a robber or a soldier! By the sacred loin-cloth of Buddha, go away!"

Again he was going to slam the door, but Bright Autumn stepped forward. "We are not from these parts, and we know not your terrors. But I assure you, we are not bandits. I am the betrothed of the Second Son of Chang Hai-teh. I have traveled all the way from Shanghai and am very weary. Will you not admit us?" Her voice was lilting and helpless. Even dressed as she was, her face all smudged with dirt, she had a dazzling smile and her posture was aristocratic.

The gateman squinted and scratched his head. "The betrothed of Chang Fengmo?"

Bright Autumn nodded. "I am worthless and it seems impossible, I know, but I have told you the truth, Old Father."

"Well," he replied, "now I am in a fix. If you lie and I admit you, I will no doubt die. On the other hand, vagabonds though you look, I dare not leave future kinfolk of the Chang family out in the cold, inhospitable night."

He continued to look at Bright Autumn, who stood modestly with slightly bowed head in the faint pool of light.

"Oh, me," sighed the old man. "I must do what I must do. I have never heard of robbers or military men taking their women with them on raids. I will take a chance. If I get a knife in the belly, it will serve me right for being a fool!"

The peephole slammed instantly shut and a moment later the entire gate creaked open a foot or two. "Hurry now!" hissed the gateman.

Once they were safely inside, he gave them hurried directions and then ran into his small hut and shut the door. Only the sound of a single barking dog could be heard as, with dragging feet, the exhausted trio made their way through the deserted streets of Tanpo.

Almost three months had passed without any word having been received from Shanghai. Hope was beginning to wither and die. Fengmo, who had helped collect funds and set up the small relief station, had searched every face and asked news of one refugee after another. "Have you spoken to any from Shanghai?"

The answer was nearly always the same. "Shanghai? Few escape *that* city! It is said the enemy holds the port in a death grip!"

Every once in a while someone would answer in the affirmative and tell of a lucky soul or two who had escaped. Some were mentioned by name, but never once did Fengmo hear the name he wished. There were families, surnamed Wong, who came through Tanpo from as far away as the cities of She-hsien or Ho-fei. There were even a few from the southern province of Fukien, but no sign or news of such a family from Shanghai. Worse, there were almost no refugees coming into the city now.

The skies had been a bright metallic blue during the past days, and the air frosty. It was always thus just before leaden clouds rolled in and the temperature went up slightly. Daily, Fengmo watched for this seasonal omen, which had never troubled him before, and prayed heaven would withhold its hand a bit longer. He could not hide his concern for the safety of Bright Autumn and her brothers. Though he had cause to worry, and though it seemed more than natural to everyone else, Fengmo wondered at his own attitude. Lately, he found his thoughts often going back to that last goodbye in Shanghai. At night Golden Willow still came to claim his soul and mind, but through the days he worried almost endlessly about Bright Autumn.

Perhaps it is the refugees, he told himself. To save my soul I cannot picture that modern girl, Bright Autumn, among them—or her wild brothers . . . and yet I know they are. Life as they once knew it is shattered. What will she be like when she arrives?

Near dusk, Madame Chang entered the family temple to find the small padded stool before the altar already occupied. Her mouth turned down at the corners as she watched Golden Willow light a joss stick and place it in the small receptacle before the Goddess of Fertility, that most stable and constant of deities.

Yes, the countenance of Madame Chang became quite flushed and ambiguous. She turned and left the dimly lighted temple without making a sound.

The lips of Golden Willow murmured in supplication. Never in her life had she prayed as she did now, not even on that stormy night over a year ago when she had beseeched the gods to free her from her troth to Kao.

"Oh, Merciful One," she pleaded, her hands clasped, "grant me this favor; give me this single desire of my heart and I will never trouble you again. Let happiness grow in my most unworthy womb. Hear me, Mother of Life! Please, *please,* give me a child!"

On and on she prayed until her legs were cramped and she could kneel no longer. When finally she stood and bowed a last time, the chain about her neck swung forward. The jade ring caught and held the light, glowing for an instant.

Golden Willow shivered in the chill air and pulled her fur-lined robe tightly about her. For weeks she had come to the temple, and tomorrow she would come yet again.

That night, the evening meal was a special affair, a time of both joy and sorrow. Sean Duncan was leaving. He had at last established communication with the American general, Claire Chennault, and would leave at dawn on the following morning to begin his journey to a small quasimilitary base located in Hunan Province.

Moon Shadow was bereft and proud. Her handsome betrothed was to become a member of those valorous Flying Tigers; it was cause for *great* pride. But for once, closely watched, she had to adhere to the customs and traditions set down centuries ago. Her family had not yet become modern enough to allow her a private goodbye with the man she loved. In truth, except for her and Sean, who would not tell an untruth, only Master Chang knew that the couple had spent even those few moments alone in the temple court.

Sean was in rare spirits and anxious to begin his new adventure. His sadness at departing was made much less painful by the knowledge that Moon Shadow and this family, who had accepted and all but adopted him, would await his return. He smiled and laughed heartily as he sat eating this final meal.

Fengmo could not help but rejoice also. To see his friend so apparently happy, with feet set firmly in a specific and personally satisfying direction, did his heart good. For that hour he tried not to think of Golden Willow sitting so silently across the room, or of Bright Autumn, or even of the Japanese.

A servant filled the cups of the men with strong sorghum wine and Master Chang rose to offer up a toast. "To my white son—may we pray daily that he return to us safe and sound, bedecked in glory!"

All in the room called out their agreement, except for Madame Chang. She sat at the head of the women's table wearing a morose and somber frown. At that moment her soul was curdled and bitter.

"Master!" Li Chi, the cook, broke into the room, wiping his hands upon the filthy apron he so proudly wore. Unmindful of proper decorum, he ran straight to Master Chang and began speaking in a booming voice. His fat face was wreathed in a smile.

"We have visitors, Master!" he bellowed. "That gateman of ours thought they were beggars at first and almost turned them away. But they are in my kitchen this very minute! The Wongs have arrived!"

Chapter Thirty-two

*B*right Autumn was placed in the apartment of Golden Willow. A small, well-padded cot was ordered prepared for Fengmo's betrothed, who adamantly refused to crowd or inconvenience her future sister-in-law in any way whatsoever. Only with the greatest urging would she even allow that the cot be set up in the regular bedchamber. She stated with all sincerity that she would be quite comfortable enough sleeping in the sitting room where Crystal had once laid her pallet.

Madame Chang, who had suddenly come to life, would hear none of it. Her dignity and dry humor were quite restored by the arrival of Bright Autumn and her two brothers. She had rushed immediately into the kitchen behind Li Chi and begun giving instructions to her staff.

The waterkeeper was set to work kindling a fire beneath his huge caldron so that the newly arrived guests might bathe the dust of the road from their bodies as soon as possible. Since all three had demurred at joining the rest of the family to partake of the meal because of their grimy and disheveled states, they supped in royal fashion right there in the kitchen. Old Li Chi was in his glory and kept heaping food into their bowls until they were sure they would explode. This done, Bright Autumn was quickly guided out of the room so the men of the house could crowd around Four and Five and bombard those weary souls with a million and one questions.

"I swear," Madame Chang said to Bright Autumn as Crystal, torch in hand, led the way to Golden Willow's apartment. "That husband and Second Son of mine have no consideration! Your poor brothers will be lucky to get a single hour of rest tonight!"

Once the three had passed through the moon gate, she turned to Crystal. "I have already ordered hot water fetched here. See that a fragrant bath is prepared the minute you get indoors."

Crystal bowed without speaking.

"I will leave you now," the older woman said to Bright Autumn, resting a hand on her arm. Suddenly, the mistress of the House of Chang was filled with affection for her future daughter-in-law. In this girl, who appeared little more than a peasant, she saw a whole new generation.

Almost the instant Bright Autumn crossed the threshold, she collapsed in a chair. All at once, she was too tired for words and grateful that the servant now pouring buckets of steaming water into an ancient Soochow tub seemed not inclined to chatter.

When Golden Willow entered a few minutes later, it was all her guest could do to stand and bow in greeting. Passively, with drooping lids, Bright Autumn submitted to Crystal's ministrations. After peeling away her soiled clothing, the servant threw them, one and all, out the front door.

The countenance of Crystal was like stone as she helped the other girl upon the bath stool and then watched as she lowered herself into the waters of the tub.

Golden Willow also watched. Above all, she wanted to feel nothing for this secret rival, neither affection nor hatred. Yet looking at Bright Autumn as she sighed deeply and rested her head against the lip of the tub, Golden Willow was moved. She knew full well this young woman was from a modern, educated home, a home of wealth and influence. She had seen the calloused soles and blistered hands and broken, encrusted fingernails. Upon entering the scented water, Bright Autumn's eyelids had fluttered closed.

Golden Willow did not want to feel anything toward this female who would soon become wife to the man she herself loved so deeply. Regardless, she was nearly overcome with sympathy. The flesh of Bright Autumn's chest and shoulders was soft and white in contrast to her sun-darkened face. That face was one of endurance, not to mention beauty. The body below it, which Golden Willow had fully glimpsed, was too lean and muscular, but its lines were well proportioned and still extremely feminine.

Crystal made no move to begin bathing their guest. She stood behind the tub holding a soft sea sponge and scowled. Uncaring, Bright Autumn appeared to be already asleep.

Golden Willow rolled up her sleeves and took the sponge. Gently, she pushed her servant aside. "Go now and pull back the coverlets on my bed," she said quietly. "She will rest there—for tonight, at least."

Crystal did not move, but stood and stared at her mistress with a shocked expression.

Golden Willow began to rub the sponge in slow circular motions over the exposed white shoulders of her secret rival. After a moment, she turned to Crystal and repeated her command, this time with a slight edge in her tone. "Do as I say. I will need salve too. Her palms are raw and bleeding."

Crystal silently bowed and obeyed.

It was dawn. The House of Chang slept as Moon Shadow pulled a fur robe around her night garments and slipped from her room. New Moon heard nothing, for she had pulled the covers over her head and was snoring softly.

Sean, having said all his farewells the night before, was just closing the courtyard gate when Moon Shadow came flying around the corner and up the path toward him. Her face was pale and timorous. Yet he could not keep from smiling. He knew she would never be the submissive, obedient wife a man of her own race had the traditional right to expect, but she suited Sean like no other. He thought her completely delightful.

Suddenly, he felt himself clasped in a surprisingly strong bear hug. "Oh, *Shawn,*" she wept. "I will miss you so much! Please come back soon!"

He tilted her chin upward and smiled into her eyes. "I will come back, little lotus, just as you see me now. And when I do, I will expect you to speak very good English. You may have need of it one day." He chuckled. *"When* you are all grown up."

Moon Shadow stepped back and stamped one foot. "Oh! You chastise me even with your parting breath! You are a very cruel and unfeeling man!" She too was smiling now.

"Touch my lips in the foreign way, *Shawn*," she begged, and then puckered her mouth and tightly closed her eyes.

He bent and gave her a quick, pristine peck. Once he stepped back and saw her crestfallen expression, however, he scooped her up into his arms and kissed her in earnest. She stood breathless and dizzy as he gently put her down again, picked up his suitcase, and strolled away. "It will get better, my little heart." He called the promise over his shoulder. "Much, much better!"

She turned only in time to see the back of his fair head disappear around the corner.

Now that they were no longer in Shanghai and under the indulgent but loving auspices of Master Wong, Fengmo and Bright Autumn were not free to meet and speak. Strangely, this did not make either of them restive.

For Bright Autumn's part, she was suddenly shy. She felt herself much less attractive than she once had been and set about a program of improvement. In addition to the price of her dowry, quite a large sum had been wrapped in those bundles she and her brothers had toted over hill and dale. A part of this money was now used to clothe her. After the hardships she had seen and suffered, she simply could not select a mountain of fabrics and fill a wardrobe as she might once have done. Still, the few gowns, tops, and trousers she did have fitted and sewn were selected with great care. She never appeared, even in the mild sunshine of late autumn, without a parasol. Most of all, Bright Autumn thanked the gods for Golden Willow, and for quiet Crystal, who was just beginning to show signs of encroaching motherhood. Thanks to them both, she was now bathed and massaged with scented oils each day until, finally, she felt soft and clean again. Her hair had been scrubbed to a lustrous sheen. Though her fingernails were still short and thoroughly unattractive, they had been shaped and buffed.

"You are too kind to me, Sister," she told Golden Willow one day, about three weeks after her arrival. "I feel pampered beyond belief!"

But when she followed this spoken gratitude with a spontaneous embrace, she was embarrassed to feel Golden Willow stiffen slightly. She worried that perhaps she had unwittingly broken some inland tradition by her open display of affection, and from that time on she showed more caution.

There were a great many things about the Chang household that left her wondering. For one thing, the eldest son, who was supposed to be deathly ill, was never once seen. She sensed that Golden Willow was not a cold or insensitive person, and it seemed more than a little strange that a wife would neither nurse nor appear to visit her ailing mate.

Then there was the puzzling attitude of Madame Chang. That grand lady treated Bright Autumn with the utmost courtesy and warmth while being aloof, almost cold toward Golden Willow.

Bright Autumn guessed that somehow these small mysteries were all interwoven, but for once she allowed her curiosity to lie dormant. In less than a moon she would be quietly wed to her beloved. They would be free and easy with one another and she could then gradually come to know all about this new family of hers.

Fengmo watched Bright Autumn and made no great effort to hide his perusal. He did not mind the good-natured teasing heaped upon him by his father and cousins, who thought his curiosity amusing and natural under the circumstances. After all, in Tanpo it was most unusual for a future bride and groom to reside beneath the same roof. But the times were not usual, and so, since the maid herself was so perfectly proper, everyone accepted the situation with great equanimity.

He often glanced at the tanned face of Bright Autumn across the dining room and decided somewhat guiltily that he liked its new hue. But what a trial these mealtimes were, and what a dilemma he found himself in! How hard it was to watch those two women, Bright Autumn and Golden Willow, sitting side by side. There was something disconcerting . . . no, downright discomforting, about seeing them seemingly so at ease together. At times, they leaned close to one another, heads almost touching, and laughed softly at some private joke.

Does Golden Willow no longer love me? He felt his heart twist painfully at such a thought, and yet he knew such was not the case. She does indeed love me, and how big is her heart to show it in just this way!

One day he passed by Golden Willow's courtyard and looked in to see not her but his own betrothed sitting alone there. Her hair was done simply in two pigtails, and she was wrapped against the cold in a robe of red and white fox. As ever, she held a parasol over her head. He almost called out for her to throw the thing aside. Instead, however, he remained still and silent.

Bright Autumn was intent upon watching a chattering pair of chipmunks, and from time to time she covered her mouth and giggled in delight at their antics. Though she was laughing and happy at that moment, Fengmo knew she was not the same girl he had met in Shanghai. With mounting horror and rage, he had listened to the tales related by Wong Four and Five. He was also aware of the grueling deprivations Bright Autumn had suffered on her trek to Tanpo. According to her brothers, she had displayed long-suffering and dauntless courage. Now, even when she smiled or sat quietly, one could see that courage in her face.

Watching her, Fengmo was moved by an emotion he little understood.

Crystal awoke. She yawned and felt the warm back of her husband pressed against her own. The desire to stay lying there and not rise to face the cold, gray dawn was overwhelming. She looked toward the single small window cut into the front wall of their room and blinked sleepily. Then, with a cry, she jerked upright, a smile upon her face.

"Lu!" She began shaking the lumpish form next to her. "Lu, wake up! The first snow has come!"

With a moan and grumble, Fong Lu rolled over and reached for her, but it was too late. She was already before the window gazing out into their courtyard like a wide-eyed child. He smiled and then left the warm bed they shared to come and stand beside her. Putting an arm around her shoulders, he also looked out at the silently transformed world and nuzzled her neck. "If I did not know better, I would swear you had never seen snow in your whole life."

"Each year when the first snow falls, I am so astounded,

I do indeed feel as if I have never seen the earth so beautiful! Look at the flakes, Husband. See how huge they are? Just think, each and every one is unique and different. It is like a miracle!"

Fong Lu reached down and placed an adoring hand over the small mound of her belly. "Just like people," he replied. "So is each person born unique in his own way."

Crystal turned toward him, and in the light of dawn he saw a flicker of fear touch her eyes. "What is it? Are you ill?"

She rested her head against his chest and a halo of tiny hair tendrils tickled his nose. Her voice came out low and muffled. "I am only too well, My Lord. It is an evil omen that I have not had a single morning of sickness. The midwife at the herb shop tells me it is always so when one carries a female."

"Paw!" He tilted her chin up, for he wanted her to see him clearly and know without a doubt that he spoke the truth. "I care not if a male rests in the warmth of your womb or a female, Wife of Mine. The child will be *ours* regardless."

Tears sparkled in her eyes, reflecting the crystalline flakes of snow cascading just outside the window. "For such as you and I, having a girl child can be terrible, Lu. I was sold as a tiny thing to be both companion and servant to Golden Willow. I am more fortunate than most. My lady has always been kind. Still, I sometimes think of the mother I never knew and how she was forced to sell her own child. I would die if that should happen to me, My Lord! I would surely die!"

Fong Lu held her tightly against him. "Never *will* it happen! You have my promise!"

They stood thus for several long moments before Crystal finally broke the embrace. She went back to where her clothes hung on a wooden peg which had been attached to the wall. Her husband watched as she quickly put aside her night garments and, shivering, pulled on a heavily quilted jacket and thick trousers. She now also had a pair of ankle-high boots, all lined with fur, which he had purchased for her. Fong Lu thanked the gods he was a servant and not a slave.

He saw how much fuller her breasts were, and the swelling of her lower abdomen. The sight was beautiful to him beyond anything he had ever seen before.

With flying fingers, she braided her long hair and then picked up the inevitable kettle. "That one who is to wed the Second Son is also an early riser," she grumbled. "Now I must prepare two baths—in two tubs!"

"Is the new one so odious?" he asked. "This coming marriage is one of choice. I am surprised my young lord would select an unworthy female."

Crystal did not, and knew she never would, tell even her husband the complete truth regarding her mistress and the Second Son. She sighed deeply. "Bright Autumn is not odious at all, Husband. I am only a lazy complainer."

With that she went to the door and opened it, but before she could leave, Fong Lu called out her name. She turned and gave him a questioning look.

"You are my heart and liver and lungs," he said. "You are my life, but you *must* have a son *next* year!"

She stood there for a moment, expressionless, with a flurry of snowflakes blowing in around her. Then suddenly she grimaced, stuck out her pink tongue, and left, slamming the door very hard.

Chapter Thirty-three

"Let me do this," said Bright Autumn as she took the drying cloth from Crystal. She motioned to the tub where Golden Willow was still relaxing. "Tend your mistress."

Though she did not demur, Crystal could not prevent herself asking a question. "Did you not have personal servants to wait upon your needs in Shanghai?" This should have been a most unusual query and yet it was not, for she had never heard of any daughter of a rich house being quite so comfortable as Bright Autumn with the idea of doing for herself.

"I would be ashamed to tell you how many servants I had," Bright Autumn laughed. "I was too lazy for words! Why, I could not even lower my wonderful self to peel an orange for fear I might muss my nails."

She held out one hand and looked ruefully at her present manicure. "However, I have learned over these past months that it is not so bad and, in fact, often nice to take just a little initiative."

Crystal thought about this as she began briskly toweling her own mistress. She was thus absorbed when her busy hands came to a sudden halt. Her mouth fell slightly ajar as she stared at the two ripening nipples she had just dried. Slowly, she raised her glance and looked into the smiling eyes of Golden Willow.

"Mistress!" It was little more than a whisper.

Busy attending her own ablutions, Bright Autumn neither heard nor saw this exchange.

Golden Willow continued to smile a sweet, secret smile, and put a warning finger to her lips to keep Crystal from saying more.

After both women were dressed, they sat at the table together and ate a light breakfast of soup and sliced winter apples while Crystal, humming all the while, poured their tea.

Golden Willow reached out and took the hand of Bright Autumn into her own. "This is a most special day in my life," she announced. "In a few moments I am going to the apartment of my husband's mother and I would like you to come with me."

Nothing could have surprised Bright Autumn more. Until now, Golden Willow had been most kind and solicitous, but never actually warm. There had always remained just a touch of aloofness about her, an almost watchful reticence.

"Thank you, My Lady," Bright Autumn replied. "I will be most honored to share any moment with you."

"There is one thing before we go," Golden Willow said. Her face paled slightly, but only Crystal, who knew her so intimately, noticed. She lifted the chain up from around her neck and unclasped it. Her fingers shook as the jade ring slipped quickly off and landed on the table. It twirled several times and then was still, a glowing circle of green and gold. Bright Autumn stared down at it with a look of confusion.

"I wish to give this to you as a betrothal gift," said Golden Willow, her voice low and controlled. "Before you put it on, however, I shall share a story with you."

Then she did indeed tell the same story that Fengmo had related to her on that glorious night, omitting only that the ring had been purchased in Shanghai, and altering the tale just enough to disguise a truth she knew would wound Bright Autumn terribly. When she had finished, she placed a single finger on the tiny circle. It felt like ice to her touch as she pushed it across the polished surface of the table toward its new owner.

"See how it glows!" breathed Bright Autumn. "I have never heard a more beautiful tale!"

"Put it on, Sister. I wish you to have it."

Golden Willow watched as Bright Autumn slowly reached out, took the ring, and then slipped it on the little finger of her left hand. Her own heart cracked and bled as she saw the beatific smile which suddenly lighted the face of Fengmo's betrothed. Yet, it was what she had expected.

Night after night she had lain in bed and tried to seal her heart against this moment.

Bright Autumn closed her eyes and cupped her right hand protectively around her left. Her entire body tingled. She felt alive with some new and wonderful emotion.

Golden Willow cleared her throat and stood up. "Come now," she said briskly, "let us go to Madame Chang."

Bright Autumn reached out to Golden Willow, and for a moment they stood smiling at one another. The two donned their fur robes, and as they left the room, Crystal saw their hands come together.

When they had gone, the serving girl bent down her head and wept.

Madame Chang looked up from her account books as Li Ma led the visitors in. She glanced from the face of one girl to the other. Seeing their clasped hands and smiles, it was all she could do not to scowl. Bright Autumn had become the center of Madame Chang's world, even to the exclusion of her own daughters. In this young woman the promise of generations was personified. Moreover, she was everything a mother-in-law could possibly desire, modest and sweet of temperament.

However, the very sight of Golden Willow grated against Madame Chang's nerves. Unlike Bright Autumn, her first daughter-in-law symbolized all her pain, dashed hopes—and guilt.

The older woman clapped her hands. "Bring tea, Li Ma, and winter melon and some of those sweet-and-sour tidbits your old bone prepared this morning."

She motioned the girls to comfortable chairs. "We shall have a small feast to celebrate the onset of winter," she said. "A new season is always cause for celebration, even in these hard days."

The meal came and Golden Willow sat quietly, listening as her mother-in-law and Bright Autumn discussed the upcoming wedding. It was to be a small and very subdued affair, a fact which did not please Madame Chang. But she knew, as did they all, that it could not be otherwise, for her husband remained adamant in his dedication to frugality.

They had finished and the plates were cleared away before Golden Willow finally stood and bowed deeply. "I have

come with tidings this morning, Mother Chang," she said.
"I hope my news will bring you a small measure of pleasure."

The mistress of the House of Chang looked upon the lowered head of her first daughter-in-law and smiled coolly.
*What news can she possibly bring me, except to tell me she
is returning to her parents? That will be a fine day indeed!
Our names will be smeared with mud! Still, I hope she does
go. Then I shall no longer be forced to look at her!*

Observing these two, Bright Autumn wondered again at
the tension and hidden hostility she sensed from her future mother-in-law. She shivered at the austere countenance of Madame Chang and silently prayed such a look
would never be turned on her.

Golden Willow raised her head with a smile. "It is my
humble honor, Mother, to inform you that for two months
now I have had no monthly flux. It seemed best to wait before coming to you, however, until I could be certain of my
happiness."

So speaking, she felt no guilt whatsoever for her deception. All had been taken from her except this one thing.
The temple goddess had seen fit to let life take root in her
womb and she accepted the gift with gratitude. The child
to be born was her future.

Madame Chang sat very still. For a moment both of the
young women in the room, and Li Ma as well, thought she
might faint. And then color rushed into her cheeks. She
stood and came to Golden Willow, laughing and weeping
at the same time. In that instant, her every animosity van-
ished. She took the startled girl into her arms.

"You can never know the joy you have given me this
day," she cried. "You can never know!"

The entire clan was gathered in the largest dining hall
to celebrate together the arrival of winter. No one could remember when it had begun, but over the generations this
meal had come to be traditional. Anticipation of the
wedding, combined with the season, made this an even
more festive occasion than usual. The food was delectable:
roast duck stuffed with rice and almonds, long noodles,
beef dumplings, sweet-and-sour vegetable dishes, pudding,
and spiced cakes. It was a rare feast to be allowed during

these troublesome days, and it was most thoroughly enjoyed.

Fengmo was the only one there who could not eat his fill. He pushed his plate away long before the meal was finished. His father, sitting next to him, saw this.

"So I have fumbled again, have I?" the older man said, not quite able to keep the hurt and irritation from his voice. "It seems not such a terrible thing to treat my family just this once."

Fengmo had meant no insult at all. Indeed, he knew how very hard his father had striven to alter his former attitude, and as a result he loved and admired him more than ever. This being the case, he felt a harmless lie was well in order. "It is a good feast, Father, and perfectly proper. My insides are simply in a turmoil this evening, and therefore I cannot enjoy the food as much as I otherwise might."

This response seemed to satisfy Master Chang. He stabbed a dumpling with his chopsticks and chuckled. "It must be the trepidation of marriage which upsets you, my son. All grooms are so as the fateful day draws near."

Fengmo smiled and at the same time let his glance cross the considerable width of the hall. Golden Willow and Bright Autumn sat together at the women's table. A twinkle caught and held his eyes, causing his heart to jump and flutter in his chest. A myriad of emotions gripped him as he recognized the ring on Bright Autumn's finger. Pain and confusion mingled together, leaving him breathless. He quickly lowered his head lest someone observe this attack of witlessness. His mind refused to accept what Golden Willow had done.

Then, almost as suddenly, his breathing slowed and his heart resumed its sure, steady rhythm. Again he fastened his gaze upon the ring, and then allowed it to travel on up to the face of Bright Autumn. Her lips were curved in a smile and there was a flush on her cheeks. Her beauty struck him full force. It was as if he had never really looked at her before, and yet at the same time, he felt he had known her forever. The most unbelievable feeling of comfort invaded his being.

He was aware of the penetrating eyes of Golden Willow before he actually met them. Across that crowded, buzzing room flashed a painful acknowledgment, an almost imperceptible nod of mutual acceptance.

Madame Chang had sent a subtle message to her husband late that afternoon intimating she wished him to call upon her before he retired. It had become the way between them. He never came to her bedchamber now unless she sent such a veiled message. Lately, those messages came with decreasing frequency. Hai-teh was not even sure the idea of visiting Peaceful Dawn appealed to him any longer. Too often she was sullen and withdrawn, making it very obvious that she simply tolerated his affection for the sake of duty. He was surprised, therefore, to enter her room and find her already in bed, all playful and kittenish.

"It is about time you arrived," she said sweetly. "You must be growing old to be so slow."

Hai-teh allowed himself a cautious chuckle. He still could not quite credit that the woman he loved seemed to have suddenly returned. "You are right, Mother of My Sons; I am old. My bones ache in this cold weather. By winter's end, I will be a cripple for sure."

Peaceful Dawn came up from her pillow. "Sit here beside me, Husband. I will rub your shoulders and at the same time give you a bit of news."

More delighted by the minute, Hai-teh pulled off his outer layer of clothing and settled himself next to her. He groaned with pleasure as she began to knead the tense, knotted muscles of his upper back.

"Bright Autumn and our first daughter-in-law paid me a most pleasant visit this morning," she said in a casual tone.

"M-m-m," he answered. But he was pleased that for once she referred to Golden Willow with respect. Recently she had begun calling the girl "that one who *used* to be my daughter-in-law," a title he was sure she used especially to irritate him.

"Those two seem to be good companions already," she continued. "I must admit to a certain envy. Golden Willow probably told her wonderful news to Bright Dawn even before she did to me!"

Slowly, he turned and looked at her.

Peaceful Dawn began to laugh in a high, tinkling voice

and nod her head. "Yes, yes, Husband. It is true. Within the passing of seven moons we will be grandparents!"

The next moments were filled with joyful embraces, which eventually led to a most satisfying and passionate conclusion. Later, tired but replete, they lay in each other's arms. The oil lamp still glowed from a corner table. Outside it was silent and still. The snow fell in a straight, silvery curtain.

"How fine it will be," she said, "when I have a babe to hold again!"

Hai-teh laughed softly. "I should think you would have had enough of babes in this house of ours. Even now the courts are filled to capacity with the children of cousins and servants. It seems they are forever underfoot, wetting and crying."

"Oh, you! It is not the same and you know it. It has been nigh onto ten years since I have held a little one of my very own."

"Is a grandchild the same then?"

"Better! I need not travail at all!"

"How wicked and mean you are, my little heart," he teasingly admonished. "You want the fun and none of the labor!"

She propped herself up on one elbow and looked down at him with a seductive expression. "I am not mean. An old woman *is* allowed her privileges."

"You will never be old," he whispered. "Not to me."

Peaceful Dawn lay back down with a deep sigh of satisfaction. "I am thinking that perhaps Golden Willow was not such a bad choice after all. She has done her duty and provided for the generations at last."

Her husband made no comment, for he still believed the marriage of Kao had been most unfortuante. But in his present mood, he could only smile. That smile dropped away, however, as he began to wonder what kind of child might come from the loins of his eldest son. I am being foolish, he thought. A son does not inherit evil from his parents. He will be beautiful and high-minded. Brought up by one such as Golden Willow, how could he be otherwise?

He was distracted from his worry by a low giggle and leaned back on his pillow, the better to see the face of his wife. "What is so amusing? Are you imagining yourself with that tot already?"

"No," she said. "Actually I was thinking of something most unpleasant, a thing which can be funny only now when I look at it from a distance." Her face grew petulant. "I knew that hairy foreign devil was a liar!"

The only foreigner Hai-teh could think of was Sean Duncan, and he was confused. "What is it, Mother of My Sons?"

Peaceful Dawn made her voice light and nonchalant. "Oh, it is really nothing, not after all these years. But do you remember, Husband, back when Fengmo and Kao were so ill?"

Their sons were all extremely healthy types, and the time she spoke of was many years back, one of the few illnesses he could recall. They had both been truly worried. "Yes, I remember well. Those little rascals were given some contagious disease by a foreign lad."

"The son of the foreign medicine man," she said, scowling. "How sick they were! I insisted upon nursing them alone."

"You are, and ever have been, a good and devoted mother," he agreed. At the same time he wondered what could possibly have launched her on this particular far-fetched subject.

"Oh, it was not that so much," she protested. "I simply could not afford to have you or the rest of the household infected. Heaven only knows how that wicked sickness might have spread!"

Her cheeks grew a little flushed now and she looked angry. "Fengmo was very ill, but not so much as Kao. At first, I thought our eldest would be lucky, for his jaws did not get all swollen like his brother's. In the end, however, it was much, much worse for Kao. He tossed and turned in a fevered delirium. Why, he even had visions!"

Peaceful Dawn looked at her husband. "I never did tell you this, but one night I was out of my mind with worry. I went myself to that ugly, flame-haired foreign doctor. 'Your son has made my sons ill unto death,' I told him. 'Now you must come and give them a cure.' "

This did indeed surprise Hai-teh, who knew how his wife disliked white men in general. "And did he help?"

"He did not! Worse, after he came here to our house, he told me a terrible, wicked lie! He said our eldest son was affected in his manhood. Can you imagine? That ugly devil told me our firstborn would never be able to have a single child, not even a girl!"

Without mirth, she laughed. "Of course, I did not believe him and I made him leave our house at once."

"Of course," Hai-teh repeated in the strangest voice. "Mother of My Sons, why was I not told of this long ago?"

She moved restlessly. "Well, why should I trouble you with such nonsense? Kao lived and the man lied, just as I have always known."

Thinking of recent hot summer nights, Master Chang began to tremble. "Do not play the innocent with me," he said from between clenched teeth. "You did not tell me because you believed every word that foreigner spoke!"

His face grew stark and suddenly she was frightened.

"Forgive me," she stammered. "I can see you are mightily upset with me. But stop and think now. If you had been convinced by that awful beast of a man, you would have canceled the betrothal! This coming grandson would have been lost to us!"

For the first time since his wedding day, Master Chang wanted to strike his wife. He wanted to scream obscenities and beat her black and blue. Yet he knew he could not. Taking deep breaths, he struggled to bring his temper under control. His mind spun. *If only she had spoken,* he fumed. *Oh, she is most certainly correct—I would have nullified the betrothal agreement. But I would also have offered my Second Son as prospective groom! Oh gods!*

He rose and dressed, and though Peaceful Dawn implored him to speak, he would not. Leaving her apartment, Hai-teh knew it would be many, many days before he would be able to communicate with his wife again.

Golden Willow and Bright Dawn sat talking into the night. At last the truth concerning the eldest son was fully told and understood. Bright Autumn's compassion went out to her future sister-in-law, but one thing troubled her deeply. She could not but wonder what kind of a babe would be brought forth from such an unloving and violent union. Golden Willow seemed to read her mind.

"My son will not be a wild seed," she said with quiet assurance. "He will be *mine*. I carry him. I nourish him with my own blood. He will be a good and righteous lad. I know it!

"The only vexation I have is that I am forced to go into the rear court, if only this once, and inform Kao of my condition. You heard the command my mother-in-law put upon me. It must be obeyed."

"Would you have me go with you, Sister?" Bright Autumn asked. "In your condition perhaps you should not be alone with him, no matter how tame he is supposed to be."

Golden Willow considered this offer for a moment and then shook her head. "No," she slowly replied, "I must do this thing alone. The concubine is there. I do not believe, as Crystal does, that she can put a hex upon my womb."

Long after Bright Autumn had gone to sleep, Golden Willow lay wide awake. Her forearm rested across her lower abdomen. Yes, she thought, this child I carry will become brave and noble, a man just like his father!

A tear escaped her eye. Even now she was feeling an echo of the pain she had experienced upon realizing that she was not the one intended for Fengmo. In the depths of her soul, she had known this was true the instant he had slipped the jade ring onto her finger. Nor had telling herself it was all superstitious nonsense helped. Fate was a true thing. Meeting and observing Bright Autumn, she had known with more certainty than ever. Day and night she had suffered untold anguish. It was only after she had missed her first menstrual cycle that she began to recuperate.

I will make this child my life, and in so doing, I will have found my ultimate destiny and joy. It was her last waking thought.

Weak rays of sun broke through the heavy, silver-lined clouds as Golden Willow stepped from one slab of stone to another. These pieces of slate marked a path between the different courtyards and had been cleared and swept. All around her the world glistened beneath a blanket of soft, new snow.

The gate of the court that Kao occupied with the concubine stood ajar, and she quickly passed through, with Crystal right behind her.

"Do not stay here overlong, Mistress," said the latter. "Your feet are damp already and you will take a chill."

Golden Willow did not answer. Instead, she stopped suddenly and looked around. In a far corner of the courtyard stood a grove of winter bamboo, bright with berries. Untended shrubs lined the walls. Even disguised as it was, she recognized the place. Her eyes sought out the boulder where she still remembered the young Fengmo, perched and flapping his small arms in imitation of a soaring falcon. Her heart twisted painfully as she closed her eyes and listened to young voices calling from the past.

"Mistress?"

Golden Willow shook herself and put dreaming aside. "Wait for me here. I will not be long."

So saying, she went resolutely to the door. A female servant answered her summons. "Who is there?" the old woman asked, squinting against the light. "Speak up!"

"It is I," said Golden Willow, "the wife of your master."

The woman jumped back and bowed low several times. "Forgive my stupidity, Young Mistress. My eyes are poor. I worked at the kitchen stove too long and the smoke has made me nearly blind."

It was true. Her eyes were little more than red slits. The inflamed lids were turned nearly inside out, a fact well evidenced by the condition of the apartment. Everywhere there was dust and clutter.

Sweet Harmony sat at a table in the dingy central room. Golden Willow felt neither disgust nor hatred upon looking at her successor. Rather, a kind of gratitude mingled with pity took hold of her. The flower girl's hair was neatly combed, but the pink satin robe she wore was all spotted and stained. It was also light and unsuitable for cold weather. Her bound feet were propped on a stool close to the brazier, and she was bent over some sewing. When she looked up and saw Golden Willow enter with the serving woman, she stood and immediately bowed. "My Lady," she murmured. "I did not know you were coming."

She turned to the servant. "Bring tea for the mistress at once, Chow Ma."

"Make no bother," Golden Willow said. "I will be here

but a short time." Her eyes quickly surveyed the room. "If your master is not still abed, I would speak to him."

Though Sweet Harmony kept her head lowered, the bright flush of her cheeks was visible, even through the heavy layer of rice powder she wore. She kept smoothing her robe. "He is not sleeping, Lady, but he rarely comes out of the chamber these days. I shall go and fetch him at once."

So saying, she placed her sewing on the table and left the room. When she returned, she was leading Kao by the hand as if he were a child.

Golden Willow nearly gasped aloud. The man now passing just feet from her was almost unrecognizable as the same who had once frightened and abused her. Sallow, dry-looking flesh hung down from his jaws and she could see his ribs beneath the thin robe he wore. With a shuffling gait, he was guided to a chair by Sweet Harmony and sat down. He looked about him in mild confusion, his eyes glazed and distant.

"Where is my pipe, woman?" His lips trembled like those of a spoiled baby. "I want my pipe, I say!"

"You shall have it, My Lord," Sweet Harmony replied in a gentle voice, "but not just yet. You have a visitor who has come to see you."

When she attempted to pull his robe neatly shut, he reached out and slapped her. "I want my pipe!"

Golden Willow stepped forward. "I have come to see you, Husband. I will take but little of your time."

He looked up and blinked several times. "So," he slurred, "my First Wife. Why have you not come before now? Did you not know how ill I have been?"

"I am sorry to hear it, My Lord."

It was as if she had made no response at all, for Kao immediately turned back to Sweet Harmony. "Yes, I feel very sickly," he whined. "Bring my pipe at once that I might receive relief from all my suffering. Ever since that brother of mine beat upon me, I have not been the same. Will you not get my pipe, Sweet Harmony?"

Golden Willow shivered. "Take him back to the bedchamber. He will understand nothing of what I say in any case. Go and then return, for I would have a word with you before I depart."

After helping Kao to his feet again, and soothing him with words, Sweet Harmony took him by the hand and led him away.

Golden Willow looked around the unadorned apartment. No scrolls hung upon the walls, and the corner where the servant obviously slept was a mess of soiled clothing and scraps of food. The old woman herself was crouched there, scratching and rubbing her sore eyes. The air was dank and heavy with the sickening aroma of opium smoke. Golden Willow wanted to turn and run from the place, but her own guilt prevented her.

When Sweet Harmony returned, she went to a chair and brushed crumbs from the seat. Her eyes were imploring. "Will you not have just a cup of tea, My Lady?"

After only a slight hesitation, Golden Willow nodded. The cup handed to her was chipped and broken. She picked it up but could not bring it to her lips. She looked at Sweet Harmony. "Must you give him such large quantities of . . ." She did not finish, but pointed toward the bed-chamber. "He is not even human!"

"If I did not, he would leave the court," Sweet Harmony replied in a low voice. "His father has spoken to me only once since I came to this house, but his instructions were very clear on that occasion. I was told that under no circumstances should your husband be allowed to leave here. Moreover, if Kao does not have his way, he becomes very violent. Forgive me, My Lady, but I do what I must."

Golden Willow stood. "And you, do you sometimes get out into the clean air?"

Sweet Harmony smiled. "Sometimes, My Lady. By late evening he is usually sated. I move about the compound then, after the rest of the house is quiet and I can be sure of disturbing no one."

Golden Willow's guilt mounted. The room seemed to grow smaller and she abruptly gathered her robe about herself and rose to leave.

"Wait." The former flower girl went to a small chest as quickly as her bound feet would carry her. She lifted the lid, closed it again, and then hurried back. Holding out a tiny pair of tiger-faced slippers, she blushed. "I know this is a most unworthy gift, but will you accept it nonetheless? I have sewn these for your First Son."

Golden Willow was taken completely aback, but the other girl extended her gift and smiled more brightly still. "Do not look so shocked, My Lady. Even a worthless thing such as I can see the happiness shining from your face."

Waiting in the cold courtyard, Crystal was not happy at how long her mistress stayed inside the apartment of Chang Kao. She was just about to go and bang upon the door when it swung open and Golden Willow stepped out.

"Come, Mistress!" Crystal cried. "Did I not tell you I should go in with you? That evil pair has treated you poorly! I can see that just by looking at your face!"

"Hush!" said Golden Willow, drawing near. "It is not the woman in there who is evil, but I myself! Come with me at once. This thing I have inadvertently done must be rectified!"

It was then that Crystal spied the little slippers, but she had no time to ask questions before her mistress marched past, heading straight for the gate. No word passed between the two as they made their way back to the warmth of the apartment. When they entered, Bright Autumn leapt up from where she had been sitting, alarmed by Golden Willow's pale face.

"Sister, are you ill?"

Golden Willow turned to them both. "Come with me," she said. "I will need your help."

Casting questioning looks at one another, they followed her into the bedchamber where she went to one of the large ebony chests and immediately set about lifting the heavy lid. She began pulling out one robe after another. "I think the plum brocade will look very well on her," she mumbled. "And perhaps the gold and white."

She turned and looked back at the two appalled faces that stared at her. "Do not look so aghast. I am First Wife to that vile thing in the rear court, am I not? As such, it is my responsibility to see his *Little* Wife cared for properly. Well, she has not been cared for at all! I am a wicked soul to have left her in that prison!"

Tears rushed to her eyes, but when Bright Autumn and Crystal ran to her and tried to put their arms about her, she would have none of it. "If you would comfort me, then help! I will not leave that poor girl dressed like a ragged

and garish doll. She too has a right to live. Yes, and I am
grateful to her beyond words for the service she performs. I
will see her clothed and accepted in this house if it is the
last thing I do!"

Sweet Harmony walked between Golden Willow and
Bright Autumn down a path and toward the family dining
hall. Both of the young mistresses slowed their pace to
match hers. But it was not only her tiny feet that caused
Sweet Harmony to hang back. Her knees, in fact her entire
body was trembling with fright. It still seemed unbelievable that *she* was going to take a meal with the great and
illustrious Chang family.

The whole of this day had been one of turbulent emotion for her. First, the beautiful lady of Kao's had come,
and not two hours later there was a scratching at her
door. She could hardly credit her own vision when old
Chow Ma came back, followed by another, younger
woman.

"I am Opal," that woman had said, bowing. "The First
Lady sends me to you as underservant. She also bids me
bring you these."

She held out her arms, which were heaped with robes of
a quality and style Sweet Harmony had never owned in
her life, not even when she was the very idol of Madame
Ying's reputable house.

Opal had briskly put her burdens aside and then scowled
around the room. "By the gods! If I am ever to return to
that husband of mine, I'd best set this place to rights at
once!"

She turned to Sweet Harmony and spoke in a rough, proprietary voice. "As for you, *Mistress,* I will fetch you water
at once. You will need time to prepare yourself for the evening meal. The First Lady would have you call upon her at
dusk."

In a state of near shock, Sweet Harmony had submitted to the overbearing ministrations of the serving
woman, who she learned was to be a permanent fixture
in her life. Opal, married to a gardener, had been a
laundress in the house for many years, but now she
took charge as if born to the task of personal servant.
She cleaned and dusted, a veritable whirlwind. At the

same time, she watched over Chow Ma. It soon became clear that her intimidating personality was no more than a ruse designed to hide the most tender of hearts. Not given to gossip, she was one of those rare persons who loved to serve. She was firm but gentle with Chow Ma, giving the old woman tasks which were well within her abilities. What was more amazing, she managed to make it appear that *she* was the underling. Even Kao did not raise her ire. She nursed him and cleaned all around him with tranquil ease. The most unique quality the servant possessed, however, was her innate diplomacy and good sense. She helped Sweet Harmony perform her ablutions with a critical eye.

"No, no, Mistress! You do not want to put powder on your face tonight." She clucked her tongue and wagged her head. "You know how these rich folks are; they will ever look down their noses at you if you appear *too* pretty. Yes, indeed! If you would win them over, especially that lofty Madame Chang, you must be unassuming and humble in the extreme. Here, let us simply put your beautiful hair in coils, with no more than a single ornament. You shall wear that darkest robe the First Lady gave you, the one which is a nice midnight blue. It is becoming and yet will not attract an abundance of attention."

Sweet Harmony was not an educated person, at least in no formal sense, but she was an apt student of human nature. She knew that she was being given a lesson in proper deportment by Opal—and she was grateful.

Nearing the dining hall, she fervently prayed those lessons would put her in good stead. A new life was opening for her, one she desperately wanted. No more for her the parade of lustful men, or the cruel badgering of Madame Ying. From this day forth, she would truly be part of a *family!* That she was but a lowly member did not matter. Even if she were to be only *tolerated,* it would be enough. For the first time, she saw a chance, a small patch of hope. She cared no longer for the adoration of men. Those beasts wanted nothing except access to her jade gate in any case. No, Sweet Harmony now sought compassion such as she had received from Golden Willow, and protective concern as given by Opal. To her, these things were *love.*

The former flower girl held her chin up and prepared to enter the dining hall with dignity. Tears threatened as she felt Golden Willow clasp one of her hands and Bright Autumn the other.

Chapter Thirty-four

The single jeep, roughly painted in a makeshift camouflage, came over the last rise and began its descent. Attached to the front of the sturdy military vehicle was a small plow, but nonetheless its engine strained as it sluggishly pushed through the snow. Two men, sitting bundled in the open rear seat, held tightly to the rifles lying across their knees. Their faces were alert and somber. A third soldier drove. The hood of his patched parka had fallen away and, unlike the others, he wore no helmet. In the cold, his face was deep red and his lips nearly blue. A wide scar ran up the back of his scalp and then over and across his furrowed brow. This scar remained a stark, vivid white. The thick spectacles he wore did not lessen the impact of his bold eyes or the thin, grim line of his mouth.

Few people were up and about to see the jeep as it made its way down the slopes and then across the valley floor, gaining speed as the road turned to slush. The gatekeeper had just opened the city when the vehicle roared past him. He jumped back and trembled as it began weaving through the quiet streets of Tanpo.

Fengmo looked across the table at Four and Five. They were gathered in the library and all wore serious expressions.

"You are sure you wish to leave then?" he asked. "It will be a most difficult trek."

"With one of your father's trucks and a pair of shovels we can manage," replied Four. "We will use our backs if necessary."

Originally the pair had planned to linger in the House of Chang until the following spring, but with each passing

357

day they had grown more and more restless. Fengmo knew the only thing that had prevented their leaving thus far was the fact that their sister was not yet wed. He marveled at the change in these two men. Strangely, they now looked uncomfortable and out-of-place in the silk robes they wore. Their bronzed faces rarely smiled. Since the wedding was to take place early the next morning, he was not surprised that they were preparing to leave.

Five rose and began to pace back and forth. "Yes," he said, "Bright Autumn will be a married woman and safe here with you, but it is the North for us. Our people are gathering there and we can be of use, if not to the Kuomintang, then at least in the Caves. It is said there is now a veritable metropolis in those stony mountains."

"I still say we should search out the followers of Mao," said Four. "But it seems I must wait forever for you to make up your mind."

Five moved to the window and looked out at the pale morning light. "I wonder what our father would advise if he were here."

The face of Four hardened. "Our father is *not* here, Brother. When will you realize that we can have no parents, no home, until the Japanese dogs are driven out? We must take a stand and fight!"

Fengmo, who had formed his own opinions over the past months, was just about to speak when a series of shouts sounded from somewhere in the compound.

The sight that met their eyes when they neared the front gate brought them all to an abrupt halt. There, near the frozen fishpond, stood the Sixth Son of the House of Wong. His feet were planted wide apart, his arms akimbo. At first he only glared at them, and then, slowly, a broad grin split his features.

"Six!"

Four and Five rushed ahead of Fengmo and began beating their younger brother happily and quite roughly upon his back and shoulders. Meantime, their hoarse cries brought half the house on the run.

Bright Autumn was among the last to appear. She looked askance at one face and then another as the crowd parted to let her through. When she approached the clearing, she stopped and gasped. Her eyes widened in disbelief and her face paled as if she were staring at a specter. Wong Six turned and the crowd hushed.

"Baby Sister." His voice was little more than a whisper.

She looked as if she might faint, but in two long strides he was beside her, supporting her slim body in his arms. Unmindful of the onlookers, he scooped her up and spoke into her ear. "Did you really believe I would miss your wedding day?"

But Bright Autumn could only sob in reply.

While Six greeted his family, Fengmo had taken the opportunity to observe the other two soldiers who had entered the compound. Never once had their faces softened or changed in any way whatsoever. Thus did they also stand now at each side of the library door. They held their rifles loosely, but even so their eyes darted about the room, probing corners and then flicking suspiciously from one face to another.

Master Chang and Fengmo sat around the table with Four and Five, while Six remained standing. He did not bother to mince words.

"I come with a warning and an offer to help," he announced. "The Japanese are grouping just southwest of this mountain range. It is unlikely they will attempt a push through the passes until after the spring thaw. From that time on, however, unless the situation changes greatly, this valley will be in enemy territory."

His words, though spoken quietly, fell on the ears of his listeners like the thunder of doomsday. Master Chang struggled to keep his own voice steady. "Do you think they will bomb?"

Six shrugged. "It is hard to say. There is no reason for them to do so, certainly—not unless they meet staunch resistance. Their army, like any other, needs food. It would be counterproductive for them to destroy the fields. So, if they send in planes, you can expect it will be for a direct strike at Tanpo."

The room was silent.

Fengmo looked at the changed Wong Six. "Is your offer of help the installment of troops in our valley? Are you, perhaps, only preparing us for those who follow behind you even now?"

The other man laughed harshly. "I wish that were the case, friend. And if it were, I would see no need to *warn* you. My troops are vicious fighters. They do not, however, pose a threat to peaceful citizens. They are a new breed, a breed of honor."

By these words, all in the room knew that Wong Six had gained fame and recognition among his peers and that he was now a leader of men.

"No," he continued, "I come, as I have said, to offer help. If you prepare yourselves immediately, you can follow us out. Anyone in the city or countryside who has conveyance will be able to move in the trail of the jeep. But there can be no delay. Another snowfall will seal us all off."

"Where do we go?" asked Four, his face bright with anticipation.

For a moment Six allowed his eyes to rest thoughtfully on his brother. His expression was unreadable. "Once we clear the mountains, the oldsters and any women who have children will be put safely on the road north," he said. "It is hoped that you others, the able-bodied men and unencumbered females, will join my comrades and me."

"Who fight their own countrymen as well as the Japanese," Fengmo flatly added.

Six's mouth pulled down at the corners. "It is not *our* choice," he replied. "Those who hold to the Kuomintang refuse our help. They fear our truths more than they do the enemy!"

He began to massage his forehead. "But this is no time to quibble. My offer holds. I suggest you meet with the other clan leaders in this city. The word should be spread. Let each family, large and small, decide its own destiny. These decisions must be made quickly, for my men and I leave at dusk."

He walked to the door. Before leaving, he turned back and looked at Fengmo. "If you are going to marry my sister, it had best be immediately. No doubt it is unromantic to rush such things; but then, these are not romantic days."

Though highly presumptuous, the suggestion of Wong Six was pragmatic and expedient in the extreme. Though

Madame Chang took umbrage, it was arranged that the immediate family, along with the three brothers of Bright Autumn, would gather in the ancestral hall of the temple within an hour.

There was none of the festivity which would normally have taken place at such a function. Lesser family members and servants were far too busy to light firecrackers. There was no bride's palanquin or shouts of celebration. For days the wedding feast had been in the making, but it seemed doubtful indeed there would be many left to partake of it. Only the beaded headdress gave formality to the occasion.

The greatest sorrow for Bright Autumn was that her own beloved parents were not there to witness her becoming a wife. Still, even this unhappiness was set aside as Madame Chang led her into the temple. Nothing could change the fact that she was about to be married to the man who had captured her heart. With bowed head, she stood next to him and paid homage to the generations of Chang. Though the family priest rushed through his incantations and exhortations and spoke in a frightened, trembling voice, she heard every word. She was greatly moved by the soft, unexpected weeping of her sister-in-law. A feeling of insurmountable joy and triumph surged through her when she and Fengmo turned to leave the hall. He reached out and clasped her hand, and it was as if she had never been completely whole until that moment. She felt vibrant, glowing. Her soul radiated a new and wonderful energy.

There was no one to regale them as they emerged into the morning sunlight. Every now and again a servant would scurry by with an armload of paraphernalia.

Master Chang approached the couple with a look and tone of apology. "Forgive the haste, my son, but you and I should be gone. The rest of the city has yet to be alerted and I would have you, my heir, beside me at such a time. We must remain calm and collected at all costs, for otherwise there will be mass panic."

Stack upon stack of hastily snatched possessions were scattered throughout the courts as people desperately tried to differentiate between luxuries and necessities.

Children cried their confusion; servants trembled and whispered among themselves. By noon the Chang family, in total, was gathered in the audience hall. With the permission of his host, Wong Six took the dais first and, amidst the sobbing of women and children, gave them the unadorned truth. To his credit he did not try to deliver, in that tormented hour, a fiery, inciting speech. He simply told them, as he had the others, of the threat and of his offer. They listened and asked no questions. When he had finished and stepped down again, they turned, one and all, to their leader.

With halting steps, Master Chang took the dais. He did not sit, but rather looked at the upturned, expectant faces and inwardly groaned. Above all others, his glance rested upon Fengmo and Bright Autumn. The newlyweds were unashamedly holding hands. An aura seemed to shimmer all around them.

"I am an old man," he began. "I will not leave the home of my forefathers. When and if the Japanese come, I will stand and fight until I drop. There are guns in the warehouse and those old cannons perched on the city walls. They are not much, but I will use them. And when the ammunition is gone, I will use a sword, or a hoe, or a hayfork. I will not leave."

He saw that many of his family had turned pale with fright.

"But," he continued, "I speak only for myself. You younger ones have years ahead of you. China will have need of your strength. There are the trucks and the automobile. I also own a few horses, sixteen mules, and a herd of oxen. Take them and go. You older women"—he looked now at the drawn face of Madame Chang—"you cannot fight and you may well come to harm if you remain. You must, therefore, decide if you are able to make the arduous journey."

Suddenly he felt exhausted. "Go now, each to his own court, and decide. But it is as the Sixth Son of Wong Cho tells you; you must make all haste."

The family of Chang Hai-teh filed out of the audience hall and into the courtyards beneath an ominous, leaden sky. Bright Autumn held fast to the hand of Fengmo.

Looking up into his face, she read his thoughts clearly and came to a halt. People fanned out all around them.

"I will not leave," she said. "Where you are, I will ever remain. If you knock me upon the head, I will crawl back. If you bind me and toss me onto a truck, I will gnaw through the ropes and leap off again. Do not think to send me away, Husband, for I *will not go.*"

Fengmo turned and took hold of her shoulders, fully intending to shake her until she showed more sense. Instead, seeing her face, her courageous and determined eyes, her tender, pleading mouth, he pulled her roughly against his chest.

"You are a worthless, stubborn woman," he murmured into her hair. "Take yourself to the courts of my mother and remain there until this is over. I must help the others before I can take time to beat you."

The streets of Tanpo were crowded and full of confusion, but outside the city walls an exodus was being prepared in orderly fashion. Wong Six and the men in his charge, along with his two elder brothers, barked orders to which the frightened populace eagerly responded. A long line was being formed. Flatbed trucks and the few automobiles were interspersed between ridable livestock. Children, bundled against the cold, were being handed up to their mothers. Those who could not or would not leave stood by and watched or bid tearful farewells to those they loved.

Within the city, before the gate of the House of Chang, remained a single, huge automobile. Beside it stood the solemn figures of two men.

"You will see they are kept safe?" Fengmo asked.

"Worry not, Master," replied Fong Lu, and he smartly slapped the rifle he held. "Not a hair on any of their heads will come to harm."

Just then New Moon and Moon Shadow came through the gate. Each carried a small wicker case and they were both weeping. "Our mother will not come, Fengmo," New Moon cried. "Even Bright Autumn cannot persuade her to budge!"

This news came as no surprise. Not for a moment had Fengmo believed that the headstrong matriarch of the Chang clan could be made to leave, not even by the threat of an enemy invasion. He could, therefore, only soothe his young sisters with encouraging promises as he tucked them into the rear seat of the car. This done, he stood and looked, first at the darkening heavens, and then back toward the gate.

"No doubt those other two will be here at any moment," Fong Lu assured him. "I hope they have enough brains not to linger over all those baby things they have been collecting!"

Even under these harried circumstances, Fengmo could not help smiling at the pride in the other man's voice. He gave Fong Lu a hearty slap on the shoulder. "I know you will have a fine, lusty son, my friend."

Fong Lu laughed. "My little Crystal thinks not, Young Sir, but I do not care either way. If there is not a son this year, there will be one the next."

He watched the face of Fengmo closely. "It is far more important that the First Lady bring forth an heir, is it not?"

For a moment Fengmo neither moved nor said anything. The words just spoken seemed to hang in the air around him. Slowly he met the candid eyes of his manservant. "What are you saying?"

Fong Lu turned away from the pain he saw. "Only what my good wife has related to me. The First Lady, her mistress, is with child."

A deep, agonized groan ripped from the soul of Fengmo. Without another word he stalked away and disappeared through the gate.

The pathways separating the courts appeared empty now, except for lighted torches and the sound of his footsteps echoing from the compound walls. All the newfound peace and happiness which had come to him at the marriage altar disappeared as he went in search of his brother's wife—and the truth.

He arrived at her moon gate just as she and Crystal were coming out. When Golden Willow looked up and saw him, she smiled timorously but did not pause or speak.

Fengmo put one hand on her arm and held her back forcibly. "You cannot leave like this," he said. "I have a right to know."

Crystal tried to push him aside, "Please, Young Sir! Let us pass! It grows late!"

But he neither felt the push nor heard her importuning. He had fixed a fierce and intent gaze upon the trembling figure of Golden Willow. She wore the silver fox robe, and against it her face was the color of ivory. Her eyes sparkled with tears.

"Let me go," she begged in a low, urgent voice.

"Not until you tell me the truth!" he repeated, nearly wild. "The child you carry is mine! I know it is mine!"

A gasp sounded from behind him and he turned to see the bloodless, horrified face of his wife. Her eyes were wide and she held a quivering hand before her mouth.

"Bright Autumn!" he cried out to her, but she turned and ran. "By the gods!" he moaned in anguish as he looked from her retreating figure back to Golden Willow.

"The child is *Kao's!*" The words tore from her in a rush and she doubled over, holding her sides. "Do you hear me, *Second Son?* This babe belongs to your brother! Go away! Let me leave this place and shame me no more!"

By now an anxious Fong Lu had appeared. He rushed to Golden Willow and both he and Crystal supported her between them. Neither looked back as they helped her down the pathway toward the main gate.

Fengmo stood rooted to the spot for what seemed an eternity before a sudden, terrible fear gave his feet and legs impetus. In his mind's eye, he could see nothing but the stricken face of his bride. He bounded toward the court of his mother. His body shook as he banged upon the apartment door with clenched fists. When it finally opened, only the wrinkled visage of Li Ma peered out at him.

"Bright Autumn?" he rasped.

"She is not here, Young Sir," Li Ma replied. "She went to say farewell to the wife of your . . ."

Without waiting for her to finish, he turned and ran away. His heart pounded as he searched one courtyard after another. Bright Autumn was nowhere.

And then it occurred to him. She was leaving. She would climb aboard one of the trucks and be gone before he could find her!

Knowing he had not a moment to spare, he ran out into the deserted street. But as he neared the city gate the way became congested and he had to push and shove his way through the throng. All the while his eyes wildly searched for a robe of red and white fox. The questions he asked only elicited hasty negative responses.

Approaching the caravan, he saw the lean figure of his father. The older man was instructing those who were to drive the trucks. Cousins, aunts, and uncles called to Fengmo, but he did not stop, for among none of them did he see the face he sought. The engines of the departing vehicles roared to life and their headlights went on. Over and over again he called her name, but his cries were lost in the din.

Working his way back to the gate, he leaned against it and ran a shaking hand through his hair. His breath came in labored gasps and he was near weeping with panic.

"Second Son!"

He looked down to see Sweet Harmony standing beside him. Her pretty face was a mask of concern as, trembling, she pointed out into the fields. She also was short of breath.

"Your wife," she said. "I saw her rush from the compound and tried to follow, but my feet! Oh, sir! I could not keep up! She ran out toward the southern slopes. I called to her, but she would not stop!"

Just as Fengmo looked toward the dark jagged mountains, a huge snowflake touched his cheek and melted.

Chapter Thirty-five

Bright Autumn was mindless. All coherent thought was frozen around a single devastating sentence spoken by her husband to another woman. *"The child you carry is mine!"*

Sobbing, she had pushed and clawed her way through a crush of bodies, not caring whether her feet stumbled along a courtyard path or a jammed thoroughfare. She knew only that she must continue, must run until she escaped the horrible devastating truth. At last she had broken free of the crowds, and her legs carried her onward and up. She did not see the villages she passed through or the startled peasants. Her feet, soft once more and shod in thin leather slippers, were oblivious to the cruel bruises they received.

Twilight gave way to darkness and still she rushed blindly on. She tripped and fell, only to pull herself up. A frightened, demented creature, she did not feel the first huge snowflakes, which drifted down to mingle with her tears.

The door of every hut was bolted tight against the impending storm—and against the unease the valley inhabitants felt at seeing the long snake of lights and humanity which slithered up the northern cliffs. It would have done Chang Fengmo no good to call out to the peasants for help, for in their present state none would have come forth.

But he did not call out. There was no time.

Mounted on the back of a roan mare too old and worn to be considered for the journey north, he rode through the fields. His only direction was the one given to him by Sweet Harmony. A loaded rifle was slung over his shoulder and he held an oil torch high above his head.

His panic was gone now, replaced by steel determination. The confusion under which he had labored for so long was also gone. In his mind there remained not a shred of doubt. Bright Autumn was, and had always been, *his.* The mate of his soul, she had been chosen by Fate to stand beside him throughout eternity.

Fate! He nearly cursed the word, the cruel deity, aloud. Yet more than the convoluted winds of destiny, Fengmo cursed his own wayward heart. Why had he not recognized the changes taking place within him? For too long he had remained a man split into two ragged and bleeding halves. Now his beloved was gone, and to lose her would be to lose his very soul. The storm could not be allowed to claim her!

The mare he rode whinnied, made skittish by the eerie shadows cast by the torch.

"Bright Autumn!" Fengmo called, as he had a hundred times before. His throat was parched and raw. "Bright Autumn! *Bright Autumn!*"

The sound of his voice rang out and came back to him from the crags and crevices, for he was now in the high country. He worked around the boulders, making trails where none existed. Twice his mount stumbled and he had to dig in his heels in order to keep from being thrown. The snow was becoming deeper, the inclines slick and dangerous. An icy wind whipped the snow in flurries around him.

"Bright Autumn!" The name tore from his tired lungs like the wail of a long-forgotten spirit.

Suddenly he halted, believing he heard a cry. His heart beat with such force his entire body was shaken and he called again, only to be answered by the wind.

He saw a movement just ahead at the edge of his flickering pool of torchlight, and the hairs on his nape rose. There, atop a boulder some hundred feet ahead, glowed a pair of fierce amber-colored eyes. In the next instant, he heard the low growl of a snow leopard.

With his free hand, Fengmo reached for the rifle. But then, as if only now sensing the danger, the mare whinnied again and reared, flailing the air with thrashing hooves and forelegs. The rifle discharged into the air and Fengmo tumbled back and over the bucking hindquarters.

It was as if he flew slowly through the velvet blackness of time and space, and even as his body hit the earth, he screamed silent protest to the gods. *No! I will not die. Not yet. Not without Bright Autumn!*

His legs touched the ground first. There was a snapping sound and a split second later he was flat on his back. When breath returned to him, he lay still and listened. The horse had fled. He could see nothing except the glittering flicker of the torch now wavering at the foot of the boulder. The world around him was silent save for the soft whistle of icy wind.

Pain shot through his right ankle and lower leg as he rolled over and came up on hands and knees. Slowly, his breath coming in labored gasps, he stood, fighting back the agony, momentarily expecting the giant cat he had seen to come pouncing down upon him. Still there was nothing, no movement or sound. He took a step, tensed, and then took another.

There was no sign of the snow leopard as he picked up the torch, and he limped to the rifle only to find the stock shattered. He groaned and threw the useless weapon aside. Looking into the blackness, the pain in his leg was drowned out by the cry of his heart.

"Bright Autumn!" He resumed his call aloud and turned his steps toward the mountains.

He had gone only a short distance when he saw the blood—crimson droplets being quickly obliterated by the storm. His heart thudded louder still as he moved on, half stumbling through the crags, now oblivious to his physical pain. His eyes never left the horrifying trail of blood. He could see indentations now too, small footprints leading ever upward.

What he spied first was only the red fur of her robe, the fine soft pelt of a fox. And next her hand, flung out against the whiteness of snow. Torchlight sparkled from the jade-and-gold ring she wore on her littlest finger.

With a wild shout of joy, Fengmo rushed forward, falling down beside her. Her eyes were closed but she was shivering. Throwing the torch to one side, he reached for her.

"Fengmo," her voice came to him in a breathless whisper.

A dry sob of relief burst from him as he gathered her close. He could see the small gash in her forehead and a mottled bruise on one cheek. Her eyelids fluttered open.

"Fengmo," she repeated. "You have come."

"Yes, little heart, I am here." He held her tenderly against his chest. "I will be here always."

He tried to sit upright, to stand, but the searing pain in his leg would be ignored no longer. It tore through him in agonizing waves until he could but drop down again. At first he was gripped by desperation, but then, suddenly, an all-pervasive peace set in. He had found his beloved. Even now she was wrapped in the shelter of his arms! There seemed to be a sweet smile on her lips.

Fengmo kissed Bright Autumn and felt their two souls melt together and become one.

"Yo-ho!"

Fengmo opened his eyes. He no longer felt the pain in his leg, or the cold. The only reality in his world was the woman in his arms, her face pressed into his neck.

"Yo-ho! Second Son!" The sound came again.

Suddenly shadows danced around their two prostrate forms. Fengmo struggled to move, to sit up.

"They are here!" came a cry. "We have found them!"

A moment later, he was looking up into the face of Farmer Fong, the father of Fong Lu. Other faces appeared behind him, open, honest faces chapped by the wind and creased by life.

"Come, Young Sir. You must sit up. We have found your horse, a worthless beast to be sure."

Bright Autumn stirred beside him and groaned softly. Together they were lifted by rough, work-worn hands.

Fengmo recognized other faces now. The innkeeper whose daughter had been attacked was there holding the reins of the horse, smiling and slapping his body against the cold.

"How . . ." Fengmo tried to speak, but all the questions seemed frozen in his throat.

"Do not waste breath, Young Sir." Farmer Fong and his companions supported Fengmo while another lifted Bright Autumn onto the mare. "You will be well, never fear. That stubborn Third Son of mine would not leave until he had my promise. A most demanding and undutiful boy he is!"

Farmer Fong walked at the head of the horse, leading it down the slopes and finally through snow-covered fields.

From behind him came the sound of male voices raised in song—a song of courage, patriotism, and victory—loud enough to be heard above the howl of the wind.

Riding upon the horse, Fengmo felt Bright Autumn stir in his arms and looked down to see her smiling faintly.

"My beloved," he whispered. There was so much he wanted to tell her . . . so many apologies . . .

As if reading his thoughts, she looked up at him. The expression on her face, the love and forgiveness in her eyes, left him mute.

She turned forward again. "Tanpo will be saved by men such as these," she murmured. "China will be saved. Our children will live to a ripe old age."

VELVET GLOVE

An exciting series of contemporary novels of love with a dangerous stranger.

Starting in July

THE VENUS SHOE Carla Neggers 87999-9/$2.25
Working on an exclusive estate, Artemis Pendleton becomes
embroiled in a thirteen-year-old murder, a million dollar
jewel heist, and with a mysterious Boston publisher who
ultimately claims her heart.

CAPTURED IMAGES Laurel Winslow 87700-7/$2.25
Successful photographer Carolyn Daniels moves to a quiet New
England town to complete a new book of her work, but her peace
is interrupted by mysterious threats and a handsome stranger
who moves in next door.

LOVE'S SUSPECT Betty Henrichs 88013-X/$2.25
A secret long buried rises to threaten Whitney Wakefield
who longs to put the past behind her. Only the man she loves
has the power to save—or destroy her.

DANGEROUS ENCHANTMENT Jean Hager 88252-3/$2.25
When Rachel Drake moves to a small town in Florida, she falls
in love with the town's most handsome bachelor. Then she
discovers he'd been suspected of murder, and suddenly she's
running scared when another body turns up on the beach.

THE WILDFIRE TRACE Cathy Gillen Thacker 88620-4/$2.25
Dr. Maggie Connelly and attorney Jeff Rawlins fall in love
while involved in a struggle to help a ten-year-old boy regain
his memory and discover the truth about his mother's death.

IN THE DEAD OF THE NIGHT Rachel Scott 88278-7/$2.25
When attorney Julia Leighton is assigned to investigate the
alleged illegal importing of cattle from Mexico by a local
rancher, the last thing she expects is to fall in love with him.

AVON PAPERBACKS